KT-425-936

ABERDEEN CITY LIBRARIES

SCAPEGALLOWS

Margaret Catchpole was born into a smugglers' world in Suffolk in the late 1700s. A spirited woman, she meets her match in Will Laud, 'hell-born babe' and wanderer, with an easy knack for evading the excise men. As the valued servant of a wealthy family and a friend of criminals, Margaret leads a double life that will inevitably bring about her downfall, and she is twice sentenced to hang – but she escapes the gallows and is transported with other convicts to Australia. A wonderful adventure story inspired by the real Margaret Catchpole – who was a slip-gibbet, a scapegallows.

SCAPEGALLOWS

SCAPEGALLOWS

by

Carol Birch

Magna Large Print Books
Long Preston, North Yorkshire,
BD23 4ND, England.

British Library Cataloguing in Publication Data.

Birch, Carol
Scapegallows.

A catalogue record of this book is
available from the British Library

ISBN 978-0-7505-2933-4

First published in Great Britain in 2007 by Virago Press

Published in Large Print 2008 by arrangement with
Little, Brown Book Group Limited

Magna Large Print is an imprint of Library Magna Books Ltd.

Printed and bound in Great Britain by
T.J. (International) Ltd., Cornwall, PL28 8RW

For Ann, Lin and Maggie

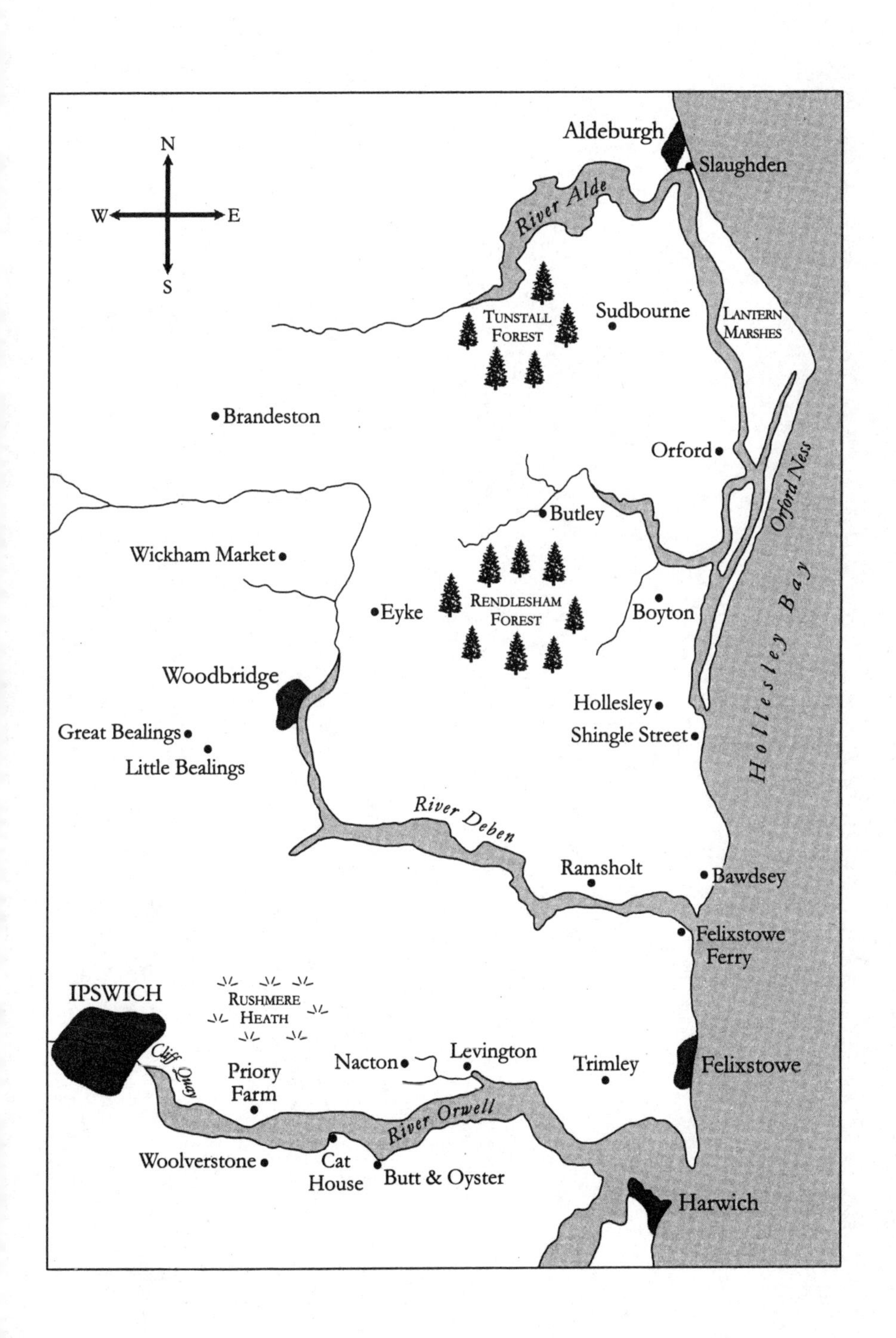
N
W
E
S
Aldeburgh
Slaughden
River Alde
Tunstall Forest
Sudbourne
Lantern Marshes
Brandeston
Orford
Orford Ness
Butley
Wickham Market
Rendlesham Forest
Eyke
Boyton
Hollesley Bay
Woodbridge
Hollesley
Shingle Street
Great Bealings
Little Bealings
River Deben
Ramsholt
Bawdsey
Felixstowe Ferry
IPSWICH
Rushmere Heath
Cliff Quay
Priory Farm
Nacton
Levington
Trimley
Felixstowe
River Orwell
Woolverstone
Cat House
Butt & Oyster
Harwich

High Water

1

New South Wales, 1817

In the very early morning there was not a movement or a sound, not so much as a bird singing. Far away, very high up over the cloud-reaches of the Blue Mountains, nervous flickers of lightning came and went.

There was an artist who used to come and sit with Mrs Cobbold on the lawn in the good old days; he was teaching her to paint. I'd take them their tea and hot chocolate, and sometimes a little cake or two. 'What do you think, Margaret?' she'd say, cocking her head over like a bird. She could make a nice enough little picture, but that fellow with the brush, he was the clever one. Short and fat and funny-looking, but the way he could paint a clump of trees. I wonder what he'd make now of the prospect from my hill over that great distance: so much of it that my eyes make it ripple like seaweed under water when I stare; and sometimes I feel I have a seven-league boot that could step across to the mountains in one stride; and sometimes it's a sea as wide as the great oceans I came over to get here, with flying fish, and the whale I saw, and the strange lights that came dancing along behind the ship. I'd need a lot of greys to paint that. Greys and greens and blues, all very soft, and I'd need to smudge them with my finger. I'd never get it right – so many trees with their big arms and the leaves that twinkle and turn together when the breeze blows. But there's not a breath now and they're still as a painting. It's dark in the west over the mountains, dusky dawn here. The heat's rising already. The smell of fruit drifts up from the patchwork plain below. The lamps are lit in Richmond on the other side of the river. The river is the like of which I never in my whole life saw before I came to this place. But then everything's bigger out of England – clouds, trees, creeping bugs – and the Hawkesbury is ten times wider than the Orwell.

'Looks like a storm, Billy.'

There's been no rain for months. It's been a very hot summer and I do not know how we got through it, him and me, but we did. Wrestling in the yard with the old kangaroo dog, he pauses mid-grapple, raises his head and frowns. 'Not today, Auntie.'

The other two dogs range along the stock-yard fence.

'There's lightning,' I say.

Billy shrugs. Matched for size, wrapped in one another's arms, dog and boy roll in the dust. Both are nine, narrow-haunched with wild pup faces in a swirl of curly hair, the dog's brown, Billy's jet black. They pant and laugh at one another, the long pink tongue of the dog dripping and slobbering.

'Tell you, Bill,' says I, 'we're in for a storm, you mark my words.'

'Not till tonight, Auntie.'

Thinks he knows. Mrs Palmer says it's in his

blood to sense the weather and she put it in his head that he do, but he is not always right, no. *He* never came up with the dreaming like the wild ones, not him. He was a baby when his poor mamma came in alone from somewhere further out, fourteen years old and all bashed up, to try and be a settler and get her certificate. She died and they put him in the Native Institute, where I got him. He's Bible-raised, a good boy so they told me, and they were right.

'Listen,' he says.

I can hear the waterfall. And now the birds, they come on sudden. Demons with their screeching and squawking. Back home they used to talk very softly in the dark – it was lovely to hear, first thing, when you were lying in your bed.

The low farmlands rising up from the river give off a strong morning sweetness. I never saw such abundance till I came over. Things grow here I never even knew existed, and I take fruit straight off the trees, fruit we never got before, peaches near the size of your head, sweet oranges, ripe lemons you can put your nose to, fresh off the tree, and breathe – ah! – and just about die with the loveliness. I tried to tell them, writing home. I thought if I could make them know just a little of what I was seeing I wouldn't feel quite so lonely here.

'Someone coming up the hill, Auntie.'

My eyes are not what they once were. I put my hands up to cut out the glare.

'Who is it, Billy?'

'A girl on a cart,' he says.

And a little nearer I see she's Phoebe Glasse,

Mrs Raby's housemaid with the bit of a twitch.

'What's up, Phoebe?' says I, walking out and down to meet her. 'This is strange, you here so early.'

The horse is a big bay. Phoebe Glasse sits on the board in a plain grey frock and shawl, very dark hair, white face and small tight lips. 'Missis says she's due,' she mumbles through her rabbity teeth, 'says she wants you.'

'She's early then. Shouldn't have heard from you lot till Sunday week at least.' I look at the clouds piling up in the sky. 'You must have seen the lightning.'

'Yis, mum,' she says, 'I been on the road two hours all on my own.'

That's bad. They shouldn't have sent her alone.

'Wasn't you scared?'

Her right eye gives a quick jolt. 'Not so's you'd notice,' she replies with a sideways look.

'Was there no one to come along with you?'

'He's gone to Parramatta for lumber,' she says. 'He's back this afternoon but *she* says she's had a show and I'm to get you and bring you back quick cos she's all on her own and she don't know what to do. I'm to bring you in the cart.'

I stand and look about. It's a long step to the Rabys' farm. I sigh. Henry Morgan's coming to mend the thatch, he'll keep an eye on things.

'Well, have some tea first,' I say. 'Billy, make tea for Phoebe, will you? And drive those cows out on the hill. Then go and wash your face and hands and get your shoes on, we're going to Mrs Raby's house.'

She gets down, puts her hands to her back and

stretches. 'Is *he* coming?' she asks.

'Certainly he is.'

He walks away, the dogs running by him with their long tails striking this way and that and their great mouths ahang like wolves. White man work and the black man patta, that's what the Darugs say – What? says I. Patter? What? – it was Amaroo said it, his great nose pitted by the pox, beard to his waist, buck naked. It was the time George (who would have married me if I'd've had him) took me on one of his trips; the time I got the beautiful feathers and saw the huge waterfalls. White man work and black man patta. Amaroo laughed and made a movement hand to mouth like eating. His bits dangling softly against his thigh, tommyhawk stuck in his belt, me trying to look anywhere else but you-know-where. Billy's a Darug boy but not lazy at all. I follow him after the cows and the sheep while Phoebe Glasse is inside drinking her tea and taking a little something. 'Shall we go?' says I to him. Already sweat runs down my sides.

'Won't rain today, Auntie.' His bare feet spread wide in the dust.

'So,' I say, 'I'll put a notice on the shop door.'

The lean-to of my cottage is my shop. Inside it's cosy and dim and smells of fruit and the musty tang of tea. I keep it nice – neat and well dusted, swept out every night. The vegetables and fruit are displayed in boxes on the floor. I sell tea and sugar and soap and such, calico and muslin, twill in bales on the shelves, and some nice wide gingham. I even sell writing paper, eightpence a sheet. I don't do too badly, we get by. Whenever was it easy? I tear a scrap from a corner of paper and write firm: Closed See Henry Morgan, and put it on the shop door and lock up, then go and get my slippers and nightgown just in case, take the musket down from the house wall and put it in a basket with a bottle of rum, calling to Billy to come quick and bring his nightshirt too in case we end up having to stay the night; and soon we are off, the cart swaying and jolting on the track. I look back. My cottage stands grey against the hill, poor enough and small but far better than it could be. We meet Henry coming to work and I give him the key to the shop and tell him to look out for the pigs that have gone to ground in the wood, the devils; and he says, 'Sure thing, Miss Catchpole, I'll do that'; then it's along Richmond Terrace on the good road, high above the river with the plain spreading out far below. Soon we're in open forest of blue gums. The river banks are wild and rocky, poor ragged trees holding out their arms over the abyss in supplication, like the watchers at the foot of the cross. The force of water has pulled them hard out of shape. Their roots cling to the banks for dear life, and captured driftwood hangs in their fingers. Something whistles out in the bush, weird and low.

'What's it like at the Rabys'?' I ask Phoebe.

She shrugs.

'Were you on the stores?'

'I was.' She drives tensely, shoulders drawn up like wings.

'At Parramatta?'

She nods. She's like a hare about the face. I'd say she's near thirty.

'I was there,' I say.

'Was you?' She sounds surprised.

'I was indeed. But I was only there two days, thank God.'

'Two days? *I* was six months.' Piqued, she spits over on to the track.

The Female Factory at Parramatta is a rotten place, a filthy stinking lousy place. I got eaten alive on the stores, ticks all over me, swollen big as currants. We were making blankets and the wool scratched me raw. Two days and I was taken off and given to the Palmers. I've been lucky. It sounds funny when you think of what's happened to me, but all in all I'd say I've had a lucky life.

'I thought you come free,' she says.

'Not at all. I come in the *Nile* sixteen years ago.'

The *Nile*, the *Minorca* and the *Canada* kept company out of Spithead. Me and Elizabeth Killet and Sarah Barker all from Ipswich Gaol clung together for fear, holding each other's heads to be sick whenever necessary. Then we got past the Bay of Biscay and found our legs and avoided each other. They were rough, the women on that ship. Barker got her a man, a sailor. I was called up to a free settler who was having a baby, because they knew I'd done nursing. And if I'd have been Mrs Rouse and a free woman I'd never have set foot on ship in the condition she was in, but I'm glad she did, because I finally knew that I would live when I pulled that baby boy from her and opened his throat and heard him cry, the timbers groaning and the floor pitching under my feet.

And here they all still want me now when their

time's due.

'When d'you get your pardon?' Phoebe asks.

'Three years ago.'

Three little years. Gone in a second. Like my life. Fifty-five next birthday, I am.

'That's when I come,' she says. 'I been here three bloody years.' As if it's past believing.

We show our passes at the turnpike and get stuck behind an empty bullock-dray, lumbering so slowly that the big bay horse has to stop completely a couple of times. She keeps jerking her head forward to eat the grass at the side of the road. For an hour we creep like this. Phoebe doesn't talk much, except when she's swearing viciously at the horse and the bullock-dray. The tongue on this woman would turn milk.

2

She could have it far worse. Raby's Hill has a lovely view across cleared ground and pasture with sheep grazing here and there, over the shining water meadow to the wide expanse of the river. They've got a vineyard running up the hill at the back, and a magnificent jacaranda tree towers over the barn and casts a welcome shadow across the yard. She's not a bad mistress, Olivia Raby, from what I can make out – only about nineteen, and quite a kind little body. I could have twisted her round my finger in no time if I'd have been Phoebe Glasse. She was up when we got there, walking about in her pretty blue shift. Billy stayed out on the veranda. She's got a nice house, not anywhere near as grand as the Rouses' or Mrs Palmer's, and shabby too, but it's got plenty of room. Mr Raby keeps building on.

'I see you brought your little picaninny with you, Margaret,' she says, rubbing her back. Her eyes look pressed-in with tiredness.

'Billy's a good boy, Mrs Raby. He'll stay in the kitchen and run and fetch things for me when I ask him. He can see to the horse now while Phoebe gives me a hand.' I started getting my apron on. 'You're early, Mrs Raby.'

'Yes, well, you needn't say it like that, Margaret, it's not my fault,' she snaps.

I smile. 'Better safe than sorry.'

'She should lie down, shouldn't she, Miss Catchpole?' Phoebe says.

'I can't lie down!' She's testy. 'When I do I feel sick.' She rubs her eyes with the back of her sleeve, making a wide, childish mouth. Her hair hangs in a long fair plait, unravelling down her back. 'Oh, damn,' she says, 'I feel foul. Phoebe, you're a good girl. Take Billy in the kitchen and give him something to perk him up. Tell him to turn Bonny loose in the field for now, he can give her a good brush down later.'

I don't always take him with me but Mrs Raby doesn't mind. Plenty do. I've only known Mrs Raby since six months ago; I met her at Mrs Palmer's. She would have me for the birth, she said, and no one else; she'd heard about me. 'Mrs Rouse speaks very highly of you, Margaret,' she said.

'Yes, madam,' I said, 'the Rouses have been very good to me.'

I brought all their babies bar one into the world, *and* all the Palmers'. God alone knows what I'd've done without the Rouses. They brought me ashore with them. 'Stick with us, Margaret,' Mr Rouse said. Sydney Cove was full of rowboats, and the men swarming onboard like hungry dogs. Scared like a girl I was, though I was thirty-nine. There was seven free settlers on the *Nile* and ninety-six of us convict women and they looked us over like horses at the fair. The soldiers from the Rum Corps were worst. 'Stay close,' Mr Rouse said. Missis was coming along behind with her little girl by the hand. She would have me carry the baby for her so they'd think I was spoken for. And they put in a good word with the Palmers. Lucky, see?

'Well, you've got to lie down now for a bit, Mrs Raby,' I said. 'I've got to look at you.'

She went upstairs heavily, holding on to my arm. 'It would happen just when he's gone away, wouldn't it?' she cried, tearful suddenly. 'I've been on pins for hours waiting for you, and all the men down at the pig runs or off somewhere, and Mr Rouse was meant to be sending me another girl but she's not arrived. I don't know what I'm supposed to do.'

'You don't have to worry about anything, Mrs Raby. Phoebe and me are looking after you.'

Phoebe came up after I'd seen Madam.

'The boy's boiling water on the fire,' she said, standing in the doorway.

'Yes, he knows what to do.'

'Shall I get you a nice drink of tea, madam?' she asked.

'I can't drink tea!'

'She needs to lie down, Miss Catchpole,' Phoebe appealed to me. 'She's been up all night. She needs to have a nice lie-down and a cup of tea, don't she?'

'I can't lie down!'

'She's all fine for now, Phoebe,' I said. 'Coming on charmingly. Let her walk about if she wants to.'

Phoebe, all spikes with the rest of the world, was obviously soft on her mistress. I left them quite content walking up and down, the one fretting like a child, the other waspish and maternal. Billy was getting on with things like a good boy, boiling cloths.

'She has a piano,' he said.

'I saw.'

There are not so many pianos in the Colony. They used to sing hymns to one in the Institute, and the Rouses let him play on theirs when I take him. Miss Mary taught him a few notes, and I showed him how to play the first line of 'Boys and Girls Come Out To Play', the first thing I ever learned myself. Mrs Cobbold taught me.

'Maybe you can have a little go on it later,' I tell him.

'How's the lady?' he asks.

'Nervous, Billy. But she'll do.'

I look in the pantry. Plenty there.

'Have you seen to the horse?'

He shakes his head.

'Do that now, Billy. Poor creature's had a long night.'

He loves horses. A horse would be a good thing for me, to get around, but we don't have one. All this walking about in the heat and then the wet and the cold, no wonder I get seedy. I'd like a nice draught horse, a beautiful great Suffolk Punch like our old Dandy, but there's none like that here. On the wall above the fireplace in Mrs Raby's living room there's a painting of a race-horse, black with a white star on its nose and white knees and fetlocks. I stand looking at it, remembering riding a horse into a river a long time ago. Above, footsteps cross and recross the floor. Phoebe's high voice somewhat lowered, trying to soothe. Olivia Raby's voice, sharp and shrill: 'I don't know what you're making such a fuss about, Phoebe!'

The painting is very dark, the black horse against a nearly black background. When I turn away it's dark in here too, dark and slightly damp-smelling. The corner of the rug has been kicked over, and the lid of the piano is open, the keys a pale slash in the gloom. From time to time I have a strange flash of displacement in this peculiar land, like waking and not knowing where you are. I daresay all of us here have something similar. But not this baby and all the other babies I've helped into the world. They won't have it, because they'll never have known anything other than this hot colony, and it will be all the world to them. And if you were to take them and put them down in a green meadow in Suffolk, they'd be lost.

Standing by the door looking out, watching as

Billy rubs down the bay in front of the barn, I get a prickle in my bones, an inkling as if the season's on the turn. The Blue Mountains are hung over by a swelling of slate-grey cloud. It's surely raining over there. God, don't let me think about floods. Haven't we had enough floods on this river? Last June was bad, but not as bad as some of them we used to get. They're always telling us to get ready and nothing happens, and no one's said a word about it lately. But the stillness. And the birds. Where are the birds? All gone back to bed? Very far, the bellowing of wild cattle from the woods. The farm buildings are a huddle of shadow. I look up. Above me the window is open, its panes catching an eerie light.

Mrs Raby says, 'Don't put it there, Phoebe, I don't want it there.'

Then Phoebe's voice: 'You are very naughty, madam. I wish you'd take a little drink.'

'Why should I?' Like a child.

A flock of lorikeets rises from the trees, shrieking as if at some great scandal.

'I think we should turn the horse loose tonight,' I say to Billy, 'put her on the higher ground.'

He looks at me, a hand on the horse's neck, then looks up at the sky. 'Splish-splash,' he says, 'you'd better get the baby out of her soon, Auntie.'

'It'll come when it comes,' I say, 'that's what they do. Anyway, I thought you said it wouldn't rain.'

'Won't till tonight,' he said. 'There's time.' And brushed away.

'Think it'll flood?'

'Could do.'

Harvest is not quite two months over and

wheat's already dear. What will we do?

'Well, it won't get up this far,' I say. 'We've got to stay till Mr Raby's home anyway. Come on in now. I'll ask Mrs Raby if you can have a little go on her piano.'

'Of course he can,' she says, 'but let him not be too loud,' and goes back to kneading her pillow with both fists like a cat. She's stopped all her walking and is lying half on her side across the bed, Phoebe rubbing her back and crooning under her breath, 'Dear dear, rue the day ever I married, Lord, how I wish I was single again,' which seems to me wholly wrong for the occasion, but the tune is very pretty and slow and fits with the moving of her arms. So I go down and set Bill on the stool, and he plays with two fingers, 'Boys and Girls Come Out To Play', smiling as he always does when he plays the piano. Reminds me of the time I first saw him, when Mr Rouse called him in out of the yard and he'd just been running about in some game, eyes still full of fun, soft little chin and the smile he has on now. And I thought: Yes, I'll have him.

I clap my hands. 'Very, very good! Now I'll show you something new,' and I guide his fingers and sing over his shoulder: 'La-ven-der's – *blue* – dill-ee – dill-ee, La-vender's – *green–'* and so on, till a sudden sharp scream calls me upstairs.

It's started.

3

Mr Raby didn't arrive that day. Late in the evening the rain started, by ten it was steady, and before midnight the baby was born. First thing she did, she licked him like the cows do when they calve. I've seen that before but not much. That was a happy birth, no trouble at all. He was a quiet baby, Thomas – a calm easy little man with loose red skin and a big fair head, who fed off his poor weary mother good as gold and very soon was sleeping soundly by her side. We were all dog-tired. We cleaned up, then Phoebe ran down and brought up a bottle of rum and some cups and we had a little drink to toast the baby. Billy was sleeping in the kitchen on a made-up cot, peaceful as can be.

Phoebe said, 'It's raining awful hard, ma'am.' She peered through the streaming window. 'I daresay the master's been held up by it.'

'That's it,' I agreed, because Missis had been fretting about him on and off, 'there'll be flooding on the Parramatta road.'

'Do you think so?'

'I'm sure of it.'

'It won't get up here, will it?'

'Of course not. You close your eyes now. Give him here, I'll take him and put him in his crib.'

She fell asleep at once when he was settled, and we blew out all but one candle and retired to the next room, leaving the doors open so we'd hear if she called for anything or the baby cried out.

'There now,' Phoebe said, 'another little drop, Miss Catchpole? Or are you for your bed? There's no getting away for *you* tonight.'

'Right enough.' It was a small closet of a room Mrs Raby used for sewing. Phoebe had made me a bed out of cushions. 'Another little drop, Phoebe. Sit down a while and have a drink with me. I don't know how it is with you but I won't sleep for a good half an hour. My head's all a-buzz.'

She sat down on her mistress's sewing chair, leaned across and filled both our cups once more, then yawned as if she'd wring herself out. We lit a pipe. For a while we rested in the peaceful purring of the rain. Phoebe's eye winked steadily.

'This is nice,' I said, 'nice once it's all done and everything's well.'

I like rum. Back home it was all gin but here it's rum and porter, and I think rum's the better. We sipped. She chewed her lip and the skin inside her mouth.

'You got it nice here,' I said. 'On a plate.'

'I miss home,' she said.

'Of course you do.'

'This is a stink-hole.' She rested her elbows on her knees clumsily. 'I hate this shitten country.'

'How long you got?'

'Seven.'

What is there to say? Few make it back and certainly not the likes of her. *I* thought I'd go back. For years I thought I'd go back.

'You should make the best of things,' I said,

'you've been very lucky.'

She gave a snort down her long thin nose. And I told her all about Norfolk Island where they shave the women's heads and hang them up and flog them on the triangle just like they do the men. Or the Coal River, where they take those poor iron-gang men you see on the turnpike.

'That's shocking,' she said, but as if she'd heard it all before.

'Mind you, they're the bad ones,' I said. 'They don't send the likes of nice girls like you to those places. See? Lucky.'

She made a face, all mouth.

She needs to get herself a man. It's very hard out here for a woman alone. No wonder there's so many whores round Sydney Cove.

'What'd they get you for?' I asked.

She blew smoke through her nose. 'Ten yards of ribbon and a pair of stockings,' she said. 'Silk.'

I nodded. I thought I could sleep now. 'Well well,' I said, 'we must get to our beds, I suppose.' But as I spoke young Thomas crowed up from his crib, and she started up as if stung.

'Heavens, Phoebe, it's only the baby!'

'I know, I know!' she said. 'I'm all of a doo-da,' and her eye winked fast three or four times.

'Ssh!'

I brought him in. Phoebe stood oddly useless all of a sudden in the middle of the sewing room.

'You need to go to bed,' I said. 'Go on, she's well away. I'll swaddle him up. Here, take him for a second while I get his blanket.' I placed him in her arms and bustled about; and when I was ready and went to take him from her, I saw that she was crying, water pouring down her face like the rain pouring down the window. She had him safe and close, rocking, one hand supporting his head, the nails all broken and bitten, and her face destroyed. Just destroyed.

'Phoebe, Phoebe.' I made her sit. 'Phoebe, there now.' She gave him up to me and I swaddled him while she shook and jerked with the effort of having to cry quietly. I let her get on with whatever misery it was that had struck so hard from the past, and I took Master Thomas in to feed from his mother, who woke and slept and mumbled and smiled, while I kept watch till all was satisfactory.

Phoebe had taken the rum and the glasses down and gone back to her own room by the time I got back. I wished she'd stayed. I could've learned her story. As I lay down it struck me hard what a broken-hearted place this was, what a world of grievers for we're ripped up when we come here, ripped like a piece of cloth right down the middle of the soul. I remembered the *Nile*. London Mary. She got life but they hanged her boy: sixteen, just getting a few little hairs on his lip. Imagine. Boy's there with his ma when she steals something and the cove takes her by the arm and calls for the law, so he punches him right in the mouth. Rip. We had one girl twelve and one hag of eighty, and *she* so addled she didn't even know who she was. Done for perjury. Rip. We used to laugh about that, you had to. She was a nasty old thing. God knows what became of her, I expect she died. And Sarah Barker crying: Oh, I never shall see my Ipswich no more, as the boat pitched.

These are old pains, but new then: not a memory, an open wound. It was like being in labour in your heart. Not a one on that ship not in mourning. And me too, for my lost lad, of course. And for England.

I fell asleep to the drumming of rain and dreamed I was on a dark ship and could not find the way back to my bunk no matter how much I roamed the rolling decks, so that when Billy woke me, standing by my bed with a candle, I felt as if I'd been wandering about for hours.

'Listen, Auntie,' he said.

It was a full-blooded storm, blowing spitefully shrill about the house, rattling the windows and doors and throwing rain like hard little pellets on the roof. Behind all this was a sound my bones and blood knew and quickened to, a gushing, rushing, *bellowing* sound, as if some great creature was in pain. The river, nearer than it should be. And somewhere too, adding to it all, the ceaseless heavy calling of sheep and cattle.

'How high is it?' I asked, sitting up.

'Can't tell. It's pitch black.'

'It won't get up here.' I felt for my slippers with my feet. The floor was freezing. 'Go quickly,' I said. 'Go see if Mrs Raby's awake. Don't wake her if she isn't.' I shivered into my clothes, stepped to the window and saw nothing but darkness and rain lashing down the glass. Pulling my shawl round me I ran next door, colliding with Billy in the doorway.

'Not a peep,' he whispered.

'Light the lamp, Billy.'

She was well away, baby too. Soon enough he'd be wanting a feed. 'In years to come,' I said to Billy as we went downstairs, 'she'll say to him, you were born the night of the great storm, when your dad was away.' I saw by the clock in the hall it was nearly dawn, but when I opened the side door and looked out it was dark as only this hour can be, and there was nothing to see in the light from my lamp but the rain hammering into the Rabys' parched yard between the steps and the jacaranda tree. The roaring was louder, a constant wild thunder beyond the darkness. Not a night to be out. There'd be no getting home this morning for sure.

'It's high,' I told him, fastening the door, 'but we'll be snug up here till the storm's passed.'

'The road'll be under.'

'Yes, in some places. We might have to wait a while. Tell you what, Billy, you can entertain us all on the piano in the morning. Keep us jolly. It'll be light in half an hour, better blow up the fire. Thank God they've plenty of fuel laid in.'

Then baby woke and Missis woke, and my time was filled up. Phoebe appeared with an apron tied round her grey stuff dress. 'The wind woke me,' she said, bleary-eyed.

Mrs Raby was sitting up against the pillows with her hair spread out loose, baby nibbling away. 'It hurts,' she said. 'Ow!'

'So it will,' I told her. 'Don't worry, they'll toughen up.'

'I'll fetch you a drink, madam.' Phoebe went out stifling a yawn.

'Listen to that rain! Listen to those poor

animals out there in all that! He's very quiet, Margaret. Is he meant to be that quiet?'

'Some are like that.'

She winced. 'His gums are very hard.'

I laughed. 'Wait till he's getting his teeth.'

'Draw the curtain back, Margaret, please, I think I can see a little light getting through.' She shifted in the bed, getting comfy. 'I want to look at the rain.'

The curtain had a pattern of tiny yellow and pink flowers winding up and up in rows. It made a rattling as I pulled it back on to the gloomiest morning you ever saw. The clouds were low and grey. There was water where there should have been sky. It had come up so quick – so quiet I might almost have said, if I hadn't known of course that the night had been all of a roaring. Yet somehow that roaring had become its own kind of quiet.

'I do hope Jack gets back soon,' Mrs Raby said. 'I want him to see our little Thomas.'

Rain fell steady on the water. There was no colour at all but the soaked purple of the great jacaranda tossing in the wind. Everything else was silvery-grey, and the fall of rain was a wonderful bright dance, a million pinpricks changing all the time like midges clouding at dusk over a stream. The river was just beyond the palings that ran across the hill below us. We could not get down to the road if we wanted to. Raby's Hill was an island, and there were other islands here and there, strange outcrops like rocks in a fast mountain stream, dividing the flow. Gradually they became recognisable as familiar risings in the landscape, certain high places where people had built for safety, planted high above the levels of the last bad floods. I picked out the Laceys and the Hilliards, and further away the farm buildings on the long ridge above.

The bell was ringing in Richmond. I've seen it bad before, worse than this. I've walked through water waist high in a house, I've sat it out on a roof and watched the river carry all away. If the rain stops we'll do well enough. If it doesn't–

'The river's very high, madam,' I said. 'I doubt the master's coming back today.'

'Oh, don't say that, Margaret.' She clucked over her baby, and for a moment I closed my eyes to shut out the sight of water. Then I turned and looked at the woman in the bed. Why deceive myself? This was a bad one, bad as any I'd known. Here was death again, shaking his old scythe at me. Here was the horror. It never went away. What am I to do with her and the babe? I ran downstairs and met Phoebe coming through the hall with a cup of warm milk.

'Have you seen it?' I said. 'It's bad, Phoebe, very bad.'

'I know,' she said. 'I told the lad to start bringing things upstairs.'

Billy appeared, struggling with a ewer of water as big as himself.

'Excellent, Billy, you're a good boy.'

'What about the dogs?' he says.

They do so love their dogs, the blacks.

'The dogs are fine.'

I know what to do. I fill a creel – damper bread, cheese, bully beef.

'I'm saving her nice things for her,' says Phoebe, white-faced, intent, feverishly wrapping ornaments in pages of the *Sydney Gazette*.

And Billy, returning from upstairs: 'But what if Henry locked them in and they can't get away?'

'He wouldn't do that. Anyway, we're a lot higher at Richmond Hill, it won't get up there.'

'How do you know?'

'I know.'

I've always dipped and dived. Keep moving. Yet as I see my own two capable hands doing this and that, whatever's needed; and as my sure feet walk here and there and my eyes continue steady, I am swirling inside. Fear's like sickness. It smells. Clings in the gut, feathers the throat. Like a returning dream, recognised. How many times have I looked death in the face? Count them, Margaret:

One. Bury Gaol.

Two, the shingle at Orford Ness.

Three, Bury Gaol.

Four. Four–

All the time my feet running up and down stairs. Too much to do, me and Billy and Phoebe Glasse, scuttling about like ants while Olivia Raby, the easiest birth I've had in years, smiled and dozed and behaved just as you always want them to, though they rarely do. She rather liked all the wild weather out there while she was so cosy and warm in her bed with baby, she said. She'd had a nice feed of porridge. 'Not to worry, madam,' I told her, 'the storm's quite bad and the river's up, but we should be right as rain up here.'

'Right as rain, Margaret!' she said, and laughed.

We both laughed.

I went down to a blast of air. Billy and Phoebe with the side door open. 'Oh, dear God!' Phoebe was saying, hands to her mouth. I looked out. The river had swelled like a grey snake. Hilliard's Farm, not half a mile away, was under water. I could see the top of the house, upwards from the highest window, and tiny figures huddled on the roof. No sign of the barns, the corn, no sign of anything. Billy put his hand in mine.

'It's all right, Billy,' I said.

Water foamed at the palings.

'I think,' said I, 'we must all go across to the barn.'

'Oh, dear God,' Phoebe repeated, 'are we all to go under?'

'Just in case,' I said firmly, looking her in the eye. 'No doubt it will prove overcautious, but we'll take no chances.'

We took stuff out of the house as fast as we could, splashing through the puddles in the pouring rain to the big barn, which was a good deal higher than the house, with a threshing floor and a ladder going up to the top level. Here amongst the hay we made a nest with all we could carry of food and water and blankets. And here we had pitchforks and reaping hooks for weapons – you never know – and a pistol from the house, and my musket and some more rum. Phoebe was silent and tight as a knot. Billy was excited, a quick smile breaking on his face from time to time. 'I ain't scared, Auntie,' he said to me as we passed each other.

'Course not, Billy,' I smiled, 'no need.'

I'd warned Mrs Raby but I think she'd finally realised something was up – her eyes were wide and scared – I don't know how, maybe we spoke too loud amid our scurrying and bustling. I made light of it, chiding myself for a fussy old thing. 'Come on now,' I said, smiling. 'We've made it lovely and comfy for you, plenty of blankets, you won't be cold.'

Thomas was crying now: brand-new, thin-as-a-blade crying.

'He's wet,' I said. 'Here, I'll change him before we go.'

'Oh, poor Margaret, you're soaked! Is it really bad?'

'It's pretty bad, but we're high enough up here, ma'am, don't worry.'

Thomas wailed as I cleaned him up, solid, healthy little creature, giving me no worries. I begin to pray in the back of my mind, quick small bursts of supplication. Please stop the rain. Please let this be the worst of it. Phoebe came in and started getting Missis out of bed with an assumed cheerfulness that struck me deep. 'There! I'll just pop your slippers on,' she was saying. 'You won't get them wet, we'll carry you over.'

'But what about the people lower than us?' she asked. 'How can *they* manage?'

'I'm sure they got away. People know what to do.'

'Oh, this country,' she murmured.

It was dark downstairs in spite of day. Her eyes took in all the marks of departure.

'The piano,' she appealed, as if I could do anything about it, tears starting in her eyes.

‘Well, we can’t take that,’ I said, and laughed to lighten it.

At the back door she gazed with narrowing eyes at the slashing rain, the jacaranda whipping, the palings not just down but broken to bits in the flood, carried away like wisps of straw. A high sea was near her door, too close and wide, unmistakably malevolent. She burst into tears. The yard was all puddles. Phoebe and I made a chair out of our arms to carry her and the baby. Billy closed the door behind us. When we reached the barn the floor was wonderfully dry and we set her down. She stood firm, clutching the crying babe, catching her breath and letting her nose run. Phoebe wiped it for her. ‘See, madam? Nice and dry. Now just up the ladder and we can have a nice drink.’

When we got up there it was warm enough but dark, and the noise of the rain was thunderous. There was one big window out of which they tossed the bales, but it was shuttered. It sounded as if fists were banging on it. Please stop, I prayed. Here are five souls who can go no higher. I wondered about the people on the Hilliards’ roof; the rain as we came over the yard was too bad, I could see nothing. It’s bad that we can’t see out. Baby’s feeding. Mother’s got blankets round her, Phoebe’s giving her water from a leather bottle. Billy and I get cosy in the hay. ‘Oh, Billy-boy,’ I sigh, ‘here we are again.’ But he’s never known this before: those other bad ones, years back, they were all before his time.

‘They’ll be sending out boats,’ I told them.

‘But it’s so rough,’ Mrs Raby said. Her voice

clipped off at the end as if her throat had closed over. She's scared, I thought. Phoebe turned her face towards me, and I saw how unnaturally bright her eyes were.

'I've seen it worse than this,' I said, 'don't worry. They'll send boats, we just have to wait it out.'

'The master knows we're here,' Phoebe said. 'He'll make sure someone comes for us.'

Good girl.

'That's right.' I nodded. 'That's just what will happen.'

'It's a good job we turned the horse loose,' Billy said. All this while beneath the wind and rain and rushing water, an animal chorus sounded, strangely, harmoniously hopeless. 'Listen to them,' he said. 'They must all have got to high ground, mustn't they?'

'I'm sure they have, Billy. They certainly wouldn't be making all that noise if they were under the water. Don't you worry about them. Animals are clever.'

4

My cottage stands high on Richmond Hill. If I was there now I would be safe, Billy and me inside with the dogs, the fire banked up, drinking tea with a little rum. 'Stead of this weary fear again, this calling to attention of all my nerves. One, the gaol at Bury St Edmunds. Two, the shingle. Three–

I've seen it all. Fires. Earthquakes. Once the hill shook itself, like a big beast shivering, a Suffolk Punch in the meadow with the flies at it. Wasn't long, just a few seconds, but after that you know there's nothing here that's safe, not even the ground beneath you. It's cruel ground, burns your feet in December. But it's not just *this* country where I am small and helpless. I realised it was so even there, in England, where the ground never heaved. It's very easy to go wrong in this world, and death comes dreadfully sneaky. I was all ready for the morning drop. Twice. I remember once walking back from Parramatta and I came up over a rise and there was the valley spread before me, and on my road a gibbet with two poor, long-dead men hanging in chains, and the crows pecking away on their heads and shoulders. The smell was shocking. They were Irish men. The Irish are always in trouble. And I had that feeling again, that feeling that comes with such sights, with such nights as those when you lie awake and think about the stretching of your throat, knowing it to be near.

I can no longer say with any truthfulness that I've seen it worse. I am hanging a red petticoat out of the shutters as a signal for a boat. The ruins of barns and houses are tossed on the swell below me, broken up like kindling. Wheat stacks race by, sheep and pigs standing on them stupid and helpless, flurries of hens crying out pitifully, made witless by the speed. Dogs howling. Our palings gone. It's up to the roots of the jacaranda so I guess the veranda's well under by now. Far out I saw a man riding a wheat stack belly-down, his arms grasping the sides. The stack was only just big enough to hold him, his feet were in the water and I could not see his face or even if he were alive, only that he wore a blue jacket and black breeches; I saw him for a few mere seconds before he'd gone, swept away, all the way down to the high rocky country round Broken Bay and out to sea.

Phoebe comes up and sits looking out with me on the broad sill. Billy's sleeping, he was up with me most of the night, we're all tired. Mrs Raby probably slept better than any of us, and she's wide awake now, singing to her baby. She's come all over with a kind of mad gaiety and keeps giggling wildly at stupid things. We have been here a long time, but time is uneven, like in sleep, so I can't say how long. It's hard to tell from the sky. Three hours? Four?

She's kept a pipe and some tobacco dry and we pass it between us, silent for some time. Phoebe is pinch-faced and serious. I smile at her. 'Bearing up, Phoebe?'

She quirks her mouth, it's not a smile. Trying, though.

'Scared?'

She nods, darts the point of her tongue out and licks her lips.

'It's easing off a bit, I think. We just got to wait. This is your first bad one, sit tight.'

'Ain't got much choice, have I?'

She shivers. 'Chilly,' she says. It's the wet clothes drying on her.

'Go in and get a blanket,' I say.

She pulls on the pipe.

'It's something to write home about,' I say, 'They got nothing like this. Where you from?'

'London.'

'I was in London once.'

'Was you?'

'Ratcliffe Highway.'

'Oh, my God.' She rolls her eyes. 'I'm Bethnal Green.' She spits in the water. 'Anyway,' she says, 'I don't write no more.'

'Don't you?'

'Nah. No point. No bastard writes back.' She passes me the pipe.

'I was five years waiting for my first letter,' I say. 'You've only been here three. Too soon to write them off. Five years all but one month, I'll never forget it, I'd writ again and again and again, thought they'd all forgot me. Fifty miles up country I was and they said I had a box from England and I walked all the way to Sydney.'

'No point,' she says again harshly, 'no point,' and I thought of how she'd cried last night.

'Who knows but you'll go back one day,' I say, but I don't expect she will.

She shrugged.

'Who'd you leave?' I ask.

'My boy,' she said. 'He was nearly three.'

I don't expect he'd remember her.

'We must take it turn and turn about to watch the water level,' I say.

'I'll watch a while.' Hard-faced, she looks out over the watery world.

5

In that weird half light we slept and woke and slept and woke, and the time passed on and on, never changing, lulled by the rushing hushing water music, whistling and whispering, roaring, moaning, till we no longer knew there was a world beyond our haven. The baby cried. Sometimes he slept. His mother wept. Sometimes she laughed, sometimes sang nursery rhymes and old beebaws. I sang to Billy:

Where have you been all the day, Billy Boy, Billy Boy,
Where have you been all the day, me Billy Boy,
I've been courting all the day with me charming Nancy Grey,
She's me Nancy-tickle-me-fancy-oh!
Charming Billy Boy.

He said, 'I'm not scared, Auntie, honest I'm not.' He ran up and down the ladder like a cat, bringing up what he could, a lantern, ropes, canisters, anything that could be saved. Two chests of tea and a ton of sugar from Sydney come only last Thursday, the missis said, laughing wildly, we could neither open nor carry, and when the foam came running in under the doors we knew the house was done for. No no no we're not done yet, I said, we've got a level or two higher we can go, and up we went to the sill and piled straw there for warmth and snuggled in like mice, all cosying in with Mrs Raby in the middle with the baby held close into her in his swaddling. Phoebe prayed silently, moving her mouth. 'Jesus,' she said over and over. 'Jesus, Jesus.'

We must put out a board, I said, so's we can see out. How high it is! And is it getting dark? Or is it just the weather, the black clouds and the sky all black and burst. Then it got so dark we couldn't see below, all we knew was the last time we looked it was up to the threshing floor, not more than seven or eight feet under us.

It swashed and slapped and chattered there.

Outside the wind was loud and joyful.

'He wants changing, madam,' I said.

'Here.' Phoebe reached out. 'Give him to me.'

Later there was a sound like great cliffs crumbling into the sea.

'That'll be the big chimney!' Mrs Raby cried sharply, and her eyes overflowed and she was suddenly half dead and yet more alive than she'd ever been, and her face was both young and old. Phoebe was haggard. And the softness of it, Billy's sweet chin, and the hand of the baby. How us three, me and Olivia Raby and Phoebe Glasse, enclosed them round, breathing life on to them.

'Auntie,' he said, 'can I hold the baby?'

I looked at Mrs Raby. She put her hands about his face. 'You are a darling angel,' she said, 'of course you can.'

Something else fell, then more, then a calamity of noise.

'What was that! What was that!' screamed Phoebe.

'I don't know.'

'It was near.'

'Yes.'

'Oh, mum, I'm scared!'

'I'm scared, I'm scared!'

'I'm scared too! I'm scared too!'

Billy with the babe in his arms crawled in under my arm. Phoebe drew in a gulp of air with the desperation of one already under the water, and Missis whimpered like a newborn kitten. Then Phoebe and the missis go into one another's arms and tremble there.

'We should pull up the ladder,' I say, much later when the baby cries again for his feed. 'You help me, Billy. Give young Thomas back to his mum.'

It didn't come easy. It was stuck and we had to haul and haul, but in the end it was up and we laid it by with all our small supplies upon it.

'It's getting dark, I think.'

Phoebe had her face to the gap where we took out the board.

'It's getting cold,' Billy said.

I reached in my basket. Time for the rum. 'Just a little each,' I said, 'nice and warm.'

The wind died down some, and the sound of the animals was less.

A little wave reached up through the boards of our loft.

Phoebe squawked. 'Oh Jesus God almighty in Heaven,' she said.

'We must get up on the roof.'

They looked at me as if I was insane.

'The pickaxe,' I said, getting stiffly to my feet. 'Christ, I can't see a thing. Where is it? The pickaxe! We brought it up.'

'There, Auntie.' Billy scampered past me, grabbed the heavy thing and staggered back with it.

'Careful, Billy.'

'I *am* careful. Here, I'm stronger than you.'

He is, I suppose. The idea of me hefting that above my head.

'Careful, Billy!'

'Oh, give it here.' Phoebe took it and set to the roof above our heads, with clamped lips, clamped eyes.

'Oh God, don't let my baby die!' pleaded Mrs Raby, the edge on her voice as fresh as a sharpened blade, and then on she went, sobbing and begging like a madwoman, while Phoebe thunked away and Billy stood on a bale ripping at the loosened thatch. 'Quick, quick!' I said and thought of the walls below us giving up the ghost, the foundations washed away, the very hill on which we'd walked sinking deeper and deeper beneath the flood. The roof itself would melt under us like sugar in hot tea.

The sky appeared, muddy slate, and rain came in, no longer pelting but steady and fine.

'Come on now, Mrs Raby,' I said, 'up now,' but she was getting useless, rubbing at her eyes and wailing like a child. I spoke sharply to her. The baby started crying. 'Up now! Give me Thomas. Phoebe, take her up. Hold on to her. Here.' And then with a tremendous crash, something collapsed beneath us and half the loft disappeared. I think we all screamed. Mrs Raby stopped crying.

'Up!' I commanded, and up she went after Phoebe's scrambling legs. I passed the screaming baby up to Phoebe, then Billy went through. 'The ladder, Billy,' I shouted, dragging it to the hole in the thatch. Hands appeared, it was hauled up and I followed. The world outside was glorious. I can't say how miraculous that twilight was, the sudden strong air so fresh and clean after our loft eyrie, and the rushing sound all around us, the sound of life. It was blowy, yes, but the wind was no longer vicious, and the rain whispered on the water. The jacaranda tree soared over us, a great blue shadow. I thought we could climb up into its branches, then I thought no, it would never support us. We stowed the ladder along the roof ridge. Perhaps we could use it to get over to the tree if it came to it, and I strained my eyes in the growing dusk to see how heavy were the upper boughs; it seemed to me they grew flimsy at the tops. Maybe the ladder would fall through them, catching on nothing. Phoebe sat astraddle with her skirts hoiked up, holding on to Missis who sat quiet with the baby subsiding at the breast. I went dizzy if I looked down at the flood running by twelve feet or so beneath our feet.

'We must stay awake,' Mrs Raby said breathlessly. 'We'll fall in if we fall asleep.'

'Have you got the pistol?' asked Phoebe.

'I have it in my apron.'

I patted it.

'Let's all stay close together,' Mrs Raby said.

'Rope.' I began to scramble back along the roof, back down the hole.

'Auntie!' Billy cried.

'It's all right, Bill, you come and help me.'

Down below was a black giddy hole.

'Stay close to the wall, Billy. Feel carefully, it's somewhere around here.'

'Here!' he said.

'Good boy! Quick, up with you.'

It was some six feet from the end of the roof to the first great blue thickness of the tree. We didn't think. There was no time. The ladder was good and long and sturdy and served well.

'I can't,' Phoebe said.

'Look,' I said, 'it's a little sideways but it's well and caught in the cleft of those branches there.'

'I can cross that,' Mrs Raby said, wide-eyed.

'We'll hold it here. Go across, Mrs Raby, and take your baby, we've got a good ten feet more on the water if we can get over there.'

Phoebe looked sick.

'Tie him on my back,' Mrs Raby said.

I gave the pistol to Billy and tied the baby with my apron. He screamed. My hands were slipping, everything was drenched. 'Help me,' Mrs Raby said, ripping away at her nightgown. There was blood on her legs, all her cloths under her drawers were soaked through with it and she needed a change but there was nothing for it, not any more. She crossed with her eyes closed, I think. Once she'd started she never faltered, but went firmly ahead on hands and knees in her drawers, Thomas bawling down her ears, till the dark bulk of the tree swallowed her up.

There was a moment of wonder. Then her voice through the rain. 'Come over, come over!'

'Go on, Billy,' I said. 'Can you manage the rope? Here, if I put it like this.'

'Are you coming?'

'Of course I am. Go on!'

He went nimbly, a squirrel.

'Go on, Phoebe.'

'Jesus,' she whispered.

'Don't think, just do it.'

'But it's not coming up any more.'

'It is, you fool!'

'Don't you call me a shitten fool,' she said.

'For God's sake, Phoebe, get over there quick while I hold this end, then you hold it firm for me.'

'Auntie!' Billy called, an edge of panic in his voice.

She swore again, viciously, then crouched herself down like a frog, skirts tucked up in her bloomers, and over she went all clumsy and astraddle, furious-faced.

'Hold the ladder for me!' I shouted.

'Auntie!'

I need someone to hold it this end. Jesus Christ, I'm too old for this. I squat. I remember. Ipswich Gaol. I've done the impossible before. Up and over with you, Margaret. Hold your breath. Go between the spikes. The ladder shakes. The water rushes beneath and the world is wild. I'm not a bad woman and I'm going to die.

'I've got my hand out,' Phoebe's voice says, close. 'A little further, take it.'

6

It was a great old tree, it held us bravely above the flood though it was not as strong as all that. We were too big, too much of a strain on its poor boughs, but it was doing its best, and it sheltered us to some degree from the relentless rain. We tied ourselves in with the rope, just before darkness fell completely. And what darkness! I don't believe there'd ever been a blacker night, full of sound, the intermittent firing of distress muskets from afar, the mournful howling of dogs, human voices coming miles over the expanse, eerie and with no direction, calling, crying out. We didn't speak any more. I slept on and off, sometimes waking with a start when the baby cried, grateful for the rope round my waist. I was very hungry. It was all gone below, the cheese, the bread, the tea. The rum was carried away on the current, too heavy to keep, and the pistol had got wet and wouldn't fire. We hung there in our separate darknesses, seeing nothing. I began to think the others were all dead, but it was such a dream, so far away, my whole life being sucked down into a well. The distant crack of gunfire made sparks behind my eyes. I think my cottage will be safe. I can see my things there waiting for me to come home. The good old dogs. My letters. My little box where I keep aunts' and uncles' and cousins' hair. I wonder what happened to the people on the Hilliards' roof.

I think we may starve. I fall. Death comes easy. No, I am not dead. I'm awake again and the tree is sighing and water cooling my toes, and what I'd really like to see now is a good old Suffolk Punch. Remember old Dandy? What a horse he was! He was the horse I rode down to the river.

I am floating like God above the face of the waters, breathing out my spirit. A baby cries. I hear a boat coming, a big big ship at harbour, the convict ship at Spithead. I sleep. The sound of oars slaps against the night. A gun cracks. Dark night, trees, the banks at Woolverstone, and the boat coming in on the Orwell, and in it Will Laud, the smuggler.

Everything has fallen away before the waters.

Salt Horse

7

Suffolk, 1768

When I was six years old I saw a woman called Jane Brewer burned in Ipswich. I was on my brother Robert's shoulders, my sister Susan was holding my hand. The Cracknell lads, our neighbours, were there, pushing one another about and shouting raucously. Georgie Cracknell pulled on my leg and I gave him a kick.

This one was different from the crowds at market days and holidays, closer-packed, milling and restless like a choppy sea, but not gay or pleasant in any way, despite the chattering voices and sudden blusters of laughter. We were a little to the side, close to the front. I could feel the pack of the bodies round my legs and was glad my head was so high above it all, like riding a monster, this way and that. Sue hung on to my hand and Robert's old ripped jacket. It was a fine bright day. A woman sold songs. I wanted a toffee apple. Near to us was a gang of young lads on the drunk, larking about like pups.

Three men already hung from the long crossbeam behind the gallows, tight and stiff like babes in swaddling, their heads hanging strangely, bent at the neck. We had not seen them turned off. I felt queasy. We should not be here. Robert would be in trouble if our mum got to know. He was fourteen, Sue was twelve and they did everything together. In front was a smaller platform, with a tall stake topped by iron rings, and a bright, clean noose hanging from the highest ring. That's where they were going to burn the woman. We'd waited a half-hour already and I wished she'd come. I wanted to see what happened.

Robert pointed out the sheriff and the hangman. 'And him there with the hat's the minister,' he said. He was a hefty boy, very comfortable for riding. He knew all about it because he'd seen when they burned Ann Beddingfield and hanged Richard Ringe for the killing of her husband; old Robinson Crusoe who goes up and down in his mad boat says he's got her rib, but everyone knows there was only ash left at the end.

I thought I saw a boy from our farm and craned to see.

'Stop wriggling!' Robert twitched his big meaty shoulders.

There was a shiver and a murmur through us all and Sue stood on tiptoe. I turned my head. A scruffy cart came past the two wagonloads of faggots and through the parting press. I saw Jane Brewer sitting upright looking at the crowd. She was young and plain and pale, very dirty and draggly with scraggy brown hair, and when she went by nearly close enough to reach out and touch, I saw that she was trembling like an old crone with the palsy. The crowd spoke, a ragged roar from which I picked out laughter and wordless shouting, her name called here and there – Jane! Jane! – and the odd few words:

'Poor soul!'

'Oh, I can't watch!'

'Look! Look!'

I strained to see her eyes. They were bright and frightened like the eyes of a horse in labour. Her mouth hung open.

'What's she done?' I asked. 'Has she murdered her husband?'

Sue said she'd tried to colour copper coins and pass them off as silver, which didn't seem so shocking a thing to me.

They drew her past the hanging bodies and she turned her face to them and I think she stared. The executioner and his man lifted her from the cart to the platform, and though I could not hear, it seemed to me that they were gentling her as you do with a nervous animal. I held my breath with the crowd, quite sick with all the waiting and the strangeness.

'Look away if you want, Peggy,' Sue whispered loudly.

But I had to see it all, how it happened. I wanted to see what changes came over Jane Brewer's face. She walked stiffly, arms pinioned. Her face was not clear any more now that she was that bit further away – I could not make out any particular expression. The minister held her arm, speaking quietly in her ear. And how he smiled at her, so gentle, a poor sad man who would, if he could, have made it all go away for her. She quivered like a thread of soot caught in the chimney above the fire, shivering with heat, trembling with cold. All's one. Then they took her and showed her what she had to do, and she went up the little stairs and stood there next to the stake. She feels funny with all these people watching her, I thought. Every single one intent on her plain face. Those Cracknell boys, eyes wide, mouths agape. Robert still as stone. You could have heard a pin drop. A woman in front of us started crying. All the time, even from this distance, you could see the trembling all through her bound body, as if it was casting her off, just shivering her away. Then the noose came down from the iron bracket, and the hangman put it round her neck, and I felt it rest upon mine.

The minister said something else I couldn't hear. It went quiet.

'What are they doing?' I whispered.

'Praying,' said Sue. Her black hair hung witchy.

I wished they'd get on with it. It was horrible waiting, hardly daring to draw breath; thinking any second now, any second; and the moment of time both long and short. When it happened, it happened fast. The hangman pulled down another iron ring and fixed it above her waist, his man handed up some big iron nails and a hammer, and at each bang of the hammer her eyes flew wide and so did mine. He fixed her to the stake with the ring and a chain. His lips moved as he yanked the noose tight round her neck and stepped down, pulling the stairs out from under her. It was a very short drop, one second. Robert's shoulders stiffened under me. Her eyes opened wide, her neck went snap, her head went sideways. A great gasp came out from the crowd, and she dangled there like a mole from a fence. I couldn't see her face – she'd swung round, but I saw how still she was at first, before her toes turned up and her poor sweet feet started jerking.

'Shame!' someone shouted, and a brawling of voices rose up all over.

The hangman got down off the platform. My brother started walking away, but I turned my head to look. She shook.

'Robert! Robert!'

But he kept walking away, and on the edge of the crowd set me down, saying I was a great heavy lump. Sue put her arms round me. 'Did you look?' she asked.

I nodded.

'Shall we get a toffee apple?'

I nodded.

'Not a word!'

'Is she dead now?' I asked.

'She will be in a minute.'

Robert went off with some of the Cracknell boys and Sue took me for a toffee apple. Later she lifted me on to a window sill to watch the burning. Jane Brewer was hanging just the way we left her, only now her feet were completely still and pointing downwards. Her body circled faintly inside its ring. They were piling the faggots round her. The crowd grew tight again. I knew she was dead, of course I knew she was dead but then again, I thought, what if something is there inside her still, some fear, some little poor flame of whatever she is, saying, please no, I hurt still, I hurt. When the flames licked up, the crowd hustled closer like dogs to a hearth. It exhaled. 'Ah!' it sighed, and again, 'ah!' Black smoke writhed up into the sky and I thought it was the soul of Jane Brewer getting away, twisting in pain. Heat reached my face. The flames spat and hissed and ran up the piles of faggots, up the stake, and up the body of Jane Brewer; and the bonfire grew wild and huge and golden like a lion, cracking like muskets. There she hung, a black chrysalis in the centre, till the rope burned through and she dropped, but the chain kept her to the stake. We stayed a while, watching, but all there was left to be seen was a black grub that hung and burned and never seemed to get any smaller.

Robert appeared.

'Home,' he said.

8

I kept waking that night. Jane Brewer was walking in our house, smiling at me with bloody teeth, dirty like she was on the cart. She kept tossing me back awake. Twice I cried out and woke Mum, who slept as light as a baby.

'For heaven's sake, Margaret, you'll wake Ned.' She plumped down on the side of the bed, her face greasy and bald-eyed from sleep. 'I've only just got him down. What have you been eating?'

'Nothing, Mum.'

'What were you dreaming?'

'Nothing.' I couldn't tell her, she'd have walloped me and Sue. She couldn't wallop Robert because he was too big, built like a bullock. She hated the crowds at those things. She said they were vulgar and it was no place for a respectable woman, let alone a child. So I told her I was scared because Georgie Cracknell told me a woman was burned in town today and vowed from the stake to come back and haunt.

'Tosh!' Mother said. 'You take no notice of Georgie Cracknell. Don't think about it.' She plumped up my pillow.

'I keep thinking what it must have been like,' I said.

'What?'

'To burn.'

'They hang them first,' Mother said, 'they don't know anything about it.'

'Hanging hurts though, doesn't it?'

'Not for long. Anyway–' She pushed me back against the pillow. It smelt stale. '–those things only happen to people who rob and kill and steal.'

That gave me a fright. I'd stolen. I took Dandy from the field and rode him down to the river. All I had was the halter, I stood on the stile to get on his back. I never could abide a saddle or any of that nonsense. You have to feel the horse between your legs, let it know the clutch of your thighs and the dig of your toes and the squeeze of your knees. I rode him all the way down the lane, over the field and right into the middle of the stream till the water was up to my knees, and there we stayed for ever so long, me and Dandy, perfectly happy with a hawk hanging over the field looking for mice, and the Nacton bells ringing. When I got back, Mr Denton was standing on our path telling my father how someone had stolen one of the horses. My mother was at the door with Ned squalling in her arms. Mr Denton's face was a picture as I rode into the yard, scattering the skinny hens that pecked here and there on the overgrown flagstones. My father's jaw fell open. Then Mr Denton burst out laughing. 'How old is she, Jonathon?' he kept asking my dad, though he knew quite well I was six.

'Margaret,' my father said, lifting me down, both proud and vexed as my mother scolded and popped a sugar tit in Ned's mouth, 'you'll be the death of me.' He was a tall stooped man, always very gentle with me. He smelled of the field.

I hadn't thought it wrong, because Dandy was like our own horse in a way, even though he didn't belong to us. But no, my father said later, very serious: we could not do just what we wished with any of the horses, not without asking Mr Denton first, because that was stealing and that was wrong. So this was what I was thinking as my mother went out and I turned sideways on the pillow to look at the darkness in the window: that if Mr Denton had not been the nice man who sometimes gave me a penny and paid all the wages for my father and brothers and the Cracknell boys, he would have called for the sergeant to take me away and they would say, Thief! Thief! and put me in the lock-up; and in a matter of time it would be me on the platform with the bright, clean noose around *my* neck. Then there'd be no hiding it from my mum.

9

I grew up with horses. Ever since I was able to be lifted up and held on the back of one I've been riding them. I'd say there were three things truly mine. My family – that is, a feeling of a nest when I think of a certain time – then my horses, and then my Will, but he came along much later.

My dad was head ploughman, and looked after the team for Mr Denton. My mother was a Yarmouth woman who came into Bury one year for the assizes, selling herring with her brother that lived at Brandeston; and there met my dad and came down here to Nacton. She'd sooner look on a boat than a horse, she said. Their great feet scared her. She liked to see the big ships come up the Orwell. All the way from Langer Point to Ipswich they come, right past us, and if you run down through the woods you come to where the river's widest, and in winter you can count a thousand thousand birds should you have the mind to. And when the decoy-ponds are frozen over, they come in their droves on the river: duck and diver, black coot, geese, swans. The river smells salt like the sea. In Yarmouth, Mum said, you could smell the sea continually. I myself was never there, and I never even saw the sea till my eleventh year, but you could not live in our parts and be unaware of its presence, shimmering away invisibly over there east where the sun rose, not so very far away. Always when we went into town, my mother would make a point of getting away from the heaving market to the docks, and we'd walk along by the boats. She'd take us down to St Clement's and along Neptune Quay, where a house stood, with a funny chimney. It was Mr Fenn's apothecary, and the butcher's was next door, and she'd go in and conduct her business there while Susan walked about with Ned, and I ran up and down the cobbles where the sailors came all a-swagger off the boats, and the cargoes were landed. Everything rang with the sounds of work, boat-work, man-work, and I wished I could grow up and go to sea and be a sailor. Either that or follow the horses like my dad and my big brothers. My mother said no, that you can't do, none of that is work for a girl, and women don't go to sea.

'Yes they do,' Charles said. 'What about Anne Bonney and Mary Reade? They was women and *they* went to sea, they was pirate women and they wore breeches a long time ago.'

My brother Charles knew all kinds of things. He was tall and dark and spiky with black staring eyes. Our sexton was teaching him because he said he was a bright boy. He could tell you all the kings and queens of England in order. Sweyn Forkbeard, the son of Harold Bluetooth, always took my fancy. It was his name. I didn't actually know anything at all about him apart from the fact that he was the father of Canute, who tried to turn the sea back.

'Well, she ain't wearing no breeches,' my mother said, 'and she ain't going to no sea so you shut your mouth.' But she said it nicely, because truth being told she'd have loved to go to sea herself.

The Widow Syers was my mother's cousin, and she lived on Rope Lane in Ipswich. She kept a house where sailors could be seen going up and down stairs all day, and when we were in town we'd go to her house sometimes and she'd give us children barley sugar and poke her scrawny dark-eyed face in Ned's and make him cry. The door was always a little open because she liked to keep an eye on the comings and goings. On this particular day, it came on to pouring with rain. It started up like a scatter of gunshot, and I rushed to the window and watched it bouncing high in the road and everyone hurrying along with their heads down. Aunt Syers says to wait it out, and bangs on the ceiling with a cane and calls down a pale-faced young sailor with cheeks as soft and naked as a baby's, who never says a word or looks at anyone, and sends him for pies and builds up the fire. She and my mum, they could sit for hours if you let them. I watched them drawing themselves up closer to the fire and settling their feet on the hearth, Mum a stout woman, the widow all bones. The widow's room was dirty and cosy and steamy, and a fine grease speckled the range.

'A little brandy for you?' Aunt Syers says to Mum, and Mum says only a little one though.

They drink out of cups, sip and sit back and slap their lips thoughtfully.

'That's nice brandy,' Mum says.

'You'll not get better,' says Aunt Syers. 'My boys they do look after me.' Then she turns her neck on which a very old, very faded yellow handkerchief is knotted, and smiles at me. 'Get yourself a sailing boy when you grow up, Peggy,' she says to me, 'you can't go wrong.'

'There's truth in that,' says my mother.

'They're out from under your feet most of the time, and they bring home the bacon.'

They both laugh.

'I told your Sue the same.'

'Oh, Sue's got her head on,' Mum said. 'You don't need to tell her nothing. This one's a different case, ain't you, Peg?'

'You're a tall great thing, Peggy,' Aunt Syers said, 'but there's nothing on you.'

'There's nothing on you either,' I said.

'Bold thing,' said the widow and chuckled, then the pale-faced sailor came back soaking wet with the pies and she let him have a pie for going.

'Thanks, missis,' he says gruffly and goes upstairs.

A sailor would do, I thought. He could go to sea and I could look after the horses, and sometimes I'd go with him. Like in the song Mum sang, where she dresses up as a boy and goes climbing up the rigging.

'Well, I never yet seen the sea,' I said. But the Widow Syers laughed and said, 'Nor have I, Peggy, and don't care a fig. You don't need to see the sea to marry a sailor.' Which is true, because she was married to a sailor before he drowned off the coast of France, and she never even left Ipswich.

Sue got a bad pie. That's what Mum always

said after, but I wasn't sure. I thought she got sick from earlier on the quay, when Mum was in the butcher's and Sue cleaned Ned's nose. You never saw a child like Ned for the snot. Always full to the brim with it he was, thick green slugs of it sitting on his upper lip; and no matter how much you wiped and wiped it kept on coming, and he never would blow it out, didn't seem to have the hang of it somehow. On this day Sue had wiped his nose a million times and she was fretting over the way he couldn't breathe at all, his mouth stuck open so he looked gormless as a johnny raw. 'Oh, poor poor thing!' she kept saying, and when he started grizzling, fell to her knees in front of him and covered his tiny nose with her mouth and sucked and spat, sucked and spat, four or five times till he was clear, making a yellowy-green frothy mess on the stones. I didn't know how she could do that. I felt quite sick. But she was like that, Sue, good-hearted; and she loved that child and hated seeing him suffer.

But Mum was sure it was the pie. Anyway, that night Sue started to vomit, and she went on and on, and very early in the morning Charles went to fetch Dr Stebbing. By the time he came she'd gone all yellow, and big grey rings had appeared under her eyes. She heaved and heaved as if some great fat snake was thrashing around inside her. The doctor was with her a long time. When he came out he said she was trying to rest and we were to leave her alone. Let her get plenty of rest but keep a good eye on her. So me and Ned had to sleep in the kitchen, all snuggled up together in front of the dying fire in the dark; we liked that. The kitchen was warm after the day, and the smell of supper lingered on the air, and after that it was me got to carry Ned around all the time and do everything for him when Mum was busy. And Mum was always busy, because Sue never really was well again after that. She stopped being sick and staying in bed all day, of course, but she just wasn't the same girl, ever. You have to have known Sue before that, how bright she was and how wide awake and always willing all the time, whatever it was you wanted her to do with you. She was a good big sister, my sister Sue. A thin dark girl like me, with a nice smile. She and me and Charles and James were dark like my dad before he went grey, and Ned and Robert were fairer. But Sue, though she went on smiling, was never so quick and hadn't the flame no more. Took to her bed very easily, and was no use at all about the place, and never wanted to do anything or go anywhere any more, poor Sue. Even Robert, her dearest because he was so close to her agewise, and so different, being big and slow where she was quick and small – even he could not get her up and doing.

10

I finally got to see the sea in my eleventh year when my mother decided to take us three youngest on a visit to Brandeston to my Uncle Willy Leader's so we could meet his new wife, an

Aldeburgh girl. She said a change would do Sue good. By this time, Sue was no child. She was sixteen, pale, black-eyed, a beautiful soft thing that never made trouble for anyone. She helped Mum about the house when she could, but then she'd get tired and have to lie down. It made you yawn just to look at Sue.

Our cottage was just by where the lane turned down to Denton's farmhouse. The woods started over the way. My three big brothers were men now. Charles took us in the cart to meet Noller's Wagon that morning. James and Robert were out with my dad in the dawn tending the horses. We went north on a very fine morning over Rushmere Heath where they burned Ann Beddingfield and hanged Richard Ringe. A little breeze fluttered over that wild place. Rabbits started up and bobbed before the cart. You wouldn't go over the heath at night because of footpads. Mum didn't even like it in the day. She said it was a scandal and a disgrace the way decent people couldn't go anywhere these days without getting their throats cut. You knew where you were with the free trade boys, she said, the smugglers wouldn't touch a poor ordinary traveller, but some of these low robbers were no better than savages. Soon we were on the Woodbridge road, and there was the carrier's wagon coming up from town full of boxes and crates, and when she and Sue were settled nicely up at the front next to the driver, Mum put back her bonnet to cool her hot red face and commenced cracking nuts in her lap and singing snatches of old songs all the way to Woodbridge. We stopped for the driver to deliver some goods and a coach going south drew to a halt nearby and struck us all dumb. On top was a string of people all chained together like you'd bind a string of onions, men and women and children, all filthy and vile. One was a boy my age, with great blue eyes that fixed on to mine. It was like talking to one another the way we just looked, like saying, hello. I swear even now I can still see that boy's face in every detail. The men's bare ankles were rubbed rough from the fetters, and the women were all draggled and foul.

'Poor things,' my mother said, 'they're away to America and they'll never come back,' and she reached out with what was left of the nuts, standing up in the wagon. One held out his hand, lifting it to us with a great effort: I saw how heavily the chains weighed him down, and I saw where a V was branded in his palm, an old mark. A guard was going about with water in a bottle.

'You're not allowed to feed the prisoners,' he said apathetically.

She tossed the bag of nuts anyway, and the branded hand, fingers splayed and flat at the ends, closed upon it and withdrew into the stinky mass. Then our driver returned and my mother blew a kiss to a poor young lad with mouth and cheeks as flaccid as a baby's, and we were on our way.

'They'll be like slaves,' Mum said, 'even the wild savages and the niggers do better than they do.'

I thought of the boy going all the way across that big sea and never seeing all the things he knew ever again. Working chained in the sun, no fun or kind words for him again. Poor boy! I said to myself, and it sounded nice. Poor boy! I put my arms round Ned. Ned was the sort of boy you could always put your arms round, he never minded. He'd wriggle and smile and preen. But now he was solemn because of the people going away to America all filthy dirty, though he tried a smile with his small soft mouth. His eyes were very bright brown. He was all of five, and his face was taking on a vaguely ratty look that was sweet and pretty in some indefinable way. From Woodbridge to Brandeston was another eight miles. My mother started to sing about poor Jack Hall who got hanged. Noller's driver joined in with her but he didn't know all the words, so mostly he just hummed. I've heard that song sound so merry you forget it's about some poor gawm getting his neck stretched, but the way my mum sang it you could've sobbed. She was very soft, Mum, she'd cry at anything, and she loved a good song. By the time she'd got to the end the tears were streaming down her cheeks and her nose was red. So we got her on to the jolly stuff instead, and soon we'd all recovered. The clouds had come over the sun. Sue sat up straight and started pointing out familiar landmarks. She turned round to me and smiled. 'Do you remember, Peggy?' she said. 'Do you recognise anything at all?'

I'd been before but couldn't well remember. In her it was all more real, because she'd seen it all the more. I shook my head.

'*I* do,' she said, and her smile was brighter than I'd seen it in ages. 'Don't you remember the garden? The lovely flowers?'

There were two red points in her white face, one right in the middle of each cheek, and her eyes seemed bigger and darker than before.

'Uncle gave you such an armful to bring home last time,' my mother said, pulling her shawl tighter. A slow drizzle began.

This time of year, Sue said, there'd be daffodils all round the house, and after the wagon had dropped us in growing rain at the Queen's Head, and we'd hurried with our gear down the lane away from the village and along the track where the trees began to grow thick, so there were – a marvellous sweep of them as if someone had thrown a yellow blanket over the hollow where my uncle's house stood. Uncle Leader, my mother's younger brother, was standing at his front door trimming his beard with a pair of enormous scissors, but he dropped them as soon as he saw us, and came running up the path to embrace my mother and take her bundle.

'I was not expecting you for an hour at least,' he cried.

'How are you, William?' she said wearily, putting forward her cheek to be kissed.

'I was going to come and meet the wagon.' He pushed his hands through his hair. 'Good God, look at this big girl! And is this our little Peggy? And this fine young lad! Ellen, Ellen, they're here!'

We were all agog to see the new aunt. She came to the door and stood smiling shyly, a very small thing in a green dress, thin of face with eyes that never settled. She greeted us all very fair and went off to make the tea.

'What do you think?' he asked my mum. 'Done well for myself, haven't I?'

'She'll not last,' Mum said, which seemed an odd thing to say though she smiled and said it like a joke, and my uncle only laughed; but then Uncle Leader never took anything seriously in his life. We'd grown up on stories of his naughtiness as a boy, and I could never think of him as a proper grown-up person at all.

'Come in, come in!' All smiles he was, all the host, and nervous because he wanted us to like this new wife who'd appeared so suddenly.

'Now, what'll it be? A little brandy? Susan, you wan little soul.' He pinched her cheeks, sat her down by the fire, poured hot water from the kettle in a bowl with some brandy. 'Here, this'll pick you up, miss,' he said, standing at the table stirring in nutmeg and sugar. 'What's been the matter with her, Maisy?'

'Oh, she's a lot better now,' Mum said. 'She was sick and it took her a long time to get over it, that's all.'

The house smelled damp. Uncle Leader blew up the fire and our new aunt brought in some lemon tarts from the pantry, and blushed but said nothing when we all remarked on how nice they were.

'Oh yes, Ellen's a rare cook.' Uncle Leader twinkled his eyes at her, and she gave a funny little giggle and looked down at her hands clasping and unclasping one another in her lap. She was not much more of a girl than Sue, I realised, very young for my Uncle Leader with his big red beard and his face all ruddy and weathered, the nose flattened by a punch. My mother looked around her as if weighing it all in the balance: the chairs and the shutters painted blue, the hearth polished, the candlesticks all clean and the candles trimmed. 'Very good, Willy, yes,' she nodded, 'she seems a nice enough sort,' as if Aunt Leader wasn't there at all.

'I gather you're an Aldeburgh girl,' Mum said to the poor woman.

'I am,' she said.

'And how do you take to life in here?'

'In here?'

'Landlocked,' my mother said.

'The Deben's nearby.'

'Willy knows,' my mother persisted. 'I've said it before, I'd die if I had to live here, I would. Where we are we get the boats and all the sailors at least. I never could abide to be without a sniff of the water.'

Aunt Leader seemed lost for words.

'Don't you miss the sea?' my mother asked.

At which Aunt Leader sat up straight and her neck stuck up and forward like a bird's. The cap she wore was a white frill about her brow and under it the thin skin of her pale freckled forehead knotted. 'Miss the sea?' she said fiercely, as if accused of a dreadful crime. 'I hate the sea! I hope I never ever in all my born days have to look upon the sea again!'

That quietened us all.

'There,' my mother said, 'as I always say, one man's sauce.'

I caught a look between my uncle and my mother. 'Ellen's lost one or two to the sea,' he said.

Mum shook her head and clicked her tongue in a way that meant sympathy. 'Very sorry, dear,' she said. 'One man's sauce.'

So no more was said about the sea, and later Uncle Leader told my mother that his wife's father and uncle had both been excisemen drowned when the free-traders shot a cannonball over their bows near Sizewell Gap.

'How terrible,' Mum said when she told me and Sue. 'How terrible all this fighting!' We were walking along the path that sloped down through the woods to the river. 'No wonder the poor girl hates the sea; there's no doubting of course it can be cruel. Though there has to be a little free trade or where would the poor man be? Why should there not be a little comfort in life, ain't things hard enough?' Mum had always given us to know that the law was unfair. It was a mess, was what she said, all a big mess and a shocking shame. You just had to do your best and keep your nose clean if you could because if not they'd string you up soon as look at you.

'How would you like to see the sea, eh, Ned? Peggy?' Uncle Leader said later as we ate our stew. His big red hands ripped a hunk of bread in half to mop up the gravy. 'Put the flowers back in your cheeks, Susan.'

'Can we go out in a boat?' asked Ned. 'On the proper sea?'

Uncle Leader laughed. 'Maybe,' he said, 'if there's time.' Then he said there was an auction in Aldeburgh the day after tomorrow, and he was all for buying a pig. If any of us wanted to go we could, but we must be up very early. Mum was more excited than any of us. 'Mary Cracknell's boy's in Aldeburgh now,' she said. 'He's in his Uncle Jack's boatyard. I must go and find out how he is.'

Mary Cracknell used to be my mother's best friend, but she was dead fourteen years now.

'Are you coming with us, dear,' she asked our new Aunt Leader in a solicitous tone. Aunt Leader was not to be moved. Hardly a word you could get out of her, though Uncle Leader clearly doted. Whenever he got up and walked past her chair, he stroked her shoulder as you might a cat in passing.

11

Charles said Captain James Cook took three years to sail all the way round the world! Imagine that! And now he was off again. All manner of strange beasts and giant plants he saw. If every day, as each brand-new horizon went on before him, he experienced even half of what I felt the first time I saw the sea at Aldeburgh, he must have been a happy man. It gave me a tight feeling in my chest as if I couldn't breathe, but Mum said that was only the fresh sea air doing me good.

Aldeburgh was a nice little town, smelling of the sea, full of taverns. There was a market in the square but the first thing my mother wanted to do, before any shopping or anything, was take us three for a walk next to the sea. So while Uncle Leader went and got his pig, we walked down between the cottages of the fishermen and out on to the wide shingle. At first it was hard to walk upon, I thought. But soon it seemed less so, and Ned and I started running about and picking up stones, all lovely, all different. The big hiss of the waves running up the shingle sounded in our ears. We shrieked against the noise. Gulls danced in the air, cruel-eyed. After a time Sue was tired and had to sit down with Mum high up the beach where it was dry. It was not cold, the sun was out and there was only a very little wind really. Me and Ned sat down too, a little way off. We played with the pebbles. I buried him up to his neck and he looked so funny with just his grinning face sticking out all pink; then he was going to bury me but Mum saw what we were about, and called across to me not to be a fool, I'd ruin my dress. So we walked up and down the shingle instead. Later, Mum took us to an inn on the beach. There was a room at the side where we could sit and look out at the sea. A man brought us some eggs, while Mum enquired outside about the whereabouts of Jack Laud's boatyard.

Jack was a rough man but a good sort, she said as we walked to the quay. Mary's poor lad lost his mother too young, left him with a right drunken pig of a dad, she did, couldn't raise a chicken let alone a child. Thank God for his Uncle Jack, that's all *she* could say.

A big ship was at the quay, and men were unloading barrels and crates, shouting to one another in a strange lilting tongue. They were tall and lithe and ran up and down the gangplank like children swarming over a fallen tree. We went in the boatyard. A hulk was half made, just ribs. My mother then thought better of Sue's presence there, in light of the fact that some of the men were naked to the waist, and she sent us out on to the quay. A boat was on the slipway, a cutter, nearly done, newly painted black. Two men were rubbing tar on the keel.

We rambled along the water's edge in the direction of the sea. Now I knew what my mother meant when she said the smell of the sea was like nothing at all you'd ever taste where we lived, not even when you stood on the quay in Ipswich and watched a fishing boat unload; not even down on the Orwell shores when the wind was blowing inland. It stung in the nostrils as if it was scouring you out. There was a boy in a boat singing a song: *Salt horse, salt horse, fifty days away, oh, salt horse, salt horse, fifty mile a day oh salt horse...* He was about fifteen, with a pigtail hanging down his back. That was Will Laud, but I didn't know it then. We passed him. We walked out to where the sea comes in on one side and the river on the other. I wanted to run and run, but Sue said she was cold.

'Let's turn back,' she said. Her teeth were chattering. As we walked, I saw my mother come out of the boatyard and track in our direction. She stopped on the quay and called down to the boy in the boat, who turned his craft lazily and brought it in close to the wall. By the time we reached her, my mother was laughing at something she'd said, and the boy was standing up in the boat. He winked at Ned.

'This is Mary Cracknell's boy,' said Mum.

There were so many Cracknell boys. Cousins and nephews and young uncles. This one didn't look much like a Cracknell. He was big-featured, wide-eyed, his mouth as soft as an infant's.

'I'm not a Cracknell,' the boy said, 'I'm a Laud.'

It sounded funny, as if he was saying: I'm a lord, and I started laughing. He looked at me as if to say, What are *you* laughing at?

'And his uncle says he's getting along very nicely, don't you know,' Mum said in the way she had, as if he wasn't there. 'I remember him when he was a tiny squalling thing in Mary's house. The lungs on him!'

'Still got 'em,' the boy said, grinning.

'Do you know where them sailors come from down there?' I asked him.

He licked his big lips and looked sideways to where the men hauled and gestured. 'Holland,' he said.

My mother was all smiles. 'You remember and come and see us.'

He raised one eyebrow sharply and looked away, smiling.

Uncle Leader came along looking for us, to take us round the town. 'Quick! Punchinello's in front of the Moot Hall,' he said. Ned was wild to see Punchinello. The town was jolly and bright. Uncle Leader bought us children each a twig of liquorice. I didn't like Punchinello. He was a hard cruel mad thing, and the light in his eyes was evil. But

Ned laughed himself silly and everyone cheered. A beggar woman went among us with her brats, staring into our faces.

Mum said to Sue: 'He's got a woman living there with him now to look after the boy.'

'Has he now,' said Sue as if she couldn't care less.

'Poor boy,' Mum said again, 'hardly known a mother.'

She liked that.

12

We bought duck eggs and butter and parsnips, and in the evening ate our supper at the Three Mariners once more, in the little side parlour where they'd built up a fire. Uncle Leader pulled the cork from a bottle of gin and told stories of the smugglers: how they dipped and dived before the law. He laughed at the tricks they played. So did my mother. You should have seen them roaring together over how those bold men outwitted the coastguard every time. It struck me as odd, considering Aunt Leader's poor father and uncle, but then he leaned forward and said softly: 'Not a word like this in Ellen's presence.'

'Oh, of course,' said my mother, wiping tears from her eyes. 'As if I would.'

I fell asleep in the heat from the Three Mariners' parlour fire. Later I was carried and put into the wagon. I opened my eyes and sat up and looked out at the little raggedy town going by, and from then on was wide awake while everyone else slept, apart from the driver and Uncle Leader, who sat with his new pig in its makeshift pen, soothing its mournful shuffle and snuffle with a softly drunken lilt.

Bareback

13

My mother taught me how to weave rushes. I used to sit and make them into baskets with Susan when she was too weak and tired to do much else, but I'm sorry to say it used to drive me mad. It sounds wicked but I became so sick of having to sit with Sue. There were times when I thought I would scream or run wild, jump up and shout my lungs out; when I'd look up in the late afternoon after plying with my fingers so nimbly hour on hour, and my eyes would swim with tears, straining at the world and seeing only twined patterns. Where had all the time gone? Time's always seemed on the run to me.

I was not a child any more. I'd grown fast in the years that had passed since our visit to Uncle Leader's. I was taller than my mother now. Georgie Cracknell had started staring at my bosom, small as it was, whenever we went to their house for our dinner after church. But I didn't fancy Georgie or any other Cracknell. I fancied getting a sailor. My mind turned on those who passed up and down the Widow Syers' back stair, some of them so young and sweet and lithe, like fresh young animals. I stood on the quay and watched them running up and down the rigging. I thought about them when I took myself off of an evening to the big meadow across the barley and sat by the hedge to watch the horses graze among the flowers. Sometimes they'd amble over, putting down their great chestnut heads to me, kissing me with gentle horse breath. Their tails were docked. When the flies landed they could only shiver, shaking their long silver manes. Sometimes I'd get on the stile and climb up on the back of one of them, usually Dandy, or a fine bold young gelding called Jem I'd seen broken in by Mr Denton. I'd watched Jem pace at the end of a rope, thinking: I could do that. I rode Jem with my knees, round and round the meadow, my hands in his mane.

It was my great good fortune that on the day Mrs Denton took a funny turn, Jem was the one in the stable.

Lucky I'd gone up to the farmhouse that day. Mum sent me with a message about Robert having come home sick from the field and taken to his bed so he'd not be working the day out. He'd had too much liquor in the sun, that's what it was, big fool. I was to say it was a sudden fever. As I came up the lane I heard an awful squawking and a big big grey goose came running to meet me at the gate with its neck out-thrust. All the dogs were barking. And there was Mrs Denton, who was always so stiff and brisk and straight, kicking and pitching on the dirty stones in the yard amongst the spilled feed she'd been giving to the hens. Her plump white bloomers were on show, her back arched. The bucket rolled. Her eyes turned white in her head. Her throat was bared as if for the knife, and a spasm moved there, a mad thing alive under the skin. One of the maids came running to the door, but just stood there frozen.

The stable door was open. 'I'm going for Dr

Stebbing,' I said.

The maid put her arm round Mrs Denton, now lying still. 'There there,' she said, 'you'll be fine now. Lily!' she shouted. A girl appeared. 'Madam's taken bad. You go and get the master, I'll get her to bed. Come on now, madam, there's the girl!'

I ran into the stable. Jem and Dandy were in the stalls. Dandy was an old nag now, pulling gently at the hay in his manger and mumbling to himself like some worthy grandfather by the fire in the evening. Jem threw up his head when he saw me. He looked as it he'd just been groomed. He was tethered loosely by the halter, no saddle or bridle. I just slipped the halter and led him out, and was up on the block and on him, and we were off. We flew. Down the lane and straight past our house, past my brothers and my father at work in the field, who stopped what they were doing and stared, thinking Margaret must have gone mad to be galloping Jem so intently with her skirts hoiked up and her hair come loose and streaming. Stones flew up from the ground. 'Margaret!' my father yelled, but there was no time. I waved my hand. We were gone. Hedges and copses flew by, clouds raced above. I could have opened my throat and let out a cry of sheer joy to be riding so wildly on such a beautiful day. But it would not have seemed right with poor Mrs Denton, a lady I liked well, half dead back there. I'd not ridden like this for years, not since I was a dusty child. A young lady should know better. But they wouldn't mind this time – this time I could ride as hard as I liked. I crouched low over Jem's neck and spoke to him, gripping with my knees, his muscles tight under mine, digging with my booted heels. His spirit was up with mine. Seven miles with no pause, no slowing, no reason. If he'd taken leave of the ground and mounted to the clouds I would not have been surprised. The heath opened wide, scored with sheepwalks. 'Ha!' I cried aloud. I was a highwayman. Stand and deliver, I've a pair of pops here will take the head off any man, and the finest prancer in the land. We will dance at the crossroads. The race ground came up on our right. Men were at work on the new gentlemen's stand. They put down their tools and shielded their eyes to watch me streak past, fast as any jockey that ever ran the course. We crested the hill and the town lay before us. St Clement's rushed up to meet us. The chestnut horse plunged. I lay back along his spine and squeezed in hard with my knees, moving with him, leaning and swaying as we plummeted faster and faster and it became necessary to rein him back a little in case we tumbled and rolled, the two of us, head over heels like a wheel.

We did not slow as we came into Ipswich, not till we'd passed the first shops and the docks were looming alongside. Along Fore Street we cantered, past the old butcher's and the apothecary where my mother used to take us years ago, all changed now and become a tavern, with people drinking in front: men who raised their tankards and cheered me along, whoop-whooping at the sight of my stockinged legs.

I waved and blew them a kiss.

I rode right into the middle of town, to Stepples Street where I knew the doctor lived. Stepples

Street had grand big houses and I had no idea which was his. People stood around gaping at me. I cried out to a respectable-looking man in a pale-grey suit: 'Sir, I'm come for Dr Stebbing. Which is his house?'

He stepped up to Jem's head. 'Here, my maid,' he said, whiskers wagging. 'You're just by it.'

I jumped down. My knees gave way and I staggered like a drunk.

'Aha,' he said, taking my arm to steady me. 'How far have you ridden?'

'From Nacton.'

'Without a saddle?'

'There was no time.'

'Let me hold your horse for you,' said the gentleman, and I gave him the reins.

So many people, the street full it seemed, all staring at me. Some had followed me up from as far as Fore Street to see what all the fuss was about.

The doctor's house was a large red-brick square, with steps leading up to a front door with a marvellous polished gold knocker made like a dolphin. In our house it would have been hung about the fire and taken down and polished once a week. I ran up the steps and knocked hard. Everything about me jangled and tingled from the ride. My breath came staggered. A maid opened the door.

'My mistress has had a fit,' I said.

'The doctor's at his lunch,' she replied doubtfully.

'Tell him I've rid all the way from Nacton,' I said. 'She's very very bad.'

Stebbing himself came to the door, still chewing on his food, a square-faced, thin-mouthed man with wispy brown hair.

'It's Mrs Denton, sir,' I said, not giving him a chance to speak. 'Mrs Denton at Nacton, she fell down in a fit and she's very bad, and there's no one knows what to do.'

'Fell down, did she? Hurt her head?'

He had an air about him, as if now everything was under control. His voice was dark and refined.

'I don't know, sir, she was on the ground kicking and her eyes rolled up.'

'Unconscious?'

'She was talking when I left. She was sick.'

The gentleman in grey stood behind me. 'The child's galloped this beast all the way from Nacton, George,' he said, impressed, 'without saddle or bridle.'

'Shoulda seen her come flying down Bishop's Hill,' said a man in the crowd.

Dr Stebbing took my arm kindly and led me through the hall and into the waiting room. Everything was so clean! The gentleman in grey followed.

'My horse,' I said, 'who's got my horse?'

'Don't fret,' said the gentleman. 'I took the liberty, George, of telling Sam to put him in your stable and give him a good rub-down and some oats. He's bringing your own horse round to the door.'

'Good, good.' Stebbing was fastening his cloak, calling for his bag. A lady appeared in the doorway with a napkin in her hand. 'Don't wait to have coffee, dear,' he said briskly. 'I'm called for.' And to me: 'What's your name?'

'Margaret Catchpole.'

'Catchpole. Ah yes...'

'Susan's my sister, sir. You know Susan.'

'Of course I do,' he said. He'd been out to our Sue many a time. 'Sit down here, please. Susanna, tell Pru to fetch her some water. See she gets home safely, Nat.' He patted my shoulder. 'You've done very well indeed, my dear.'

Stebbing gave me a crooked smile and was off without more ado. The maid brought me a cup of biting cold water that went straight to my head like wine, and I was left alone while the gentleman in grey, who introduced himself as Mr Southgate, took himself off to the stable. I looked about the room, which was high and dim, with chairs all round the walls, then I went to the window and saw a small yard full of pots of pink flowers, and blood-red geraniums that trailed from a window box. The paving stones were white and clean, as if a maid went out there every day and swept and scrubbed and scoured just as she would inside the house. I looked up. A great white plaster rose adorned the centre of the ceiling. The door stood ajar and there were comings and goings in the hall, and a smell of beeswax and polish and a perfume like faint lavender. Dr Stebbing's house was not so grand as all that, I know now, but it seemed so to me then.

Mr Southgate returned after a while and said if I was quite recovered and would be pleased to step into his coach he would take me back. Poor Jem was for a rest now. Someone would fetch him home later. And so I rode for the first time in a coach with a gentleman, in comfort all the way back home. He went right out of his way to get me home, though he was such a big man himself, a farmer, but not in the way of our Mr Denton, who was only a tenant. Mr Denton hadn't such a grand coach as this; he had only a cart for ferrying his girls around. No, Mr Southgate was somewhere between Mr Denton and our Squire Broke up at the Hall at Nacton.

He handed me down from the coach in front of our house with all of them looking on, and he came right into our yard and got chicken shit on his boot. When he heard that Dr Stebbing had already been and gone, and that Mrs Denton was poorly but safe and surely would have been a whole lot worse were it not for me, he gave me a whole guinea and told my father I was worth my weight in gold.

Hell-born Babe

14

The next time I saw Will Laud I was fifteen years old, and I'd been working away in Great Bealings for two years, as a dairymaid to that same Mr Nathaniel Southgate who'd spoken up for me to Dr Stebbing. I grew like a stalk at the Southgates'. Sue screamed when I went home the Whitsun of the Cracknells' party.

'You're enormous,' she squealed.

They all were in front of the house when I got down from the cart, all except James who was up on Rushmere Heath with his gun, after whatever he could kill. My brother Charles was lean and tall, a bolted plant like me, and pale, paler even than Sue, so much so that his melancholy eyes seemed too dark for his face. So strange and familiar it all seemed, such a messy commingling, Mum never having been a good housekeeper and Sue too drooping to help her any more: the smoky kitchen, my dad with his long legs crossed, smoking his pipe by the fire, Mum stirring the stew and everyone but my quiet father talking at once. Ned was only ten, but he'd grown near as tall as me, skinny and bony. His bashful, boyish air was getting hard at the edges. Susan was on a bed made up under the stairs, and Robert had stationed himself on a stool by her side. Funny the big lunk looked on it, too big for it. 'Come and sit with me, Peggy,' Sue said, and I did, and from there held forth a while about my life.

I was never really in a house with books till I went to the Southgates. Charles had six books on a shelf next to his bed but the Southgates had whole walls covered with them. I only ever saw Mr Southgate reading them though. Uncle Catchpole, my dad's brother who lived near us, said Charles would never be satisfied because he read the wrong things. He could go to the ends of the earth, Charles could, and it still wouldn't do. If I was Charles I'd be sick of labouring too, I told Uncle Catchpole when he said that. He's too quick for the life he's got. Too quick in his mind. I never got to look in any of those books at the Southgates'. I learned not how to read books but people. A lot of quality came to the Southgates'. Some you could be familiar with and they'd laugh, like Dr Stebbing. Stebbing was great friends with Mr Southgate, and was often at Bealings. He'd ride up from Ipswich on a bay pony, and the two of them would go shooting together. He always remembered me. There I'd be with a bucket of milk, crossing the yard.

'Margaret, isn't it?' he'd say, with a big smile. 'Our bold horsewoman!'

'Good morning, Dr Stebbing.'

'My goodness, that looks heavy! Let me carry it to the door for you.'

'And spill it all down your nice coat? Don't you be a silly man.'

Others, you must not smile too widely and you must not say any more than you need. Some required a bob of a curtsey, some far more, though they never got it from me. I'll not scrape. I'd not work for someone I couldn't look in the eye.

It was the first time I'd ever been in a big house and I learned how to be a good servant. I watched all the people who came and went on business with Mr Southgate, and all the men who came to work for him; and I learned that money talks very loud in life. Money has big elbows. I learned too that although you might get on nice and pretty with the higher sort of folk, it was always master and man at heart and never the twain shall meet. Or rather, meet they shall, but never the twain shall stick. They were good people, the Southgates. They paid fair.

15

Mum had a long-tail in the pot. When James got back, he had a big hare from up on the heath. He took it out the back and cleaned it into the bucket, hung it up in the outhouse then sudsed his hands and face before he gave me a hug. James had a bit of Ned's rattiness about the cheeks, and his nose was very long and sensitive and twitched sometimes. I suppose he had to be a poacher. That's what we all said about him, and we laughed. His black brows that met in the middle in a lovely fan over his nose. Sue got up from her bed and came to the table, and we all ate together as if no time at all had passed. I must give this place a good clean before I go back, I thought. The stew was as rich as anything I ever tasted when the Southgates had company and we got the leavings. But Sue couldn't eat the stew. She had beef broth Mrs Denton sent over from the house.

'Mrs Denton's been ever so good,' Mum said. 'Scarce a day goes by she doesn't send a little something for our Sue. She's a nice woman. You should see what she's got for the baby. She took me in and showed me.'

Tomorrow was a Cracknell's christening party and something of a great occasion.

'Who'll be there tomorrow?'

'I don't really know. Your Uncle and Aunt Catchpole and their lot anyway. The usual from the village, I suppose. She's invited Stephen Laud and his boy but I doubt they'll come. Mary's lad.'

'We saw him at Aldeburgh.'

'That's the one.'

I had not thought about that boy from that day to this but I swear his image came into my mind then so clear and sharp it was as if there was a picture of him hanging in the air in front of me. A boy standing up in a boat. Salt horse, salt horse, fifty days away, *oh,* salt horse, salt horse, fifty mile a day *oh* salt horse ... and I swear there was a kind of quickening, as if something somewhere beyond the air had shifted. Fate's easy to feel when it happens like that. So I was ready for him.

16

It was a mile or so over the fields to the village. It was a lovely day, warm, fragrant, blue. The flowers were scattered all over the meadow, strewings of red and pink and yellow as fine as spray. The bell of Nacton Church was ringing as we walked back down the lane. The party was in the house at the back of the shop, spilling out into the garden and the field behind. A long table stood under the tree, with pies and cakes on it, and a big bowl of punch. Everyone from the village was there. There were barrels and boxes from the shop to sit on, and a couple of benches, and dogs and children running about, and Mrs Cracknell resplendent in her best gown and the baby resplendent in foaming acres of white, fast asleep in her mother's arms, sweet and pink and wizened with a mouth like a wet flower. Uncle and Aunt Catchpole were there and all the cousins. My father and my brothers went to drink with the men and Mum and me went into the kitchen to see if we could help, but all was done. A girl was stirring junket. My cousin Betty, stern and steady as a rock, was carefully laying out lemon tarts. I wandered out into the garden and saw my brother Charles drinking from a flagon of cider and talking to a rangy bold-faced man with a ruby face and a look of disorder about him. The man wore a high-collared jacket, very dingy and crumpled, and his hair was sparse and colourless. His eyes roamed constantly about.

'Hello, Peggy,' Charles said to me as I walked near.

'Charles.' I put my arm about his waist.

'The sister, is it?' said the man, very drunk but capable.

'The sister indeed. One of them.'

'God bless sisters,' said the man.

'Here, Peggy,' Charles said. 'Shall I get you a cup of punch?'

'Do.'

The man stood tall and perfectly still, an unnatural stillness, the stillness of a drunk who is only so because not to be so would mean collapse.

'And who might you be?' I asked him.

'Stephen Laud's my name, madam,' he said with exaggerated deference, 'and you are Margaret, I do so believe.'

His eyes were too familiar.

'Is your boy here?' I asked, looking round.

'Where is the clod?' he murmured fondly.

Charles handed me a cup. The punch was warm and spicy and went down into the pit of my stomach.

'There he is. Will!'

I didn't look, I drank. He came and stood beside me and still I didn't look. He was a man now almost, but he was not so tall. We were head to head.

'This is my sister,' Charles said.

He seemed to know Charles already.

'I've heard of you,' Will said, turning to me. 'You rode a horse into Ipswich.'

Charles smiled at me. 'Your fame goes before you, Peggy.'

'Anyone'd think I'd ridden to the moon,' I said, 'the way they go on. It was only Ipswich.'

'Don't decry it,' Will said. 'People like stories.'

I turned my head and looked at him then. He smiled. Big lips, big eyes. Blue, humorous. His hair was long and messy and fair and everything about him was perfect. I suppose it was then really that both our fates were sealed.

'I remember you,' I said. 'You were in a boat on the Alde and my mother spoke to you.'

He nodded. 'Yes.' A dimple came and went on one side of his mouth.

'Do you remember?'

'Yes.'

'You were singing a song that went: Salt horse, salt horse...'

He laughed. He had a very free and open laugh. It made me feel strange, the way you feel when you see something like a newborn pup and want to touch it. He had no mother. He'd never had one, I knew that.

'Are you not with your Uncle Jack any more then?' I asked him.

'No,' he said, 'I'm in the shipyard at Harwich now. But not for long.'

'Why, what are you going to do?'

'I'm going to sea,' he said proudly. 'Plenty of work between Harwich and Holland.'

He'd been offered a good berth, he said. He knew a captain.

17

There was so much clapping and cheering and everyone drinking to the baby, and more punch and wine being brought out, and junket and syllabub frothing with lemon and cream. We were all whipped up in the crowd and stirred about, so that I ended up with my cousin and his girl, and a couple of village children who wanted me to make them dandelion chains. So I sat on the bank with them, slitting green stems with my thumbnails, watching Will go here and there. There were handsomer boys there, and maybe cleverer too, though I doubt it, unless it be my brother Charles. But it was Will I watched, fooling about with the children, drinking with the men, flirting with the girls. The dogs followed him too, nuzzling their wet black noses into his palms and pockets and receiving his cuffs and caresses. I had no doubt that he and I were bound now, no doubt at all. No fear that either one of us would ever get away for better or worse. The very set of his round head upon his shoulders was thrillingly familiar. He came up to me later, when the afternoon was drawing on towards evening. He put his face very close to mine. His eyes were bright, pale blue. 'Your brother tells me you're no longer living at home?' he said.

'That's true.' Our faces swayed about each other, you could say they hovered. I drew back. 'I have a position in Great Bealings.'

'Ah!' He nodded his head as if something was clicking into place.

There was a burst of screaming laughter from the children running wild in the field above.

'I sometimes visit my uncle in Aldeburgh,' he said, 'and I have a sister at Sudbourne. I could call on you if you like. When I'm passing.'

This made me laugh. 'It's nowhere near.'

He laughed too. 'I know. But I travel about a fair bit. I've walked from Felixstowe Ferry today.'

'That's not far.'

'Oh, is it not, my girl?'

'Ten miles is all.'

'Aha. It seemed longer in company with the old man.'

'You have a sister,' I said.

'I am not quite the unlicked cub your mother takes me for,' he said, looking around, mock nervous, for the ample presence of my mum. 'She descends upon me regularly,' he said, 'and tries to look behind my ears.'

'Here's old Robin,' someone said. Will grinned and bounded away. 'Whatcheer, Robin?' he called out.

The old man's real name was Tom but everyone called him Robinson Crusoe. He stood just beyond the gate with his long pike held over his shoulder like a scythe, and blue-green mackerel hanging from it at intervals, pierced at the lips.

'I know you,' he said. 'Will Laud.'

He was like a wild sea-thing come up from the deep, with his three-pronged stick dripping weeds. His clothes, though rags, were curiously clean because of the constant washing of the weather.

'Of course you do,' said Will, opening the gate for him. A crowd of children gathered to look at the spiky old spectre with his naked arms as brown and thin and knotted as a dead tree in the wood, hung all up and down with his barbarous jewellery. Human bones, horse bones. Three hag-stones hung against the wiry grey hairs in the V made by his collar.

'I know you,' he said softly, 'you hell-born babe.'

Will laughed. 'That I am.'

My mother bore down upon us. 'Well now, Robin, have you come to see the babby?' She beamed and linked her arm through the old man's, having to tilt her head right back to look up the distance into his hollow harrowed face – a face like a saint gone wild in the desert.

'You're looking very well, my dear,' she said. 'How are they treating you?'

'Shocking, ma'am,' he said, declining his head to her and shaking it sorrowfully.

He meant his demons. That's what old Robinson Crusoe had. Other people you'd say: And how's your mother or son or wife or whatever, but with old Robin it was his demons.

My mother showed sympathy. Tutting and clucking, she walked him up the path, crying, 'Look! Look who's come!'

Bones clanked as he walked, and the amulets tied about his knees jangled together. 'Boy,' he said to a Cracknell, 'take these fish and give them to your mother.' The boy took his pike and set about unloading the mackerel. Mrs Cracknell came from the kitchen with the baby still asleep in her arms. A crowd gathered by the punch table to see baby Susan laid gently in the old man's bone-decked arms.

'Will you have a cake, sir?' asked Henry Cracknell, and Betty got him a drink. Old Robin with the baby had the look of an eagle hanging over its nest of young. He looked fierce in the eyes but he was not so at all, or only when he was shouting at his demons. I heard him once raging at them out in his boat on the river when I was on the bank, and it was a fearful sound. Such a roaring and bellowing as if a soul were being dragged down into hell.

'Aye.' Robin made the sign of the cross on the baby's forehead with his thumb. His hands were gnarled, but gentle and graceful. On every finger was a ring or two or three.

'Those are lovely fish,' Mrs Cracknell said.

The mackerel boats came up the Orwell, passing us here and going on to Ipswich. But most of us got ours from Robin as he went about.

'He sings them up from the deep,' Will said.

Robin got fish when no one else could.

'Patience gets fish,' said Robin, 'not magic.'

The baby went back to her mother and Robin drank a good draught of punch. So did Charles, who'd had plenty and more already and was getting how he did when he was tipsy, wilder of eye and darker of brow and reckless in a quiet sort of way. When Robin went back to his boat, Charles said he'd walk down with him, and then so did Will. Both of them were merry, and me too, and I didn't want to be left so I tagged along. It would be dark soon but there was a big moon up already in the blue sky, fragile as sugar. Words were written on Robin's back, weird nonsense words, or maybe some foreign tongue. I wanted to ask Charles what they meant but I didn't. It was dark under the trees going down to the shore. Will Laud and I walked closely, side by side, Charles and the old fisherman going on before.

'So what's it to be?' asked Will. His fingers brushed against my shoulder, almost touching my neck. The shock ran down from my left ear, right through the centre of my guts and into the deep pit between my legs.

'What's what to be?'

'She feigns innocence,' he said. 'Shall I visit you at Great Bealings?'

'You can't. I'm not allowed callers.'

'I can meet you in Woodbridge.'

We came out on the shore where the river was widest. Far over on the other side, the white-washed wall of the Butt and Oyster shone clear at Pinmill where all the boats were moored. The trees of Woolverstone were dark already. Robin's old boat was pulled high up on the shingle, its single tattered brown sail pointing with a drunken air at the moon. It was home-made, banged together out of this and that – doors and table-tops and any old bit of wood nailed askew. It was all over horseshoes and charms, just like himself. How he survived in it I'll never know.

'Where you off to, Robin?' Charles stood with one foot up on the side of the boat.

A flight of birds took off. Waves slapped on the

shingle. Stowing his long fishing pike in the bottom, Robin nodded seawards, then looked at Will. 'I can take you part way home,' he said. 'You's best get you home.'

'Not tonight, old man,' said Charles. 'Will's staying with us tonight.'

Is he now, I thought. Is he so? No one told *me*.

'What about your dad?' I asked. 'Is he staying too?'

Will turned his eyes to me slowly, a faint smile round his lips that seemed to mean something. I got an urge to pluck his lower lip as if it were a fruit, to pluck and place it gently between my teeth. 'He'll bed down at the Cracknells',' he said.

Thank God for that. I didn't want that old soak round our house.

Robin looked at the sky then across the river. 'There was a light in the Cat House last night,' he said.

We all knew what a light in the Cat House meant. Free-traders.

'Watch out for yourself, Robin,' said Charles, as the two of them pushed the old wreck down to the water.

'I've nothing to fear from any human devil,' Robin grunted. 'It's these–' He waved an irritable arm above his head as if swatting flies. The boat met the water and Robin got in. 'You's better get you to your home,' he said, suddenly glaring at Will. The boat drifted and he dipped an oar. 'You's best do as I say. Don't you go running about tonight.'

'I will, Robin,' Will said, 'soon as I pass a word

or two with the Cracknells. But I shall walk back. You're not getting me in that tub.'

'You are hell-bound, Will Laud,' the old man said.

It made me shiver, but Will laughed. 'But not in your boat.'

Robin looked at me very sharply, then back to Will. 'This Margaret Catchpole here,' he said, 'she's not afraid of old Robin's boat, are you, mawther?'

'Not at all,' I said smartly, which was only the truth. I used to go in his boat when I was only small, and I never had no fear of it. Robinson Crusoe was the most skilful boatman on the Orwell. I enjoyed bailing out. He used to give me a little bucket and I'd be happy for hours while he fished from the helm. Once, he jumped up and flung both his arms out over the water with all fingers spread, crying, 'Begone! Begone! I charge you be gone!' then sat back down and went on fishing as if nothing had happened.

The boat moved out into the reach.

'Take care!' Charles called.

'They'll not touch him,' said Will.

'Some would.'

'*They'll* not touch him. I know them,' Will said again. 'They'll do nothing to a man who's light in the head.'

'I'd say he was very heavy in the head,' Charles remarked, and we all laughed.

We walked back slowly to the party through the gathering dusk under the trees. It was a beautiful evening. Tiny bats flittered here and there. We walked separately but together in some wordless way, and by the time we reached the Cracknells' something had changed, though nothing that you could see. Betty and my mother were lighting lanterns. The punch was gone but there was still plenty of ale, and my brothers James and Robert stood drinking with Georgie Cracknell in the light from the open back door. My father and Uncle Catchpole were inside smoking pipes by the fire.

'You should get back to Sue,' my mother said to me quietly. 'She'll be lonely. You go on and I'll follow soon.'

'We'll walk Peggy back, shall we?' Will said to Charles.

'Peggy, is it?' I said.

'Peggy it is,' he smiled. 'That's what your brothers call you, so I will.'

'Wait for me,' I told them. 'I'll bring her a bundle.'

My mother was already standing by the hob packing up a cloth of tarts and a piece of pie when I went into the kitchen. 'I don't suppose she'll eat them,' she said, 'but still...'

I went up to her and whispered so my father and Uncle Catchpole couldn't hear: 'The smugglers are about.' I liked the sound of it. Oars dipping on oily black water. Shadows on the shingle. 'There was a light in the Cat House.'

She nodded.

They used to take Dandy. He was a good sound horse who wouldn't make a noise, a horse of sense. They came so quiet in the night, I never heard them, not once; never woke up at the rattle of a harness or the kick of a footstep. You'd never know they'd been if you didn't go out in the field early that morning and see the sweat drying on Dandy's flank. Did the Dentons know? Or did they close their eyes? I'd sit on the fence and put my arm round his neck and feel him throb, and whisper in his hairy ear: 'Had a good time, Dandy, have you? Out on an adventure?'

My mother gave me a look as she passed me the bundle. 'Gone sweet on Mary's boy, have you?' she asked at the door.

'You could say that.'

She laughed at that. 'You could do worse,' she said.

They were waiting for me at the gate. We went down through the village, by the blacksmith's shop, all closed up, at the low point of the valley. Charles was drunker than I'd thought, staggering from time to time, but Will walked steady, smiling, and the two of them talked together very easily. I'd never seen Charles like this before. He was not a man easy in himself as a rule. We passed a bottle between us. They talked about navigation and astronomy and mathematics and something they had both read called *Roderick Random*, which made them laugh hilariously about a scene where some poor body gets a chamber pot emptied over his head. He was in very high spirits, and when we got back went straight to Sue, who was sitting sewing by the fire, and took both her hands in his. 'They shouldn't have left you alone,' he said, 'we should have brought the party here to you.'

Sue frowned. 'I don't think I know you,' she said.

'Oh Sue!' I placed the bundle in her lap.

'My hem! Here, let me finish off.'

'This is Will Laud. Don't you remember the Cracknell boy in the boat at Slaughden Quay?'

'Could you not have come?' he asked, as she turned back the folds of the cloth.

'I get tired,' she sighed. 'Too many people...'

'Oh, but now there's only me,' he said, seating himself beside her, 'and I'm practically family.'

'You are not!'

'I am. Aren't I, Peggy?'

She exclaimed at the tarts and set about the pie, one of Mrs Cracknell's finest, with the best of intentions. 'Very familiar, isn't he?' she said to me, ignoring him. 'This pie is nice.'

'So now we have brought the party to you,' Will said, and waved the bottle. 'A small drink?'

'What is it?'

'Brandy.'

'A little,' she said, 'with water.'

He jumped up obligingly.

'Warm the water,' she ordered, enjoying herself.

He swept her a low bow, grand as a lord. I laughed. 'Grand as a lord,' I said.

By twelve everyone was in bed apart from Will and Charles, who'd gone a little way behind the house and sat talking long into the night, with their pipes and whatever remained in the bottle. I could just about hear them if I lay on my back and strained my ears, not what they were saying but simply the distant soothing hum of steady talk. I couldn't sleep. I wanted to be with them, so raised myself up very quietly and tiptoed downstairs and got my cloak on over my nightgown, then slipped out of the back door to run wildly and recklessly barefoot through the dewy grass. There was a hollow before the lower pasture, where a bank of primroses and bluebells sloped gently up. Charles lay on his back at the top of the slope, chewing on a blade of grass and looking at the stars. Will sat below in the hollow, his back against the thin trunk of a thorn tree, the bottle a-dangle from his fingers.

'But I'll go farther,' Charles was saying. 'I won't stop till I reach somewhere where the people have never even heard of England.'

Will drank gracefully. 'Come to Amsterdam,' he said. 'I can get you a berth.'

'Holland doesn't interest me. Much too close,' Charles said.

Will turned his head and looked straight at me where I stood in the shadow. 'Hello, little Peggy,' he said.

Charles lifted his head.

'I couldn't sleep.' I walked across the grass and sat down on a stone. Will looked at my bare feet.

'Margaret Catchpole,' Charles said, 'you are a shameless bold girl. Go back to bed.'

'No.'

'Suit yourself. Here, Will, toss over the bottle.'

We stayed up till three or four or more. Charles got all fired up like I'd never seen him – something to do with this young boy Will Laud all set to sail the seas, even if it was only Holland he was going to – here was Charles now twenty-seven years old, and never been out of Suffolk. Charles began to talk with a passion about islands in the far south seas; about strange and wonderful people who never worked and lived on giant fruit you could pluck off the trees, and forests bigger than all of England, places where the sun burned like fire and fierce wild beasts roamed free. He talked as I'd never heard him talk before, then fell silent. We all did. The Dentons' cockerel kept crowing, an echo on the dark.

After a while, Charles started snoring.

'We should get him to bed,' Will said.

'Yes,' I replied.

He stood and came over to where I still sat on the rock. 'Are your feet cold?' he asked, kneeling in front of me.

'Not at all.'

He began rubbing them in his big warm hands.

'Did your sister use to look behind your ears?' I asked him.

He smiled. 'No.' A small snorting laugh down his nose.

'Did no one ever make sure you'd done your washing?'

He laughed softly. 'No.'

'Shall *I* look?'

He put his head down obligingly, and I pushed the hair back and looked behind his ears. He had nice neat ears. There came a moment beyond my ability to tell. Nothing happened. I held his warm head between my hands and he, smiling, let his face sink down into my lap, my thin nightgown between him and me. And nothing. Silence, and my thumbs caressing the spaces behind his ears. If God came to me and said Margaret, you can have anything at all, all blessings known to mankind, but you can't have this moment, I would have told God to leave.

He lifted up his head and looked me in the eye. 'I'm very fond of you, Peggy,' he said.

'I'm very fond of you, Will,' I replied.

Nothing was said for a while.

'Shall I come and see you?' he asked.

'I can't have callers.'

'Come on, Peggy,' he said, smiling, 'don't be like that. When shall I see you? You know I'll be thinking about you till I do.'

'Will you?'

'Yes. And so will you, I think. Thinking about me, I mean.'

'Oh, I will, will I?' I kissed his hot dry brow, the hairs lying across it.

He laughed.

'Yes, you will.'

I never held a baby to my breast amongst all those I brought into this world that I felt the tender feeling I had for Will Laud. So I kissed him on his big warm boy's lips and it was like a deep warm fall into sleep and when it finished the whole world had changed. The Dentons' cockerel crowed, splitting the darkness before dawn. Charles woke up with a splutter and a sneeze. We three went into the cottage and Will went off to bed down with the boys.

I crept into my own bed upstairs behind the curtain and lay gazing up at the roof. Sleep came with a soft summer morning rain that crooned about the house.

18

He came to see me once while I was still at Great Bealings. We went down an alley in Woodbridge and he pushed me up against a wall, not hard, but hard enough; and his face came at me, his big smiling opening lips, his grinning teeth. We kissed frantically, as if this was our only chance ever, kissed and fondled a full half-hour till both of us was burning. There was nothing like that. Nothing.

'We will always be together now,' he said, when finally our time ran out and we drew apart.

For a few minutes more we walked up and down the town, my arm in his. He said he was waiting for the call to go to sea. It was a man called Bargood took a shine to him, he said, a big trader used to get his boats fitted out at his uncle's yard in Aldeburgh. I don't know how many ships Bargood had. Lots. 'Says I'll make a captain,' Will said. It was a nice little run across to Holland and back and he'd be often home, with silver in his pockets.

I saw him that one time in Woodbridge and he said he'd come again and send word, but it was only a week or so later I got the message through Noller that Sue was very sick and Mum was not well enough to cope, and I was to come back home at once. Uncle Catchpole was coming for me. Mrs Southgate said she was very sorry to lose me. She called her husband, and he said I'd been a splendid dairymaid and he'd always known since the day I rode that horse down to Dr Stebbing's house that I would go far. And they gave me an extra half crown, and some lovely yellow ribbons for Sue. Uncle Catchpole came with the cart and carried me back, up over Rushmere Heath and past the gibbet, where something fresh was hung. 'Look away,' Uncle Catchpole said, and I did. Back home, it was as if I'd never been away, except that the house had turned into a pigsty. Everything had a coating of dust, and my father's old brass pipe cradle that my mother always polished with vinegar was ashy and stained with something dark. It was foul to me after the Southgates'. Sue still had her cot under the stairs, with a curtain she could pull across. I felt angry with her at first. I could not understand why she had let herself get like that, so thin and old-looking. She was only just twenty-two and she looked thirty. She'd been pretty, but that was all gone. But her eyes were still the old Sue's eyes, still soft. I went straight to her and gave her a kiss. I didn't know whether I was glad to be back home or not.

'See how you all fall apart without me,' I said.

She laughed. 'We do, Peggy,' she said, 'we really do.'

My mother had grown very stout of late and was short of breath. Her eyes had taken on a harassed, accusing look. 'I've not been able to cope,' she said plaintively. 'Not feeling so well myself, you see,' and burst into tears.

I looked around. My brothers and my father

were out with the team. 'What's been the matter, Mum?' I asked her.

She wiped her nose. 'I get very heavy,' she said, 'very very heavy inside me. Dr Stebbing's given me some powders.'

'She does too much,' Sue said.

'Well, never mind,' I said. 'I can help now, can't I?'

Work. I'd get my breath, go for a walk and see the horses, say hello to Mrs Denton then go through the place inch by inch scrubbing everything. It would take time. I'd get a capon from Mrs Denton with my own money, and I'd roast it beautiful. Mum could peel the potatoes. I'd get Sue up off that bed and into a chair by the fire, change all the sheets, get the water on for washing. I did all that and more. It was easy. I was blessed with strength. When I lifted up Susan she was like a doll to me.

Everyone said what a good girl I was. Mrs Denton said it, my mum said it, Sue said it; and when my father and brothers came home from work and found hot water for their washing all ready, and a savoury smell in the air, they said it too. So of course then I realised what I'd missed at Bealings. It was the way my kin made much of me. Not that the Southgates were remiss to me at all, but there I did what I did because it was my employment, and the praise was no more and no less than warranted. Here, I did it for Sue and Mum. And I could be near Will.

19

I was a good girl, and I was happy and yet not. Happy. That sounds terrible, that I could be happy while my sister grew weaker and sicker and my mother's wheezing grew louder. But I did, and the reason was that Will Laud by this time was running tame about our house, and whenever he could, would walk up from his father's at Felixstowe Ferry. He and Charles were great friends. They'd got into the habit of sitting talking of an evening on the fence or out in the long grass in the meadow with the horses. I think they talked quite deeply, about life and death and big things, and when they were doing that I stayed away. It seemed to me that was only between the two of them. Charles had never talked like that to any of *us* as far as I knew, certainly not to me; and I was quite sure he never talked like that to James or Robert. But Will had a talent for getting along with people. Of course he was not a smuggler then, well not really, though he was already set on the path that led to it. Even if I'd known it wouldn't have made any difference though. Half the stuff we got came through the free trade one way or the other and it was the same for everyone we knew. You just didn't talk about it. What I mean to say is that I knew he was a bad catch. That he sailed close to the wind. I was never a fool, I just loved him. Maybe if I'm honest it was even because of that.

We sat down one evening as a mist was forming over the shingle, and the lights were winking over at the Butt and Oyster on the other side. Everything was very still. We sat a little way apart with our cloaks wrapped round us, he a little further down the shingle than me, in perfect silence for so long I had fallen under a kind of spell from the lapping of the water and the greatness of the sky where a few stars were faintly beginning to appear. What made him turn his head and look at me at that moment I don't know. His face scared me. For a moment I thought he was turning into something, and my heart froze. But it was just another Will, one that had always been there but that I hadn't seen yet. Will could make a look like a kiss. Like a kiss, it could be gentle or brutal. This one was raw, fierce in the way a child is fierce, and with a great deal of fear in it. I took it all in, and it gave me a sharp little pain.

Next minute he smiled in a foolish way, as if he was laughing at himself, and we got up and walked back to the house.

20

One day a sailor came to our door and asked for him. Will was out in the field with Charles and I sent the man out to him. Will came in looking all excited. 'This is it,' he said. 'I'm going to Amsterdam.'

'What, now? This second?'

'I'm to report to Captain Bargood at noon tomorrow at Felixstowe Ferry.'

He was to go on board a cutter called the *Alde*, he said. Some of the crew were laying over at the Butt and Oyster tonight and he was to join them there and get his uniform, ready for the off first thing in the morning. The sailor had a boat waiting on the shingle to take him over.

'Come over to the Butt and Oyster, Pegs. Drink my health before I have to go. I'll row you back later.'

'You're not taking her over there,' Mum said without much conviction. 'That's a rough old place.'

'She'll be all right with me, we'll stay in the front parlour. Come on, Pegs, I'll treat you to a good feed. It's my last night, your mum can manage without you for an hour or two.'

'Let her go, Mum,' Sue said.

'Oh, go on.' Mum waved us both away with the dish cloth. 'Take no notice of me, I'm only your mother what brought you up.'

We ran all the way down to the shore. The sailor was waiting, leaning up against his boat with his sea boots in the water and a curl of smoke rising from his pipe.

'Pegs,' Will said, 'meet John Luff, Mate of the *Alde*.'

He was a small man, hard as oak. He wore a brown george wig, old-fashioned, and his eyes were cool and hard as he looked me over.

'Pleased to meet you, John Luff,' I said.

He sniffed and nodded. Luff the gruff, I thought.

It was so still, the water as fair as can be as he rowed us across, and I was so happy that nothing could keep the smile from my face. It didn't matter that Will was going away. I never had that feeling of wanting to keep him at home. He and I weren't like that. A big ship was in for unloading on to the barges for Ipswich, so the Butt was packed with sailors; but we got a cosy place in the parlour where one or two of the better sort were having supper. The sailor went off through a door which swung back to reveal for a second a room full of blue uniforms. Here and there was the brighter flash of a dress or an apron.

'Can't we go in there?' I asked Will.

He looked over his shoulder. 'I promised your mum.'

'Go on, Will.'

He sat across the table looking at me thoughtfully. 'Let's eat something first,' he said. 'Maybe later.'

We ordered fish stew and ale. The stew when it came was steaming and peppery, rich with shrimps and mussels, and the ale was strong and soon went to my head in a wonderful way. A fire crackled merrily nearby. It was dim and sweet in the parlour, and the way the firelight danced on the jugs and spoons was a delight. He said I had the loveliest brown eyes in the world. A whistle played in the other room, a slow but jaunty air.

The door swung open and a tall gangly fellow with a pigtail came out.

'Luff said you were here, Will,' he said.

Will stood up grinning.

'I'm for the *Alde*, same as you,' the man said.

'This is my Peggy, Rube,' said Will.

'Peggy.' The man bowed. 'Come through.'

That was my first time in such a place as this. Will knew everyone. Robinson Crusoe was there, sitting in the corner very stiff and upright like a scarecrow, and so was one of our Cracknells, and a couple of girls who used to go to our church. A little boy of about seven, all dressed up like a sailor, was standing on a barrel and playing a whistle.

'*He*'s never going to sea, is he?' I asked. 'He's a baby.'

'Of course not,' said Will. 'Not yet.'

We sat at a table with Rube and Luff. Others came to sit with us, and Will knew them all. I saw one of the girls I knew eyeing me and gave her a wave. She waved back. It was like being at home with my brothers, as easy as that. Rube had been to America. It was a beautiful country, he said, but a dangerous place. They had terrible snakes there, made our adders look like tiny eels. The fighting over there was filthy. Robinson Crusoe walked by our table. 'Margaret Catchpole,' he said, 'what are you doing here?'

'I'm seeing Will off.'

'I'm off to Holland tomorrow, Robin.' Will stood up. 'Have a drink.'

Robin stood there staring at me as if I was the only one present, and I realised it was not me he was looking at, but something a little to the left of my right shoulder, as if an imp was crouching there. It gave me a shiver.

'Stop it, Robin,' I said.

Robinson Crusoe's hair and beard were very

long and matted, knotted here and there with tiny shells and fragments of delicate bone so graceful they must have come from skylarks or doves. At that moment John Luff walked behind him, drew a knife and hacked off a thick grey ringlet that held a tough but thin brown bone about two inches long.

'Stupid old fool!' Luff dangled the clot of bone and hair in front of Robin's face.

'Leave him alone!' I shouted.

Robin's charms were his protection. If he lost one something would get him. His mouth caved in. Luff laughed and passed behind him again, tipping the old man's cap down over his eyes. 'Hocus-pocus! Shite!' Luff spat.

I jumped up and whacked him a light clout round the head. 'Give it back to him!' I ordered.

A great guffaw arose. Luff froze. His grim mean little eyes were steady on me. For a moment I was afraid, but then he gave a snickety laugh and tossed me the ringlet, which I handed to Robin. It vanished somewhere into his rags.

Luff sat down.

'You'd better tell her, Will,' he said slowly, with a peculiar smile, 'she'll not always be so lucky.'

Flying Boat

21

After six months Bargood had made Will captain of the *Alde*. That was very fast, him being so young, but there was something, some charm about him in those days. The first time he came home he brought us all a little something – a plug of baccy for Daddy, sweets from Amsterdam for me and Sue and Ned, good rum for the boys, and a lace cap for my mother. The second time and the third time the same kind of thing. But after that he came as Captain Laud of the *Alde*, and he was earning more. We got candlesticks and dresses, a pretty carved box, a fine fowling piece for James. A very flash boy he could be, indeed, striding in all lovely in his white and blue uniform, with the brass buttons all polished up, like the most respectable of seafaring sorts, except that his face could never be that. His face was not right for respectability.

I swear time changes, slows and speeds. It seemed a long time, but it may have been only a year or two: those nights, a footstep, a knock on the door, then a voice, one of the boys: 'Will's here, Peg.' My mother loved him, her unlicked cub. It strikes me now she didn't care about the things some thought she *should* have. I heard Mrs Cracknell say once to my father – soft, she thought, but not soft enough – is it quite right, do you think, your Margaret running about with Mary's boy?

The way she does? My father pulled a mouth and said, 'Well, there you are.' As if he wasn't at all sure himself. I knew what they meant. Will was not the man a stolid matron would want for her daughter, not steady, not safe. But my mother was not really a stolid matron, for all she looked like one. She'd settled on my dad, but I'm sure she still pined in some way after a lad like Will. She was strong, my mum. She was the cock in our barnyard, and she let me have my head. There were those who blamed her and my dad and said they let me run wild, but I worked hard for my family; why shouldn't I have a little fun now and then? That's how I saw it. Where was the harm? As long as my work got done and all got fed and watered, and all went along smooth and sure, as it did till I reached seventeen and Sue died.

She just caught a bad cold one day. God knows where she got it from, none of the rest of us caught it. It went on her lungs and she started coughing up green. After that it went very fast. She went to bed, and by morning the green was drowning her. Her nose began to bleed before Robert could get back with Dr Stebbing. Stebbing bled and steamed her, but she just went down. We sat up all night, all of us, holding her hands and making her cool and telling her what a good girl she was. I saw her die. Robert was holding her in his arms. The light went out of her eyes. It was just after four of a very cold winter morning.

We put her in the hard earth in Nacton Churchyard. It was freezing cold and there were tiny particles of snow flying about in the air and birds gathering on the river. I pitied the poor gravediggers in this weather. My father and Uncle Catchpole went at the front of the coffin, then Charles with Uncle Leader, and James and Robert at the back. We all cried. All except Robert, who'd been closer to her than anyone else. His face was blank.

Will was at sea and didn't know she was dead. Seven nights after her funeral, there we all were sitting about and suddenly he was there at the door, his yellow hair tangled over his brow. He came in and put his bundle down on the table and looked for me, smiling. I went straight to him. I could not help the happiness I felt, and took him by the arm and told him at once: 'Sue died.'

His smile faltered. His eyes stayed on mine but changed. He looked sideways to where she used to be and stared at that spot for a moment or two. Slowly his eyes filled with tears. When Will cried, the blue got bluer. He'd known us two years, Will, but you'd have thought we'd nurtured him from birth, our family. He had no mum or comfort at home and he'd burrowed under our wing. Sue might have been his sister. But then he wiped away the tears with two fingers, took off his heavy brace of pistols and laid down his cutlass; and he and my father sat side by side smoking.

Everything was changed with Sue gone. It was hard not to keep turning your head and looking round to the place where she no longer was, there under the stairs, her nook where we'd all gather sometimes as if round a fire, except that it was she that was cold and we that were trying to warm her.

'She was lovely, your Sue,' said Will.

I was on one end of the settle, he was lying at length, his head sideways on my lap. I started unplaiting his pigtail. I combed his hair and he looked at me upside down and his face was so unearthly upside down, like a goblin, not human at all but so alive and strange it made me want to scream. We went for a walk, both of us very drunk. Who knows the time? It didn't matter. Sue was dead and all was changed, and Will and I had changed too though we didn't know what we'd changed into. It was so cold. So white and wintry and hard. We stood shivering, hugged up together very close under the tree by the gate, and he told me that he'd brought her a special sweet from Amsterdam, one that she loved. He always tried to bring her some. And here she was dead seven days. We kissed, our wet faces colliding. There was nowhere we could go but home to our cottage, where Mum was damping down the hearth and everyone drooping quietly away to their beds. Will went in with the boys as he always did and I went and lay in the pitch dark with my eyes wide open for a long time.

In the middle of the night he woke me very gently and said wrap up warm, he was taking me to see his ship. We went out in the dark. He whispered it was all right, he'd left a note that Charles could read, they'd know I was with him, and we'd be back in mid-morning. The skiff was on the shore. We rowed down to the mouth of the river, black water smooth, stars sharp and crisp, not a light to be seen anywhere on the banks till the sentinel at Langer Fort, where Will raised the oars and let us drift silent; then on up the coast past Felixstowe and the ferry, to where the *Alde* lay darkened under Felixstowe Cliff. A fog was drifting in from the open sea. I did not see the ship at all till we were pretty well upon her, then her graceful bow appeared above us like the neck of a great beast. The skiff ran alongside the fo'c's'le where a sleepy young sailor was on watch, grinning down at us, leaning dreamily on his arms.

'King George for ever,' said Will softly. The lad sniggered. That's what the excise men said.

'There's none but thee and me and Mr Luff,' the boy said. 'They's all gone ashore.'

'What about Adam?'

'He's below.'

'Tell him to put wine in my cabin,' Will said, little king of this world. And I stepped on board and was taken by the hand and led proudly about the decks, the captain's lady, and shown everything, urged to throw back my head and look up the length of those great masts rearing into darkness, note the tautness of her rigging, the long-barrelled guns on her spotless white decks. They kept her beautiful, those tough rough sailors. I saw John Luff very briefly, sitting at a table near a window in the fo'c's'le eating bread and cheese and drinking from a wooden tankard. He acknowledged me with a smile of the eyes and a raising of his drink, but did not stop chewing.

22

I grew to love the *Alde*. There were those who would have trembled with fear to find themselves on her, though I didn't know that at the time. But to me she was always a haven, a beautiful, beautiful ship. Will's cabin was home to me. We couched there many a time, sometimes here, sometimes there over the years. With the cold winter beyond us in the dark, or the summer of a fine afternoon, the window open for the soft sea breeze. That first time there was a candle in a horn lantern, the remains of a slab of bacon on a platter, and the dregs of small beer in a jug. It was warm and snug, with a smell of leather and spice. Adam Hare was setting wine on a small table near the stove. My heart jumped when I saw him. Adam had a stumpy body and big strong shoulders and arms. His head had been so hacked about with a knife, the ears and nose and lips cut off, he scarcely resembled a human being at all. The eyes that looked out of the ruin were mild and moist, steady and fixed in a way that made me think he was simple.

'Good man, Adam,' Will said. 'This is my Margaret.'

Adam nodded, courteous.

'Hello, Adam,' I said.

He bowed and went up the stairs on to the deck, sighing loudly.

'Pillory,' Will said, looking into the wine jug. 'The good burghers of Lynn made that of him.'

'What had he done?'

'Don't know.' Will poured the wine. 'He can't say. No tongue. He's been with the ship for years.'

'The poor man.'

'Don't fear Adam,' Will said, giving me wine. 'He's gentle.'

I hate the things people have said about Will. How shall I say what I know? He was a bad man, some said who knew him less well than I, some who cared about me and wished me well. If you'd not met Will Laud you could have been a good woman and got married to a good man and raised up the young just like your mother did. Oh, there was bad ones, sure there was bad ones. Luff was a bad one, but there was worse. All got tarred with the one brush. No one's telling *me* Will ever cut a throat. He'd no stomach for that kind of thing. It wasn't his fault I met him. Wasn't mine. Might as well ask life itself to stop as wish away the meeting of me and Will. I knew what he was. There would not be a hearth and home with winking china and the familiar round of day on day. I knew what he did, even before that night when I sat on his knee in his cabin and he proudly read me the manifest: flour, starch, manilla rope. He pointed out the letters, said he'd teach me to read one day, and kissed me over and over. The first cargo he brought in was gin. He showed me all the records going back and back. Bargood insisted on order, he said, he was very particular about his papers, so if the coastguard ever did come a-calling all was fair. All was fair. Then he pulled me in towards him and his tongue came softly gliding in between my lips. 'Come to bed, love,' he said, lifted me and carried me to his bunk. We'd done it before, here and there, where we could, in fields, in woods, in our house once or twice when everyone else was out, and once, in silence absolute, when everyone was in but fast asleep, and the night was dark and thick like velvet. Here, at last, was a bed, a real bed. We were blessed. We jumped into it, a wild place where we played, wolves a-tumble in the pack. There's no heaven better. No heaven I'd want. Afterwards, we lay talking and eating the Amsterdam sweet he brought for Sue. He said he'd stay with the smuggling two or three years. He'd worked it all out. Bargood didn't care if Will had his own little business on the side, tobacco, snuff, gin or whatever else. There was money in it, and fast money too. 'Long as I steer clear of the coastguard,' he said, 'and she's fast, she is, the *Alde*. She can outrun anything.'

'Life's short,' I said. 'Think of Sue. Be careful though, Will.'

He sat up on one elbow on his side, his long hair rough round his head. 'You know, Pegs,' he said, 'I'd give it up if you really wanted me to. But what should I do? I could stay in the shipyard or I could get my dad's old job when he's too old or drunk. I've done it once or twice anyway when he's been incapable.' He laughed and his eyebrows arched. A quick face, Will had. 'Will Laud, the Felixstowe ferryman like his daddy afore.'

'Good job that, as my ma would say. Government post. Lovely.'

'I'm already doing better than my dad. And my

uncle. Bugger King George, you wouldn't have me go to war, would you, Pegs? I've no stomach for that.'

'No, no, no!' I cried and grabbed his face and kissed it.

'You know me, Pegs. I won't be satisfied with – with–' He sought the phrase. 'I won't be satisfied with the common grass.'

Would I have had him any different? No.

We slept a while. When I woke mid-morning, though it was cold and rainy out there and the boat rocked gently, we two were combined in the single sweat of our bodies. He was still asleep, his big dry lips parted, breathing on my shoulder. It made me remember the old ballad where she wakes up in bed with her lover, and the sheets are damp and she says 'wake up, wake up, the sheets are all asweat', but when she looks it's not sweat but blood in the bed. It was her brothers run him through while he lay there. My brothers would never do a thing like that. No blood for me and Will, no deep dark fate, no sorrow of an old song.

He woke up as I was looking in his face, focused for a moment and smiled. 'Hello, Face,' he said.

'Hello, Face,' I replied.

'The sheets are asweat,' I said.

He threw them back. 'So they are.'

There were sounds of voices on board.

'One by one,' he said, snuggling down, 'my hungover crew returns.'

He rose up naked and beautiful, took some keys from a jar over the door and squatted down by a great black chest at the end of the bunk.

'Look!' he said. I moved down and peered over the lid of the trunk. Swords, pistols, powder horns and muskets, cruel cutlasses.

'I can have whichever I want,' he said. 'Look at this!'

He waved aloft a pistol with an ivory handle. 'This for today,' he said with relish. 'See, I'm the only one can get to them, I'm the only one he trusts. I hand 'em out.' He laughed and tossed the pistol on the bed. Then he pulled on his big sea boots and belted on the sword and pistols he shed last night, and walked about the room laughing, naked but for those things. To me it's all the same, men and children. There's not too much to choose. He made me laugh.

There were men on board when we left, just one or two, and a boy high up in the rigging. All of them were dressed like plain merchant sailors. Rube was there, he smiled very nicely at me, very warm. I liked him. He was quiet and friendly, and his eyes were clever. Rube was a navy deserter. If they got him, they'd hang him. The rain had stopped. Over the low rail the sea was sparkly, the sky bushy with thick white cloud. Birds flew inland, a whistle of wings. Adam Hare stood by the galley door. He may have been grinning, I could not tell; at any rate the mouth of teeth was parted, and I'm sure it wasn't a snarl.

My comrades now, part of my share in this world.

23

Two weeks later I met Captain Bargood. He wanted to see me; after all I'd been on his boat.

'You're getting a reputation, young lady,' he said, wagging a finger at me and puffing smoke out of his pipe in little bursts.

'Am I?'

We were in the Neptune, on the Quay, the place with the funny chimney that used to be the apothecary's. You wouldn't have known the place. It had been knocked into one, and they'd built a new stable. It was a good rousing inn where the sailors came straight off the boats. The people of the town came too, the sort who wanted a good time. We'd gone upstairs into a little room where the captain was sitting chewing chicken wings and drinking red wine. You could look out and see the ships on the river. Bargood was huge – I don't just mean he was big as a man of the world, I mean his size, the bulk of him like one of his ships, the size of his balding head (he never wore a wig), the monolithic widening column of his throat before it sank into his shoulders, the span of his massive pink hands. He said he had some sweet-meats from America in the *Alde*, which was here in dock, and sent Will out to get them. Then he poured me red wine.

He knew all about me. He knew about the time I rode Jem down Bishop's Hill into town. He knew I was at the Butt and Oyster, and here and there with Will; he knew who my father and mother were, and my uncles; he knew my brother James was getting married soon to Polly Rawl of Bucklesham, and that Robert had started keeping company of late with fat Dinah Parker, my friend who worked over at Wakes's farm at Downham Reach. He knew Charles was a bit of a scholar. He admired that, he said. 'There's always a place for a clever young man,' he said. 'Look at our Will.' At the mention of Will's name his narrow little eyes positively twinkled. He knew my Aunt Ellen Leader's father and uncle were in the preventive service and killed by free-traders.

He put down his great bull head and moved it from side to side sorrowfully. 'That was a terrible thing,' he said, 'a stupid thing that should never have happened.'

I agreed.

'Of course she was upset,' I said. 'I would be if it was my dad and uncle.'

He leaned over the table and stared into my eyes very seriously. 'We don't want trouble,' he said. 'All this fighting is pointless.'

'You're right.'

'Your aunt,' he said, 'is there anything she's in need of?'

I stared back into his pale eyes. 'My Uncle and Aunt Leader are not wealthy,' I said, 'and they have four little ones and another on the way. Might even be twins by the look of it. Any little helps. But she'd never touch a thing if she thought it came through the free trade.'

Our faces came closer. Almost touching. He's

not that old, I thought. Not as old as he looks, but ugly.

'Will tells me I can trust you,' he said, 'and I trust Will.'

We weighed each other up. 'Do you think I would ever do anything that would put Will in the way of harm?' I said.

'No, Margaret,' he said, 'I don't believe you would.'

'There then,' I said, 'take your chances with me.'

He smiled. Will came back with the sweetmeats and more wine, and we had a very merry time of it all told, till Sy Cracknell came calling that if I wanted a lift it was now or never.

24

There's some wax indignant about anything. And there's hypocrites too.

The Dentons, now I always liked the Dentons and I can see their side of things, they have to be careful, don't we all? But even they turned a blind eye when it suited. They let their horses be used. But then they were never short of a good cask of brandy or gin, were they? And how good it was those years after Will joined my family as an honoured friend. We had so much. When he was away for a long time he'd send us things by a marsh boy from Bawdsey, or by sailors, who'd pitch up by our gate. I loved to see a sailor at the door. Imagine, on a tedious day when your mother's been in her bed with the croup, and your father's back's indifferent to any amount of rubbing and the rain's not been able to make up its mind since Sunday – and suddenly, there before you, a strange brown man with foreign places in his eyes. Mention something you want. There it will be. Magic. Say, for example, my father sitting by the fire of an evening, Will and the boys playing faro. My father knocks his favourite old pipe against the pipe-stand and pokes it and shakes and goes tut; give it a week or two or less, and there's a nice new meerschaum pipe for him. A sack at the back door, could've been flour, and under the chaff a shawl, silk, lovely stuff, cost a fair bit. Nice tea. Snuff. The brass candlesticks my mother loved to polish, James's gun, the bolt of cloth that made winter waistcoats for my brothers. All presents from Will. And when James finally married Polly Rawl at Nacton Church, it was Will who provided the beautiful red jewel she wore at her throat.

By this time we'd known Will for about three years. So much a part of us he was that James and Polly made sure of a wedding when he'd got a run ashore. He was very thick with John Luff by now. The two of them came up the river in a sailing skiff, Luff to the Butt and Oyster, Will to us. I could have wished for a nicer best friend for Will, Rube maybe. He was a gruff old thing, Luff was, and he drank too much. Will appeared at our gate early the morning of James and Polly's wedding day. A haze of heat already trembled in the air. He was afire, full of fun. 'Look, Pegs,' he said after he'd kissed me and hugged me so hard he'd taken all the breath out of me. He pulled a watch out of his pocket. 'I've been in London. I got it from a man in Clerkenwell. French, it is.'

'What were you doing in London?'

'Seeing the sights! We were off Southend so me and Rube took the skiff up the river. What a river that is, Pegs!'

It was the most beautiful watch I'd ever seen, with all kinds of large and small circles overlapping on its face and a complicated fob tied up with a thin red ribbon.

'That's a magnificent watch, that is,' he said, 'and I've got a present for the bride. Where's James?'

'Margaret!' my mother called, all aflap over cakes and tarts. 'Bring him in. You've no time to stand out there.'

Will followed me about telling me his adventures, like a talkative child that's been out playing all day. I was trying to do five different things at once. It's not fair, I thought. I want to go to London. It was then I first got the thought in my head how it would be to dress up like a sailor boy and go on board with him one day for fun, and see how many people I could fool; and see Holland and France and London and all the places where things happened. I must put it to him, I thought, but I couldn't get a word in, he was so full of himself, and my mum like a silly girl all ears so that he swaggered and boasted more and more.

'We'd offloaded at Felixstowe and got everything away, sweet as silk, forty horses with tea, eight wagons of brandy. Right under their bloody noses we were, we could hear them talking in the lookout. And there's another three hundred tubs of gin in a barn at Trimley Common Farm with Humpy Cole keeping an eye on it for us. Well, Humpy sends that there's a revenue man going round trying to drum up a couple of dragoons and he thinks someone must've blabbed, so what do we do? We dump the brandy fast in this place at Colden Green – this is the cleverest thing, the cleverest thing, wait till I tell you – and we get back there with the wagons out the back and just as we've got about twenty barrels on the wagons here come the preventive service men with a couple of dragoons and hail us with a loud-speaker. *Lay down your weapons! In the name of His Majesty!* So me and John and Rube and Adam Hare, we always have him around because he scares them, we go out front as bold as can be without our guns, innocent babes, and engage them in talk!' He laughed wildly. 'That's all we do! And all the time the goods is going out the back! What idiots! Even I would have thought of that one. Straight out through the hayloft and on to the wagons and off to Colden Green while I'm showing him my papers. Captain Laud of the *Alde!* Very respectable. "Don't come that with me, Will," one of them goes, "you're Steve Laud's boy." So I am! And see how I've made good. Been studying navigation with my uncle and now I'm a captain, and this other one knows my uncle so we're all chitty-chatting away and I'm telling them how our ship's up being fitted at Harwich, which is nearly true, and we've come over on the ferry and on our way to see some friends at Bucklesham, which is sort of true also in a way;

so by the time we get in the barn, all's clean as a whistle. We were just resting having a smoke and a bit of a break. Hot weather for walking. And of course all in order, he's looking through my papers and it's all sweet.'

He sat down and put his feet up on the hob and my mother swiped them with her cloth.

'That's the great strength of Bargood. You're well covered. Not a thing out of place.'

'I think you were just lucky,' my mother says, serious-faced. 'Supposing you'd got someone with a bit more pluck and not those oafs? Some would have blasted your lights out and checked your papers later. Don't you be a fool. Something's gone wrong there and someone's not been careful. You take care.'

'That's what I'm saying! All in order. Oh, we do take care, Mum. But wait till you hear! This place at Colden Green. It's a secret cellar. It's got a trapdoor. You'd never know it was there and do you know why? Because it's under a dung-heap. A dung-heap! Who's going to go digging around in a dung-heap, eh?'

'You, Will?' I asked him drily.

He laughed. 'Not at all! I get someone else to do that. This farmer, though, he's a good man. Soon as it's all stowed he drives his sheep over so's there's no tracks at all. Magnificent!'

'Who talked, Will?' I asked. 'That's what I want to know.'

'John's looking into it.'

Then he showed us the lovely red jewel on a chain so thin I was scared to touch it, but Will said it was strong as a rope. He never said how he came by it and no one asked. And I got to ride Jem over to Bucklesham to give it to Polly's mum so she could put it on for the wedding, and you should have seen the fuss in *her* house. It was worse than ours because Polly had lots and lots of giggling little sisters who no one ever told to shut up. When Polly got the jewel, she went quiet. 'Is that for me?' she said, with tears coming in her eyes. 'Oh – is that for me?' She stopped still with it in her palm, gazing down, as if the beauty of it made her sad somehow.

That's how good Will was.

We were lucky with the weather. After the wedding, we all went home to our house to eat and drink. Robert drank God knows how many flagons and lurched about with his mouth open, then sat down under the elderberries and burst into tears, as sudden as a baby that's just dropped its rattle. I think it surprised him more than anyone. I went up and put my arm round him. 'What's to do, Robbie?' I said.

'Sue's not here any more,' he sobbed, and I gave him a hug.

We were diminishing. James and Polly were going to live at Bucklesham.

'Shall I get Dinah for you?'

He nodded.

She was sitting quietly on the bench by the door with a smile on her round moon face, all on her own watching everything that went on. They were a funny couple. She was a soft, mild-spoken girl, very respectable, and Robert was just a drunk when all's said and done; but Dinah never had expectations, and she never had anyone to call her own but the people she worked with. Anyway, I don't suppose anyone else would have had our Robert. She was a good girl, Dinah. *She'*d never have come across to the Butt and Oyster with the boys like I did later that night after James and Polly had gone off to Bucklesham and Robert had fallen into his loud snoring sleep leaning up against the great cushion of her arm. I remember the night and all of us merry after eating and drinking; and the moon bright and high, almost full; and the night cry of a bird, and Charles talking about America. That's what he had a yen for. America. He'd met Rube once or twice and was all for soldiering, but not against Spain, he said, not at sea, no, he'd go for a soldier in America. When Rube heard my brother talk about America, he said, 'It's filthy fighting. Too much for me. The Indians fight different. And I've no stomach for going after women and children.'

I remembered he was a deserter.

'I wouldn't go west,' said Charles.

'You go where they tell you.'

'Or the East,' Charles said dreamily, 'if not America, the East.'

'Any news on who squeaked?' Will asked Luff.

Luff licked his lips slowly and wiped his mouth with the back of his hand. He looked at me as he said: 'I do believe we will have some news quite soon. Several ears are to the ground.'

Will told me once about a time when he and Luff were walking through Rotterdam late at night and a man passed by with a violin under his arm. Luff just walked up to him and hit him in the mouth. The man went down and sat with his legs splayed out on the ground, his back against the wall and one hand holding his face. The other hung on to his violin.

'What did John Luff want with a violin?' I asked.

'He didn't want it. He didn't even try to take it.'

'So why did he hit the man?'

Will widened his eyes and drew down the corners of his mouth.

'That's what I asked him. He just said, "I hate fancy friggers with violins."'

'Didn't you try and stop him?'

'How could I? It only took a second.'

'Luff's mad,' I said. 'You be careful, Will.'

'Oh, I am. Anyway, he wouldn't tap me. I'm his captain.' Will laughed. 'He's not bad, I mean not really bad. He thinks he is but he's not really.'

'Soft, you are,' I said. 'Not wise.'

25

Two days later the excise men shot three smugglers at Sizewell. One of them was from Dunwich.

None of us knew any of them, but the fear ran through us like a shiver through a hay field. Will and the boys had been in Ipswich cooling their heels at the Neptune, well away from the action, but the *Alde* pulled anchor and crossed over to Holland till things blew over. They were gone about three months. Every night I woke up thinking of Will shot. When he finally came back he said he'd got the use of one of Bargood's cottages to lie low in for a while, at Levington, a stone's throw away. I thought that was really funny because it was right near Broke Hall where our Squire lived, the Dentons' landlord who I never saw. Sir Philip. And Sir Philip was all for the excise men. I could walk to Will's in half an hour. It was tiny, two little rooms but big enough for me and him. We'd eat bread and cheese and drink porter and make love. I told Will about my idea for dressing up as a sailor and he laughed and thought it was a fine jape and dressed me up in his clothes. I made him put on my dress. I wore his pistols and sword and marched up and down, and we laughed ourselves silly. And time – ah, time – the shortest can be bigger than all the rest, and the small mean times stretch out like long lanes at night.

I knew this sweet time was passed the night Will came to me and said he'd gone for the quartermaster.

No one had a thing on our boys.

They'd been sitting outside the Neptune of a lovely summer evening having their brandy and milk, when the quartermaster walks up and tells them to put out their light. It's only a light in a lantern, for lighting the pipes.

'I will not put out my lantern,' says Luff, and the quartermaster shoots idly, randomly. Bang! Luff's hit in the thigh.

Will jumped up, reaching for his pistol, but Rube and a couple of others stopped him. Thank

God, or he'd be dead.

A couple of times I'd thought that. He'd be dead if not for this, if not for that. In the darkest points of the night I'd wake up with my mind in a dead fear.

Luff was looked after. Stebbing himself took out the bullet and the quartermaster was committed for trial at the next assizes. And so he should be. Of course he was acquitted in the end. Luff was laid up in another of Bargood's cottages. He had cottages all over the place, I realised; the man's wealth was beyond me. So well he lived on free trade, Will said. Fortunes were out there. Two more years at most, Will said, as he had said from the very beginning – how long ago? – so that when it came about that they began saying free-traders could get a pardon if they'd go in the navy and fight, Will didn't want to.

'I want to knock on like this for a while,' he said, leaning down for the tongs. 'I'm not a soldier. Anyway, they've got nothing on me.'

Thank God for that.

We were sitting in our house of an evening, coming up to Christmas. The door burst open and in came Charles with a wind-bashed face and the smell of winter on his coat. He was wild, sparkly-eyed, though he'd only been in Nacton playing chess at the sexton's house.

'Did you win?' Ned asked, a lovely gingery boy of sixteen, like my Uncle Leader might have been at his age only more slender.

'No.' He threw down his hat and unwound his muffler. 'Listen to this!' And while I mixed him a nice hot grog he told how he'd been reading in a paper about two men going up in the sky in a little boat pulled by a giant ball that sailed in the air. They'd looked down from the sky, he said, and taken their hats off to everyone in Paris. He said at the sexton's they were talking about nothing else.

'I don't believe it,' Mum said.

'It's true! They flew right away up in the sky. Imagine!'

'What, and no rope?'

'No rope.'

'How did they get down?'

'I don't know. They're men of science.'

'I don't know what they'd want to go up in the sky for,' my dad said. 'It's not natural.'

'I'd go,' said Charles. 'I'd go now. This second.' These two men doing this momentous thing in Paris had made him happy. My brother did not have a naturally happy face, though his dark eyes were soft by custom. But this had made them dance and dart.

'You wouldn't!' Mum said.

'I would.'

'*I* wouldn't,' said Ned.

'Nor me,' said Will.

'I would,' I said; and Charles looked at me and smiled his very rare and beautiful smile.

I would. I would, though the very thought of it filled me with terror. I would, to see what it was like. We were alike, me and Charles.

My father shook his head, amused. 'You're mad,' he said.

He left us next day. I don't know why he did it

that way, not telling anyone. I suppose he just thought it was easier. If he'd told Mum she'd have wept and tried to make him stay. He went down into Ipswich and enlisted at St Mary Elms, and the first we knew was a message sent up by a boy, that we were not to worry, he was on his way to Portsmouth, bound for India. He'd always fancied America, but we'd lost America by this time, so India it was.

Mum cried for weeks. On and off, on and off, weeping in corners, snuffling as she fed the ducks or took in the washing. I cried too, but not for long. Charles should have gone years ago. I thought of him often in the weeks that followed and knew that I must soon make my escape too.

And it all came to be, and sooner than I thought because of a horrible thing that happened.

First I heard was when Mrs Denton came by and stood whispering with Mum at the gate for a long time, and then Mum came in with a look of dread and anger and said it was a sick sad shame that such terrible things were done and wouldn't they all get tarred with the same brush now, just you wait and see. She shed a few tears. 'I'd wring their necks myself with my bare hands if I got hold of them,' she said.

'Who? Why? What's happened?'

There was a miller near Bungay killed. He'd locked his horses away at night so they couldn't be used, even though they'd warned him three times; and the free-traders come in the night and taken him from his bed and put him on his best horse backwards and ridden him down to the mill and cut his hands and feet off and left him there, and he bled to death.

'They should hang! They should hang the bloody lot of them!' my mother cried.

I ran down to Nacton and got the news from the Cracknells. It was the Stowmarket lot, everyone was saying. Bloody murderers. 'Kill a man, maybe, but don't torture him,' Georgie Cracknell said sadly. 'A bullet in the head maybe, yes, but not what they did to him. Not to any man.'

'It's foul,' I said.

The whole country was up in arms, the coastguard and surly dragoons were suddenly everywhere, and whenever people met, they'd say, 'Have they got them yet?' The miller was taken from his wife in bed. He had four children. I couldn't stop thinking about the poor man, whoever he was, whatever he'd done, how horrible to look down where your hands and feet used to be and see the red blood pouring out. The *Alde* was on the other side, thank God, when all this happened. They must have got word because they stayed away.

Then one day in the lane I met Big Lily from the farm. She'd been maid there since ever I could remember and we always chatted. So we stood a while until we got on to talking about how terrible about this poor miller, just as everyone else did, and I thought she looked at me in a funny way.

'What's up, Lily?' I said.

'Oh, nothing.'

And she went on her way. But after that I kept thinking I was getting funny looks from people, and I was. I couldn't understand. No one had ever minded about anything before, nothing had happened with any of our people. It was the Stowmarket ones that did the terrible thing, everyone knew that. But people have funny minds, and people like to yatter yatter yatter. Then I met her again and she told me she'd heard it from Mrs Denton that they'd got three men for the miller's murder.

'Thank God for that,' I said.

She looked at me closely.

'They'll hang them.'

'Of course they will,' I replied.

There was a peculiar pause.

'I would have thought that might have bothered you, Margaret,' she said.

The air between us quivered.

'What do you mean?'

She looked away.

'Well,' she said, 'I would have thought with some of the company you keep...' and she turned sharply and walked away.

The Turnspit Dog

26

I was twenty-two when I went as servant-of-all-work at Priory Farm, and some things had become clear. One was that I would never marry Will Laud or any man. The other was that I'd never bear children. The first I knew because if it wasn't Will it wouldn't be any, and Will wasn't the sort you married. The second I knew because Will and I had never had no talent with cundums or any of those tricks, and still nothing ever happened.

I stayed just over a year at Priory Farm, near the river at Downham Reach where the big ships anchored and offloaded their gear into the lighters for Ipswich.

Dinah Parker worked alongside me. Every night I had to dust and sweep out the keeping-room and kitchen, scour the flags, clean the chimney piece and make sure there were plenty of logs stacked ready by the fire for morning. I was last up and had to make sure all was snug and safe, and when everything was quiet I liked to slip the latch and take Bosun, the turnspit dog, for a walk down to the wooden bridge. A moat surrounded the farmhouse, where the ducks and geese swam, and the bridge crossed the stream where it emerged from the moat over a small weir. If there was a moon I'd sit down for a while and look at the pale light on the water, and listen to the whispering of the tall trees and the snortlings and huffings of poor bandy-legged little Bosun running here and there in the dark.

The only one I ever met those nights was Philip Broke's gamekeeper going home to his cottage, a nice enough old cove who always stopped for a chat. God knows what he'd have thought if he'd known what my brother James got up to nights.

'You don't want to be about this late, miss,' he'd say. 'They'm's some funny folks about.'

'I'm all right, I've got Bosun.'

And we'd laugh and he'd puff on his long-stemmed pipe which made a spicy fragrance on the night air. Then he'd shoulder his gun and off he'd go, and me and Bosun would return to the house. I'd take the poor creature in for a little while before blowing out the candles, all but one to take upstairs with me. There used to be monks in Priory Farmhouse. In those still, quiet, late hours I used to wonder if the place was haunted, sitting there on the settle in the big kitchen with Bosun next to me, his tiny pointed chin resting on my thigh. 'Sweet little boy,' I'd whisper to him, 'sweet little boy,' and feed him a sop of bread soaked in leftover gravy. He had a pretty face and was a hard little worker and deserved his treats. His feet were soft and gentle, like rabbits' feet, and seemed too small for all the pacing he had to do in turning the spit so the household could have its meat. I'd cosset him a while then put him out in his kennel and go up with my candle to the tiny attic where I had to duck my head whenever I got into my bed. From my window I could look out and see the river and the lights on the ships. I'd think of the sailors out there swinging in their hammocks and looking forward to tomorrow when they'd row ashore and walk the four miles down to Ipswich; how they'd stop at our farm for a drink of water and sometimes, if it was hot, put their heads under the pump. Whenever I could, I'd go out and chat a while and hear the news. They were always full of it. Some knew Will and could tell me of a good night's carousing in Rotterdam or Antwerp, and sometimes there'd be a message – he'll be home Thursday week – or a trinket from Amsterdam wrapped up in a fragment of lace. Sometimes the preventive men would come, by twos and threes. I'd see them from a distance with their blue coats and white stockings, and I gave *them* water too, ladling it from the crock. They were just lads, like my sailors.

And Will himself of course, appearing unannounced. What did we do? We walked in the night with the turnspit dog. We rowed over to the *Alde* moored out in the river and went to ground in his cabin – still, after all these years, in dreams I wake in Will's cabin and am complete at once, filled – or walked in the moonlight along deep, dusty Gainsborough Lane, slipping our arms around each other's waist. He'd say: I say, Pegs, what would you do if I was popped off?

'After the sailors again, are we, Mags?' That was Mat Sampson, the cow man, a leering fool of a creature.

It became a problem. Wherever I went in the end it became a problem, me and the sailors. One or two of them look a bit rough – and you know what people are like. One night they were making a hell of a din on the beach. Then one day, when me and the dairymaid went into Ipswich, it seemed we met a sailor or two every few yards and they all knew me and said hello; and the dairymaid, a very silly young girl, giggled like a fool each time and went home and told Mrs Flitch the cook that Margaret knew every single sailor in Ipswich. Mrs Flitch, a thin beady-eyed woman, told everybody else, of course, even Mrs Wake, our mistress, so there was talk already by the time my brother Ned came asking for me one day, and I ran down and saw at once by his face that something was up.

He was seventeen now and his lip was getting a downy look.

'They've put us off, Peggy,' he said.

'What are you talking about?'

'The Dentons. They've put us off. You're to come and help, Mum's in an awful state.'

It was the beginning of the bad time.

'What? Why? *Why?*'

'Because of Will.'

'Because of *Will?*'

'Two preventive men came, Peggy. They treated us like criminals.'

'Jesus Christ almighty.'

My blood rushed. What had my poor mum and dad ever done? The Dentons couldn't put us off. Mr Denton liked to sit and smoke of an evening out under the elderberry tree with my dad. We'd been their tenants for – I don't know – long before I was born. Since Sue was a babe. I'd saved the bloody woman's life, for God's sake, when she was down in a fit. I'd pulled her tongue out and stopped her choking, I'd gone for Dr Stebbing;

Mr Southgate said I was worth my weight in gold. They wouldn't turn us off. They wouldn't.

'I'll go and see them,' I said. 'They won't do it.'

'They have, Peggy! Keep your voice down, you don't want them knowing about it here.'

'Oh, Jesus!'

I said I'd follow on. My mother was sick, I told them, grabbed a few things and ran to try and catch up. I was breathless when I came alongside him, striding out along the road with his arms swinging and a grim set to his mouth. He was near tears. 'I don't know what we'll do,' he said. 'I don't know where we'll go.'

'What happened?'

'Three men came.' He kicked a stone viciously. 'They said they were looking for Will. Get away, they said, you know you know where he is. He's here all the time, isn't he? They threw all the beds over as if they thought he was underneath. Dad keeps saying: What's he done? What's he done? And this bastard turns round and looks at him as if he's a clump of shit stuck on his shoe and says: I don't know, *you* tell *me*, what *has* he done?'

I had to run to keep up with him.

'I tell you, Peggy, I'm going mad. I feel like thumping someone.'

'Oh my God, what's he done?' I said, going cold. 'What the hell has the stupid boy gone and done now?'

'You said he was always careful, Margaret.'

'He is!'

'Where is he now?'

'He's in Ipswich. Is that where they went?'

'How should *I* know?'

'Well, don't shout at *me*, it's not my fault!'

'Why couldn't you have walked out with a normal boy, Peggy? Why couldn't you have walked out with Georgie Cracknell or someone?'

'Georgie Cracknell? Don't be ridiculous.'

'What's wrong with poor old Georgie Cracknell? Not good enough for you?'

'Don't be stupid. There's nothing wrong with Georgie Cracknell but he's not Will, is he?'

'No, thank God.' I'd never seen Ned so furious. 'Thank God for the Georgie Cracknells of this world.'

'Don't you get like that about Will! I never see you turning down his stuff! Useful, isn't he?'

He made a banishing gesture, one arm stiffly cutting the air.

'We'll be better off than you,' I said nastily, burning inside, 'when he's through with the trade and I open my little shop.'

'No, you won't!' he exploded. 'Are you completely mad? You're never having a shop, Margaret. He's never leaving the trade. Don't you see? Surely!'

He was getting ahead of me and I had to run to keep up.

'Are they putting the Cracknells off too?'

'No, Peggy,' he said bitterly, 'just us.'

Our house was over. I knew as soon as I set foot over the threshold, the air had changed. Things were out of place. The settle was up and Dad and Mum were kneeling by the big chest, taking things out and looking at them in a bemused way before setting them down pointlessly again. James stood glowering from under his black brow, hands in his pockets in front of the fire. Robert sat round-shouldered, one hand loosely balled on the table.

'I'm so sorry!' I blurted.

Mum looked angrily at me. 'What's the girl talking about?' she said to Dad. 'What's she got to apologise for? It's not her fault.'

'Peggy, love, nobody thinks it's your fault,' Dad said.

I started to cry. 'Ned does.'

'I didn't say that.' Ned glowered.

'You did. More or less.'

'Rubbish,' James said. 'We're all angry but not with you.'

'With Will then. What did they want with him?'

James shrugged. 'Who knows? Someone somewhere talked, I suppose.'

'What were they looking for?'

Another shrug. 'Contraband.'

'Wanted to know where we got them candlesticks.' Mum was sad rather than angry. Tears enlarged her eyes. She'd been looking so well lately. Now this. 'I said they were a present from my cousin. You don't think they'd check, do you?'

'Course they won't, Mum.' James looked at me. He'd grown into a lovely-looking man, our James, very dark of eye and brow like Charles, only prettier. 'There's no point going up there, Peggy,' he said. 'I've been up. I've been up there all morning just about, and I spoke to them both, him and her. Both very very very sorry, of course. Both down in the mouth. Must understand if it was up to them blah blah blah. Must understand they could lose the farm. Must understand...'

'It's not fair,' said Ned.

'How long have we got?' I asked.

James sighed. 'Month.'

'You should have seen the gaffer when he told me,' Dad said. 'Didn't know where to put his eyes.'

Ned snorted. 'My heart bleeds.'

'Makes me sick!' James suddenly exploded. 'When you think of all the years we've put into this place. And for what? What have we done? What's Mum done? What's Dad done? Nothing. Aren't we allowed to have visitors? Just because Will came to see us?'

Robert had said not a word. Now he stood up and walked to the door. 'I'll get the cart out,' he said. 'I'm going into town. Someone needs to tell Will.'

'You go with him, Peggy,' Mum said. 'He'll not know where to go. There's nothing to do here, me and your dad are just sorting through a few things.'

Robert went to bring the cart round.

'I'm so sorry, Mum.'

'Not a word! I don't blame you and I don't blame Will. One of the family, he is, one of ours. Not another word.'

'Where will you go?'

'I'm looking around,' James said. 'Polly's brother knows a lot of people.'

'Don't worry, Peggy,' Dad said. 'The gaffer feels bad enough, he'll not put us off till we've somewhere to go.'

That evening I walked out in the meadow with the horses. Dandy was long gone now, Jem no wild thing these days, but a sober and dignified creature. He came straight to me and laid his huge head against my chest. I was afraid. I was wrong, wasn't I? Ned was right. I should have married a steady man and been normal. They should have blamed me. Too good to me, my family, spoiled me always. Something huge was closing up for good. All of my previous life.

27

Two weeks later they'd moved to a cottage on the edge of Nacton Heath. Two months after that Mum was dead.

Bargood took things in hand. Me and Robert found Will playing faro with Adam Hare and Rube on Neptune Quay. He cared nothing for himself. 'Ha,' he said, 'this is bluff. They've got nothing on me and they know it. They was hoping you'd all squeal, that's what it is. The bastards! Come!' He took us inside and up a twisting staircase to a deep-blue room with a pargeting floor, where Bargood and another man sat reading their newspapers and drinking coffee. The other man, a thin, serious sort with grey hair, looked straight at me for a few seconds then drained his coffee decisively and rose.

'You have business, Josiah,' he said discreetly and was gone.

Bargood was all crinkle-eyed geniality till he heard the news, then he banged the table and swore and promised that my family would not suffer.

'It must have been the Shingle Street raid,' he said to Will. 'Someone must have recognised you.'

'What Shingle Street raid?' I asked, but I was soon to hear about that, as the whole country was talking about it a day or so later. They'd loaded sixteen wagonloads before the coastguard attacked, then they'd scattered, but the load was taken and locked up in a stable at Bawdsey. It was dark. Will said no one could say for certain they'd seen him, or anyone else for that matter, they all had their handkerchiefs over their faces. And indeed, apart from us losing our home, nothing else ever came from this incident. Will was away within the hour across land to meet the *Alde* down off the coast of Essex. You had to admire Bargood. A messenger here, a word there, and in a day he sent a purse of money to suffice till my father and brothers had work; and in two days, word came he had a place for us. That's one thing I'll say for the smugglers. They took care of you, if you were one of theirs.

I don't know how many cottages Bargood owned. All over the place, Will said, in Holland too. He lived in different ones at different times. I knew he had one at Ramsholt and one at Eyke, but there were lots of others. Ours stood all on its own right on the corner of the heath, near where the road runs up towards the decoy-ponds. It turned its face away from the wilds and looked towards the high road running down into Nacton, as if trying to ignore its own rough and lonely situation. The sheep cropped here and there before it.

That year. It was as if God was looking down on us like he did on Job and saying now what else can I send to these Catchpoles? And it hardened me and made me determined to survive. Will and the boys stayed Holland-side a while. Ned got work as a shepherd and Dad found some labouring. Robert was useless, he just drank. He was getting worse. Got a bit of labouring now and then but always ended up with the push. I was still at Priory Farm but going home a lot to help, and Dinah too, such a good girl she was and so foolishly and quietly devoted to that poor big babby with his drinking bottle forever in his fat fist. But the funny thing was Mum, how she rallied and seemed well, and made new yellow curtains and put her best foot firmly forward with good cheer. She made it just like home till you stepped out of the door and saw that there were no trees, no palings, no elderberry, no meadow where the lovely horses grazed. And she did all that and then died, and it was nothing to do with the asthma in the end, it was a stupid accident.

All our stuff had come over on the carrier's cart. It sat alongside Bargood's bits and pieces that were already there, pots and pitchers, a broken time-piece and two high-backed chairs, a bench and a stool and a gong from foreign parts; and Mum was forever moving things about, still waiting for them to slot into their comfortable places. One tall recess, hard by the rack where the washing hung, had three little shelves high up where old things gathered greasy dust: broken things, forgotten things, boxes and candleholders smothered in wax, cracked bowls holding spent cartridges, bottles long since hopelessly clagged with unrecognisable dirt, and a nest of canisters with a faded daisy pattern on. It was these she was reaching for. She'd said once or twice they'd scrub up nice, those canisters. She was standing on a stool and it slipped under her and she fell and hit her head a great blow on the iron hob and never got up again. Only Ned was there and he was in the yard washing up for his dinner. He could see Dad and Robert just coming over the brow of the heath. He went in and found her dead. Quite gone.

Her funeral was well attended. So many people liked my mother. It was nice in a way, all of us together, the Cracknells and the Catchpoles and the people from the village. The Dentons came. Both of them squeezed my hand and said how sorry they were and what a good woman she was. I missed Charles. He never wrote. He'd been gone two years and not a word. She'd worried every day. The sexton wrote to his regiment but we never heard a thing. He should have been there. James stood with his wife and baby. Polly had another on the way. An old piece of crêpe was wrapped around Dad's old hat, and his poor face under it was long and grey. And there was Will, home at that time, standing with his head bowed and his hands clasped before him, tears streaming down his face. It rained, that same sweet soft rain there had been the evening of her death, and the rain-mist clung on his eyelashes. He raised his head and looked at me. Such looks

Will had. Such eyes. Even there, then, we could go soft on each other like that, over a distance.

When Sue died he took me to the *Alde*. When Mum died, he took me on the river, across Downham Reach and over to Woolverstone. Half a mile in the dark upon the Orwell, with the rain now no more than a moistness of the air and the moon at the full. I was warm in my cloak. We said nothing. Will rowed. Moonlight twinkled all around us on the tranquil water. We drifted into the far shore, along the shadow of the thick woods that ran down to the water's edge, to where the tall trees gave way to Woolverstone's parkland. The park boat was moored at the edge of the lawn below the Cat House. Far above glowed the lights of the big house, softened by the moisture in the air. The Cat House was like a little white castle with battlements, an odd house with many walls, and it occupied a pretty spot. The estate's gamekeeper lived there, and he was one of ours. All his lights were out so you couldn't see the stuffed cat in the window facing the river, a huge white malkin with yellow eyes and a pink nose that had belonged to the gamekeeper before. Our man had him on a stand on the sill, with a table behind on which he placed the lamp to shine out a warning on certain nights. But all was peaceful tonight. The shadows of deer grazed the high ground. A night bird called plaintively. Mum was gone for ever.

We lay down under the trees and made silent love.

We sat upon the wooden jetty and leaned together.

'I should not come and go as freely as I have. Not for a little while.'

'Things will get better,' he said. 'You wait.'

'I know,' I said uncertainly. 'I know'

28

'Ha ha, they're coming for you, Margaret!' Mat Sampson again, always teasing me. Had a mean streak, he did, and too fond of his own silly voice, which was high and undisciplined, sometimes tra-la-la-ing on, interspersed with giggles, as if it couldn't stop.

I was scouring out the frying pan, scrubbing away. I ducked my head and saw out of the window two preventive men in the yard, the sun shining on their silver buttons and the buckles of their shoes.

'They'll be wanting a drink,' I said, slung the dish clout over my shoulder and went out. A sweet-mouthed farm boy stood in the yard, and the old gamekeeper of my nightly rambles sat on the bench to the right of the kitchen door with a jug of beer, ankles crossed, long double-barrelled fowling-piece resting up against the wall. The first preventive man was brown and hard-eyed. The second was a golden boy.

'What'll it be, lads?' I smiled. 'Beer?'

'You darling,' said the hard-eyed man. 'Beer indeed.'

'Yes thank you, miss,' said the boy, loosing the

collar of his cloak and sinking on to the other bench.

When I returned with the flagon Mat Sampson followed me out. 'Any activity?' he asked as I poured for them.

'Activity?'

'Of the free-trade kind?'

'There's always activity,' grinned the golden boy.

But the hard-eyed man stared Mat out, slowly taking off his three-cornered hat and setting it down on an upturned barrel that served as a table, before saying, 'Now why would we be telling you all our business?'

'No reason at all,' Mat replied jovially.

'No activity for us for a while anyhow,' offered the boy as I handed him a drink. 'We're for a run ashore, thank God.' His blue eyes met mine, he smiled broadly and my insides turned like cream turning under the spoon.

'You're too young for this game,' I told him.

Everyone laughed; he did too.

I thought of John Luff and his cronies. 'You're too young.'

'I know you,' said the hard-eyed man. 'You're Margaret Catchpole.'

'So I am,' I replied, smiling brightly at him while my pulse quickened. 'And who may you be?'

'I worked once with your brother.'

'Which one?'

'Charles. How's he faring these days?'

'I wish I knew. He listed two years ago and went east but we've not heard a word.'

'East, eh?'

'India.'

'Good man, Charles,' said the man, no longer hard of eye but steady only, and he smiled for the first time. He was not so bad. 'Rafe Cumber, ma'am,' he said. 'Remember me to him when next you see him.'

'I will, sir.'

'You rode bareback into Ipswich when you were scarce more than a child.'

'Oh, our Margaret's a one all right.' The gamekeeper drained his beer and stood up, reaching for his gun.

Mat Sampson smiled his leery smile and made circles in the dust with the scuffed toe of his shoe. 'If she was a boy she'd be out on the high seas.'

'I would.'

It was all pleasant till Mat said, 'But not on your side, boys,' and laughed a stupid great laugh. I hit him one with the dish clout and he ducked aside, chuckling. The sweet-mouthed farm boy hovered near me. 'Did you?' he said. 'Did you ride bareback into Ipswich?'

'It's no marvel,' I said briskly. 'I had to ride to fetch the doctor. There was no time for a saddle.'

Mat sniggered down his nose. 'Captain Margaret!' he whinnied. 'She'd make 'em walk the plank!'

'Shut up, Mat.'

'Forty lashes, Margaret! Please!'

'I'll give you more than that,' I said, 'but you won't like it.'

'How did you stay on the horse coming down Bishop's Hill?' asked Sweet Mouth. 'Without a saddle.'

‘You hold on with your knees,’ I said defiantly, staring him in the eyes, aware it would raise another knuckle-headed laugh from Mat. It did. The venerable old gamekeeper, uncomfortable with this kind of talk, shouldered his gun and cleared his throat. The golden revenue boy smiled ear to ear. Rafe Cumber put a coin on the barrel for the beer. ‘May we fill up our flasks, ma’am, with some of your good water?’ he asked.

‘Of course.’

Then they were off, all of them but Mat, who stood in the yard bouncing from foot to foot. He followed me into the kitchen where Dinah was stirring the broth, sweat glistening on her wide brow, and the silly dairymaid poked straws at a bee that revolved on its back on the sill, buzzing loudly. I picked up the frying pan, half scoured, with a view to finishing it off. ‘If you ask me,’ Mat said, ‘those excise men are wasting their time. They should be out there fighting the mounseers rather than gallifragging about after a bunch of scabby turds who think they’re Captain Kidd.’

‘Shouldn’t you be working, Mat?’ I asked him pointedly.

‘I say, Margaret,’ he replied. ‘Did you know there was a price on Will Laud’s head?’

I didn’t think. I swung the frying pan through the air, suds and all, and bashed him a fair blow on the side of the head.

‘You’re mad!’ he bellowed, covering his ear with his hand.

‘And you’re a liar,’ I cried, wielding the pan as if to land him another.

Mrs Hitch came bursting out of the pantry, a

skinny fury waving a spoon, shrieking at the top of her voice: 'I will not have this! I will not! Out of my kitchen! Out of my kitchen, both of you!'

Dinah had stopped stirring and watched as if frozen; the dairymaid looked up from the poor spinning bee. Mat retreated to the yard, scowling now, stood just outside the door nursing his sore ear and staring at me with a look of hatred.

'Am I to go too?' I asked the cook boldly. 'Don't you need me for the puddings?'

'Don't give lip, she snapped.

'I'm sorry, Mrs Flitch,' I said, 'but why should I have to let him insult my friends and say lying things about them?'

'*You* don't know,' Mat said through the door. '*You* don't know what's a lie and what isn't. I might have seen a handbill for all you know.'

So then of course I knew that there was nothing in it, and I breathed more free. 'He tries to annoy me, Mrs Flitch,' I said. 'He shouldn't act the martyr if he succeeds.'

'Can't a fellow have a bit of a joke?' he appealed, wounded, venturing in again.

'Away, you!' the incensed dame commanded, pointing imperiously with a big iron spoon, and he sloped moodily out of sight. She turned and gave me a little push. 'And you,' she said, 'to work. Any more of that and you'll be out.' I flounced a little as I nodded and turned away, got down to chopping the onions very fiercely, very small. Dinah cast me a little sweet smile, twitching her eyebrows. Mrs Flitch stomped out and after a second or two we giggled quietly, the three of us, me and Dinah and Dora Todd.

'You're awful,' Dora Todd said, 'you're really awful. Did you see his ear was bleeding?'

'Boo hoo,' I said.

'Served him right,' Dinah added softly.

'He was only larking like he always does,' said Dora.

'For God's sake, Dora,' I snapped, 'will you kill that blessed creature and have done with it.'

'What did he mean?' Dora asked. 'Will Laud's your beau, ain't he, Margaret? What did Mat mean? What did he mean about a price on his head? What was all that?'

'All that,' I said, 'was bilge. Balderdash, bilge and blather if you must know. Mat Sampson's a fool. He's a clod you'd scrape off your shoe.' And that set the daft girl off giggling again.

29

It started again, the talk. Can't have talk. It was Mat Sampson got them stirred up, with all his blather about the smugglers did this at Hollesley and that at Eyke, and this one slit a gizzard, and that one got hanged, and so-and-so's got a hundred pounds on him and many a one would sell their own grandam for that, let alone a bloody free-trader, wouldn't you say, Margaret? Of course, you'd know all about that kind of thing. And so the looks started. And the tongues spawned poison, but it was at harvest home that all hell broke loose. That was never fun for us, harvest home, not for the likes of me and Dinah. For us it was hard work. The Wakes were very keen on showing a grand largesse-spending. We'd been getting ready for weeks. I must admit Mrs Flitch excelled herself at this time of year. She wouldn't let anyone else do the harvest loaves, and they were magnificent. When finally they were set out on the table on the lawn for all to see, they were like suns rising. She put faces on them, and leaves, and ears of corn, and little field mice and ladybirds and swallows. Seemed a terrible shame to cut them open but we did, and delicious they were too. We had the tables set outside, and when the reapers and mowers and gatherers were all done hollering largesse, and the last wain had lumbered over the field and the last load of corn was in the barn, here they all came raggling and taggling along from the fields like a wind-blown banner.

'Come and look, Margaret,' Dora called from the open door, 'they're bringing the bough.'

The kitchen was hot as hell. We were cooking for thirty-seven, if you included all the children. I'd been draining potatoes and was wet and red from the steam, sweating like a pig, but I dumped the cauldron, straightened my cap and went out. The leader was a big brawny reaper called Lawrence, riding on Mr Wake's skewbald. Behind him the green bough was carried aloft. A band walked alongside, pipe, fiddle, drum, and all the men from the farm were there, the wives in pretty pinks and yellows and sky blues, the children ajog. They came up from the river in a long snake, crossing the bridge, singing and dancing with their hooks and sickles on their shoulders. They went to the barn to lay the bough on the corn, and we rushed, me and Dinah and Dora and Mrs Flitch and a girl or two that had come to help, to have all ready all at the same time, the potatoes, the cabbage, the turnips and carrots, and the roast beef all red and succulent, a sight I had not seen since this time last year. I set little Bosun free. Out he ran, shaking himself, with his red bush a-wagging to greet the men already gathering by the barrels with their jugs, drawing off the strong brown ale. Dora stirred frantically at the gravy. The table was crammed, we'd been baking since four. We had pies of veal and mutton and pork, buns and dainties and fourses cake of lard and currants, well spiced and sharp with oranges and lemons. The pantry was a picture, jewelled red jelly, soft yellow custard, apple pies oozing syrup on to their sugared tops. I kept going and sneaking a look because it was so cool in there and smelled like paradise. I could have eaten those lovely sweet cool things. I could have died for a drink of the cold lemonade my mother used to make in summer.

Mrs Wake came through the door that led from the parlour, smiling her rare smile. 'Ready, my ladies?' she asked.

We served, the three of us and Mrs Wake, while surly Mr Wake and his boys drew the ale. The men all got drunk, and many of the women too. Then we brought out the plum puddings and the sweets, and Mr Wake emptied the largesse bag on to the table and counted it out, five shillings for the men, half a crown for the women, two bob for the boys.

The musicians set to. So at last we could get our own, while two of the wives made a huge can of tea, and the first barrel was rolled out of the yard and the second rolled in. We put back our caps and wiped our faces and ate under the trees. I had beef and turnips and plum pudding with blancmange, and a big piece of harvest cake, and I drank a jug of beer. Feeling very merry and rested, I joined in with the stepping, all hands joined, with Sweet Mouth on one side and Mrs Flitch on the other. Away we went skipping around the yard and out on to the green like a ribbon taken by the wind.

30

The sky was just beginning to turn dark. Lanterns shone on the moat, and the third barrel was on its side. A fat man danced on a bench. Someone had been sick near the pump and someone else was swilling it away with water. Mr Wake saw us. 'Girl, fill the cans!' he said, pointing to the table, but I was having none. I was for fun, but only till I saw Mat Sampson come staggering and lurching through the dancers with a wide sloppy grin on his loose lips.

'Dance, Margaret?' he slurred.

'Oh well,' I said, 'come on then, Mat.'

But he took that to mean he could start grabbing and groping, so I gave him a bit of a push and he went flying off his feet and landed on his back on the green slope near the gate. He grabbed my ankle and pulled me down, laughing like a fool.

I hit him and leaped up, he jumped to his feet and made after me. And there at the garden gate I saw suddenly an unexpected face, John Luff all dark and serious against the revelry. His eyes stared straight at me, unblinking, a look in them I had never seen there before in that hard man, one I could only call fear. Something was terribly wrong.

'Why, John,' I said, starting forward.

Mat grabbed my arm; I swatted him off like a fly. He laughed.

'He's hurt, you're to come,' John Luff said.

The blood drained from my veins.

Mat flopped on to my shoulder; he was worse than I thought. He stank.

'Is this parasite troubling you, Margaret?' Luff asked softly. He was deadly, the softer the deadlier. I never saw steadier eyes. Stop it, John, I would say, as I always did, and he'd look at me in that way, and smile and stop it, but slowly, in his own time. Stop it. But before I could answer Mat sealed his own fate. 'Largesse,' he yelled, stumbling from my shoulder, 'largesse or revolution!' straight into John Luff's stricken face, and Luff downed him, quick and sharp, one mighty blow to the face that sent him sprawling backwards. Blood burst out of his face. A great drunken roar went up from Mat's fellows.

'Come now, Margaret,' Luff said, deadly fearful. 'He's badly.'

Mat raised up on an elbow and put up one hand to cover his smashed nose. Blood came through his fingers and ran down his chin and gathered on his shapeless lips. 'You fucking whore, Margaret Catchpole!' he bellowed. 'You fucking whore!'

I looked in John's eyes. I took nothing with me. We went over the green and down to the bridge. Bosun galloped along with us and a few of Mat's friends came chasing drunkenly after, bawling abuse, but soon turned back when John brought out his pistol.

In the lane were children playing drop-handkerchief.

'What happened, John? Tell me how bad?'

'Shot,' he said. 'Bad. Sent me.'

It was dark under the trees and the river was dim. The skiff was on the shingle.

'What happened?'

We were in and away. Back on the beach the turnspit dog ran here and there at the water's edge. His forlorn howling accompanied us out into the reach. Luff never looked at me. His eyes were to the sea. He told me they'd met with the coastguard on the North Vere by Havergate Island. There'd been a battle, and Will was shot. That's all he'd say. It grew full dark as we rounded Langer Point and turned north up the coast. She was a good fast little skiff, the breeze was with us, soon we passed the sandbank at the mouth of the Deben and saw across the flats a light in the church at Ramsholt. It was a false light, John Luff said, and spat overboard. Not till we'd passed the coastguard station at Bawdsey did he tell me more, how the coastguard were drawn off to Sizewell Gap, or so they thought; how they'd fixed a glass on Shingle Street for a day or two and all was quiet at the station there, the only movement on that wild stretch being the builders at work on the new Martello tower; and how, when they landed the goods on the long spit of the North Vere, a score of excise men rose up from the shingle like corpses from their graves and shot dead a man called Daniel Peake from Sudbourne and a Dutch lad called Joris, and slit the throat and shattered the head of poor Adam Hare. The rest scattered, melting into the night. Will was challenged and emptied his pistol into a pipsqueak exciseman, whose comrade came at Will with his sword and dashed the pistol far across the beach; so he drew his own sword and they fought, and Will was hurt.

'Lucky I went back for him,' Luff said. 'He was out cold and two or three more of the bastards coming up the beach.' Small as he was, John Luff was strong. Later I found out he'd thrown Will over his shoulder and run with him, splashing over the narrows and into the marshes, where any man who was not a fool could become invisible.

31

Will was in a house with green shutters, a nice cosy little place, one of Bargood's. Rube was there, teary-faced and filthy, gnawing his nails in the chimney corner and waiting for the kettle to boil. He smiled weakly when I came in. 'Here she is now, Will,' he said, 'here's your Pegs.' And I saw

Will lying bloody and naked on a bed. A very old crone with a withered face and turned-in lips, a bow-backed witch of a thing in an old-fashioned cap, was putting steaming flannels on his feet. A pad of red dulse was set over his left eye and cheek; the other eye, terrified, stared straight up at the ceiling, while his teeth rattled like old bones in a diceman's palm. His hands were clasped upon a running red mess on his right shoulder. Will was whippet-thin about the buttocks but his legs were strong and wiry, every muscle in them tensed, all of him slick with sweat, shiny and bruised and dirty, heels thrusting into the coarse grey blanket like tent pegs. His neck was arched and there was snot on his lip.

'Sweetheart,' I said, going to him, 'sweetheart.'

My heart cracked.

'It hurts, Pegs,' he choked out.

'Yes, yes, but it will be all right.'

'C-c-cold,' he whispered.

'We'll make you warm.'

Rube brought a bowl of warm vinegar, a bowl of hot water. 'I'm boiling cloths,' he said. 'We undressed him because he was burning up.'

'The doctor,' I said.

'No,' said Luff. 'No doctor. They've gone for Hans Meyer.'

'Who?'

'He knows what he's doing. He was a barber.'

'When will he be here?'

Luff licked his lips. 'I don't know. They have to find him. He'll take the bullet out.'

'When?'

Luff shook his head.

The old dame, pottering about with her cloths, wiping and cleaning his body, paused to pour whisky between Will's bloody teeth. 'He's lucky,' she said crisply. 'He'll live.'

'Let me see,' I said to Will.

'No,' he said. 'I'm trying to stop it bleeding.'

'Please, Will.'

'He won't let us near it,' Luff said.

Will started to cry. I parted his shaking hands and saw where the white bone lay in splinters against the mess. With fascination I saw sinew, shiny and bright, and the bullet sitting in amongst it all like a great fat burrowing slug with its tail sticking out. Not too much blood but there would be when it was pulled. I looked about. 'Give him whisky,' I said, and got up, walked about and found a pantry off the kitchen, a barrel of flour, found tweezers under the stairs and set them boiling, told Rube to roll through the barrel, washed my hands and waited. We took turns holding Will's head, dribbling the amber liquid into his mouth and stroking it down his throat, till he was lolling half dead. I said nothing to no one, just got about my business. Rube and Luff held him while I did it. He tried to buckle, all of him, and the whisky came spluttering back up his throat. The bullet came out thickly coated in blood, and a great flooding came after. I dropped the bullet on the floor and it rolled. Handfuls of flour, quick, one after the other, on the uprush. So much blood. It swelled up through the flour, made a vile pink pastry you could knead. We threw and threw the flour, John Luff and I, till the room was like a mill and the body on the bed was like a white clown with a huge pink sloppy growth that swelled by the second. We tended it like clay. And somehow it stopped growing under the great weight we threw on it, and the weight of our hands, and we could rest a little. We looked at each other. Both of us were sweating.

Luff's lip curled. I smiled. We held eyes, mysteries one to another for ever, stuck together by Will.

'Jesus Christ,' said Rube.

'There you are, Moggy,' Luff said to the crone. 'Have you ever seen the like of that before?'

Rube was sick outside. Will was dead to us but he was breathing, his mouth wide open and the air rattling through his lungs. We washed him down and cleaned up and settled him and sat around the lamp talking and sipping on the whisky. Moggy Mitchell, an ancient spy of Bargood's, went out sniffing for news and was back by midnight. It was all up. They had his name and the name of Luff. The man Will shot was a youngster, a lad of twenty, not dead but shot in the thigh, and very sick. I thought of the golden boy who came that day with Rafe Cumber and drank his beer and passed on. Too young he was. Too young. She said there was a price of one hundred guineas on Will's head for the attempted murder of an excise man, that there were handbills as far as Lynn in the north and Essex down south.

32

There was no going back. For nine months, Will and I lived in the house with green shutters between Orford and Shingle Street. The wound healed slowly; Hans Meyer could not be found and it was left to me to pick out the fragments, clean it up, cover and bind it. Cleaning a wound is no different from cleaning any other mess; when you'd done as much skivvying as I had it came easy. Poor Will shook and tossed in fever for a week, while Rube and Luff joined up with the *Alde* and the rest of the crew lying off Aldeburgh, lacking a cook now Adam Hare was gone and faring for themselves till they reached Amsterdam, where the ship was to be put in quarters.

Will nearly lost his sight. He was, as Moggy Mitchell said, lucky in the end. His wild blue eyes still looked at me as before, but there beneath one was a great slice out of the cheek, a hole in the face like a crater that puckered over dark red and drew down the lid strangely. That became his one sleepy eye.

My brothers came, bringing food. Bargood called and told us not to worry about a thing. He'd had words with certain people, certain very important people. Just lie low,' he said, and all would come well in the end. We were safe, and when Will was recovered he'd be better out of the country for a while. A long voyage.

'What about me?' I said.

God knows who'd employ me now.

'What, Margaret?' His fat face smiled. 'Shall we make a sailor-boy of you now?'

Will was lying in bed in his bandages. He laughed. 'She'd make as good a one as any,' he said, but we all knew Bargood would never countenance a woman on board. Bargood said when Will took sail I should go home. He'd provide. We'd put it about that I'd been away helping at my Uncle Leader's, whose wife was with child again and gone very sickly. That much was true. My Aunt Ellen Leader *was* pregnant and she *was* sickly, and there was even some saying she might die and leave the poor man with all those young ones. I should stay quiet at home till all tongues had left off their wagging, and by then Will could venture forth again, if only he was careful.

So we were left alone, apart from Moggy Mitchell who came by sometimes with gifts from the smuggling crew, a box of raisins, a capon, butter and cheese, coffee, tobacco. Will was changed. It's when his madness began. He knew he could die now. He'd seen Adam Hare's ruined head hanging back from the shoulders, pulped bloody on the strand like a burst pumpkin.

We went walking on the empty singing beach, miles with the shushing tread of our feet on the shingle, slate sea, huge sky, booming bitterns in the wild marsh grass. The shingle was brown and grey, made of a thousand gentle shades of pink, of silver, of gold and blue. Along the ridges grew ramparts of odd green flowers with regal spikes, sea cabbage and yellow poppies, sudden purples, and the blue thistles of sea holly. Sometimes we'd sit and stare at the waves. He wept. A great melancholy overcame him, so that he could not eat or sleep. He said John Fuller, the man he shot, grew up with Rube's cousin, and it made no sense. He said we're the ones who die, the likes of me and John Fuller and Adam Hare and Rube and Luff and your auntie's uncles. No one takes a pop at the likes of Captain Josiah Bargood. No. And he's not the greatest of them, there's those in the know as high above him as he is above us. And that's the way the world goes.

He lay in my arms nights, grinding his teeth. His dreams were vile, they pitched him here and there, pinched and poked and bit like Robinson Crusoe's demons, held him low in suffering deeps from which his voice would mourn and entreat. Or he'd wake in the night and sit smoking, staring at the laden darkness with horrified eyes.

'What's wrong with me, Peggy?' he asked.

'Hush. Lie down. I'll get you a drink.'

'Oh, Pegs, let's leave it all, let's go to Holland. We'll run a tavern and the lads can keep us provided.'

'Yes, we will.' I smiled.

I washed his long yellow hair and cut his nails and urged rest, conspiring with Moggy Mitchell to mix a sleeping draught. I thought he could sleep away this worm in his mind, but it proved as chronic as fleas.

'A man's head,' he said thoughtfully, 'all that a man is, all that there is – no more than a mess for flies.'

'No, no,' I said, 'much more than that. The soul

isn't in the blood, Will.' And she came back to me, Jane Brewer. A blackened chrysalis swinging slowly in raging fire. There was no sign of the soul leaving, hovering with wings over the spitting flames. 'What's important is invisible,' I told him.

Once he sat bolt upright in the middle of the night and shuddered like a reed. I touched his back and he flinched.

'Go to sleep, my sweet,' I whispered, and gentled him down.

His breath was hot and scared.

'So much blood in a man,' he said, 'you wonder how it all fits in.'

'Don't think.'

'He was like a bottle,' Will said. 'Like if you shook a bottle and took off the top. It flew. The blood. Came out in a great fan, a great curtain, like this!' He made a movement with his hands near his throat as if shaking out linen. 'Splash!'

'No more of that! Don't think of it.'

'It's not thinking. I don't even have to think. It's there whether or no.' He laughed. 'I swallowed something too big.'

'Give it time, give it time. It'll pass.' Like a nausea, or a bad cold. Poor Will, unmanned by blood. I'd've made a stronger witness.

'We'll go to Holland,' I said. 'I'll take care of you, my boy. We'll have some peace.'

So the months passed, and I learned what it felt like to love the ocean as my mother had done, to walk along where the damp fringe of the sea meets the shelving stones, millions upon millions, each one the only one, with the wind whipping and the gulls crying and the saltlick of your lips on your tongue. At night, the dove-grey roke rolled in from the sea and lay thick as wool on the marshes. You could wade in it.

I loved him more than ever now. Big strong thing that he was, it was me that carried him through those times. We could have been happy. We had visits from friends now and then, from sailors, and once, Will's sister Lucy came with her man Keeley and drank tea with us and talked about the state of their dad, who'd lost his job taking the government packet between Harwich and Langer Fort due to going up and down Felixstowe Ferry bladdered so many times that no one trusted to sail with him no more.

'Take care he don't find where you are,' Lucy said. 'He's got a mouth on him like a dribbling arse. And not only that, he'll be tapping you for money, he was scrounging round our door two days ago. God knows where he is now, probably at Uncle Jack's.'

Lucy was a plump fair curly-haired woman as little like her brother as you could imagine, with a round impassive face and a steady gaze, a woman who never returned a smile.

Will told me she used to cry singing him off to sleep with Barbara Allen when he was six years old and she was fifteen. I think she had a weariness.

'Take care, you, Will,' she said. 'You know you can always come to me if you've the need.'

She didn't say anything about me.

I found a pebble of amber and gave it to Will for luck. He kept it always about him in his pocket after that. I gathered the prettiest stones and shells and made a show of them on the window sill. I put wild flowers in a jug and made soup and hung fish to smoke, and in time he came round. In time he gazed less at empty space and began to talk of getting us a pheasant or two. There were one or two lads home, here and there-abouts, all kicking their heels, lying low.

'You take care, Will,' I said.

He laughed. 'How can anything happen to me now?' he said, and took out of his pocket the piece of amber and held it upon his palm.

I was so pleased to see him showing some of his former liveliness that I let him go. He had a fine long night with his friends, returning with a brace of pheasants. Things went better after that. Friends were important to Will, and it was best he didn't think too much. Those he had he stuck to. People he stuck to, not things. That's why he stuck with John Luff even when he shouldn't have, and now he owed John Luff his life. Things he'd give away. All but that watch from Amsterdam, which he loved to take out and polish and fiddle about with. As he grew stronger in mind and body, he grew restless. I was restless too. Bargood came. He stayed in the house with us for a few days like a visiting uncle, though of course it was *his* house, so all was strange. He joined us in our walks along the beach and it was plain our days here were numbered.

Bargood gave me a fat purse. 'Now, Margaret,' he said. 'You take this home to your father and brothers and Will takes a voyage, a long one, maybe a year, and when he comes back everything will be just as it was.'

A year! That took me by surprise. He'd never been away that long before.

He was gone three and a half years.

A Good Servant

33

May 1793

The first time I was in Dr Stebbing's house was when I was thirteen years old and getting help for Mrs Denton. The second time I was a young woman just turned thirty-one, still an innocent, I now think, though at the time I'd never have said so. I caught him as he returned from his first round of the day. There I was on his doorstep, all neat and bright and early.

'I know that face,' he cried heartily. 'Don't tell me!'

It had been a while. He tended Robert in his last hours but I had not been there.

'I've been away,' I said.

'Margaret! Margaret Catchpole!'

He always liked me, Dr Stebbing did. You'd have thought I was his long-lost daughter. He put down his bag and gripped my shoulders, beaming all over his red, well-fed face. He'd changed more than I: he'd filled out and got a tight look under his eyes, and his hair was paler and thinner than before, well back from the temples. 'Look at you,' he said. 'Just look at you, you're as tall as me.' Then his eyes became serious. 'I am so sorry about your brothers, my dear,' he said softly. 'They were good young men, each in his own way.' It was nice of him; there's some would have looked down on us for the things that had happened.

'They were silly boys, Dr Stebbing,' I said, 'each in his own way.'

I'd cried all my tears for Jack and Robert, and a great many there were.

'Both these things can be true,' he replied.

'I know, sir.'

A very young maid came to the door.

'Now,' he said, as she took his cloak and bag, 'surgery isn't till ten but as it's our intrepid horsewoman...'

I heard the sound of children on the upper floor. A thick meaty smell pervaded the hall, the good doctor's breakfast sausages, I assumed.

'Oh, it's not about a health matter, Dr Stebbing. It was something I wanted to ask you about. I'm sorry, I think your breakfast must be nearly ready. Shall I come back later?'

'Not at all, not at all.' He rubbed his hands together vigorously 'Becky,' he said to the maid, 'I'll take breakfast in twenty minutes. Will you bring coffee to the drawing room? Very good. Now, Margaret–'

And he showed me graciously into a room off the hall as if I was a lady, a lovely green room with a big white fireplace and a massive china dog, all curls and spots, that lay in the hearth where the cat should be. A tall clock with pictures on its face ticked merrily on the mantelpiece, and there was a picture on the wall of a meet, with ladies and gents on horseback, and hounds with tails aloft.

'Now, Margaret,' he said, 'what can I do for you?'

We sat in pretty chairs with rose-sprigged trim and drank coffee.

'Well, Dr Stebbing,' I said carefully, setting down my bowl, 'I'm looking for work and wondered if you could help me to some. I hope you don't think I'm being forward, but you know such a great many people, don't you, sir – you know – from your rounds and all – and you were always very nice to me and I just wondered if you might have heard of something.'

His eyebrows shot up. 'Well,' he said, 'this is new.' And put his chin in one hand and thought hard. After a moment he gave me a long look. 'What have you been up to, Margaret?' he asked. Oh God, I thought, what's he heard? But the look in his eyes was kindly, and it was nothing. He wanted to know how I had been employed these past few years, that was all, and the truth was easy to tell; that I'd been living at home for a while and then gone up to Brandeston to my Uncle Willie Leader's and ended up staying five years as nursemaid. 'He'd give me a good character, sir, but as he's related I don't know if it would do.' And I numbered all my skills, the ones I'd always known I had, and those I'd learned at my uncle's; such as my mother's great talent for looking behind ears, a necessity when you're caring for a brood of seven.

'My aunt died, you see,' I said, 'and she left him with seven, and one a baby. She died in labour, and then he couldn't cope. But he's married again now, sir, and my new aunt and I don't get along very well.'

He smiled at that. There was a whole story

there that he was guessing at. In how few words I buried away five years. I do believe in looking forward. Some storms had shaken us, and I missed those children something sore, but they'd got a new mother now, one that brought money and a bit of land to their dad; and there's only one direction ever and that's straight ahead.

'It so happens, Margaret,' he said, 'I may just know of a place. It's a very nice lady of my acquaintance, a very clever and respectable lady, and I believe she has need of help. Will you excuse me for a moment?'

I was not as hard as I thought. Suddenly alone, for a moment, all the old pain welled up and I bit my lip hard to stop the tears. Not just for James and Robert, but for the little Leader cousins I'd looked after. They hadn't wanted me to go. I couldn't stay though, not after what that woman said to me. I'd been happy in Brandeston. No one knew about me and Will, no tongues flapped. I always loved my Uncle Leader's house, always had since I was little, that green bowl of earth, the daffodils, church bells across the fields, the sound of voices from the Queen's Head at the end of the village. The house was out in the fields alone, where the woods began, a little way from the river. We got no sailors round there, just the odd one, and Uncle Leader and I, we got along fine. He treated me good and he paid me a fair wage for all I did. I liked the Brandeston people, not a one of them talked, or at least not that I heard; and I was treated well when I went about the place. They saw what good I did. The place was filthy when I got there, a stink-hole full of ragamuffins, Uncle Leader moping about like a wet fish. He looked so tired suddenly after Ellen died, a grizzled old lion with sad eyes. The kids were all lousy. I rubbed and scrubbed and made the place shine, and wiped their noses and combed their heads with paraffin. And when Will had returned from America with a cargo of skins for Bargood, and gone once more to his Uncle Jack's in Aldeburgh, we saw each other all the time, just like before; so that even when those stupid boys got themselves dead, the one with a bullet, the other with drink, these things were like great scars on a pleasant lane that still rambled on.

And now it was gone and I was weary.

But I blinked away the tears and rubbed my nose, and I was smiling when Dr Stebbing returned and handed me an envelope with a name scrawled on it. 'This is a letter of introduction to a lady called Mrs Cobbold at the Cliff,' he said. 'She has a great number of children, and I happen to know she's just lost a nursemaid. If you take this over there and have a little chat with her, she might just have something for you.'

'Where's the Cliff?' I asked.

He was surprised I did not know. It was Ipswich's great brewery.

34

We'd been dossing at the Widow Syers', me and Will. They'd taken the price off his head when John Fuller left to go a-pioneering off for Canada, as well a man as ever, and the only one who could identify Will as the one who shot him. So there was no more evidence. Will had come back brown and hard and wild, with something in him that scared people. It was the scar, livid on one cheek, and the mad look which sometimes came in his eyes. And his mouth. You could have taken his mouth for cruel if you hadn't known him. He'd fallen out with John Luff somewhere along the way, which did not displease me. Luff had been for staying in America, but Will wanted to see me. He would tell me no more of this, only that they'd come to blows one night on the banks of the Congaree River. America was a marvellous country, Will said, bigger than you could possibly imagine.

'Pegs,' he said, 'you and me'll go wandering one fine day.'

When I had to leave so sudden with that woman's curses in my ears ('I'm not having that smuggler in my house! And you! You're nothing but a trollop. A smuggler's trollop, he'd come down to see me placed, saying come what may he wouldn't go back to sea without knowing I was settled.

He was still in bed when I got back.

'Here,' I said, 'I want you to read this letter for me.'

'Success?'

'Said Dr Stebbing liked me, didn't I? I'm to make a good impression now on this grand lady at the Cliff.'

'The Cliff? That's a fancy sort of a place, isn't it?'

'Come on now.' I sat beside him. 'I want to know what he says about me.'

He yawned and scratched both hands through his hair. 'Get me some tea, Pegs,' he said. 'We'll go to the Neptune. We'll need fresh sealing wax.'

It was a small thing to break the seal.

'My dear Mrs Cobbold,' he read. I leaned on his shoulder. I could pick out one or two of the letters now; there was a school in Brandeston these days, and Charley, Uncle Leader's eldest boy, had been teaching me. Will cleared his throat.

I would like to recommend to you one Margaret Catchpole. A very good hard-working woman who is seeking a position. She has been acting as nursemaid to her uncle's seven children for the past five years and has a great deal of experience in all areas of domestic service. I have known her for more than eighteen years and think highly of her character. She has had considerable hardship in her life and has borne all with forbearance and a courageous spirit. I can vouch that she is intelligent and resourceful and therefore have no hesitation in recommending her for service.

'My dear Dr Stebbing!' I exclaimed.

Will laughed. 'How can she refuse you?'

I chivvied him out of bed and made tea, and off we went to the Neptune and got sealing wax from the landlord to make all good. I downed a dram for courage before setting off in high spirits, east along the quays for the Cliff. It wasn't far to where the farmlands began. By the landing place at Orwell Park I met old Robinson Crusoe, a basket of fish on his shoulder.

'Hello, Robin?'

'You hag,' he shouted, 'get back to hell. I will not! I will not!'

It was not me he addressed. He was watching a space high in the air before him.

'What a lonely life,' I had once said to Will. 'Poor Robinson Crusoe!'

'Not so,' he'd replied. 'He has plenty of company as he'll always tell you.'

Will had talked to him about his demons. He said Robin knew all their names and natures and they were all different and all related and he could recite you their genealogies and histories and never ever get anything wrong. He said it was as complicated as the Bible or the Greek and Roman myths.

'Begone!' cried Robin in a wild throaty voice; then a most peculiar twitching came over his face, and he began batting furiously at himself. They were poking his eyes, pulling his nose and ears, pinching his arms and legs. This went on for some minutes whilst the mad old man danced about, his bones and amulets clinking, as if assailed by a swarm of wasps. At length it seemed the spirits left him, and he noticed me standing there.

'Last night,' he said, 'they pelted me with dung.'

'Oh, that's shocking!'

'They're at it night and day, after me to do their wickedness.'

'But you're a good man, aren't you, Robin?'

'They won't take no!'

'You're a good man so they can't hurt you.'

'Margaret Catchpole,' he said, 'where have you been?'

'Brandeston, Robin.'

'I've been to Brandeston,' he said. 'It was there they ran old John Lowes near to death and hanged him for a witch. The acorn foaled a mare.'

Above us the brewery resounded with a hollow sound, as if a giant was rolling a barrel across rough boards. Men's voices called to one another back and forth.

'Do you know the house?' I asked him. 'The Cobbold house?'

He peered fiercely over the edge of the landing place, where baby eels played like young otters about the black stones. 'What do you want with the Cobbolds?' he asked.

'Employment,' I replied.

He nodded to the steps ascending from the water, then trailed me up them from the landing place. There stood the high walls of the brewery, and a warm malty smell was on the air; beyond, a big lawn with lime trees, and a grand dwelling house with windows that watched the river, and the land high behind, hilly, with a path rising to a farm, and cattle grazing. I had never been inside so fine a house before but I thought of what the doctor said about my courage and resilience and stepped out with bold purpose along the path that bordered the lane and led to the side of the house; not so bold as old Robin though, who strode without a qualm straight across the lawn to the front door, which stood open to the bright late spring noon. Still, I knew my place. I did not have the immunity of the mad. I went to the kitchen door. A girl came out of the heat and steam and asked what I wanted then called out to a stout matron who sat shelling beans at a large table: 'Mrs Potts, here's a woman says she's got a letter for the missis.'

The matron peered over her spectacles, fixing me with a steady eye, sighed deeply and got up as if weary. 'Is it about the situation?' she asked, coming to the door. A bunch of keys as big as a man's fist hung by her apron.

'It is indeed.'

'Well then,' she said, not returning the smile I lavished upon her, 'Ursula, go and see if Madam's seeing anyone.' She motioned me in with her head. The girl clattered up a flight of stone steps, showing her heels. It was a grand big kitchen. Mrs Potts bade me sit down and wait in a chair that stood next the wall by the side of the fireplace, where a massive black cauldron squatted in boiling flames and steam. It was devilish hot in there. Four long spits gleamed above the fire, and several saucepans bubbled away on the hob. Something fine and gamey and rich was on the air. A grinning lad and an old man sat smoking on the far side of the wide table. The old man nodded and tipped his hat. A fat round-eyed footman in a blue livery sat supping tea from a saucer.

'Morning, miss,' he said, 'or should I say afternoon? What time is it?'

'Time you got off your arse and went back to work,' answered a handsome woman of fortyish I took to be the cook, for she was active about the saucepans. She tipped me a wink and a quick smile.

It would do me fine, I thought. House like this, close to the town and the river, a congenial place by the look of it. Turn on the charm, Margaret. And when the girl came back and said I was to come up and wait in the hall, Madam would see me shortly, I knew I was in. Just let Madam talk to me and she'd see how useful I could be, and if she paid me a decent wage I would be too; and I'd have my own money again and save myself a little nest egg. The hall was wide and gracious, with a grandfather clock and a tall mirror with a gilt frame that shone against a wall of duck-egg blue. There was a pretty walnut table, polished to a high shine, where a bronze cupid stood with bow poised, his giggling baby face quite startlingly real and animated, with dimpled cheeks and merry slits for eyes. Five or six doors opened off the hall. The front door stood open, and there at the top of the steps was Robin showing off his catch to a fine boy of sixteen or so with brown hair that fell straight and limp across his brows.

'Any crabs, Robin?' the boy was saying.

Someone somewhere played scales falteringly on a piano. I heard men's voices raised in conversation in one room, and then a door opened and Mrs Cobbold herself came sweeping out on a burst of laughter. She was laughing a little too as she came towards me. I dropped a quick curtsey. She was younger than me, with a broad friendly face and dark hair.

'Is it about the situation?' she asked pleasantly.

'Yes, madam. I have a letter from Dr Stebbing.'

She took it and read it through. I watched her face. She smiled as she read, her eyes going back and forth rapidly. 'You've had care of seven children,' she exclaimed, looking very pleased.

'Yes, madam?'

'How old were they?'

I numbered them on my fingers, my Leader cousins.

'Excellent,' she said. 'Do you know how many children *I* have, Margaret?'

Four or five, I thought. 'I'm sure I don't know, madam,' I said, and smiled, looking her full in the eyes.

'Fourteen,' she said, 'and another on the way,' and laughed gaily, patting her stomach.

'You've never had fourteen children, madam,' I said. 'You're not that old.'

'Quite so,' she said. 'I am the *step*mother of fourteen children, I should say. What odds?' She shrugged. 'I have fourteen children to all intents. And that means, of course, that the position of nursemaid is a very important one in this family. Do you think you would like to work here, Margaret?'

'Very much, madam.'

She regarded me closely, then read through the letter one more time, whispering to herself.

'Mother,' the young boy called through the

open door, 'Robin's got some crayfish.'
'In a while,' she said, then smiled at me very warmly. 'That young man out there would not fall under your care, although he is still a big baby in many ways.' And then she numbered on her fingers, as I had done, the charges that would fall to me. There were a great many; I lost count. The youngest was nearly two, a babe. The eldest was fourteen. She asked about my family and my previous situations, and she nodded and hm-hm-ed in her throat a great deal, then straightened her back and folded away the letter in a decisive way. 'Can you start tomorrow?' she asked.
'Certainly, madam.'
'Excellent!'
So I was taken on as under-nursemaid in the daytime and under-cook in the evening for six pounds a year and my keep. She said it would go up if I stayed with her and worked well; and she let me leave through the front door, coming out with me to talk to Robinson Crusoe and look over his wares. It seemed he was a great favourite with her, for she bestowed upon him the most dazzling of smiles. 'There now,' she said, 'my favourite fisherman. William,' to the youth, 'this is Margaret who joins us tomorrow.'
William was a gawky bony boy with a big Adam's apple. 'Can she cook?' he asked his mother.
'I'm sure she can.'
'*Can* you?' he asked me cockily. 'Can you make a cherry trifle?'
'You wait and see.' I smiled, bobbed a curtsey and took my leave. As I passed by the stable yard, a big dog ran to the end of its chain and barked

at me.

'Pompey!' the boy yelled.

'Watch yourself,' I told the dog. A big jowly hound it was, with tragic eyes. No threat. I could tell by the ready wagging of his tail when he heard my voice. 'Pompey, lie down,' I told him.

His kennel was near the entrance to the stable yard. I could see two tall coach horses, one a bay, the other a strawberry roan, a picture of patience side by side on the cobbles. Each wore a grey blanket that steamed. The sight filled me with happiness. This was a good billet, no doubt at all. I practically skipped back to the Neptune, and there we made merry on my last night, but not too merry as I had to be up and about very bright the next day. We danced in the courtyard where they hanged a poor young thing called Rasmus Young a hundred years ago, a boy smuggler and not so clever, they say, because he drank too much like my brother Robert and that's what did for him in the end. His ghost walks the long room. You'd not get me there after dark alone.

35

After that old bitch in Brandeston, Mrs Cobbold was a jewel. She saw something in me, took a shine to me, you might say. I felt sorry for her too. She was nearly as new as me in a funny sort of way. She'd been at the Cliff – what? – eighteen months? Two years at most. And she wasn't much more than a girl. I don't know why I felt sorry for her, I shouldn't have done. After all, she had a head on her, she knew what she was doing; she made two old men very happy and she got rich doing it. Down there in the kitchen, they talked about her, nicely for the most, because she was a good lady to work for, a very kind lady. Her husband, the brewer, was a grey and solemn gentleman, pleasant enough, but old enough to be her father. Yet even he was nowhere near as old as the one she'd buried. They said he was sixty when she married him and she just twenty-three. They said she was an actress in those days. Imagine that. Sickly he was too, because he left her a widow after six months. Then straight away she married my master. I suppose he'd have been about forty-five then; well, I can see that a man of forty-five is a different proposition from one of sixty. At least if he's kept himself trim and able, as the master had. But a man with fourteen children!

The house teemed. There were twenty-two of us under that roof, not counting the coachman who slept over the stables. A boy came in and ran errands in the daytime, and two girls came in from town to help. I had my own room. I never did work in a better place and I never will.

I wondered about my mistress. To hear them talk you'd think she'd come up from nowhere but she talked like a lady and she had that kind of grace a lady has. Still, there was something about her, something none of my other mistresses had had – and that was how she'd touch your arm as if you were her friend, and you only a servant. And how she'd sing and run up and downstairs, and sometimes kick her heels on the porch, and sometimes laugh immoderately. And how, for all that, she was imperious and ran that house with a rod of iron.

I watched her painting on the big lawn, sitting there with two men. I was walking in the shrubbery with the little ones assigned to my care. Looking at her, I could see she was one for the men. I don't mean that in a rude way, I'm sure she was as good as gold. But she did like to have men around her, and they liked her in return. A scruffy old artist in a long green coat was making a most lovely picture of the view over the river. Between them was a board with the paints and brushes and water, and a small table standing off to one side with the remains of tea. A thin dark man with a long nose sat there, smoking and talking rapidly in a foreign language. She laughed as she dabbed at her easel, replying in the same strange tongue. The way she held her big flashing teeth when she smiled was showy and slightly tense.

I had three-year-old Georgie by the hand. Four-year-old Freddy, defencelessly insolent, plodded alongside. Their big sister, a sweet dreamy girl of eight by the name of Sophia, drifted before us on the path. I'd been getting them to tell me the names of the flowers, the honeysuckle along the fence, the toadflax on the wall, but I stopped, enchanted, to listen to the foreign talk lilting along like a stream. I could have listened all day. But the artist, a rough sort, told them to speak the King's English, for God's sake, what did they take him for, an educated man? And they all laughed.

‘What language is that?’ I asked Sophia. ‘Do you know?’

‘French, of course,’ she replied languidly.

The baby was down for his sleep. The head nursemaid had the rest of the children, those that weren’t at their lessons or old enough to be out and about on their own. So far my duties had been pleasant. As we ambled along, I listened to the talk on the lawn, all in English now, and all of the pardon of Mary Bryant, who’d run away from the new colony and sailed halfway round the world in an open boat with her babies and her husband. They’d all died apart from her: and they’d put her in Newgate. Mrs Cobbold thought it was marvellous that she was pardoned. The dark man agreed, but the artist pursed his lips and said, ‘I suppose so. But then if you make an exception for one...’

From the brewhouse came the distant voices of men. Pompey lay with his nose upon his paws, looking up at me with soft brown eyes. Three big lads, nearly men, larked about in the stable yard. I wondered if Mrs Cobbold ever looked at them and reflected how they were so much more of an age for her than their father, and how funny it was that they should have to call her Mother when she was only six years or so older than them.

Mrs Cobbold laughed and tapped the old man’s arm with her wet brush.

‘My dear Elizabeth,’ he said, ‘refrain from drenching me.’

‘Oh dear,’ she sighed, throwing her brush back into the water with a delicate frown, ‘I’ll never get this sky right.’

That night she asked for chocolate, and I took some to her in the sitting room. She was lying on the chaise longue reading a book.

'Have you had a good day, Margaret?' she asked, looking up and smiling, laying by her book.

'Very good, ma'am,' I replied.

'Excellent.'

'Will there be anything else, madam?'

She sipped the chocolate. 'Oh, that's wonderful,' she said, closing her eyes with both hands round the cup. 'I think I shall drink lots of chocolate while I'm pregnant.'

36

Now surely, I thought, looking out of the window that night in my own room, the bad times are over. I felt another surge of anger at my brothers. The fools. What did he expect, drinking himself stupid day after day, silly Robert. Raving about the night inside his head, creatures crawling out from the dirt under his fingernails. Leaving all of us bereaved, and dear Dinah Parker – who would have thought it? – big with child. Bigger I should say. How could he do that to us? Why should my poor dad have more grief in his old age? My eyes swam with tears and the river swam before them in the moonlight. A small boat tacked against the current. The coastguard were abroad. This time tomorrow Will would be in Holland. Soon there would be money. Gifts. I could be happy here. I thought of that girl escaping the colony. My brother James might have ended up there. Would that have been better? To go out there alone to that terrible wild place of naked cannibals and wild animals and snakes that leap like dogs. Or to be shot instead, as he was, with a brace of Admiral Vernon's pheasants in his bag. Some fellows laid an information against him. I let all my tears go that night looking at the river and thinking of my lost brothers. There are no letters from the dead, but Charles should have written. Unless he was dead too.

I shook myself briskly – this would not do – and went to bed.

Next morning the master turned up while I was taking the children to their lessons. They had a governess, a pale reedy woman with fingers like willows, and a small light room that smelled of chalk and wood and faint lavender, at the end of the long passage upstairs. Upon the wall there was a map of the world, and on a small round table, a globe, the first I'd ever seen. This fascinated me. While the older girls took their places and Miss Flowers wrote diligently on the board, I was able to study it, turning it slowly and letting my eyes drift here and there over its amazing surface. It was old and brown. All the world was brown. Africa. China. Great oceans.

'Look, Henry,' I whispered to the heavy baby on my arm. Georgie and Freddy were in the passage.

Here and there in the oceans a whale blew. Had Charles seen whales? And there was India, where it was very hot. I looked up, and the master was there in a high black collar. His eyes were pale and his hair grey, and he looked vaguely familiar. He smiled absently.

'Apologies for disturbing you, Miss Flowers,' he mumbled. 'My wife thinks she left a book in here.'

'Is it this one, Papa?' asked Harriet, the eldest girl.

'Ah! Good girl!'

She was very clever, Elizabeth Cobbold. The number of books there were in that house; I'd never seen so many all in one place, and she'd always got her nose in one or another. This one looked heavy and dull. Mr Cobbold glanced at me shyly, nodding and reaching out to touch for a moment the podgy hand of young Henry Gallant, the baby, who beamed with delight. As he left and I gathered my younger charges in preparation for a walk, I wondered if my new young mistress ever imagined herself in the arms of a nice young man like Master John or Master Thomas, those lovely big lads I'd seen in the stable yard, or even Master William, he of the big Adam's apple and soft brown hair, though he was only sixteen. It's not as if they were blood to her, is it? I'd have been tempted, I know.

A good time followed. They looked after me, the Cobbolds, she and he. They looked after a lot of people, like Robinson Crusoe and daft Davy Waring in town, who'd had his nostrils slit when he was a boy and breathed like a blocked bellows. Well, any poor fellow can get his nostrils slit. They never did like my poor sweet Will though. Why? What blindness? They were nice people even so, and that's the simple fact of it. It became clear to me as time passed, and as those children grew dearer and dearer to me with each day they came to me with their tears and grazes and bruises, their funny talk and funny thoughts – that I loved them like I loved my Leader cousins, whose noses and bums I'd wiped, whose fears I'd soothed. They were all the same to me. I have no truck with the differences that are set between us, nor will I ever. My babies were always my babies, no matter how high or low they might be. And they remember me now, I am sure, as I remember them. There was a baby in Mrs Cobbold's belly, under her pretty gown. She'd put her hand on it as she lay drowsing and reading her book of a long afternoon. 'Oh, Margaret,' she'd say, 'I could just fancy a little chocolate.' It was her first and she was nervous. 'Oh, Margaret, I hope we're settled before this one comes.' The whole household was moving from the Cliff to a house in town. There was a place not ready yet, and she wanted to be there before the baby was born. There were so many people she could talk to, so many friends, some of them very high indeed, and yet she became my friend. That's what I thought then, and now I know it. That's a strange thing. She liked to talk with me, here and there as we met about the place. She, of course, knew infinitely more than I ever could; but still there was a lot I knew she'd not an inkling of. And sometimes she'd be overwhelmed, though she was good at not letting on. When the house was full, and she'd missed her afternoon nap; when the two older married daughters were on a visit with their offspring and there was no peace anywhere, then, if I was standing with her with Henry in my arms, she'd hold my arm lightly and take a deep breath and smile and say, 'God help me, Margaret, is there no end to it?'

'Oh yes, madam,' I could have said, 'of course there's an end to it. My brothers and my sister and my mother, all are gone. There's an end to it, madam, so never say die. Onward!' But I never did say such a thing, because it would have sounded silly.

She started to like me with her when she was down in all the hurly-burly. I was there to look after the little people, but sometimes I felt it was to look out for her too, in a funny sort of way. She had no need of protection. But I did feel sometimes that when she laughed too loud, or drank a bit too much (she never disgraced herself, never), a tightness of the nerves quivered below the spotless perfection of her appearance. She loved to entertain. I never saw such nights before or since, and never will, as those we had at the Cliff. After she had squeezed my arm and perked up her smile, forth she would go, sweeping like a glorious wave down the staircase, brilliantly smiling, to greet her public. We were on show, all of us. The master hung around with his hands behind his back, loitering here and there with his faint smile, always upon the fringes while she held court. Some very grand people came. Sary Turner said the Cobbolds were the biggest family hereabouts, and the brewery had been here as long as anyone could remember. The master's grandad began it. Master had a finger in many pies, and in every pie there were men of worth, those who thronged the rooms with their shining wives whenever there was a party, bankers and shipowners, men who sold corn, men who sold coal – and those the mistress loved, the artists and writers and poets, real ones who came up from London wearing fame in their faces.

In the early part of a fine evening I'd be allowed to see all that went on, for she liked to show off the children. I'd turn them out very prettily and take them strolling on the lawn amongst the gentry to be kissed and questioned and admired.

One such evening Master William attached himself to me. 'What do you think, Margaret?' he said. 'I'm to go out with Robinson Crusoe to-morrow. She finally persuaded the old man.'

'About time too,' I replied. 'You'll come to no harm with Robin.'

'I'll bring you some mackerel to smoke,' he said, stepping ahead, grabbing Georgie by the arms, lifting him off his feet and swinging him round and round. Georgie shrieked.

'Can I have a go?' yelled Freddy.

The other little ones came running, all wanting a turn. Henry lurched in my arms, excited. I set him carefully on his feet, hanging on to his hand. 'Don't forget baby!' I cried. 'Mustn't leave baby out.' Henry was just beginning to totter but he fell over all the time. The big girls started chasing him. All was tumble and fun for a while, then Master William got tired and said, no more, his arms were coming out. That day I'd cooked six ducks he'd shot on the decoy-ponds. A big child-man he was, very sweet, a great favourite in the kitchen, where he'd sit for ages picking at the food and getting slapped by Mrs Potts, yarning with John Pride, the fat footman.

'I'd love to be out there now,' said Master William, looking over the river. 'I'd like to sail down to Woolverstone and go night fishing.'

He'd had a couple of drinks, I think. His eyes were shining.

'Say I slip off now...' he began.

'No such thing,' I said. 'Your mother wants you for the entertainments, as you very well know.'

He rolled his eyes and turned down his mouth. 'Spare me, God,' he said.

Soon it would start getting dark. I had to round up the younger ones for bed. If I could settle them all in time, maybe I could get down and watch the entertainments for a little while. I'd never seen such stuff. Everyone was accomplished. A small orchestra was setting up in the big room for the dancing later on, but first Master John would play the piano beautifully, while Master Thomas and Miss Harriet would sing a duet; then Master William would play his flute. Madam herself would read out some of her poetry from a small leather-bound book, a real book with proper printing. She was so clever. She'd even written a novel. Imagine. She showed it to me once in the library. Some of the poet fellows would read too, and a lady called Mrs Sleorgin would recite something classical in a deep, thrilling voice.

But it was not to be. Freddy had eaten too much and whined for an hour, stuffed full like a lapdog by the well-meaning guests. Sophia spilled her drink all over the sheets and the whole bed had to be remade. By the time I got down, the orchestra had struck up and the floor was a bright whirling show of waltzing couples. The old painter was there, and the dark man with the long nose, a frequent visitor, someone from the Ipswich newspaper, I think he was.

Master William saw me standing at the door and came over. 'I say, Margaret,' he said, 'I played like the great god Pan himself.'

'Oh, I'm sure it was lovely.'

He blew out his cheeks. 'Dear Mother has outshone herself tonight,' he said in a not altogether nice voice. 'Genius rubs shoulder with genius wherever you look. Do you know who that is?'

'Who?'

He indicated a man with a neat wig and an abundance of lace about the cuffs. 'That's Mr Wilberforce,' he said, and whispered conspiratorially: 'Bigwig! And that–' nodding towards a pleasant-faced balding man '–is the great George Crabbe.'

The poet. I'd heard of him.

A lady came and bore Master William away. Heigh-ho, I thought, back to the kitchen, and pulled away from the lovely music. At the foot of the stairs two men sat and smoked.

'Crabbe read well, I thought,' said one.

'Indeed,' said the other. 'So did our hostess.'

Then they looked at each other and sniggered in a nasty way.

I didn't understand, but I knew that they were being nasty. In time I would learn that there were those who came and drank her wine and ate their fill, counting themselves fortunate to be her guests, while laughing behind their hands. Her poetry was poor, they said. Nay, worse than poor. And the paintings. Mediocre at best.

What did they know? Had they books with their names in print on the spines? Had they her spirit? She had a gift for life they never had.

37

Six months of my new life passed, and no word from Will. I cursed him. Berated him in my head.

Sometimes as I lay in bed at night I worried about the press-gang. Surely not, I thought. Surely not just now when everything is set so fair. Then I would take myself in hand and say: come now, let it go. You didn't choose a safe man, the kind to hang upon your every minute and keep you well informed. You chose a rake and a charmer, a rambleaway, heigh-ho, heigh-ho. What did you expect? You chose, and you'd choose him again. Will can take care of himself. Then I'd shake with anger and a kind of grief. And sometimes I'd think: so what if he *is* pressed? Who knows if it might not be the making of the boy. A pathway from the smuggling if it were wanted. *Was* it wanted? I don't know if it's what *I* wanted, let alone him. He'd get his pardon if he served. But I didn't want him harmed. He'd be a man on the right side of the law again, a proper sailor walking on the deck, a King's man. It was possible. They weren't picky, they wanted men, millions of men for the war, and Will was a bloody good sailor, say what you will. People talked about how good he was.

But in the end it came down to pure worry.

I found myself one evening, when all my duties were discharged, asking leave of Mrs Cobbold to run into town quickly and have words with a relative. I'd say it was the Widow Syers, if she asked. She said yes readily, but it was no relative I ran down to, it was the Neptune. I met Rube between the front and back hamlets of St Clements. He'd just returned from a Danish run. I asked if he'd heard anything of Will and his crew, but he hadn't. He'd seen John Luff though. He was at the Neptune. We walked down there together. I hadn't been to the Neptune for ages. It was heaving. The light from its mullioned windows spilled over the darkness, figures passed to and fro, men and women, drunk and happy. From the quay came the strident sounds of a concertina and an accordion playing together. Rube had to duck his head to get into the big room, and there I saw John Luff through the crowd, sitting by the great fireplace with a drunken look about him.

I walked straight up to him.

'John,' I said, 'I thought you were in America.'

He'd not changed, except that his whiskers were longer and more matted. His wig was dirty, and his eyes were bright and insolent. 'You see I'm not,' he said.

'How long have you been back, John?'

There were brand marks all up the side of the fireplace, where they tried the irons for the casks; he kept running the tip of his knife up and down them as we talked, like a child running a stick along railings.

'Have you seen anything of Will?'

He laughed as if I'd asked something audacious, looking away with studied indifference. Then his eyes dragged back to me. 'No, I have not,' he said. 'Run off and left you, has he?'

I held his eyes. 'Got a wolf in the breast, John? Biting you is he?'

He drank deep, never blinking or taking his eyes off me. Rube brought me a drink. We kept up this eye battle, Luff and I, and I don't suppose either of us knew what it was truly about. He could have snapped my neck easily if he'd wanted to, some dark night, some alley. He'd laid many a one down for far less than the kind of sauce I gave him. No; I think after all he liked me in his own way, but he was not a man who had any other way than a rough way, and never a way at all with women. There *was* one somewhere, I believe, a small quiet little mouse of a thing that bore his kids and lived all lonely somewhere down south. He can't have seen much of her. As for me – I did not dislike John Luff. A strange thing to say about a man like that, and yet I say it, and I don't really understand why. He was a bad man, a deep and a miserable man, but he'd carried Will on his shoulders from the shingle and saved his life. And I liked something about him, knowing I shouldn't. Maybe there was pride in it, the way you'd feel if you could handle a wild dog.

'And what's the matter between you two anyway?' I asked.

He just kept quiet. That's how he was. No

answer to anything, save for the hardness of his eyes and mouth. I never did find out what it was they argued about. One wanted to stay, one wanted to go. What of that? No call for all this sulking.

'So did you get enough of America?' I asked him.

Again that stare, and a short snigger. We sat in silence for a while, till I grew bored and went to talk with Rube and enquire a little here and there if there was any news. Not a thing. I was back at the Cliff by ten. It was a bright starry night and I could smell the river. Old Pompey ran out of his kennel and woofed low, then saw it was only me and did a clumsy dance of welcome. Mrs Cobbold was playing whist with some ladies in the drawing room. The master was just coming out of the library with two or three books under his arm, and it came to me suddenly where I'd seen him before. It was in the Neptune. Ages ago. When I first went there with Will all those years gone, he was with Bargood. Or maybe it was not him, it was a long time ago, and one old grey gentleman looks much like the next. It could have been him though. Captain Bargood was as honest a man as the next as far as the world was concerned. He had many respectable friends.

'Oh, Margaret,' said Mr Cobbold. 'Will you tell Mrs Potts I'll be away most of the day tomorrow. I'll be at the new house if anyone wants me.'

'Yes, sir.'

He smiled and turned away, his shanks thin in their white stockings, then turned back. 'Have you been out, Margaret?'

'Yes, sir. I asked Mrs Cobbold, sir.'

'Oh good,' he said absently. 'All well, Margaret?'

'Oh yes, sir.'

I knocked on Mrs Potts' door and told her the master would be up in town tomorrow at the new house on St Margaret's Green. They were getting ready to move in whenever the builders had finished their work. I checked on the children before I went to bed. Henry was snuffly. He must have been not much more than a newborn when the mistress married the master. I wondered what the master's first wife had died of. Was it the birth? Then I went to bed and lay tossing and turning, thinking again about the press-gang. Salvation of many a smuggler. Would they take him? What then? A free man: Will. Free to come and go. Me and Will, free good citizens as we had never been before – free as the wind, all roads open to us – well, life was a peculiar fickle thing.

38

There was a pretty walk at the back of the Cliff to Sawyer's Farm. I used to take the little ones, sometime six, sometimes seven or eight, me carrying the baby. You can go alongside the river to the Grove or Hog Island, or through the farmyard and up the sandy hill. At the top there's a lovely view over Ipswich. That's where we had our picnics. I made them dandelion chains, I gathered lords-and-ladies into bundles for the hearth, made strings of the ladies-hair. The children thought I was a wonder. Beyond Sawyer's Farm was Greenwich Farm, a quarter of a mile south. That was another favourite walk. Up there on the high ground, the air was always fresh and soft. You could see the river at its widest, with the boats coming upstream. Coming back from here one day, we passed close by a place where some of the brewhouse men were digging into the foundations of an old shed. The men were out on the hillside taking a rest, passing a flask between them. Henry toddled. The girls dawdled along behind us. Georgie and Freddy ran on ahead and vanished inside the doorless building.

'Come out of there!' I yelled.

Their voices came hollow, laughing from inside.

'Keep an eye on Henry,' I told the girls and went after them. Half the foundations on one side had been deepened. The boys were down in the pit, jumping about wildly.

'Up now!' I clapped my hands. 'Out!'

They came giggling then ran round the back. You'll not run me ragged, you little devils, I thought, aware of the brewhouse men watching all this from the hillside. I followed with dignity. There they were crouching in the dust by the wall, poking away with a stick.

'There's a hole, Margaret,' Freddy said.

'It's a rat!' Georgie got down on hands and knees.

'Listen!'

'Come on *now*,' I said.

There *was* a noise.

‘What is it?’ I said.

‘A big rat,’ Freddy said.

‘A *very* big rat.’ Georgie flashed me a toothy grin.

Big as a dog, I thought. In the same second I realised what that settling, grating sound was. It was the sound of stone against stone, shifting and rumbling, like thunder clearing its throat in the distance. I dashed forward, grabbed each by a skinny arm and flung them as far away as I could. Then I ran. The wall came down like Jericho. It sounded like an army falling off a cliff, and it made a cloud that thick-coated us and stopped up our throats. A rock hit my foot. Down we went in a mass, me and the boys, holding on to each other. Then the men were there.

The mistress, holding up her skirts, was already tearing up the hill with her hair falling down and streaming out behind, summoned by the wailing of Georgie.

‘My God! My God!’ she cried, pulling the boys into her arms, clutching them to her.

‘They’re not hurt, ma’am,’ one of the men said, ‘just shocked.’

She looked up at us all. ‘How could this happen?’ she asked.

The foreman stepped forward. ‘Ma’am, it’s not safe to have children playing round building work. If it weren’t for this here young woman they’d be under that there,’ and he jerked a thumb at the dust settling slowly over a great mound of rubble.

She looked at me. ‘Margaret,’ she said sternly, ‘what were they doing playing here?’

'They ran on ahead, madam.' My throat seized up with tears.

'Them was naughty lads, ma'am,' the foreman said stoutly. 'She called 'em back, she did, we was up there and we saw it all. She told 'em, she did, and they ran away, and if she hadn't of grabbed 'em and thrown 'em clear they'd be under that there, they would, that there. Them was poking with a stick, ma'am. She got 'em away.'

'She did, ma'am, aye,' said another, and a general murmur of assent arose from the good lads.

A fine procession we made back to the house, a brawny brewhouse man carrying me in his arms to save my foot, and another two following with Georgie and Freddy. Mrs Cobbold walked alongside carrying Henry, and the girls brought up the rear. There was no need at all to send for Dr Stebbing but someone had already gone for him, and the master was sent for too. They made such a fuss. First thing I did was clean myself up and put on a clean frock and apron, but then Madam made me lie on the chaise longue with a pouffe for my foot, and she had Ursula bring me sweet tea. Then she sat down by my side and told me her husband had closely questioned the brewhouse men and was quite satisfied I had behaved in a most sterling manner. And if anything had happened to the boys she didn't know what they would have done. In came the culprits, clean and glowing, and she told them they must kiss me and say they were very sorry for being such naughty boys, and thank me for saving them from a very nasty accident. 'Why, you might have died,' she said sternly. And when Dr Stebbing arrived and gave me leave to stay off the foot for a few days, and Harriet brought me a cake, I thought life could be far worse than this. The master came and thanked me very properly. Dr Stebbing chuckled and recounted my exploits on the day of Mrs Denton's fit, of which they knew nothing.

It seemed I was worth my weight in gold again. How it must be, I thought, to live like this all the time, and be waited on. They let me stay on the chaise longue in the drawing room till it was time for bed, and all the children came in and sat with me and we ate toast and jam.

Well, after that I could do no wrong. You might almost say I was like one of the family. No, that's silly, I never was like one of the family. It's not as if I ever sat of an evening with them except on that one occasion; or as if we ever partook of food together or anything like that, except if we went for a picnic to Hog Island. But I could speak very free. Often Mrs Cobbold would send for me just to talk. She seemed to value my opinion, especially when it came to the children. Of course I saw more of them than she did. She'd have me sit with her sometimes, in quiet times, while she got on with her sewing, and she liked to get me talking about my life and how I'd grown up with the horses. I left out a lot, but she became acquainted with my family, both the living and the dead. I was quite honest about my brothers and the manner of their deaths. 'Poor Margaret,' she said, 'you've been through a great deal.' I remember her sitting to get the best light from the window, making a dress for Sophia, a lovely soft green muslin sprigged with tiny pink roses. I could not take my eyes off the lovely thing. I'd seen nothing like it; it seemed to shine. She was very nimble with a needle. 'That's beautiful, that is,' I said, and she asked me would I like to have the offcut. I kept it through the years but never made anything of it. I just liked to bring it out from time to time and run my fingers over its softness. She liked me very much and I could make her laugh. I never had trouble believing there could be friendship between the two of us, so far apart in station; I never cared about that. And then one day she met my father and Ned, and I realised how different they were with her, how put out by her grandeur. They appeared at the kitchen door all dressed in their best, very ill at ease. They'd seen nothing of places like this.

'It's your dad, Margaret,' Mrs Potts said. 'He wants a word.'

'Dad!' I said and kissed him. Then I kissed my brother Ned, so strange to me now, grown quite away from me. His sweet rat face had grown thoughtful and stern of nature. He smiled awkwardly, briefly. I was almost tearful to see them so unexpectedly. Lately I hadn't been getting home much.

They'd brought me a letter from Charles that nobody could read. Dad said he thought maybe I'd have picked up enough by now to have a go at it, but I hadn't. Will had always been going to teach me to read but we'd never got round to it. The thought of him stabbed my heart. I wished it had been a letter from him and not from

Charles, and then I felt guilty.

I left them sitting in the kitchen drinking tea, Ursula taking care of them, while I took the letter to Mrs Cobbold. I asked her if she'd be so kind as to read it for my father and brother and me. Her cheeks turned pink. 'Oh, Margaret, why of *course!*' she sighed, as if I had deeply gratified her. And she greeted my father and brother so kindly, quite as if they had been her equal. 'Why, Mr Catchpole,' she said, 'I am so pleased to meet you. I do hope you realise what a great credit to you your daughter is! Why, Margaret has become a positive boon to me since she came here. I don't know what we'd do without her, I really don't.'

My father smiled, eyes downcast. 'She was always a good girl, ma'am,' he whispered.

'And you are Ned!'

'Aye, ma'am.'

'I'm very pleased to meet you, Ned!'

'Thank you, ma'am.'

They were so shy. All smiles, never knowing where to look. Why, look what our Margaret has become! See how well she's thought of. And what a grand lady! Oh she was, my mistress, that she was indeed, a very grand lady. But she said to me once: why, we're all cut of the same cloth when all's said and done. Didn't God make us all, all from the same clay? Of course he did!

She received us in the library. There was a good fire crackling in the grate. The children had been in with Molly Briggs, the older ones reading and the younger ones doing jigsaws; some of their mess had been shoved into corners. Old Pompey had been brought in by Mr Cobbold and given a big bone, and was lying gnawing it in a loud and slobbery way on the rug.

'I'm so sorry for the mess,' she said, looking around. 'Please, do sit down.'

My father and Ned had never sat in such good chairs. Wing-chairs, green-grey. Passing through the house sometimes when no one else was around, going from here to there, many a time I flopped down in the chairs of this house, on the sofas and even on the beds. Oh, soft! We didn't have soft like that. The soft of money, what it could buy. Soft like the remnants of the green sprigged muslin.

'My dear Mother and Father,' Mrs Cobbold read.

It is with great pleasure I take up my pen to acquaint you that I am very well and in Hindustan with my regiment. I am a good soldier and am now a captain and may become a sergeant-major. The East is very different. I am learning to speak some of their language. I like it very much here. I have sent you a picture, I make many pictures. I have tried to draw the Orwell looking over towards Woolverstone from my memory but it is hard to catch. This one is of looking over the sea from where we are stationed. I hope you are all as well as I am. How is my Uncle Leader? And Uncle Catchpole. I think about you all. Please say hello to all my dear brothers and sisters from me, their dear brother Charles, who remembers them very constantly. I have had lots and lots of adventures. The sun here is very hot, and there are lots of big insects and flowers and plants, some of them very beautiful.

I have ridden an elephant. I will be home I hope in a year or two. Your very loving son,
Charles.

We listened, rapt.

'Shall I read it again?' she said.

'Oh please, ma'am.'

So she did, and one more time again.

'Well, fancy that,' my father said. 'An elephant.'

'Your brother writes very well,' Mrs Cobbold remarked to me that night as she fastened her cloak in the hall. She and the master were attending the theatre in Ipswich and I'd brought Henry down to say goodbye. The coachman was bringing the carriage round to the front. The door stood open and there was a sharp nip in the air.

'He's very clever,' I said. 'He's always wanted to travel.'

She smiled a little thoughtfully. 'I did too,' she said. 'But I'd not like to go so far as your brother. I'd like to see Italy.'

'Well, maybe you will, madam.'

'Who knows?'

'As for me,' I said, 'I'll take it as it happens. I'd like to see Charles on an elephant though.'

She sniffed the air. 'We're in for rough weather, they say.'

The coach arrived at the door and the master came down. Young William was riding up front with our coachman, old deaf George Teager. William jumped down and came running up the steps. 'It's going to freeze!' he said, as if it was good news. 'Robin said.'

'Margaret,' Mr Cobbold said, 'tell Mrs Potts we'd like a fire in the morning room first thing, would you?'

'I will, sir.'

I was looking forward to a warm cosy night downstairs playing whist with Ursula and John Pride. Like as not William would join us. He did, and a great night we had of it. We built up the fire and got out the good brandy and the gingerbread, and laughed, I can't tell at what, just that we all laughed a great deal those nights down in the big warm kitchen. When the rain came and tapped on the dark windows, that made it even better. If I were to stand at the door now, I thought, I'd see the dark river all tossed and torn in the wind. We will have snow for Christmas, Master William said, and it must be true because he'd heard it from Robinson Crusoe and everybody believed Robinson Crusoe because he looked so wild and strange and lived so much alone on the river.

39

The morning after my father and Ned brought Charles's letter Mrs Cobbold announced a history test. She liked to do this sometimes, to gather the children in the schoolroom and play the governess for a bit. You could tell she'd been an actress. She still loved to perform. I see her standing in front of the board in a blue dress with white trim, her dark hair slightly awry. 'Now!' she said brightly. 'We're going to find out what you know about our kings and queens.' Henry was dozy and I was sitting in on the lesson, with him sleeping on my knee, thumb in mouth. We often sat in. We'd been doing the Plantagenets. This morning of the test there was some debate about Richard the Second. Miss Ann said he wasn't a Plantagenet, he was a Lancastrian. Mrs Cobbold said that didn't mean he couldn't be a Plantagenet as well.

'I always thought the Plantagenets went all the way up to Richard the Third and the end of the Wars of the Roses,' said Harriet.

'No,' insisted Ann, 'they ended with *Edward* the Third. After that they're all Lancaster and York.'

I remembered Charles as a boy going over his lessons. Sweyn Forkbeard, William the Conqueror, Edward the Second. I still always got the Henrys mixed up.

'Look,' said Ann, 'it says here,' and she started flicking the pages of her history book.

'No books!' said Mrs Cobbold, holding up one finger. 'Now. Let's go right back to the beginning and the first Plantagenet. Who can tell me the meaning of the word Plantagenet?'

Blank silence.

She wrote it on the board. 'Anyone?'

'We haven't done that with Miss Flowers,' said Sophia.

'No? *Plant – a – genet.*' She enunciated it clearly in her lovely French, looking round with raised eyebrows and a smile, and when no one offered anything wrote two more words on the board in her neat sloping hand.

'From the Latin,' she said. '*Planta* – a plant, *genista* – a species of – what lovely bright-yellow plant do we know that flowers in the spring and summer. Harriet?'

Harriet twisted her mouth. 'Daffodils?'

'Not a flower, a shrub,' the mistress said, and wrote again, in capitals this time. I recognised B and OO.

'Broom,' she said. '*Planta genista* becomes *Plant – a – genet* in French, meaning the broom plant. And a sprig of broom was the emblem of the French House of Anjou.'

Oh, the way she pronounced Anjou. Lovely. I tried to remember it so I could try it out myself later. Aw-n-shew, like a lingering whisper.

'Geoffrey, Count of Anjou, the grandfather of our first Plantagenet king, used to wear a sprig of broom in his cap, and so he was named Geoffrey *Plant-a-genet*. And so – Plantagenet! And the first Plantagenet king adopted it because of his Norman heritage. Now Sophia–' but then she had a thought and said, 'Did you know that *genet* means a horse in, what is it? Spanish, I think. *Planta-genet* can also therefore mean plant-horse. Now, what on earth is a plant-horse?' She laughed. 'That sounds very odd, doesn't it? But it only means earth and air. So the Plantagenets, or so they'd like us to think, were the perfect combination of spirit and matter. There! My goodness! We have wandered quite away from the subject. *Now*, Sophia. Who, Sophia, are we talking about? Who *is* this first Plantagenet king who adopted the sprig of broom as his symbol?'

Sophia was sitting by me, open-mouthed

because she had a head cold. She frowned, thinking hard.

'You should know this, Sophia,' Mrs Cobbold said.

Sophia pulled a face.

'Henry the Second,' I whispered.

Mrs Cobbold's eyes shot to me.

'Sorry,' I said, and everybody laughed, including the mistress. 'You mustn't tell her, Margaret,' she said. 'She'll never learn.'

She called me to the library in the afternoon.

'Margaret,' she said, 'don't you think it's time you learned your letters?'

'I know one or two, madam. A B C and this and that.'

'I'm sure you do, Margaret, but I can see that you are capable of far more. In your family, how many can read?'

'Only Charles, madam. The sexton took him on because he was bright.'

She looked at me seriously for a moment or two, her lips moving slightly as if she was making calculations.

'Would you *like* to learn to read?' she asked.

'I think so, madam.'

'I think you should. If it suits you you can learn alongside Master George and Master Frederic. It would benefit *them* too, I'm sure. Where did you learn your kings and queens?'

'At home with my brother Charles. He used to recite them out loud.'

'You're an intelligent woman, Margaret,' she said. 'Look.' And she set before me a crooked pile of books. She spread them across the table, opening each one and flicking the pages. A red book with gold lettering on the spine and a raised flower on the front cover. 'Here, all the plants and flowers, their charming Latin names and all that they mean.'

She was mad about books. She'd read for hours on end. When she read, her face moved unconsciously, her eyes smiled, her lips moved, she frowned and sometimes grew tearful, and now and then laughed out loud. She put her books down all over the place. She'd walk here and there: 'Where's my book?' she'd say. 'Has anybody seen my book?'

At the bottom of the pile was a small blue volume with a golden sword down its spine. She smiled, resting one hand on the growing mound of her belly. 'This is mine,' she said softly. She laid the book in my hands. 'Look,' she said, leaning over and turning the first few pages till we reached a page with the title and a couple more small lines. 'That's me,' and she pointed at the name under the title. 'Eliza Clarke, that's me. That's what I was called then.'

I looked at the words. Eliza Clarke. They were the first two words that jumped out of a page at me.

'Is that you, madam?' I was amazed. She was even cleverer than I thought. Her name all proud there, printed fancy on the page of a real book from off a shelf. 'Did you write all that?'

She laughed. 'Anything's possible,' she said.

'What's it about?'

'It's called *The Sword.*' She sighed, fingering the sword on the spine. 'It's a novel. I loved writing it. I'm not very good.'

That's what they said about her, those snig-gering men at the edge of the dancing. That she wasn't very good. But she was so proud of it.

'The Sword,' she repeated, *'Or: Father Bertrand's History of his Own Times*. It's a story about those times we mentioned. Now, you tell me, *you're* good at kings and queens. It's set in Norman times. Who was our first Norman king?'

'William the Conqueror.'

She clapped her hands. 'Bravo, you do better than any of my children. I'll hear you read twice a week.'

So began a wonderful time, those first weeks of learning to read and make my letters on a slate. Me and Georgie and Freddy side by side. Miss Flowers was a good teacher. The schoolroom remains for ever a place of great warmth and great safety to me. My happy days. My almost happy days. If I'd only known for sure that he was safe. Still, I did well. Mrs Cobbold gave me a Bible, a small fat one I could hold in one hand, with pictures here and there, of Samson pushing out his big fists against the columns, of the Saviour on a hillside with his flock, a beautiful shepherd; and of the great flood of Noah, a massive grey wave with foam on top, and riding its spumy crest the boat that carried all the world. The stories I grew up with. She gave me other things too. A long long poem I never could fathom. A pretty book with a pink ribbon at the front, and on every page a single sentence, along with a picture, often of a flower, or a tree, or a hill, or a bird on a nest. In time I would make out a sentence here and there.

Once I had a sprig of thyme. It reminded me of Mrs Cobbold's story about the Plantagenets and the sprig of broom. *Oh, the lark in the morning she rises from her nest.* And Aesop's Fables. I loved those. She showed me books about ancient things, books of science and philosophy, things I knew I'd never read in a million years. 'That's not the point,' she said. 'One must be aware that these things at least exist. The point is that things must always be written down.'

Mrs Potts said I wasn't the first. 'You're clever, Margaret,' she said. 'She loves it when she gets a clever one.'

40

When Molly Briggs left us to marry her sweetheart I became head nursemaid and to work under me I got Jane Wells, a big hearty creature with a booming voice that carried for miles. She used to sing 'A-Hunting We Will Go' and chase the children round the shrubbery, making them shriek. She'd stand at the door and clap her hands: 'Come on now, Mistress Ann! Mistress Sophie! Lunch! Lunch! All brisk and smart now, one-two, one-two!' Master William called her the Major-General.

It meant more money for me. By now I was firmly fixed as part of the household. It's true to say I'd taken to the comfort of living in so fine a place, the quality all around me, the silky furnishings, the shining polished wood of the staircase and the high-backed chairs that stood in the hall. And the warmth! The lovely food so plentiful that we supped on many a grand evening feast in the kitchen, washed down with claret. And when that dreadful winter came on, and the sleet began to gel in the air, and the clouds blew out fat black cheeks, and the wind whined and whistled and bit into your skin, how delightful it was then to climb with a full belly into my warm bed in my own room, the candle aglow on the bedside table prettily covered with the sprigged green muslin she'd given me. I'd try for a few more words in the book with the pink ribbon, before blowing out the candle and falling asleep. Will, where are you, you big fool? I'd think as the rain hurled its lonely, locked-out self against the window.

As the days marched on, getting ever wilder and stormier every day, our walks no longer took us so far afield. I was always about when the men came up for their pay; I liked men's company, and they liked mine. No sailor with a message for me had appeared at the kitchen door for a very long time.

It was the kind of winter people remembered much later and talked about. Great sheets of ice lay over the Orwell. We had so many birds that year, the mudflats crowded with snipe and redshank, widgeon and teal, and very many brown geese that took off from time to time in lofty, mournfully crying flights along the estuary. The world turned grey, the sky massed cloud, the garden shivered in a constant rain.

The house was crowded. The married daughters descended one afternoon with their children, while Mrs Sleorgin, the mistress's friend, was in the music room playing duets on the piano with Master John. At six o'clock, the master told me to have the children ready for tea by half past. When I ushered them into the sitting room, Mrs Cobbold was standing by the streaming window looking out at the wild darkness and rubbing her hands together. 'It's turning to sleet,' she said. Far away I heard a rumbling, a giant's yawn that might have been the awakening of thunder. The family drifted in bit by bit, gathering about the fire where Ursula had drawn up the tea table and set it with mounds of hot toast and bread and butter. 'Margaret,' Mrs Cobbold asked, pulling the curtains and turning from the window, 'would you feed Henry?'

The sitting room was a large airy room with three or four little seating arrangements here and there. It was quite a sight to see the entire party, seventeen all told if you counted Mrs Sleorgin, who'd been invited to stay, spread itself all over the place and set about the business of scoffing. The oldest was the master, in his slippers and yellow waistcoat, running his fingers through his fluffy grey hair; the youngest his new grandson, a babe in arms sleeping soundly on his mother's knee. Henry and I were with Mrs Sleorgin, a small birdlike lady in a lilac gown.

'How's my little Henry?' she cooed. I'd heard her sing. She had a strong contralto that could carry all the way down the hall and up the stairs when she sang, but her speaking voice was a tiny flittery thing. 'My dear' – she twinkled her bright eyes at me – 'do you think he'd sit on my lap?'

'Of course,' I said, gratefully handing him over. He'd go to anyone that wanted him, and at once delighted her by snuggling his head under her chin, settling in as if she were a comfy chair.

'Where's William?' asked the master.

Ursula was pouring the tea. 'I'll do that,' Mrs Cobbold said. 'Run and see if you can't ferret him out, if you would.'

'Shall I go?' I said. 'Henry seems very happy with Mrs Sleorgin. If you don't mind being left with him, ma'am?'

'Not at all,' she replied, only too pleased, holding in one hand a half-nibbled slice of toast. 'He's my darling, aren't you, Henry-sweet?'

Henry sucked butter from his finger.

I ran up and looked in William's room, I searched all around the house and down in the kitchen where I thought he might be sitting with the servants as he so often liked to do; and last I took a lantern, threw my cloak over my head and dashed across to the stable yard, thinking he might be with the horses. The sleet fell thick and fast now, and the path was all puddles frozen solid, so that I had to skip around them and wet my feet in the mushy white of the lawn, the wind tearing at my cloak, which I held wide to shield the lantern. Light glanced over Pompey's kennel.

The coachman was in the stable, mixing mash for the horses.

'Have you seen Master William?' I asked.

George Teager was a small bow-legged man, deaf as a post. 'Eh?' he queried, cupping an ear and grimacing.

'Have you seen Master William?' I shouted against the sound of the beating on the roof.

'Not since this morning.'

Such a silly boy, William. Sixteen and thought no one could teach him a thing. Was he out in all this? Off somewhere stupid probably without a coat, I thought. I'd seen him come home soaked to the skin. 'Well, it wasn't raining when I went out,' he'd say, standing dripping on the hall carpet, grinning at a scolding. I met Ursula by the front door.

'Master William's taken the boat out!' she said, and her eyes held a kind of alarm that turned me cold.

'No!'

'Oh God but he has!'

The sitting room was in chaos. Sophia was crying. Harriet looked at her feet. Their father thundered. 'Why didn't you tell anyone, you stupid girl!'

'He said not to.' Harriet was sullen.

'He's gone fowling,' Mrs Sleorgin whispered urgently to me.

'It wasn't so bad then,' Sophia told her father miserably. 'He said not to say anything or you wouldn't let him go.'

'Dear God!' Mr Cobbold said.

I'd never seen his face sick with worry like that before.

'He's gone out in *this!*' he cried furiously.

As if to galvanise us, a great blast shook the windows. The fire leaped up. Then all was activity. The brewhouse men were called up and John Pride sent for, and he and the master, with Master John and Master Thomas, all wrapped themselves up in their cloaks and mufflers and set off with their heads down and something of panic in the way they walked. I ran after, still in my cloak. That boy was dear to me. At the landing stage we met with two of the brewhouse men, about to shove off in the skiff.

'All set, Tim?' asked the master.

'He's taken the oars,' Tim said heavily. 'That's bad that is, sir. He's taken the big boat and the little oars. Look.'

Ridiculous, those two big men in that tiny skiff with those great heavy oars. Mr Cobbold groaned. More ridiculous still to think of that stupid boy, armed only with the silly little oars from the skiff, all on his own in a boat made for twelve. Even Tim and his mate would have struggled with it in this weather. You could have blown poor William away at the best of times. I know what we all thought. We were girding up our loins for the worst. I met Tim Lee's eyes and we both knew. If we get him back alive, we said wordlessly, he'll be a lucky lad.

'Tide's going out fast,' Tim said.

I saw William in my mind, the oars ripped from his grasp, crouching helplessly in the bottom of the boat as it sped him along the estuary and down to the open, pitching sea. That's if the ice – which we could hear grinding and cracking out there in the dark – didn't tip him up before he got there. He'd be frozen stiff. Snow was on the wind. We set off, me and John and the boys and Mr Cobbold along the shore.

'If he's any sense,' I said, 'he'll have gone ashore.

Bet you anything we'll meet him on the path.'

'He *hasn't* any sense,' Mr Cobbold said shortly. I think he could hardly speak.

Tim and his mate had rowed out in the channel very wide to get round the frozen ooze. At first we could just about see them. For a while we heard them calling to each other; but after we'd passed the Grove and crossed over Hog Island there was nothing but a huge howling blackness over the river, and thunder at sea, louder than before. The wind tried to lift us off our feet. We couldn't speak. It became a kind of madness, the five of us struggling on calling 'William! William!' into the fury, three or four miles and not a soul, till we were come alongside Downham Reach and would very soon reach the place in the woods where you turned in for Priory Farm.

The boat had gone across nearly as far as the other bank.

'This is hopeless.' Mr Cobbold shouted against the wind.

We stood in a huddle, the wind tearing at us.

'We should go back,' the master said. 'What can we do?'

'We can't just give up, sir,' cried Thomas.

'We could go right past him and not see him,' John reasoned.

I was on Thomas's side. 'Sir,' I said, 'at least let's go as far as the trees. At least then we can get our breath. There's a little beach down there, you get a good view all along the river.'

The master blew out his cheeks. It began to snow in earnest. 'Come on!' he cried, and on we ploughed.

Call it stupidity or faith of a kind, I don't know. I just knew we should go forward. Everything told us that if the boy was not gone ashore and sheltering somewhere, he was most likely dead, but I could not think it. I ran ahead. The trees began.

'Wait, Margaret!' cried Master John, running after me.

'Listen!' I stopped still in the first shelter of the trees.

'Let's wait for the others.' Master John stood with me. I was conscious of him, a man I did not know very well, very close, and the wild night.

'Listen!'

I was sure. Someone coming through the darkness. Invisible. 'William!' I yelled.

'William! William!' we both called.

The others arrived.

Someone called back, a deep hailing from the shore. We ran. It was very dark under the trees. We came out on the beach where John Luff and I had taken our leave of the turnspit dog. There was the skiff drawn up, and Tim and the other man trudging up the shingle. The others were behind us.

'We found the boat,' Tim said. 'She's out there drifting empty.' He gestured with his arm. 'She's taken in a lot of water.'

'No sign of him?'

'No sign.'

'Oh God!' Mr Cobbold looked wildly up and down the river, as if there was anything to be seen. He's dead, I thought. He must be.

'He might have gone ashore,' said John Pride.

'He's maybe gone to some house for shelter.'

'I'll run up to Priory Farm,' I said, 'I know them there. If he came ashore anywhere round here that's where he'd go.'

'Go with her, Tim. No sense in taking the skiff any further. We'll go as far as where the wood ends.'

So we splashed up along the path through the wood and parted ways, but no sooner had Tim and I come out on the road than we saw a man come lurching towards us with a great burden on his back. 'Help, friends,' he called out. 'Help me with this lad.'

Tim ran forward.

'Will?' I shouted. 'Will?'

Impossible, I was mad, but it was his voice. Wouldn't I know it anywhere?

Tim caught the boy as he slid from Will's shoulder.

It *was* him. Terrible though it was, even then not knowing whether William was dead or alive, I laughed out loud. Master William made a dreadful noise, doubled out of Tim's grasp and landed on his hands and knees, retching and groaning horribly.

'He's swallowed half the ooze,' Will said.

'Look at you!'

They were all mud. Foul-smelling monsters.

'Oh, Will!' I was angry. I hit him.

He caught my hands and laughed.

Tim must have wondered, but all he said was, 'Thank Christ. Let's get him up to the farm. Shall you go and tell the others, Margaret, while we deal with this young idiot?'

But they'd already heard and come running up from the trees.

'He's here, Mr Cobbold!' I greeted him. 'He's here,' grinning all over my face like a fool.

41

It was very strange to walk up once more through the copse and over the wooden bridge that crossed the stream. The rill where it left the moat was still and frozen, and the moat solid, snow settling on it. The thunder had moved further out to sea. I was all a-tremble and felt a sudden urgent need not to see anyone from the farm, so I said we'd run back home and take word, me and Will; we'd not all fit in the wagon anyway. The sailor was a friend of mine, I said, a very old friend of my family. And before anyone could gainsay us we'd slipped away and were together under one cloak, and the wind behind us coming in from the sea now, sweeping us along the shore and over Hog Island like a broom. By the time we got home I was all mud like him.

He told me the news on the way. He'd been taken from his ship six months ago along with three others, pressed on board a man-of-war called the *Briton* and bound for three years. He couldn't send word, he said, they'd been Holland-side all this while and no one given leave, and were only now returned. The *Briton* lay in Harwich Harbour, he'd got leave for a week.

He'd rowed up as far as Nacton Creek before abandoning the boat because of the weather, and it was near there he'd come across that fool of a boy stuck in the mud, no mud-splashers, nothing at all, trying to wade in through the ooze and sunk in right down to his waist almost. His lips were blue and he was crying for his mum, Will said. At first when Will got him ashore he'd thought he could walk but the boy was beat. Will carried him the last half a mile, and not a soul out on such a night until he saw us on the road.

We got home a full half-hour before the others, who took Mr Wake's wagon and came back by the high road. The mistress was informed of our arrival and came running down the kitchen steps, stopping short halfway down when she saw us standing there like two wild gypsies. 'Margaret, you've got mud all over you!' she cried.

I've been cuddling this sailor, madam. I didn't say it but it couldn't have been more plain. Her quick eyes took him in, and he looked away.

'This is my friend, Will Laud, madam,' I said. The brewhouse men had been back a while and already told her what had happened.

'I'm pleased to make your acquaintance.' She nodded at Will.

'The boy's gone for Dr Stebbing,' she said to me. 'Oh, poor Margaret, you're soaked to the skin, run up and get changed, dear. Mrs Potts, hot water and warm blankets! Has Ursula lit a fire in the bedroom?'

'Yes, madam, it's all in hand.' Mrs Potts couldn't take her eyes off the wild man who'd appeared in her kitchen. 'Jane's filling the slipper bath.'

'Mr Laud,' Mrs Cobbold said graciously from the steps, 'we are in your debt. Do make yourself comfortable. Sary, a hot drink for the man. And some food.'

He was struck dumb and bashful. He never looked at her.

I ran up to my room and found hot water in my jug, and made myself just about presentable in my dark-blue gown. The sound of voices came up through the shrubbery. Breathless, I went down to find Tim and John Pride supporting Master William in. Mrs Cobbold threw her hands to her face when she saw him. 'Oh, William, William, William!' she cried, swaying from side to side.

He retched right over the hall carpet but nothing came, thank God. I suppose he'd voided most of it. They'd thrown their coats all over him and he started flinging them off, moaning like a child. The children lined the banister and gaped. Mrs Cobbold clapped her hands. 'Out of the way!' she ordered. 'Let's get your poor brother up to bed!'

'Is he going to die?' asked Freddy.

'Of course he isn't. Shoo.'

Dr Stebbing arrived. They put William in the slipper bath, not too hot, the doctor said, not at first. Mrs Potts tested it with her elbow as if he was a baby. 'Now, now,' said Stebbing, scolding cheerfully as he opened a vein in William's arm. 'What have you been up to, Master William? Thought you'd bag a few ducks, did you? On the worst night of the year? That was intelligent, wouldn't you say?'

A drop of blood showed.

'Good, good,' said Dr Stebbing. 'Margaret, a little hot water if you please. That's right, pour it slowly, just here. Very good, very good. Brandy?'

We soon warmed him up but he was still sick and acting the baby when they put him to bed. I left them all fussing around him and returned to the kitchen, where Will was standing by the fire trying to scrape drying mud off his clothes. John Pride went up and begged a pair of Master John's old trousers and a shirt of George Teager's for him, and Ursula scrubbed his blue jacket and trousers and set them out to dry by the fire. It was that time in the evening when all the servants gathered for a bite and a tipple. Everyone wanted to hear about the rescue. Quite the hero they made of him, and he grinned his wild-eyed grin and laughed and fooled around like a boy till the door opened and Mrs Cobbold appeared above us once more on the steps.

Something was wrong. I couldn't have said at the time what it was, but I knew. It was something to do with the way she stood halfway down, straight-backed and lofty, the way Will was obliged to raise his face if he wanted to look at her, the way he would not, preferring to gaze at a spot on the flagstones a little way in front of him.

'My husband tells me you are a very brave young man,' she said fulsomely, flashing her teeth. 'Thank you so very much for all your help.'

He gave an awkward shrug and mumbled, 'Oh well, ma'am…' and shrugged again. There was a strangeness in the air. No one spoke for a moment. Will licked his lips and vaguely smiled, sheepish as a schoolboy in front of the mistress.

He was very dirty, hair all over the place, eyes rimmed with black. Suddenly he was small.

'My husband sends you this guinea,' she beamed, reaching over the rail.

He flinched. 'Not at all, ma'am,' he said gruffly. 'Give it to Margaret instead.'

'Oh.' She straightened, frowning and smiling together. 'Oh well then ... if you say so.' She winked at me. 'Catch!' she trilled, tossing the coin.

I raised my palm and caught it.

'Wonderful,' she said. 'Now, I'm sure you won't want to venture out again tonight in all this, Mr Laud, so I'm having a bed made up for you in Mr Teager's room. Margaret will take you over there after supper, won't you, Margaret?'

Still, he would not look up and meet her eyes.

'Thank you, ma'am,' he mumbled.

42

Will and I sat up late that night in the kitchen, long after the others were in their beds. His sleeves were rolled up past the elbow and the veins in his arms filled me with tenderness, so that I ran my finger ends slowly up and down them, up and down.

'Hey, listen, Pegs, it's not so bad you know,' he said. 'The *Briton*'s not a bad old tub and the captain's taken a shine to me.'

'They always do,' I said, squeezing his slender waist.

'I'm a good sailor,' he replied cockily, 'and they

know it. But listen, Pegs, what do you think? If I do my three years I'll get a full pardon. How about that?'

'Give up the free trade?'

'Who knows? Fact is I could if I wanted to now. That wasn't so before. What do you think?'

I did not know what to think.

'We could get a little shop in Brandeston, you'd like that,' he said. 'One day when I'm through with being a King's man, I'll come back with gold and silver, and with the money you'll save here we could set you up nicely. You always said you'd like a little shop. Like the Cracknells.'

He was so reduced in the presence of very grand folk. I'd never seen it before. In the kitchen with us he was full of himself, a fine boy with his wide laugh and the firelight in his eyes; but before Elizabeth Cobbold, he was a strawhead. When I slipped upstairs to see Master William I'd heard them talking as I passed the sitting-room door, laughing over their belated tea and toast.

'What a wild savage-looking creature he is, Margaret's beau,' Miss Harriet said.

'He has no manners, I agree,' Mrs Cobbold said, 'but I'll hear nothing against the man. Anyway, what do you expect? He's a rough young salt.'

'His teeth!' piped up Sophia.

'Poor Margaret,' Master John said. 'She's a good sort.'

'Coming back, do you know what he said to me?' That was the master, warming his shanks by the fire. 'He's hoolly froze, he is, sir! Hoolly froze!' He made Will sound like a fool. There was more I did not catch, and then a great bursting tide of mirth; and I hated them, all of them, their bright golden faces laughing at Will, for all he'd damn near killed himself hauling their fool of a boy in out of the mud. I felt for the guinea in my pocket. A guinea, I thought. He saves their boy's life and they give him a guinea. Here boy, take that!

The Winter Cold

43

It began then, when they laughed at Will. The big folk had no time for sailors in their houses. Sailors on the quay, sailors in town looking rakish in the vicinity of the inns, yes, but not indoors. Will was always too rough for them.

He was gone away now on the *Briton,* and we got along very well till after Christmas and the long-awaited removal of the entire household to St Margaret's Green. I loved our new house and I loved being right in the middle of town: no more than a step to Carr Street one way, where the sailors loitered day and night outside the Salutation, and a step the other to Christchurch Park, where all the toffs went on a Sunday. The old Christ Church bell had a solemn tongue, but the bells of St Margaret's just across the way made the air golden even as the snowflakes fell, and seagulls shivered and screeched on our two big gables. Our house was one of the grandest in town, with a beautiful garden at the back, a pond, weeping willows, a herb garden that smelled of heaven when summer came. A creeping vine, sometimes red, sometimes green, ran all over the front, and the big windows looked out over fields towards the Woodbridge road and further to where the hills began. Oh, it was the best of all worlds for me. Our stable was by a cow-keeper's yard and a blacksmith's forge, so all day I heard the soft rattle of horses and cattle coming and going, like home. The very air was soothing. And no one had a thing to say if I took a little time occasionally and mounted me up on sharp-eared Crop, the master's strawberry roan, and rode a little way along the Woodbridge road, or even just around the Green. They were kind, the Cobbolds. The mistress said she liked to see me ride.

It was here that Master Rowland was born. But not before that nastiness we had the last night at the Cliff, when she was huge with him in her belly, looking like a partridge poor thing and hardly able to walk. I've sometimes wondered if it was John Luff brought him on. I was putting the little ones to bed in the new place. We were just about getting straight, though it was all a bother of coming and going still, all running up and down and here and there and no one knowing where to find anything, and the children so buoyed up and wild, running round and round their big new nursery. It was the devil of a thing to calm them down. What a weird echoing sort of a house the Cliff must be now, I thought, emptied, the life of it drained away. Only Mrs Cobbold, Master John and Master Thomas were there this last night, to close its eyes, as it were.

Ursula came in, mad to tell me the news. Delight in her eyes. Sary Turner and she had been talking to George Teager, who'd been going backwards and forwards all night with the coach between here and the Cliff, and the master going back and forth with him too.

'The mistress was attacked by a drunken sailor in the garden!' she announced.

'No!'

'She was! He shook his fist at her, and made as if to swing a punch. And he called her a dirty word.'

'Is she hurt?'

'Not *hurt*, as such. Scared, I suppose more like. But fancy such a thing! She heard Pompey raising the dead and tried to get the boys to go out and look, but they said they couldn't go because they'd got their slippers on. So she said *she* was going, someone had to, and they said, up to you, but *we're* not going out in our slippers just because Pompey's barking at a rabbit. And now the master's ever so upset with them. Only you know I thought I'd better tell you, Margaret, because you know what people are like, and now there's Mrs Potts saying I wonder who that sailor was, I wonder if it was Margaret's beau Will Laud, that nice young man that came that time, I wonder if he's looking for Margaret and had one or two too many on his way along the river. Some men do turn a bit nasty when they're bladdered. She said George told her it might be him.'

At first my heart leaped up. Will was back. But immediately I realised it couldn't possibly be him.

'Why should it be Will? He wouldn't do a thing like that. Who says it's Will? Did Mrs Cobbold say it was Will?'

'I don't know.'

'Just because it's a sailor doesn't mean it's Will,' I said. 'If Mrs Cobbold saw him, she'd know. I won't believe it's Will till she tells me so herself. Gossip!'

'Oh yes!' Ursula agreed, nodding her eager head violently. 'It's terrible! All just gossip.'

'Tell me what happened. Everything you know.'

'She went out and saw a man in the shrubbery,' said Ursula, 'and she called him out. Come out where I can see your face, she says. And he comes out and she sees he's reeling drunk and tells him to get on his way, and that's when he comes at her and calls her something wicked. So she goes to let Pompey off the chain and the man's off straight down the shore shaking his fists and away in a boat.'

44

Later, it was said she'd been grabbed at. That he'd snarled like a dog. They were all agog in the kitchen.

'It's not Will!' I shouted. 'Hear me? He's not even here, he's serving his country, I'll have you know.'

'Soft now, Margaret,' John Pride said. 'No one's accusing your Will.'

'They'd better not!'

'Course not.' Sary Turner was worrying away at the fire. 'He wasn't that sort of a young man at all if you ask me. You can tell. You stick up for your boy, Margaret.'

Good old Sary.

I couldn't sleep. That night was bright and sharp as a jewel. When I rubbed the frosty stars from my bedroom window and looked out, the world was soft blue, St Margaret's Green snowy, and the fields bundled up in the dark, the palings opposite thickly rimmed with luminous white. I looked for a figure, a sailor standing in the freezing night. Who wanted me? Was there news? But there was no one. I woke in the night three times, each time listened for the chiming of the Christ Church bell, staring into the pale dark in my room and wondering how far it was to morning, how much the man may have frightened her, how dreadful those boys for letting a woman about to drop a baby go out in the snow like that; and how if she'd been their real mum they wouldn't have let her go. How strange to try and be a mother to those great lumps. Then I became angry, with the boys, and with the sailor for threatening and in so doing throwing doubt upon me. For who but me in that household had a pull for the sailors? And by morning when I woke unrefreshed in that strange house, my anger was hard and solid like a ball inside me, somewhere behind my heart, and went out in snaps against all and sundry, even Will who was cursed in my mind for being so far away. And when she came sweeping in from the coach, pink-cheeked from the cold with snow on her boots, and said not a word to me about it though she must have known how anxious I would be, and scarce looked at me but with a vague and unpleased eye, then I felt the anger become fury and had to turn sharply and swish away into the breakfast room where some of the children were still about their eggs and kippers.

It was mid-morning before she sent for me. The children were in the new schoolroom and I was going over my letters, spelling things out. Ursula popped her head in and said Madam wanted me in the drawing room. When I entered she was all cosy on the chaise longue in front of a blazing fire with her books and a cup of tea and her feet up, the big belly a hard round dome before her. She smiled up at me but the look was one of a little reproach as if I had done something wrong.

'Margaret,' she said. 'What do you think of your new home?'

'Very nice, madam,' I replied.

'Yes it is, isn't it?' She laid by her book. 'Much better for the children, I think.'

I waited.

'I wished you were with me last night, Margaret,' she said.

I said nothing.

She sighed. 'I suppose you heard about my little adventure.'

'Yes, madam, everyone has.'

'It was nothing.' She stifled a yawn and looked away at the snow falling steadily on the Green. 'Just a drunk. But very unpleasant.' Again, a long strange pause. 'I do hope it doesn't happen again.'

'Why should it?' Perhaps I said it a little roughly.

'Why indeed? Do you think you might have any idea who this unpleasant person might be, Margaret?'

A small red cloud burst inside me.

'Why should I, madam? My type, was he?'

She coloured. 'Oh, Margaret,' she said. 'Of course I didn't mean that. I just meant that you know so many people, so many – oh dear, you are taking this in quite the wrong spirit, and we're all very tired what with the move and the–' she raised both white hands and flapped them above her belly, frowned and suddenly spoke strongly '–for heaven's sake! I've been sworn at and intimidated on my own property by an intruder. I just wanted to know if you might have any idea who the rogue was, that's all. What's so terrible about that?'

I licked my lips. 'Nothing, madam, nothing at all. Just wondered why you thought I might know, that's all. Do you know what they're all saying, madam? And it's as if it come from you. They're saying it was Will Laud, my friend, who scared you and was drunk and all that, and it's not fair. He's not like that. It's just not fair.' My voice quivered.

She pulled herself more upright. 'Of course it wasn't Will Laud,' she said. 'That's ridiculous. *I* never said that. Who says so?'

I made a disgusted sound. 'People.'

'Is that what you thought I meant?' she asked. 'You thought I was implying it was your friend? Now, that's not fair, Margaret, I never meant any such thing.'

I believed her. 'Oh, they'll say anything,' I said. 'The whole thing's garbled. It must have been nasty for you; you should have sent those boys out, madam. Tell you, if I'd been there I'd have got them off their lazy arses.'

She laughed. We were back like before. I'd had no other mistress I could have spoken to so freely.

'Describe him,' I said, 'this sailor.'

'A dark rough little man,' she said. 'Nasty hard little eyes and a beard.'
'Was he wearing a wig? An old brown-george?'
'Oh, I don't know, Margaret. Yes, I think he might have been.'
'Sounds like John Luff,' I said.
'You know him?'
'He's not a friend,' I said quickly. 'I just know who he is. Everyone does. He's not the sort you want to know, madam.'
'I'm sure he isn't.'
'Was he after game?' I wondered.
'In our garden? On a night like last night?'
'Drunk anyway.'
'Oh, absolutely.'
'You shouldn't have gone out, madam,' I said.
'Why? Do you think I was in any danger?'
'I doubt it. But you don't want to take chances, madam.'
'Pompey would have had him,' she said, smiling. 'Plenty of life in the old dog yet.' She stroked her belly. 'I think I'll have a little sleep,' she said. 'I know it's early but I can hardly keep my eyes open. Perhaps you could ask Ursula to bring me a drink of chocolate in an hour or so.'
'Certainly, madam.'
And she wriggled about getting comfortable on the chaise longue, sighing at her great unwieldy bulk.
Master Rowland was born two days later. He was given over to me almost entirely. He was my favourite. I loved him so much it was like a small pain. He wasn't the most handsome of those children, he wasn't the best or the brightest, but

he had the softest heart and the sweetest eyes and he loved me back right from the very beginning and always wanted me. Jane Wells took over much of the work of the other children from me now, and for a while I was content, rocking and dandling and singing and tickling, and would have been completely happy if it hadn't been for Will. I worried sick about him every night when my head finally touched the pillow, thinking of the war against the French. The ports were full of maimed soldiers. Every night I prayed. Make sure he's got enough to eat, dear God, and don't let his poor feet be cold. I swore if he ever came back I'd not let him go again.

Luff worried me too, though he hadn't shown his face again. What did he want, hanging round the Cobbolds? I was sure it was him. I asked in town and found he'd been seen just after Christmas but was gone again, some said down to London to ship for America but some said only as far as Stowmarket. It was surely me he was hanging round for. Why? Not for me alone. It must be that he had word of Will, or that he *wanted* word of Will. John Luff was a dangerous man. He always had been, but not to his friends. I think he'd been too fond of Will. When they parted, his friendship turned to hate. And he was a good hater, Luff. He missed the past too much, that was his trouble, the good old times when the salty comrades of the *Alde* ploughed the main and put gunpowder in the rum.

It was a dreadful winter, one of the worst ever. The poor froze. Mrs Cobbold sent Sary Turner and me with blankets and a barrow of coals to the

Black Horse. They were collecting all over Ipswich, a soup kitchen was set up between the front and back hamlets, and another by the Buttermarket. Sary wanted us to walk by the barracks since we were close. She had a lad in there who was getting his discharge soon and marrying her and taking her up to Norfolk. She was a Norfolk girl herself and couldn't wait to get back. But the parade ground was empty. We stood looking through the gate.

'There he'll be,' she said, smiling. 'In there keeping his pretty toes warm.' And wriggled her own in her black boots, and stamped them vigorously against the hard-packed snow. 'I'm not a town girl,' she said.

'Nor am I,' I said, 'but I can live anywhere. I like to see all the people and the docks and the streets.'

'What about you and your Will,' she said as we turned away, trundling our empty barrows before us. 'When are you two getting spliced?'

'Never! He's too much of a wanderer.'

'Why not? Don't you want your own little baby like Master Rowland?'

That made me laugh. 'But Sary,' I replied, 'there'll never be a dearth of children wanting me. I'll never be childless.'

'It's not the same.'

'It's as good as,' I said. 'Maybe better. Children grow up and break their mothers' hearts but they always keep a soft spot for their old nurses. I've seen it.'

As we passed near St Margaret's Ditches there was some poor idiot getting whipped, his thin bare back less white than the snow. The blood welled up along the stripes, freezing as it did so. Hardly anyone was watching, too cold. Warm work though for the flogger.

'Can you tell me why it is, Margaret, that they're flogging that one there for being a beggar, while we're trundling coals for the poor?'

Me and Sary hurried along, bundling our mufflers about our faces.

'Don't expect sense from this world and you won't be disappointed,' I replied.

Those words to Sary were lightly spoken but how deep they stuck in my mind, how often they walked through my thoughts in times I could never have foretold, times when the world was all gone mad. It's a good thing we do not know what lies ahead of us.

Sary smiled. I believe she lived happily ever after with her soldier in Norfolk, by the sea somewhere. I imagine it, a brood of pretty children and Sary the cook's good food. I believe it but I do not know. I wonder if she ever heard what happened to me? She'd have cried, I think. Certainly she had a good heart. When we came back along the edge of the Green we saw Robinson Crusoe coming out through the tall folding gates of the cow-keeper's yard, clad only in his old coat and his bare hands blue.

'Robin!' she cried. 'Cold weather indeed to bring you in off the river. If you come round to the kitchen I'll give you a hot drink.'

'Brandy and water, ma'am,' he roared. 'Brandy to keep the foul fiend away.'

'That's what I always say,' she called cheerily.

She lowered her voice as the old scarecrow trailed along after us, picking our way through the deep drifts that skirted the garden. 'Poor man looks starved.' The big girls were chasing the younger children about in the snow and there was much shrieking. Georgie was running in ever widening circles that brought him closer and closer to the frozen pond. Jane Wells was there but she was preoccupied in smoothing down a rather fat snowman with a parsnip for a nose. 'Stay away from the pond!' I yelled. Little Henry dropped the snowball that was melting in his mittened hand, and hurtled clumsily towards us across the snow. He rammed my legs, laughing. I picked him up. 'What a very bright red nose!' I exclaimed.

'That pond's a menace if you ask me,' Sary said.

'Nothing wrong with the pond,' I said, 'if only people are sensible. Children must be taught sense.'

It was very deep and the sides were turfed, smooth and slippery like a slide. Six steps ran down to the expanse of ice, fractured here and there by thrown stones, pelted with snowballs. The willows' trailing arms were caught in the ice.

'Sense?' Sary snorted.

'Sense,' I said firmly, 'in the face of chaos. Jane, please make sure they don't go near the pond.'

'I've told them, Margaret,' she said. 'You don't know how many times I've told them. Soon as my back's turned…'

In the kitchen we stood gratefully thawing. Sary gave Robin a chair by the fire and warmed some brandy, and he settled nicely, sipping away, setting the cup down from time to time to perform a peculiar mime with his hands, a sweeping back and forth, quite graceful and rhythmic. He was weaving stockings. Charles told me once he'd been a weaver before he went mad.

'The mistress wants you,' Ursula said.

Mrs Cobbold was on the chaise with Rowland tucked in between the cushions. Her playing cards were strewn on the table.

'Darling's gone to sleep,' she said. 'Play a hand with me, Margaret, I'm bored.'

Out-at-heels

45

It was the first of June. I know because later, when we heard the news about the great victory at sea, Mrs Cobbold counted back and said, 'Do you know, that must have been the day you pulled Henry out of the pond.'

I'd gone out to pick a few herbs for soup, and there was Jane Wells, with Harriet and Ann, all jumping up and down and screaming their silly heads off, and a great commotion in the pond.

I ran. It was Henry. He was three now, a great lump, splashing like a whale. I tucked my skirt into my drawers, jumped in and grabbed him. The great wailing he set up as soon as he knew I had him convinced me of the health of his lungs. I hoisted us out by the willows.

'What were you doing near the pond?' Mrs Cobbold, who had run out at the first shout, pulled Henry to her and hugged him, getting her gown all soaked. 'How many times do you have to be told? All of you?'

'It's impossible, madam,' I said. 'You can't stop a child from running about.'

'God, you're soaked. Go and get changed before you catch your death,' she said. 'Jane – see to him. Ursula – hot chocolate.'

It was a warmish day, but my teeth were chattering.

'Margaret,' she said, taking me by the arm and

walking with me back to the house, 'what would we do without you? It seems you're always rescuing my idiot children. Quickly, get yourself dry and go and sit yourself down by the fire till supper. Jane and Ursula can manage.' She smiled, brushing herself down. 'Oh dear,' she said to the ladies she'd been entertaining in the parlour, who had gathered eagerly by the French windows, 'I'm afraid I must get changed too. Do excuse me.'

'Of course.' Mrs Sleorgin smiled a big toothy smile. 'Well done, Margaret!'

'Oh, I felt like a swim,' I quipped, and that made them laugh.

The mistress read to me out of *The Times*, and showed me the headline: IMPORTANT NAVAL VICTORY!!!! 'Glorious victory obtained on the first inst.,' she read, 'by his Majesty's Naval Forces under the command of Earl Howe, a victory which we may say with confidence has so crippled the navy of France, that it will be impossible for the French to send another grand fleet to sea, at least during the present campaign.'

I went down town that night. I couldn't rest when my work was done, late as it was. All Ipswich was going wild, the streets a riot of shouting, laughing, whooping, fooling fun. They said it was the same everywhere. They said in London every bell was ringing and all the flags aloft. They said six French ships were taken. Hundreds of our men were dead; but thousands of theirs, even though we were outnumbered. A thousand Frenchmen were taken prisoner. Beneath the crazy chimneys and beetling brows of the Neptune's mullioned windows, a crowd drank and danced and caroused. Hundreds of our men were dead. Word of Will? Anyone? Anyone with a brother, a friend returning? Anyone hear of Will Laud, who went out on the *Briton* but changed ships at Torbay? Or so I'd heard. Anyone at Torbay last March? Will Laud, able seaman, thirty-six years old, blue eyes, yellow queue, scar on the left side just under the eye. Nothing at all. I met Rube and many another familiar face, many who knew him – no word. So I drank till two on the quay and rolled home sore at heart, thinking now: 'He is dead for sure'; now: 'He'll be home tomorrow, next week, soon, soon.'

Two nights later a boy came to the door and said there was a sailor down at the Salutation with a message for me. Ask for Jack Carr, he said, the landlady's nephew. So off I dashed to Cross Keys Street and there was this Jack Carr in a room with all his friends around him, and his aunt the landlady and all her girls and the men of the town hanging on his every word. He waved a beer mug and shouted as if we were all hard of hearing, but it was because he himself was half deaf from the thunder of the guns. 'They was good fighters, give 'em that!' he roared, 'but we sent 'em flying. Three days' fighting. You can't see! Can't see a thing. Tears streaming down your face. It's the smoke. The smoke.' A long-nosed, lanky sort of a man he was, with a high fever in his eyes and raging on his brow.

I stood at the back and shouted: 'Have you got word of Will Laud?'

That got through.

'Are you Margaret Catchpole?'

'Yes.'

'Will Laud sends he's well and safe and coming this way soon as he can get free!'

Eight months I'd lived with his death in the back of my mind. Now I knew he wasn't, I let in the thoughts that had always been there. Will Laud is dead in battle. Will Laud is lost, no one knows where. Will Laud has lost his legs. All possibilities rippled through me in a second, and the world was a fearful place. I felt my eyes grow bright, licked my lips. A girl I knew in the crowd lifted both her fists in the air and smiled wildly. 'Three cheers for Will Laud!' she yelled. Everyone was pot-merry: three drunken hoorahs rose up to the beams.

I pushed through to Jack. 'Where did you see him?' I asked.

'Portsmouth.'

'He's well?'

'Very well.'

'Not hurt?'

'Not hurt.'

'And coming home?'

'They'll not let them go yet,' Jack said, 'not risk losing them. Half of them's pressed men.'

'Did you talk with him?'

'We manned a gun. Can't say we got much talking done.' He laughed.

'How long?'

'Eh?'

'How long did you man the gun with him?'

'All of it. Three days. We were chasing the French.'

I nudged in as near to him as I could. 'Tell me,' I said. 'I want to know all about it. What did he say? How did he look? Was he thin?'

'I don't know,' he said. 'He looked like he looked.'

'Three days?'

'Terrible weather. Bloody fog. A wonder we weren't all blown to hell. We followed through the lines and they was firing broadsides, full broadsides, both sides, two hundred bloody guns all blasting away. You think you're in hell. Can't see a thing. All you see is the flashing! We give 'em a good pounding though. They'll never forget!'

'Was he in good spirits?'

'He says damn all to hell with this weather. For Christ's sake let a man sleep!'

'He couldn't sleep?'

He laughed. 'Sleep?'

Someone took away his empty mug and handed him another and he sucked furiously at it. 'Slept next our guns,' he said, throwing an arm round my shoulder. 'Three days and three nights on the deck. Would you like that, hey? Three days and three nights on deck next your gun, and the fog and the drizzle and the old tub pitching?' He chuckled and his eyes crinkled pathetically.

'Did you hear anything of Nicholas Blunt?' a woman called.

He frowned. 'I don't know the name.'

'Jacob Rose?'

He shook his head.

More names.

'Let me alone,' he snarled. 'I don't know every man in the navy.'

I was lucky.

'But that's nothing as to the battle!' he suddenly bellowed, right down my ear. 'We hauled up under her stern! Hundred and twenty guns. Shot like hail. Two went down next us. I got this here.' He took his arm from my shoulder, pulled back his coat with a filthy brown hand and displayed a great wedge of bloody bandage. 'Then this ball comes, thirty-six-pounder it was, and the boy at the next gun–' his eyes popped '–head's gone! Head's gone and legs still there! Six of their ships we took!'

'The most ever!' said the landlady.

'Couldn't see a thing! The smoke. Down below, the smoke, you think you're in hell.'

'Why are you back and Will not?' I asked.

Jack pulled his coat aside and showed me his wound once more. 'I came on the *Phaeton*,' he said, as if that explained everything, and took a huge drink.

'Sir,' I said nicely, 'when you're rested, tomorrow maybe, can I come and talk to you again?'

He slid his arm around my waist. I felt him tremble, a fine quivering very far inside his body. 'You come and see me, sweet,' he said, 'you come whenever you want to.'

46

She turned against me.

It happened slowly and strangely. It was the sailors. Jack Carr used to come up to the house to see me, and sometimes Rube. There were others, a few lads from the Neptune, not a bit of harm in any of them. They never came till late at night when all my work was done and the children settled, and then it was no harm – we just sat in the kitchen with Sary and John Pride and Ursula, talking or having a small nibble and a drink, passing the time. What was wrong with that? Didn't she have her friends in and out all the time, and the parties and the dancing and the big people up from London?

It's easy to mistake the kindness of a good employer for friendship. I didn't think she'd mind. Sometimes Sary's young man was there too, and nothing was ever said about *him*. But then *he* was a dragoon.

One day she came across me talking to Jack Carr over the palings, and she gave him such a peculiar look. I suppose he looked odd. Poor fellow's wits were addled if you ask me, not that I knew him before the battle but I'm sure he can't have been as muddled as all that before. True, he was shouting rather loudly but that's only because he was deaf. Later she said to me, 'Who was that you were talking to, Margaret?'

'Jack Carr,' I said. 'The fellow from the Salutation who brought me the news about Will.'

'Ah.'

'He was in the big battle,' I said.

'Oh yes, that's right.'

Of course, she'd had that nasty experience with John Luff the last night at the Cliff. But it wasn't fair to judge them all by him.

'Shall I bring Master Rowland to you after his bath, madam?'

'What?'

I drew the curtains. 'Master Rowland,' I said. 'Shall you see him after his bath?'

'Oh yes, of course.' But she was distracted.

As far as I was concerned I couldn't have too many sailors round the house. To me they were just like family. And mad Jack with his garblings about the Glorious First was my word of Will. Not that I found out much more than I did that first time in the Salutation; there was nothing more to know. They'd manned a gun together, that was all. Then Jack had been injured and transferred to the *Phaeton* and sent home, and Will was waiting for his discharge and would come as soon as he could. And after that, nothing. I kept waiting for him to turn up but he didn't. When I went out I wondered if I'd see him walking down the street. Never.

Never any word.

Still, he was alive. I thought of how terrible it had been for him when poor Adam Hare got killed. How was he, now he'd seen the mess the cannons could make? Again and again Jack Carr threw bits and pieces of the battle at me. The stench of black powder. Smell of blood, decks slippy. Fire. Hell. I thought of Will there; day and night, I thought of it. If I could have gone there and been with him, if only I could have been there. Why would they not let the men come home after all they'd been through? When he was a smuggler, after a particularly hard outing he always got a run ashore. Surely they'd not send him straight back into battle? More danger, no end to danger. There was no way but to be strong about it. So I talked to my sailors and kept up with the news, and Madam continued in some way I could barely define to sniff at my friends. The look on her face told me. Not that she was ever anything less than gracious with them, if ever she encountered one by chance on the path.

Then one day as I was passing the cow-keeper's yard I glanced in through the gates and there standing in front of the cow-keeper's cottage was John Luff. He didn't see me, but it gave me quite a turn. What does *he* want, I thought. If she sees him she'll go daft on me. But he never came near that day. I went into town and asked here and there and found him staying on a ship of Captain Bargood's by the Custom House. I saw him on deck and he saw me. He waved. I beckoned with my arm. He smiled fleetingly, looking around himself this way and that and playing with his pipe in a leisurely way, as if deliberating whether to speak to me or not. Then, very insolent, he strolled down the gangplank. He came up too close, a way of his, and put his face near mine, a game of intimidation he had. He was like a dog, John Luff. The trick with his type is never showing fear.

I stared him hard in the eye, so close I could count the red veins breaking over the shiny whites. 'What a thing you are, John,' I said. 'Here's me known you years, and here's you acting like we're mortal enemies, and I still haven't got a clue what it's all about.'

He laughed down his nose. 'You're not my enemy,' he said, pushing his chest against me. 'What makes you think you're that important?'

'There you go proving my point.' I put my hand

on his chest and pushed him back a little. 'Will's coming home,' I said, 'did you know? Will you and he be friends or silly enemies?'

'Search me,' he said. 'He'll not be back in ages. They're out between Ushant and Scilly.'

'You know that?'

'I know that. Don't you?'

'He's due leave.'

John snorted.

'How do you know?'

'I know things,' he said. He smiled then, almost like old times when he was Will's friend and as tame as might be expected with a man like him. 'I will drink with you tonight if you're there,' he said.

'Where?'

'Where else? The Neptune.'

Many of the old crew were there. Bargood came over and stroked my face. There was much good cheer. The captain sat at table with John Luff and me, and we talked about trade. There was a place for Will on the *Alde*, Bargood promised, whenever the navy let him go. 'He was safer with us, Margaret,' he said, patting my hand.

John Luff raised his mug. 'They'll never let him go. Let's drink to the fool. To Will, for keeping the seas clear of the French for us.' His eyes danced. We all drank but he downed his in one gulp and immediately called for another.

There was no doubt. Captain Bargood kept abreast of things. Will was out there at the mouth of the Channel, or even tossing like a top in the Bay of Biscay. Though I could laugh and drink along with all the rest my heart felt pierced, as if a great hatpin were impaling it. The *Alde* came into my mind, Will's cabin where we made love and dressed up in each other's clothes, the mewing of seagulls, the decks scrubbed spotless with sand and saltwater. When he was captain of the *Alde* he'd got home fairly regular. But now it seemed the King could take him and keep him as long as he wanted on black bloody decks with the rain pouring down and weevils to eat. Enough returned to tell us about it. Sometimes I wished he'd got shot like Jack Carr. At least then I'd have had him back safe.

'Margaret,' Luff said, suddenly gentle, 'don't fret. One of these days the fool will turn up at the door and expect a grand welcome after being so stupid as to get himself caught.'

'He'll have a free pardon.'

Luff laughed and made a crude sound with his lips.

Bargood's piggy eyes were merry. 'There's always a place for Will on one of my ships,' he declared, standing and patting us both on the shoulder as if we were children. He left, and I got tipsy so as not to feel the pain of the hatpin, and we sat and reminisced about the old days like a couple of ancient things, me and hard John Luff, who was at the stage of drinking that made him sentimental.

'By the way,' I asked, the two of us leaning together across the table, 'was that *you* came and scared Mrs Cobbold at our old house?'

'What?'

'Our old house, just after Christmas. Was it you hanging round in the garden?'

He laughed, a quick humourless laugh.

'You dare come near her again!' I shoved him.

He shoved me back.

'You'll get me dismissed!'

'Oh, Margaret,' he said, almost fondly, 'have another drink.'

I got home at two. Next day Mrs Cobbold asked me to bring Rowland to the sitting room. She liked to see him on the rug, pushing himself up on his two pudgy hands and looking around as if perpetually amazed by the world. I kneeled beside him.

'Well,' she said. 'Well, Margaret, haven't you got anything to say to me?'

'What, madam?'

She perched forward on her chair; her hair was pinned up in curls and a few locks strayed down around her throat and shoulders. She had that thin smile on, looking up from under lowered brows, indulgent. It riled me. 'Nothing you want to say, Margaret? Nothing at all?'

'I'm not sure what you mean, madam.'

She sighed and sat back. 'Margaret,' she said softly, shaking her head.

I hate it when people do that. Why can't they just out with things?

'What's the matter, madam?' I felt forced to ask.

She looked at her hands. 'What time did you come home last night?'

Aha.

'Near two, madam,' I said and looked her in the eye.

'And?' she said softly.

I don't know. Was there something of insolence about me? Listen you, you're only a girl, I couldn't help but think. Don't you speak to me as if you're my mother. Not that my mum would have ever been so coy about a telling-off, she'd just have clouted my head with the dish cloth.

'I'm sorry, madam,' I said steadily. 'I didn't realise you disapproved.'

'It's too late, Margaret,' she said, putting sternness in her face. She looked Grecian with her hair dressed up like that. 'How can you look after the children adequately if you've been up half the night?' she said.

'Sorry, madam.' I hauled Rowland up on to my knee, sniffing him discreetly. 'I don't need so much sleep, you see. I've always managed well on very little. It doesn't affect me, a late night don't. I forget it's not so for all.'

'There are certain things we have to make clear, Margaret,' she said, leaning forward, long arms twisted gracefully upon her knees. 'You're one of my best people, and I'm sure you know that. But I have to tell you that things have been said.'

'Said?' The old anger surged. Why couldn't people keep their fat mouths closed? Who said, who said? John Pride? Mrs Potts? Ursula? The gardener? Maybe the gardener, he saw me one night coming out of the Salutation.

'Don't look like that, Margaret,' she said sharply. 'I have to tell you. A neighbour made some comment to Master Thomas about the large number of sailors coming and going these days about St Margaret's Green. Now, I'm quite sure your friends are perfectly pleasant, but please understand that I cannot allow this house to be seen in a bad light. You do see that?'

'I see.'

'Now leave little Rowland with me for a spell. I want you to hear Sophia's Latin before tea.'

'Right, madam.'

'Of course you may have the occasional visitor in the kitchen; you know I'm not an unreasonable mistress. Learn to exercise restraint, that's all. Just don't let me hear talk about this house.'

She held her arms out for the boy.

'He wants changing, madam,' I said.

'Change him first then.' She smiled, all brisk and amiable again.

I hoisted him on to my shoulder and he sucked his fingers against my neck. I began to walk away but turned back and said, 'What about when Will Laud comes back?'

She looked perplexed. 'Oh!' she said as if I'd surprised her then, as if she wasn't thinking. 'Oh, but are you sure he's coming back?'

'Sure! Of course I'm sure!'

'Oh, I suppose he can visit.'

'Did you not know, madam,' I said coldly, 'that he and I are *very* good friends?'

She studied me for a moment, frowning. 'I had no idea,' she said as if she had a headache, 'that he meant so much to you. I'm sorry if I said anything wrong.' Then a thought hit her. 'You're not going to marry him, are you?'

'No, madam,' I said clearly. 'I have no inclination towards marriage and neither has he.'

She could make of it what she liked.

'Thank God for that,' she said lightly, smiling broadly to ease the situation. 'I'm about to lose Sary, I don't want to lose you too.'

'I'll change Roly.' I turned to go.

'Though I do think you could get someone better than him,' I heard her add, almost under her breath.

I spun round.

'Don't look like that,' she said, reddening. 'You're an intelligent woman. You have nice ways. He's too rough for you.' She smiled, thinking to sugar it with humour. I'd have none.

'Sorry to differ, madam.' I turned on my heel.

What does she know of Will and his like, or any of my sort for that matter? She said she loved the poor. She said she loved the sick and the needy, the widow and the orphan and the fallen woman, and she loved old Robinson Crusoe, and the little scruffs that came selling besoms and wooden pegs. But she never liked Will, and that wasn't fair. Will could've died saving their daft boy, and all he got was a measly guinea. The more I went over it in my mind the angrier I got. For days I fumed. She knew something was wrong. She was all charm and smiles as if nothing had happened, but she couldn't take back what she'd said. I wanted to kick something. A great weight of injustice lodged hard in my chest. And him out there could get shot any time, all for saving us from the French. *Why* should I smile all the time and act as if my own affairs are nothing? Imagine if it was one of *theirs* out at sea. Can only they feel?

That's how I thought.

47

She started picking on me. At first I thought I was imagining things but soon I could doubt it no longer.

'Margaret, are you sure he should be putting that in his mouth?'

'Margaret, are you sure he's warm enough in that?'

'There was rather a lot of noise coming up from the kitchen last night. I don't want to seem unreasonable, Margaret, but I don't remember erecting an inn sign outside my house.'

'Margaret, Sophia told me you took her and Harriet on to the Quay yesterday afternoon. Are you sure that's quite suitable?'

'Margaret, please! Would it hurt you to smile? I declare you're making miseries of us all. Why the long face?'

She'd look at me and sigh. 'What can we do with you, Margaret?' A friendly arm upon my shoulder. He could be dead for all I knew. To her, to all of them, it was as if Pompey had lost his bone and was sulking in his kennel. 'Cheer up now! It's not as bad as all that.'

I dare say.

I could take no more. She called me to her and heard me read. It was Marcus Aurelius; she always gave me things that were much too hard: *Time is like a river made up of the things which happen, and its current is strong*. When I'd done, she clapped her hands. 'That's lovely, Margaret!' she beamed. 'I am so pleased with your progress.'

'Thank you,' I said.

'Sit down,' she said. 'Let's have a little talk.'

I sat.

'What is it, Margaret?' she asked me, in a very kind manner.

'You know, madam,' I said. 'You know I've heard nothing from my friend. Of course I worry.'

'Yes, but Margaret,' she said earnestly, leaning forward and taking my hands in a firm grip, 'life has to go on. How many women in this town have a husband or a son or a brother at sea? How many, Margaret? Should we all stop and go into mourning?'

'It's not just that,' I said. I was hot. I could've cried. I'm going to say whatever I like, I thought, surprised at myself. Hark at her, giving me advice and her a chit of a thing. Sometimes, when she was all glittering and brittle in company, I felt old enough to be her mother. 'It's you.'

'Me?' She leaned back, amazed.

'I can't do anything right for you these days. You never used to complain but you moan about everything now.'

'I do not.'

'Yes, you do.'

'What are you talking about, Margaret?'

'Everything I do, you complain. You're always watching to see if I'm doing anything wrong.'

'Oh, don't be ridiculous!'

I'd said too much. Suddenly I thought: this is my job and it's a good one. Better than living in

Uncle Leader's cottage. Shut your stupid mouth, woman.

'It's not me,' she said, 'it's you. You're the one who's changed. You're the one walking round with a long face all the time. I'm just behaving as I've always behaved. Your mood's affecting your work. That's what's wrong.'

'Oh,' I said, 'is my work not good enough any more then?'

'Don't be silly,' she said. 'It's not as good as it used to be, if you want the plain truth, but I'm sure you know that. Listen.' She stood and walked briskly here and there. 'Mr Cobbold has connections in the Admiralty. If you give me the name of Will's ship I'm sure we can make a few enquiries and set your mind at ease. In the meantime I have to run a household and you're a part of it. Now – what are we to do?'

I stood too. 'Thank you, madam,' I said. 'It would be wonderful if you could find out anything for me.'

'I'll try. Now – to business. Here's what I've been thinking. You and I have had our differences but I don't want to lose you and that's a fact. I was thinking, maybe a change. Sary leaves us at the end of October. I want you to take her place.'

'Me? Cook?'

I didn't want it.

'It will mean an increase in salary naturally,' she swept on. 'It makes far more sense for you to take over the kitchen, you know the ropes already. I'll get another girl as under-nursemaid and Jane can have your position.'

She looked at me expectantly.

'Thank you very much, madam,' I said.

I'd have a bigger room. I'd be head over all the girls. I dropped her a curtsey and left in a daze. Jane was in the hall with Freddy and Georgie. 'I think I just heard Master Rowland,' she said.

'Like enough. It's time.'

He was standing in his cot, holding the bars, gurgling lustily and bobbing up and down. When I picked him up he was warm and heavy; his arms went round my neck and his mouth blew bubbles against my ear.

'There, little Roly-Pole,' I said, sniffing his silky fine hair, 'are you a hungry boy?'

Sweet thing. You won't be mine any more, I thought.

48

I missed him very much. I missed them all.

I was cock of the walk now and nicely provided for, thank you very much. I earned enough now to take something home to Dad and Ned once in a while. They were still living up by the heath. Dad was sanguine enough, hale and hearty; Ned was still shepherding and looking likely to do so for the rest of his days. I wondered about the continuation of us. There was Polly had James's two, Jim and Sam; and Dinah Parker had little Doll. Polly was married again to a fellow from Dunwich. Dinah passed herself as a widow and worked as a washerwoman in Bealings. Maybe

Charles would have a child still. His last letter, in July, I'd been able to read for myself. Dad and Ned were ever so impressed. Charles had left the army and had some sort of government post. He said he'd come home in a year or two when he'd saved a bit more money, but he loved India and would always want to go back. He had a pet monkey called Rice.

I never heard from Will. Mr Cobbold wrote a letter to Portsmouth like Mrs Cobbold said he would, but nothing came of it. The King was cruel to keep the men away.

49

More than a year passed. I turned thirty-three in March. Thirty-three! A very great age indeed. How had the river flowed so quickly? How many seasons had I seen change from the window of my room? The willows in spring, pale and fragile. Shaken by gales, lashed by the rain. Heavy with snow. Spring again, all awakening, and me a very great age. Time's march, faster with every passing year, frightened me. Would it *ever* bring him back? Suppose he was gone for ever? Dead. Met another. Loved another. Suppose he'd forgot me?

Never.

'Will Laud, I hate you,' I said aloud one night. The willows were silver. And I shook with rage too cold for tears.

I ruled the kitchen with total attention, saved them money, wasted nothing, kept the endless round of meals for all, three times a day, running along smooth as silk: dinner for the nursery and the parlour, dinner for the kitchen crew, dinner for their friends when they came – and they had so many friends, so many evenings full of music and clever people and fancy dress; and always a good hot supper for all who happened to be about the place, every single night, come what may. So what if it sometimes included loopy Jack Carr or Rube passing by with the news, and even on one or two occasions John Luff. The kitchen was mine now and I could do what I liked. I worked hard enough, didn't I? So what if nosy neighbours saw me coming out of the Neptune? Sometimes I had to get out of the place just to breathe new air, air that smelled of the river and ships; just to walk and walk and look at the boats, hoi polloi milling about the docks, foreign sailors, dark-skinned and restless, canny dogs scavenging rakishly, tough women with knowing eyes. I never did take much account of the differences in people, not so's it made that much of a difference anyway. That was my trouble. The Cobbolds or the life down the Neptune and the Salutation, it was all the same to me. I could knock along nicely with all kinds, but others couldn't.

I hardly ever saw Madam any more. The older children came into the kitchen now and then, William and Harriet, occasionally Sophia, tall and bonny as can be, outgrowing the green dress with pink roses her mother made; they liked to hang about and chat and poke their fingers into things and lick them. But the younger ones weren't allowed. Too dangerous. Oh, I had no illusions. She liked me, Mrs Cobbold did, she liked me very much, but what it boiled down to was she thought I was a bad influence. The kitchen was a way of promoting me and being nice to me while putting me at arm's length. I thought about this a lot. Had I done wrong? Not by my lights. I worked hard for the Cobbolds and they did right by me as a servant. I never meant them no harm, never. They were tolerant people. I'd have got the sack posthaste anywhere else, I suppose. It would just have been: No Callers, and no arguments. At least I'd have known where I stood, but they confused me. My mistress made me a friend. She gave me a great deal of freedom, in speech and in my comings and goings, far more than any employer before or since. She had me taught along with her own family. But when my real life came calling, she dropped me. And I was hurt. And I thought, I'm going to have to leave here if Will comes back. Him coming round here all the time, that simply couldn't be. So when I saw her in those days, and it was little enough, I was just the servant. Not surly – she said I was surly, but no, I was not – I was only behaving formally, like a servant, like I was supposed to behave. It was all right for her, you see. She could change as she wanted, be my good friend or walk past without even seeing me when she was with proper people. She didn't mean any harm by it. But I got confused as to how I should be, and I hated that I had to hide my feelings for fear of being scolded.

'Oh do buck up, Margaret, please! You're very strange these days. You always seem miles away.'

'I am.'

My heart's broken, I felt like saying. Do you know what it's like, the months dragging by and by and by, crawling? I think he's dead. How am I supposed to look?

Far away? I was in a million places, on a ship at sea, bleeding on a deck, in my own shop in Brandeston, my own mistress and able to act just as I pleased. And I was back home, young again, and all my brothers were still alive, and Sue and Mum; and I was riding dear old Dandy bareback down to the stream to drink. Thinking it before her now, called once more to answer for myself, I almost cried.

'I wish I didn't have to say this,' she said. 'Things have gone missing.'

'What things?'

'Things from the stores,' she said. 'A couple of loaves. A pot of meat.'

'Oh, the pot of meat,' I said. 'I know about that. I gave it to a friend of mine, I didn't think anyone would mind. It was about to turn, and no one here wanted it. It's all right, madam, it was for the kitchen staff, not the household.'

'I don't care who it was for,' she said. 'Was it accounted for?'

'Accounted for?'

'Mrs Potts has to keep the accounts. How can she do that if the stores go willy-nilly?'

'Madam, I'm not sure I understand you,' I said. 'Am I not to dispose of perishables in a way I see fit without consulting Mrs Potts?'

‘What about the loaves?’ Her brow was stern.

I drew myself up straight, looking her hard in the eye. ‘I gave one loaf to a beggar, madam,’ I said, ‘for his family. It was stale. The other one I have no knowledge of.’

Actually I’d given the potted meat to a penniless fellow from the Neptune who was shipping on board a freighter bound for Holland next day on Will’s old route. The bread had gone to another, setting off for Harwich with nothing but hope and pride. As for the second loaf, a horrible suspicion was creeping in. John Luff had been around two nights ago.

‘Look,’ she said, ‘I’ll say this once. I’ll have no more sailors in the kitchen. I’ve been more than tolerant, Margaret, but enough’s enough. I’ve got my children to think about, don’t you forget, and I’m sorry to say that I place their welfare before your feelings every time, Margaret.’

She had worked herself into as angry a state as I’d ever seen her in. There was no arguing.

‘Of course, madam,’ I said, ‘I understand, madam,’ and walked off without a curtsey. Why the hell should I curtsey? All this about loving the poor and needy, and here was me not allowed to help out my friends. It was all froth, I thought. Froth. I’d kill bloody Luff when I saw him, him and his light fingers, getting me in trouble. Him and who else? So when, as I was supping leftover soup with Ursula and the new girl a few nights later, nine o’clock or so, I heard his voice outside the kitchen door, my temper flew up and I ran to the door and threw it open and called out into the darkness: ‘Don’t you dare come round here no more, John Luff! I know what you're about.'

A laugh answered. John Luff's deep melodic laugh like the devil in the darkness. But it was Will stepped into the light cast by the door, a rough old leather bag slung over one shoulder, a great smile like a sunburst over his face. Drunk as a hog. It was a shock, a big stab in the heart.

'You swine,' I cried, bursting into tears. 'Why have you never sent word?'

He burst out laughing and made a grab at me. He was mad. His face, I mean, was changed. My heart was beating very hard and sick and some of it was fear. He was changed. I took him by the shoulders and shook him furiously. 'Are you back for good or what?' I kissed him, hard and angry.

'How she welcomes me!' he laughed. 'Yes, I'm back for good. I got honourable discharge, Pegs. Me!'

John Luff hovered on the path. I wanted him to go away. Will and I hung close together.

'Can we come in, Peggy?' he asked.

'No!' I said. 'You're getting me in trouble.'

They came in anyway. The new girl, a large, shy creature with a tame air, was all eyes. Will sat down in John Pride's chair next to the fire. His hair was long and shaggy. I brought a chair over and sat by him, staring into his face. His eyes were naked in a way I'd never seen, dancing and merry and free, but not happy. Then he looked at me in the old strange way, a look like a cut, and put up his hand to touch my face. A very gentle touch.

Luff was helping himself to soup, making a mess. I looked at Ursula, who raised her eyebrows. She wouldn't tell, but if Mrs Potts came in, or if the girl said something.

'Drink your soup quick, John,' I said. 'We'll take a walk, we three.'

Will leaned from his chair and crushed me. He smelled wonderful, a dear sweet mixture of salt marsh and tar and long-worn clothes. 'Peggy, Peggy,' he said, 'we'll have a good time now, mawther.'

'Tell him to hurry up,' I said. 'I could lose my position.'

'No, surely, she won't mind, the missis, she gave me a guinea. She won't mind if it's me.'

'It's not you,' I said, 'it's him.'

'John. He's all right, aren't you, John?'

Luff, stiff and straight, tight as a knot, was drinking straight from the ladle and getting it down the front of his dirty coat.

'Up!' I said, taking charge the way I used to do with the children. 'Come! John, we're going. Ursula, I won't be late. Just tamp the fire before you go up.'

When Will stood up I realised how ridiculously drunk he was. He swayed and grinned like an idiot. When he walked he lurched and frightened the maid. I saw how that large timid girl must have seen him; one part beauty to two parts gargoyle. His eyes popped. His nostrils flared. The cruel lines of his lower face had deepened, scoring themselves in. His foolness was about him like a radiance. To me it was as if he was calling out for shelter. But I suppose by now he looked ugly to some. I saw him as he'd always been. That boy. Lovely sweet boy. I took him and propelled him to the door. He kissed his fingers to the room. I pushed him out.

'John! Now!' My tone brooked no complaint.

On the pavement I drew them both together and scolded them in a whisper. 'Drunk like this! It's not fair!'

'Pegs,' Will cajoled, nuzzling my neck, 'can a man home from bleeding hell not have a drink?'

'Ssh!'

Luff came very close to me and looked me in the eye with steady controlled mirth. Then he pushed me. Quite hard on the shoulder.

'What?' I gasped.

He pushed me again. 'Leave him alone, you bitch,' he said, and his eyes never changed. 'See what I could do with this fist?'

'Don't you ever dare speak to me like that!'

'John, John.' Will grabbed his arm. 'None of it!'

I shoved them down towards the cow-keeper's yard. 'If you ever dare threaten me again, John Luff, I'll kill you,' I said.

'You're not his mother,' Luff said, steady as ever. 'He can drink if he wants.'

'Foul your own nest, John. Leave mine alone.'

'Dear Christ!' Will reeled against the cow-keeper's gate, it folded open and he fell through into the yard and went down on one knee in a heap. 'Can't you agree, you two? Here we're all met together and we could be dead. Soon will be. God sake, friends!'

Luff put his hands under Will's armpits and pulled him up. 'Come on, man,' he said, brushing at Will's shoulders. He had to reach up a little to do so. 'Let's go to the Salutation.' And there he was turning Will around. I lost my temper.

'Why are you here anyway?' I asked John. 'This is me and Will's reunion. Why are you here? You should know better. Just go away.'

He raised his eyebrows as if I was an idiot. I was too angry to be scared. Will stepped in front of me and put his arms round me, all soft. 'Take no notice of John, Pegs,' he said. 'He's all right, aren't you, John?'

'I'm very fine,' John said. 'Come to the Salutation.'

But as we surged through the gate and back on to the pavement, there was someone standing on the other side of the Green watching us.

'Have you got any money on you, Pegs?' asked Will.

It was strange wanting to hit him and yet being overjoyed at the same time. It was like twin fountains spurting to the sky.

'Money,' I said, 'no, I haven't. Where's yours?'

'What, my money?' He started picking through his pockets.

'What's in your bag?'

'She's after your money.' John laughed.

'My clothes,' Will said.

'What about the money?' I said. 'The money you were supposed to be bringing back? Your discharge money? You wrote.'

'There wasn't as much as I thought,' he said.

I saw my shop in Brandeston rise like smoke to the heavens and vanish.

I stood back. 'You've drunk it, haven't you?' I said. 'The pair of you. You've drunk the bloody lot.'

John gave a great bellow of laughter, a huge

insulting knuckle-headed roar that broke my dam. I hit him hard on the side of the head.

Well, you could see that she couldn't keep me after that. All the neighbours looked out of their windows or stood at their front doors to see the brawl. Everyone heard the bawling and shouting and watched the Cobbolds' cook and a drunken sailor like two fighting cocks trying to get at one another with their claws, while an even drunker sailor tried to get between them and ended up engaging them in a stupid triple dance that skittered this way and that on the pavement. I was knocked about a bit by Luff, I suppose, but I got in a knock or two myself.

'Friends!' cried Will, panting between us. 'Friends!'

Then there was a convergence upon us of good outraged citizens, whereupon Will and Luff melted away into the night, running down into the town like shadows; and I of course was left behind to face my worried and deeply embarrassed employers. They were fair with me, I think. Their first concern was for my well-being.

'Did anyone hurt you, Margaret? Should you like to see Dr Stebbing?'

'Not at all,' I said. 'I am no more than shaken.'

He'd left bruises on my shoulder and arm but nowhere else. Big blue bruises that went on changing colours for days.

Their second concern was to call in the Justices of the Peace. They were there first thing in the morning, scotching any plans I had for running down into town on the first pretext. There were three of them. I remembered all I'd heard about

JPs. Everyone knew they were the biggest thieves of the lot, Will always said. I had to give a deposition but I wouldn't tell them anything. They were just sailors, I said, I didn't know their names. They'd had too much to drink. Ursula and the girl never said a word. I never got to thank them for it, because the third concern of my employers was to inform me I was finished, only they didn't say it like that. She said she was very sorry. She hated having to do it. 'What you need,' she said, 'is a change. You're a restless spirit, Margaret, and I don't think we can manage you at the moment. Here's what I think you should do. I'd like you to leave by the end of the week. Don't worry, I'll pay you till the end of the month. You can go to your father's for a while, or one of your uncles. Think very carefully about your future. There may still be a place here on my staff at some point in the future, in spite of last night's unpleasantness, but only as long as you're prepared to abide by the rules of the house. Do you understand?'

She was not putting me off completely.

'Think about it. Come and see me in a couple of months,' she said.

I didn't wait for the end of the week. It was too awful. I asked if I could leave at once, said I was sure Ursula could manage, that the new girl was very good. She seemed relieved, I thought. 'Of course,' she said, 'if that's what you really want. Come and see me in the drawing room before you go.'

There didn't seem to be any question of me taking a formal leave of the family. Dad's or Uncle Leader's? I thought as I threw my things together.

Neither. I would go to Will, what else could I do? Someone had to look after him, and it couldn't be John Luff. *He* wasn't having him. When I paused outside the drawing room, I heard William: 'You can't do that!' he cried. 'You just can't!' I saw him, his blunt young face in profile. He was eighteen now, losing his gawkiness.

I couldn't see her.

'I know it's dreadful, William, but what else can I do? Your father's had to go about speaking to all the neighbours and personally apologising for her behaviour.'

She sounded truly upset.

I coughed and rapped on the door.

'You can't go, Margaret,' William said.

'Oh, it's all fine, Master William.' I smiled. 'Madam's right, I could do with a change.'

Now it was all over and I was leaving, I wasn't angry with her any more. She'd done the best she could by me according to her lights, what more can anyone do? I felt sorry for her at that moment, seeing tears in William's eyes. I was more like the mother he'd lost than she was, and she knew it. Of course I was, I was closer to the right age than she was.

She gave me a book as a keepsake. A little one, just a single poem, with funny pictures. It was one she'd had published, a proper book with proper binding, and it was about a mince pie. By Carolina Petty Pasty, it said. That was her, she said. In the front she'd signed herself several times in a graceful flowing hand. Elizabeth Knipe. Eliza Clarke. All her names. And I left her in friendship, she feeling bad.

50

So I was back at the Widow Syers', me and Will in a room up the back stairs, but not for long. We got by. Will's dad had died while he was away, but that old reprobate had not left a thing. Still, with the money the Cobbolds paid me off with, and a bit of help from Bargood, we went up to Aldeburgh where the old *Alde* was fitting out at Uncle Jack's boatyard.

For two years it was almost like the old days, but for the difference in Will. Something of death had rubbed off on him – him and many another. The Three Mariners at Slaughden Quay was full of fighters and madmen, and Will was at home with them. He'd developed a fondness for teasing death. Whenever he came back from a run with Luff and Rube, there were tales to turn my blood. I saw old Robin's fierce face, the Orwell shingle: 'Will Laud, you are a hell-born babe.' His ship was fast like a good horse and made him invulnerable, his daring became a thing talked about in the inns and taverns. Daring, they said, but actually it was madness. Sometimes, Rube said, he walked out along the jib-boom and talked to the sea as if he was having a conversation with it. He could have gone straight about now, but there was no going straight any more for Will after the war, there never had been really, I suppose. But if ever there was a time he could have, this was it, with his free discharge and certificate of good character in the service. 'I'm a respectable man now,' he sometimes said and laughed at the very idea.

When he was not on a run he worked in his old line with Uncle Jack. Luff was constantly hanging round. They were always waiting for a word from Bargood, for another run, another sniff of adventure, but trade was bad because of the war. There was not much money. As for me, I liked Aldeburgh well enough but I knew I'd have to make my own way. I tried this and that, stayed at Uncle Leader's once when the lads were away on a long trip Dutch-side, but it was not a success. Brandeston just made me restless. I wanted my shop when I was there. I knew exactly the spot where I would have had it. I used to see it there, and think about its set-out; and from there my mind would wander far over to Amsterdam and a tavern on the sea front, and from there to the open sea, and me and Will upon the fore deck.

It was in Brandeston I got word of the great event of those two years, Noller's Wagon bringing news that Charles was back. Straight away Uncle Leader took me to Dad's in the wagon. We were agog all the way, but when we arrived it was strange. Charles was not my old Charles any more, but a stiff stranger, a much older person, dark-skinned and serious and a little intimidating. His eyes did not smile. We were all shy. We were all so much older, so much changed. I wanted to know all about India and his travels, but he was never a talker, was he? Except sometimes after drinking with Will Laud. 'Will's doing very well,' I told him. 'He's working in his uncle's boatyard.' Charles smiled but said nothing. When he was last here Mum was alive, and Robert and James. We sat with strong absences in that tiny house of Dad and Ned's, and I wondered what had happened to my family, that we were so broken up.

He was on business but would say nothing about it, only that he had to go to London and thence to Portsmouth where he would take ship once more – he seemed not entirely sure as to where – but the journey would pitch up in India in the end. He was not married. He had no children.

He stayed two days. He felt awkward too. On the second day he went to the churchyard to visit Mum and Sue. He was sad to find the old sexton gone. When he left us, I remembered I had not told him I could read and write now, like him; so I ran after him along the lane and grabbed his arm.

'I can read and write now, Charles,' I said. 'Let's always keep in touch.'

'Where will you be, Peggy?' he asked. 'At Uncle Leader's?'

I had not much idea where I would be. 'You can always send here for me,' I said.

We kissed, and he was off, a tall black figure retreating over the heath, loping, gone.

I did not go back to my uncle's. I was sick of being short of money. I walked down into Ipswich next day and knocked on the Cobbolds' door.

'Knock me down,' said John Pride. 'Look who it ain't.'

'Is she in?'

'She's having a lie-down,' he said, but just then she appeared, crumple-faced, peering over the banister. 'Margaret?' she cried. *'Margaret!'* and came running down with her gown loose and embraced me like a long-lost sister. 'All this time and not a word!' she said. 'What have you been doing?'

'I've been ill,' I said. It was easier than going into detail. 'I've been at my uncle's. But now I'm looking for a position again.'

She'd take me again, I saw that. She took me on trial, if I could only give her to understand that there'd be no more sailors, helping where I could, mainly in the nursery; all that time I was good as gold, never went near an inn, lived like a saint, till the under-cook left and I was back in the kitchen. It wasn't what I'd wanted. I'd much rather the nursery; particularly as there was another baby, not hers but Master John's, a married man now and staying in his old quarters with his wife while his own house was got ready 'Me!' Mrs Cobbold said. 'A grandmother!' She was only thirty. For a while – maybe three months, not more – things were good. Everyone was pleased to see me. William was a man, Sophia was turning into a swan, Henry Gallant was a lanky boy of five or six, and Rowland was running about on great sturdy legs. Miss Flowers was still there, and Mrs Potts of course – *she'd* only leave in her coffin. Ursula and Jane Wells had gone, and there was a new nursemaid, pleasant enough. George Teager's deafness had become as near total as made no difference. He was useless as a coachman if the truth were told, but they kept him on out of charity still, in his old room over the stable, where he could sleep with the comforting horse-smell of his best days. I loved the stable. Strawberry Crop remembered me, and there was a magnificent new hunter, a tall grey by the name of Rochford. Often I strolled down there with this new big Rowland, lifting him up to pat the horses' great warm noses. How much does a horse like this cost to buy? I thought. A hundred guineas? That would be cheap. They had a new man helping George. I envied him. In a different world, I thought, I could have done this, spent my life in a stable and lived with horses. I'd have loved that. It's what I would have done if I'd been a lad. You could do far worse than George Teager's life, I thought, living up there and waking in the night from time to time and hearing the sleepy horse-sounds of the night.

51

It didn't work out. She said my work got sloppy. She said I was letting myself go. Hoity-toity. As far as I was concerned, I was just the same as ever. Trouble was, she knew me better now. Could I change? So completely and still be Margaret? It wasn't the sailors this time, at least as far as having them come round the house was concerned, because they never did. I made sure of that. But when Will came back and lodged himself at the Neptune, what should I have done? Cut him off? I could still go out, couldn't I? If I passed an old friend in the street, what was I to do? Look the other way? Why should I do that?

I met the Widow Syers one day as I was walking down to town with Harriet and Ann. Poor old soul, the state of her! She was old when I was a child. She'd grown stark and skinny and fierce, and her hair was a wicked nest, her gown cut low in front to show a crazed and cracked expanse of ancient flesh, flat and ruddy and freckled. 'Oh, aren't these young ladies lovely?' she crooned at the girls, reeking gin and showing her grey stubs of teeth. 'Aren't these just the most sweetest little darlings? Very dainty, ain't they?' The girls smiled wildly. I couldn't help it if I knew these kinds of people, I always had, I couldn't change that. I wasn't going to get like some of these servants in big houses, greater snobs than their masters. Some of them, you'd think it was their own arses getting wiped.

I got my final warning when I was sick on the morning of one of their garden parties. A very grand occasion it was, with a band playing under the willows, and a troupe of green-clad dancers on the lawn. I'd been up baking since five. At eight I started feeling funny. I think it was some oysters I'd eaten the night before with Will and Rube outside the Neptune. Suddenly I had to run. Mrs Potts had to take over from me even though she had so much else to do, and Miss Flowers and the nursemaid had to help out with the jellies. I took to my room and was deathly sick.

No one came to see me because there was no one to spare, but I was glad of that. I hate fuss when I'm sick. When I was all spent and finished,

Mrs Potts popped her head in, tut-tutted and set about emptying the bowl. Later, when everyone had gone and the house was quietening down, Mrs Cobbold came to see me.

'How are you feeling, Margaret?'

'Terrible,' I said. I wanted her to go away

'Do you know what caused this?' she asked, sitting down on the side of the bed.

'Oysters.' Saying the word almost made me heave again.

'Oysters,' she repeated thoughtfully.

Next day when I was up and about, she said she knew I'd been drinking the night before. She knew I'd not been in the house at midnight because she'd checked. This would not do.

'Please don't compel me to dismiss you again, Margaret,' she said sorrowfully. Pointless to say she was wrong. I don't know, maybe the beer did have something to do with it but without the oysters I'd have got away with it, I'm sure. Who knows? What matter? It could never have lasted. One night I know I would have rebelled; would have brought Will into the kitchen and served him the leftovers along with whatever delicacies had returned from the dinner table. I may even have gone down to the cellar and got a decent bottle of wine. Didn't he save the son of the house? Hadn't he a right to warm himself now and then by their kitchen fire?

But it didn't get to that. It was a matter of language in the end. The cow-keeper's boy left the gate open and a massive black bull got out of the yard and walked on the Green. The nurse had only brought the babies in five minutes earlier.

When I put my head out from the porch and saw the cowman's silly boy standing there with his mouth open, picking his nose and doing nothing, I told him to get the bloody thing in at once before it killed someone. He didn't like my tone.

'Fuck off, mawther,' he said.

Of course no one heard him say that. Everyone heard what I shrieked back at him though. It echoed round the Green and bounced off the noble front of St Margaret's Church, reaching the ears of the Cobbolds, who at that moment were assembling in the drawing room with a few select guests for afternoon tea. I agree: such words should not have to be listened to by young ladies. Not to mention a city councillor and a JP and a high-ranking officer of the Suffolk Militia and his sensitive wife. It was too much. She paid me off till the end of the month and that was that. Will was furious.

'So much for them!' he raged. 'You're mad, Pegs. They never gave a damn about you. You were a jester. Some little rag they could laugh about. In the end you're nothing to them.'

'What did you expect, Will?'

'Nothing. Nothing at all from any of their sort. More fool you.'

I wasn't bothered, I'd expected nothing else. Of course I couldn't work for her any longer, but she still liked me. So did they all in spite of themselves, and I know why. Because I saw no differences in them. No, I didn't. I saw no differences in them and us and the whole bloody lot. See them as babies, they're all the same, naked puling things brought into this world which is so cruel. And it *is* cruel. Sometimes I've given up, put down my head and, making no sound, moaned like the devil, like a hungry ghost, a sorrowing ghost. Just like a little thing moaning along against all of that pain.

After that I really was ill, and I couldn't work. I don't know what it was, just some very big tiredness, I think. I went up to Will's sister's at Sudbourne. Lucy dragged up Will some rough and ready way, but did him some service, I always think, because the man had good in him, no matter what they say. I heard strange things in time. That he was a murderer. Will was no murderer. That he was mad and wild and was going to get himself killed. That he was a terrible bad man. Well, he wasn't, never to me.

Lucy had married Bill Keeley the shepherd and they had a cottage on the edge of the salt marsh. Always we heard the whistling of the curlew. We had no money; trade was bad. Will came. We slept in the shed, over the sheep, and every morning Bill Keeley would drive his flock out on to the marsh. A letter came from Ned to say Dad's back was bad. Will worked for Uncle Jack and gave me some money. I sent it to Dad. Night and day the salt marsh moaned and brooded outside. Birds called, their voices in the dark lonesome and pining. We knocked on fine with Lucy and Bill. Lucy was heavy and fair, smoked incessantly and spoke like a man. Bill was round and tough and bluff, and hated the revenue men. They were hard people who didn't say a lot, but they loved Will; so they loved me too because I was with him. The four of us lived quietly as the weather grew wilder and stormier. There were many days we scarcely went out. The world whirled madly beyond the windows of the cottage, and time passed strangely disregarded, and we became poorer and poorer and poorer, and there was no trade, and no sign or word from Bargood, and sometimes we were freezing and stayed in bed all day, me and Will wrapped up tight together against the winter cold.

When spring arrived at last, we were so out-at-heels we'd forgotten there was any other way; and all the world was salt marsh and sounding sea and swollen sky. Then Uncle Jack died and left the boatyard to Will.

52

He set off on a bright windy May morning for Aldeburgh. He was gone three days, and on the fourth two sailors came by and told us he was laid up in his uncle's house with a bloody wound. John Luff had cut him down crossing Sudbourne Heath. I set off at once.

'I've been trepanned, Pegs,' he grinned when I walked in. A bandage was wrapped round his head. He was very pale.

'That man's mad,' I said. 'He's dangerous, Will. Where did he cut you?'

It was not a great wound. A long sword-slash ran diagonally to the hip from just under his left collarbone, but it had bled a lot, and the surgeon had put in stitches. Then he'd trepanned Will to ease the brain, which was fevered and full to bursting. 'I feel most light about the brain now,' Will said, lifting the bandage to show me the scar.

I'm not saying it was all John's fault. Too much drink and stupidity, that's what happened, and that was both of them. But Luff went too far this time. They'd fallen in at the Mariner's Compass in Orford, got unholy drunk in the course of an afternoon and a long evening, and in their cups agreed a plan for Will to sell up his uncle's house and business and quit England for ever for America. The three of us would go, me, Will and Luff. They'd been coming over Sudbourne Heath to tell me the great news, had just entered Gap Lane, when a moment of sanity was visited on Will.

'She'll never agree,' he said.

'Make her', was John's advice. I could imagine his sneer. And at that moment Will realised America was not for him and that he never really had intended to go. When he tried to explain this, John flew in one of his terrible quiet rages and drew his sword. So did Will. Round the fools circled and goaded each other unsteadily till a full fight broke out and Will's sword was broken. John chased him towards the marshes and cut him, thumped him in the face, stole his beautiful French watch and ran away. Will couldn't remember how he got to Aldeburgh. First thing he knew he was in his uncle's house and the surgeon was threading his needle.

'Is Luff mad?' I asked.

'He's always been mad.' Will smiled weakly. 'That's well known.' He was going through a kind of grief for his old friend.

Of course he'd always been mad, but he'd been like a barely tame dog you knew would never turn on you. But he'd turned. Where was he? Would he step out of the darkness one night with a knife?

We stayed in Uncle Jack's house a week or so, talking about what we'd do now there was money. Suddenly there were possibilities. The shop in Brandeston. Holland. America. America was too far for me. 'I could do what Bargood did,' Will said. 'Be a big man. Carry on in the timber trade and have boats going out.' But he kept coming back to Amsterdam. 'You'd like Amsterdam,' he said, 'I know you would. Me and you in Amsterdam, Pegs!'

Yes.

'A whole new life with this money,' he said. 'I'll sell up and first we'll go to London. We'll buy new clothes and go on the rant. I know people. And then we'll sail from there to Holland.'

Adventure. Yes.

'Tell you what we could do – we could get an alehouse in Amsterdam.'

Oh yes, better than a shop!

And Will would go to sea sometimes.

'But would John Luff turn up?' I asked.

'He's set on America,' said Will. 'That's where he'll go.'

'Why did he take your watch, do you think?'

'As a keepsake,' said Will.

53

In May the mackerel boats were coming up the Orwell. Robinson Crusoe was out and about, rattling his bones. I was at my dad's and Will was in London finding a place for us to stay. The boatyard was sold; we'd kissed Aldeburgh goodbye.

A boy came from the Widow Syers' and said there was a letter, so I packed myself up and off into Ipswich all ready to take the coach at a moment's notice, and there in the widow's kitchen was a scrawled note from Will: *Come immediately. Am in Newgate. Bring money the Man in the Moon Wapping. Am stuck in hell you must come and get me out. Sixty guineas to free me. Will pay all back when out. Had a knock on the head. Come immediately. Boat sails Holland late 25 May. COME NOW.*

Oh God, what's he got into now? In Newgate? That terrible place. Oh God. Bring money? What money? *He's* got the money All I had I gave my dad. What's he done with it?

I could have strangled him. He'd never grow up and be a man. Sixty guineas? Why do I bother? Sixty guineas?

The widow set about making tea, shaking her woolly head. 'Sounds like trouble. I wouldn't go near if I were you,' she said. 'If you ask me I think he's had his time. Leave him to stew.'

'I think you're right,' I said. I dared think it.

'Where does he think I'm going to get sixty

guineas from?'

'Well, you can't, dear, it's impossible. Perhaps he imagines you can borrow it. Who do you know might have that kind of money?'

Crazily, Mrs Cobbold came into my mind. The very idea of trying to explain a thing like this to her! She'd probably think it a good thing he was in Newgate. Then I thought of Bargood. Far better. Bargood liked Will, he'd hate to think of him stuck in that place.

The widow placed the tea in my hands, patting them as if I was a child. 'The top front's free,' she said. 'Kip there tonight if you want.'

After my tea and some of the thin brown broth she was simmering up for her lads, I went looking for Bargood, but he was nowhere to be found. Someone said they thought he was off on some northern business. I went to bed that night and lay listening to the boys in the kitchen keeping the widow's old age sweet with their amiable carousing. I knew I'd never sleep. All I could think of was Will lying in Newgate, on straw I imagined. What had he done? Where was the money? He said he could pay it back. The money must be somewhere he couldn't get at it and he needed me to fetch it. Maybe it was at this Man in the Moon place in Wapping. Next morning I enquired, but there was no London coach that day. I walked up and down the waterfront, asking here and there if anyone knew anything of Captain Bargood, if anyone knew of a wagon or anything at all going to London I could beg a ride on. Nothing. I even walked several times in the direction of St Margaret's Green and each time turned away before reaching it. At last, sick and tired and angry, not just with him but with me for not just washing my hands of him, I went deep into the park and sat down under a tree. There were deer grazing a little distance away. Lovely creatures, lovelier than horses in their way. There were eight or nine fallow youngsters and a magnificent stag who faced me from afar with regal interest and no fear. You couldn't possibly ride a stag. The idea of a wild thing like that letting you mount was unimaginable. And yet what a dream! I lay down on my back and closed my eyes. Sunlight through the leaves flickered over my darkened vision. I dreamed myself drifting over to where the big stag waited, watching me approach. I dreamed that he stayed for me and let me stroke his face, then stood patiently while I climbed on a stump and mounted. And we rode all the way to London swifter than the wind.

When I woke up I had an inkling of what I might do. I went down to the Neptune and filled myself up with a fine chowder, then back to the Widow Syers' and up to rest, saying I had a sick headache. When I lay down on the bed and closed my eyes, I drifted between sleep and waking, floating side to side like a feather. The inkling stayed outside, tapping at the window. At ten I went down and found the kitchen full of sailors. The widow was knocking back gin. I joined her, making them give up a seat for me by the fire. They were young lads, wet behind the ears, smooth and pretty and graceless. One or two could have been my sons. They filled a cup for me, and we drank an hour or two and were merry. The best times of my life have been simple times like this, food and drink and company, a good fire, laughter. Rough sorts. The Cobbolds would have saved me from rough sorts, but I didn't want saving. I loved these lads. At midnight I slipped out into the lobby and silently quit the house. I walked about a bit, away from the crowded parts of town where the taverns still hummed, turned my face towards the darkness where the fields began. It was a fine night. The sky was bright, stars appearing between the great inky masses of cloud slowly scudding westward.

Sixty guineas. A hundred guineas for a horse.

I knew I could never come back. I had in my pocket thirty shillings, all I had left. My brain felt clear and sharp. 'I'll do it,' I said out loud, turned and walked smartly back to the widow's and asked for a pair of scissors. I said I just wanted to mend a little hole in my stocking before I went to bed, took the scissors with me up to the room and there cut off my hair just under the ear. I had no mirror. Was I now a man? I laughed. All the time it was there, whispering, a little voice sweetly whispering, disturbing the tiny hairs in the approaches of my ears: *They hang you. Hang you by the throat, make you dance; life's horrible.*

Why live if not to die? A long time since, I chose risk.

I got over a low wall at the end of the Cobbolds' garden, then over the lawn to the stable yard. Pompey, my dear, why did you not bark and rouse the household and have them all rush and scold me, bring many tears and terrible things, but nothing so terrible as what really happened. For Pompey betrayed me with his slapping tail and soft eye. He let me through to where Crop and Rochford slept standing, warmly mouthing the air with their big soft lips. The door was locked but the wicket at the side by the muck-bin was unhanked. It was easy to nip in there. I stood a moment in the dark inside, listening. The sound of a great beast slowly moving. George Teager snoring upstairs. I knew where everything was. I found the lantern, lit it and placed it on the bottom stair, then eased back the bolt and unlocked the stable door. I was not afraid. George Teager was deaf as a post. 'Good Rochford, good boy,' I whispered. The big grey shifted his feet. Crop nudged me with his nose. 'Hello, my Crop,' I said. 'Are you the one? Are you ready for a ride?' Crop threw up his head. It was time to turn myself into a groom, so I took the lantern and tiptoed upstairs. George was fast asleep, snoring gently and steadily, a motionless lump on his cot under the roof beam. I set the lantern down on the table alongside the remains of his supper: a few crumbs of bread, cheese rinds, scattered egg shells and an empty tankard. His coachman's livery was laid across the back of a chair but his everyday stable clothes – breeches, jacket, shirt – had been tossed in a heap on the floor. I had to search for the boots. One was under the bed, the other in a corner of the room. I bundled everything up, once more took up the lantern and tiptoed back down. Two minutes later I was a man. St Margaret's clock was striking one. He was small, George Teager, the breeches were a little short for me, but they'd do. The boots fit well. The new groom's hat, hanging on a peg, soon covered my ragged hair. My own clothes I rolled up and stuffed into a seedbox, shoved as far back as I could under a manger and overlaid with straw. Then it was saddle and bridle on Crop, straw on his feet to mute the ring of hooves in the stable yard, out into the meadow and on to the road.

The Man in the Moon

54

I walked him past the front of the house. At the end of the Green I climbed upon a step to mount. His ears were cropped, hence the name, but the stumps of them quivered as I dropped lightly into the saddle. He was the most beautiful horse I ever rode without a doubt, a most tall and graceful strawberry roan coach horse, high stepping and full of spirit, proud like the stag in the park, yet gentle. His tail was cropped like his ears, but his mane flowed free. Six years old and strong as a lion, he, like me, was under an enchantment. We trotted briskly through town with straw shedding from his feet. The stirrups troubled me so I slowed him and kicked loose of them, dragged them up and crossed them over the saddle in front of me. When we got on to the London road, his head flew up; when he smelled open country his great muscles lurched and we went into a gallop. It was my dream again.

The great ride of Margaret Catchpole. That's what they would say in after time. That other ride, my wild descent of Bishop's Hill to fetch Dr Stebbing, paled in comparison, and yet I've thought since that in some strange way the second could never have happened without the first. If I had never furthered my acquaintance with the doctor in such a way, I never would have gone with his letter to the Cobbolds, never laid eyes on strawberry Crop nor sailed mile after glorious mile through this fine blowy night, a whispering, billowy place of indigo cloud flowing like a stream over the running moon.

We saw no one for miles. That horse was running for joy. He was a coach horse, a beast accustomed to standing between the shafts and ambling here and there in town. I gave him his head. There was no skill in riding him, no matter what they say, which is not to say that I had none. Only that he carried me so perfectly I had no need of it. My urgency infected him. Like the clouds we streamed; we soared, we clawed up the dark road before us.

Just before Colchester I saw the light of a coach advancing. I gave him my heels; we'd fly so fast we'd be invisible. My breeches were too short, they'd ridden up and showed my stockings as far as the knee. What must I look like? Someone's groom? I sat proud, George Teager's stick in my hand, resting on my horse's neck. We passed the coach at a steady gallop and I raised my hat. It was dark, who knows what I seemed to be. The coach had lanterns swinging front and back, cutting the darkness. We rode on. Time vanished.

Hours.

I had no idea how far it was to morning.

We had slowed to a luxurious canter and had been peacefully ploughing the night thus for some time when the light of an inn sprang upon us from the dark roadside, demanding that we stop. I rode into the yard and dismounted, shaking down my breeches till they reached my ankles once more. No one was around apart from a sleepy ostler's boy, who yawned as he took the reins from me. 'Give him a quick rub-down,' I said, keeping my voice low, 'and a feed of oats. I'll be on my way in half an hour.' And I went in to find the place deserted except for two men silently drinking together, and an old woman in an old-fashioned cap, sitting next to the fire with a big pile of socks to be darned. She put by her mending, standing and enquiring with a look what I wanted. 'Brandy,' I said, taking a seat at one of the tables. Without a doubt, brandy for warmth and strength and bravery. And water. She had some nice buttery biscuits, she said, if I'd care for some. I ate five.

'Have you come far, sir?' she asked.

'Only from Colchester.'

She nodded.

I asked the time. 'It struck five not long since, sir,' she said, resuming her darning.

The men took no notice of me. I felt the brandy go down into my stomach, heat all the way. This heat is making me brave, I told myself. I am a man. A youngish man, smooth-faced. I am my master's groom, taking his horse to London for him, with instructions to get a good price. I asked for more brandy. For the first time I thought about what I was doing. I would find the Man in the Moon, and when my horse was rested I would sell him for a hundred guineas, certainly eighty, buy Will out of gaol and we'd sail for Holland. Five, six – what time did George Teager get up? How long? An hour? Half an hour? How could they follow? They'd no idea which way we'd gone. Some horse thief had taken Crop, that's all they'd know. They'd get another horse, just as good, they could afford it. After that I'd be a girl again. It was a boy stole the horse, not me. A boy drinking brandy in an inn in the middle of the night.

We did not stop after leaving the inn. The light came up over the Essex plain. More and more people passed us along the road. I thought like a boy, moved like a boy. I *was* a boy.

55

I rode in through Bow and made for the Thames, dropping the stirrups and slotting my feet into them, not wanting to attract attention. Wapping was on the river, I knew that much. As I came deeper into the city, waterlogged fields and muddy lanes gave way more and more to tangled streets and cluttered alleys, that covered me and kept me safe. I was no one here. Rags and scruffs were all around – who'd notice me with my trousers too short? What a fine stew of people this was. I'd seen black men on the Ipswich quays once or twice. I'd seen Lascars and Chinamen, and even a wild Arabian, or an Indian with shiny red breeches and rings in his ears and a sash about his middle as blue as a kingfisher. But nothing like this. Never such a Babel of strange tongues, such variety of faces, so many kinds of the men of the world, white, brown, black, yellow, united by the sea; and some of the women too. And here was me, a smooth-faced man amongst them, riding my grand roan horse nearer to the salt smell of the docks, the heart of sea-town beating away, causing an equal drumming in my heart, but not from fear. It was more a kind of joy made up of all the old familiar smells of tar and fish and strong liquor from the open doors of all the queer little taverns with their ship's prows and figureheads; of the banging of hammers from boatbuilders' yards, and the sight of a four-oared cutter being tarred in the middle of the pavement in front of a church.

At last, above the rooftops, a great pattern of masts and sails and rigging spread itself across the thin white sky. I had reached the river. I went into a baker's shop and bought a pie, and asked if anyone knew of the Man in the Moon at Wapping. A fat woman told me this was Limehouse. Follow the river for Wapping, she said. The waterfront was a maze of courts and alleys – narrow, twisting byways, shacks, huts, rickety buildings leaning this way and that, their doors spilling out sailors and frowsy women, mucky urchins, labourers, porters, men in wigs. A great many cast eyes on Crop, spent as he was, and all grimed from the road, but noble and wonderful for all that. As for me, I was beyond tiredness. I could see Will here. I could see him and me drinking sangaree together at a waterfront tavern, pleasing ourselves, a room with a bed to which we could retire, a late morning awakening to the sound of ships acreak at their moorings, the cry of gulls, the distant lilt of a squeezebox. Then we would stroll along the Highway and see the shops and I'd keep from him the sharks after your money round every corner.

The Man in the Moon was in Dog and Bone Court, just off Ratcliffe Highway to the north. South towards the river was all new building and mess from a big fire three years ago. I've known many speak ill of Ratcliffe Highway, those who opened up their nostrils but not their hearts. The Highway was not safe, but it was fun, and I loved fun. Say what you will about it, wherever you looked there was fun. I could read very well by now and the signs outside alehouses and eating-houses spoke to me:

Grand concert here tonight!

See La Belle Marie walk the tightrope!

So I was happy, seeing me and Will here. I lived in many places, but throw the dice now between the Cliff and Ratcliffe Highway and, do you know, I think I'd go for the Highway any day, rats and all.

Dog and Bone Court was entered by an arch between a Jewish watchmaker's and a ship's chandler's. Sagging creels of shells were displayed on the pavement outside the chandler's. I dismounted and led my horse under the arch and through a dark tunnel – which, by the smell of it, served as a urinal – into a large courtyard of slippery clay, with a paved drain running down the middle. On either side was a hotch-potch of buildings, some ancient, some seemingly thrown up last week with whatever was to hand – straw, a few planks, clay, old palings and doors all higgledy-piggledy. Most of them were sailors' lodging houses. At the end was the Man in the Moon, a low rambling building with mouldering green shutters and steps running up the outside to a gallery that overhung the yard. The whole court had grown up around this place. People swarmed in and out of it, up and down, like maggots around a cheese. I approached. A great babble and roaring came from within. There above the door hung a picture of the man in the moon himself, with his dog and staff and a wild grinning face that put me in mind of madness.

A stable boy came out and I promised him an extra half crown for himself if he cared well for my horse; for I intended to sell him for my master, I said, as soon as he was well rested. Three seamen, one with the smooth gold skin and narrow eyes of a Malay or a Chinaman, lounged at the door of the inn. Their eyes followed my beautiful Crop as he was led away, head adroop, and then they looked *me* up and down, the dusty groom about his master's business.

'Fine nag,' one with a green handkerchief remarked.

'I'm selling him for my master.' I lounged with them. 'Interested?'

He grinned, shook his head. His friend, an older man with bloodshot eyes and a huge red nose, shot out some noxious black oil from between his teeth. 'Too fine for you,' he croaked to Green Handkerchief. The black stuff splattered the step.

'I'm looking for a friend of mine,' I pushed on. 'Name of Will Laud. I think he was staying here.'

'Only docked last night,' the first man said. I could not place his accent. 'That's not a name I know.'

'A sailor,' I said.

They laughed. 'Whatever made you think you'd

find a sailor on Ratcliffe Highway?' rasped Old Croaky.

The Man in the Moon was mad inside. A great room was crammed with all sorts, sailors and labourers, rag-pickers, raggy men, bad women, fat dames, young girls, little children, dogs, all apparently roaring drunk, reeling about in a thick blue smoke that plateaued in a great shifting cloud in the region of the beams. I stood tall and shouldered through to where a fat man stood with his hands like slabs of meat on the counter, golden buttons drooping by long loose threads all down the front of a dragoon's livery. His jacket was so ancient it had the appearance of a cushion habitually clawed by a particularly restless cat. Beneath it rose a massive mound of belly heaving unhealthily up and down under a filthy leather apron.

'Rum,' I said.

He drew the cork from a brown bottle.

'My friend Will Laud told me to ask about him here,' I said. 'Do you know him?'

One of his eyes looked always to the left while his nose looked to the right. He had a face that could not smile. 'You know anything about that woman in the cellar?' he asked.

'I have no idea at all about any woman in any cellar. What are you talking about?'

'Hi, Bets, there's a fellow here asking after Will Laud.'

A heavy-jawed woman with blonde ringlets and pocked, rouged cheeks glanced up from collecting pots. 'He's in bloody Newgate,' she said.

Not one of them in there looked at me as if I

was a woman. Now I was here I could be a woman again if I wanted to but I was enjoying myself too much to stop. Did it make me safer? I don't know.

Bets said Will had been lodging in a room in the cellar with his wife and children. He'd had some sort of fight, it started here in the court with some nasty little fellow. The nasty little fellow got away but Will didn't, so they put him in Newgate for brawling. And now his wife and children were still down there, and that woman was a bit queer in some way, Bets thought. *And* there was rent owing. That was all she knew.

His wife and children! What was this? As I groped my way down the dark stone steps I laughed out loud, boiled with fury and tears: believed and wholly disbelieved, all at once.

It was a warren underneath, a great cellar that must have extended back under the next street or whatever was at the back of Dog and Bone Court. The front bit was storehouses, but the rest was divided into rooms, and every single room was crammed with lodgers. The wife and children, I'd been told, were about halfway down. I knocked on the door but there was no response so I tried the handle and, finding it unlocked, walked in.

They were not Will's wife and children, they were Luff's. With great relief, I saw that straight away. The two little girls both had his cast of features, though weirdly innocent. Their mother didn't look at all surprised to see a stranger enter her room. She was standing with her youngest – a scared-eyed baby, golden-haired, limp of lip, dreadful and doomed – held before her like a shield. Of course: the mousy little wife of whom I'd heard tell, once, twice, long ago. The unimaginable children. I'd never quite believed in them. There was nothing in the room but a rough table on which stood a jug and some wooden bowls, a slop bucket in one corner, and a straw pallet with a couple of soiled blankets rumpled over it. High in the wall was a grating where I saw feet walking in another street. The face of a child of about three peered out from the neck of an old flour sack on the pallet.

It broke my heart to look at the children. How could I not think of Henry Gallant and Rowland? How could I not see them here? Then I looked at her, and my heart went out. She was very young. A small slim pretty thing with a face marked by three enormous flesh-coloured moles, one above the lip, one in the crease of the nose and the other below her left eye.

'Mrs Luff,' I said, 'my name is Lucas Clements. I'm a friend of Will Laud's.'

She didn't say anything. She looked as if she thought she ought to smile but wasn't very good at it.

'What happened?' I asked. 'Did they fight again? What happened?'

She said nothing so I closed the door, came in and sat down next to the child on the pallet. The child turned her head, gold-ringleted as an angel's, and regarded me with wary interest from her sack.

'What's your name?' I asked the mother.

Nothing but a shy look.

I thought she was mute. Might even have had her tongue cut out. A bit daft. Someone should take her out of this place and look after her.

'Where's John?' I asked.

Nothing.

I looked around. There was nothing in the place. No fire in the grate. A stink came from the slop bucket.

'Is there any food?'

She shook her head in a vague way.

'Are you hungry?'

They all looked at me. It was like talking to dogs.

I addressed the child in the sack. 'Are *you* hungry?'

She looked shocked.

'Listen,' I said, 'I'm going to go out and buy some food and bring it back here. I've come a long way and I need to rest. I need to go to Newgate Gaol and buy Will Laud out. You know Will Laud?'

Of course she did, he'd been staying with her while he searched for our passages to Amsterdam. What had happened? Luff turned up and they fought, I suppose.

'I won't be long,' I said. 'I'll get someone to come in and light a fire for you.'

I saw Crop well settled, gave the stable boy money to take fuel and soup for Luff's sad little family and told him to get a fire going for them; then I ventured out of Dog and Bone Court and walked along the Highway. It looked like rain, and my pockets were now lighter than they should be. All along the way were little shops selling peculiar things from curious places, masks and fans and trinkets, a cape of feathers, tiny stuffed birds with long pointed beaks, artfully poised on delicate perches and filigree swings. I saw a shop with cages hanging all over the front of it full of real birds, canaries, parrots, strange crested things, and plain black birds that whistled shrilly as if their throats were pipes played by master musicians. The money would have flowed if I'd been flush. I could have gone into one of the grog shops or a dance-house, and indeed, more than once I was propositioned by painted ladies and almost tempted to go on the rantan just for the fun of it. Life's different as a man.

Giddily awash with possibilities, in the end all I did was go into a ship's grocer's and see some more of my hoard run away on a loaf and some cheese.

When I got back she'd closed the shutters over the narrow strip of window where the feet walked. A fire crackled in the grate and a new candle burned tall and steady on the table. They'd had their soup. Its savour lingered in the air and made my stomach clench. When I gave her the bread and cheese she smiled faintly. 'A bit now,' I said. 'Save the rest.' Then I left them for a time while I went up into the saloon and ordered soup and bread for myself, and some rum. First thing in the morning I must sell Crop now, come what may. The ringleted landlady came to my table and sat down, leaning on her arms. 'I'm owed sixteen shillings,' she said. 'What am I supposed to do? Can I cast babies on the streets? It's a shame but what am I supposed to do?'

They talked funny down here, I thought. That's Cockney.

'I don't know,' I said. 'Life's hard.'

'Oh it is,' she agreed, 'and you don't get nothing for nothing, young man.'

She asked my name and I said Lucas Clements. She wanted payment in advance for a bed. Another shilling from my pocket, and a promise of all amends to be made tomorrow when I sold my horse. She told me to go to Black Bull Yard at Aldgate to get a good price, and said she'd have another pallet sent down to the cellar. The place roared about me and I began to feel nervous. I drank more ruin for courage. Two fat women ripely abused one another in screeching tones. Some dark foreign sailors reeled about with their arms around each others' shoulders. I had not slept since last night and now it was getting dark outside. Suddenly a great wave of weariness overcame me, irresistible.

A surprise awaited when I returned to my lodging. The man of the house had returned from work; not John Luff but a seven-year-old replica, who had laid upon the table next to my bread and cheese a few pennies, a cannikin of oats and a twist of something like tea. He accepted my appearance without a blink, as if the coming and going of total strangers was an everyday occurrence, and asked my name in a friendly manner.

'Lucas Clements,' I said. 'What's yours?'

'Chuck,' he replied, and told me he worked at the tannery on the other side of the wall.

'What wall?'

'The big wall over there.' He pointed vaguely.

Clearly he was by far the most sensible person here. I asked if he knew Will Laud and he nodded.

'And where's your father?' I asked.

'I think he's dead,' said the woman, standing just as she had before, with the baby held in front of her like a shield. I could not have been more surprised if the baby had addressed me.

John Luff? Dead? I felt grief. Surely not John Luff! Bad as he is.

'Ma thinks he's dead,' said Chuck, 'but he's not.'

'Why do you think he's dead?' I asked her.

She went dumb again.

'Why does she think that?' I asked Chuck.

He shrugged.

I went right up to her and looked her full in the face so she had to answer. 'What's your name?'

In the same small thin voice, the voice of no one, she replied: 'Catherine.'

'Will Laud had some money,' I said. 'Money from his uncle's boatyard. Do you know anything about it?'

She was blank. Chuck was blank.

I must sleep. I ached all over from the saddle. My pallet and a blanket had been delivered and awaited, scratchy and hopping with fleas. To me at that moment it seemed a bed of down.

I was woken from a deep sleep by the opening of the door and the sound of a man's voice. Chuck was shaking me by the shoulder.

'I am looking for one Will Laud,' the voice said.

I sat up, dazed. A fellow with an earring and curly brown hair stood in the doorway. The candle had burned low and the fire smouldered, giving off spirals of thin grey smoke. Catherine and the two little ones lay under the blanket on the other pallet, all of them awake and quietly watching. I never knew such silent children in my life. Perhaps she dosed them with something.

'Are you Will Laud?' the fellow asked.

'No,' I replied, rising on to one elbow. 'Who wants him?'

'I was told I'd find Will Laud here. Are you not him?' He seemed slightly at a loss.

'I'm a friend of Will Laud's,' I said. 'Who wants him?'

'There's one John Luff sends for him to come to the *Pelican*. She sails at dawn.'

'For Amsterdam?' I said, confused.

'For America.'

I didn't understand. I sent the fellow away with the assurance that Will Laud would not be sailing at dawn, which was true enough, then lay down and sank back into a still deeper sleep, one full of roads that went on for ever under a blue moon. Next thing I knew the door slammed back against the wall and there was John Luff himself, glowering down at me like an owl, till recognition dawned in his eyes.

'What are *you* doing here?' he asked, amazed. His tone was all surly dog, and fired me up for the game.

'Hello, John.'

I sat up.

He came into the room and closed the door, sat down upon the ground and looked round at his silent family. Chuck got out of bed and padded to his side.

'How are you, Chuck?' Luff said, man to man.

'Well, Pa.'

Chuck sat down and Luff glowered at me. 'Cat,' he said dully, without looking at her, 'put some wood on the fire, it's freezing in here.'

His wife got up at once and fed sticks to the embers, coaxing a small flame.

'What do you want here?' he asked me.

I stood, trembling. Cold, fear, fury. 'Will's in Newgate and we have to get him out.' That was all that mattered. 'What's he done with his money? Do you know? The money from Uncle Jack? If you know where it is, tell me.'

My words came out tight, hard. I'd kill John Luff if he didn't give me the money.

'Will's in Newgate?'

'You didn't know?'

'No.'

'For brawling. With you.'

He laughed.

I stepped forward and spat the words into his face: 'He sent for me to get him out. If you know where he's lodged his money...'

'Are you mad, Margaret Catchpole?' he said. 'Do you really think I'd let you get your hands on a penny of his money?'

I was speechless. I had no idea what he was talking about. I looked into his eyes, for something, some reason; but all I saw was that familiar look of his, amused, lofty, so guarded it was arid.

'I never did anything to you, John,' I said quietly.

'No more you did, Margaret,' he said. He jerked his head towards the door. 'Come. Let's go for a drink.'

We went into the saloon of the Man in the

Moon. I had no idea of the time but thought it must be getting on towards morning. A few people still huddled here and there, very addled. Two played chess on top of a barrel, very rarely shifting their ivory chessmen but spending long minutes silently gazing at the board.

'Is it money you want?' he asked. 'Do you want paying off, is that what it is?'

'What are you talking about?'

'And why are you dressed like that?'

'It's safer. What are you talking about?'

He leaned over the table and took my hand and squeezed it till it hurt, pushing his face right into mine and speaking very fast. 'You think a man like Will's going to smother himself in a flimsy-flamsy shop? With a nagging woman? You think he'll ever settle down with *you?*' His lips were wet. '*You're* not his real life.'

He let go and leaned back, cool again. My hand burned where he'd held it. I felt sick. Tears sprang into my eyes and I was horrified that he might think them tears of weakness.

'You're a fool,' I spat, hating him. 'You're a fool and you're evil. Give up. You have no hold on him.'

'He's going to America,' he said, smirking. 'His passage is paid.' Then he took out a watch and squinted hard at its face. His sight was poor, I realised for the first time. Then I saw that it was Will's Amsterdam watch, and I remembered how Luff had cut him down with a sword.

'That's Will's,' I yelled, jumping up. 'You're a bloody thief, you are, John Luff, and you're a bully. And you're deluded. Will isn't going to America.'

Everyone looked towards us. I glared. My raised voice, I realised, was too girlish. I must stay calm. The blood in my head hammered. I sat back down.

'Will isn't going to America,' I repeated, forcing my rage down till it showed no more than in the trembling of my balled fists under the table.

'He's a fool then,' said Luff, called the boy and ordered up some Arrack punch.

We sat on, in silence.

I left most of the drinking to him. I needed wits. Wits for the morrow, wits to watch him slowly get drunker and drunker, for the hollows of his eyes to seem presagers of age, for his head to sink a little lower. Some great matter oppressed him. Rage would not serve me now.

I took a long drink and looked him in the eye. I told him we were for Amsterdam and he chuckled mirthlessly. Amsterdam was a shit-pot, he said. He could get a piece of land on the Potomac. Now was the time.

'That's a hard voyage for little ones,' I said. 'Still, your poor Catherine will be glad to get out of this hole, I shouldn't wonder.'

He had reached a state of vague incoherence and dead eyes. His wig was filthy. 'They ain't coming,' he said, a grin attaching to his face but not touching his eyes.

I reached for the punch.

'You're leaving them?'

'I am leaving them.'

He held my eyes. 'Don't play holy,' he said. 'It's no great matter. They do very well without me.'

'The rent's owing,' I said.

'Fear not, Saint Margaret. I'll settle.'

'What's the time?'

'Nigh four,' he said.

Jesus, I thought, for a nice cosy bed.

'They'll go on the parish,' I said.

Luff's ringleted tykes on the parish. Here. Couldn't be worse than what she had. The great God only knew that if he left her in holes like this for months on end, she was better off without him.

'You are a horrible man, John,' I said steadily, as one old friend to another. 'They've all gone, your saving graces. I can hardly remember what they were. More fool Will that he called you a friend. I know what you've done. You've taken his Uncle Jack's money for America. You are a worm, John Luff.'

He carried a knife and a sword at all times, and he was more than a little mad. He could cut me down in a second, easy.

My words actually seemed to cheer him up in some peculiar way. He laughed. 'A worm with money,' he affirmed, and drank. I will walk with him down by the docks, I thought, and there I will knock him on the head as he did Will and take back our money, for our new life in Holland. But would he carry it all on his person? Or was it in a coffer in the hold of the *Pelican?*

'You can't do this,' I said.

He leaned back, fully at ease, to light his pipe.

'I can do whatever the frigging hell I want,' he said.

I leaned back too. 'How terrible,' I said, 'to be you.'

56

He left four sovereigns on the table before he left. I know because I saw them there when I came back in after my long morning walk. I assumed he'd also given the landlady the rent. Cat was up, standing just like before, with the baby in front of her. The older child played with the dust on the hearth, sweeping it up into drifts and mounds with her fingers. Chuck had gone to work.

'I'm going to Aldgate to sell my horse,' I told her.

She showed no sign of anything, no interest, no enquiry. I hesitated. The *Pelican* had sailed an hour since; I knew because I'd asked a sailor at the tobacco dock. I prayed I would never have to look on John Luff's face again. I was going to ask if she knew he'd gone for good this time, but she probably wouldn't have answered anyway.

It looked like rain. Crop stood ready in the court, the stable boy holding his head and waiting for another penny. I strode out for the new day. The old had been most strange, but I had slept, and I had cleaned my boots and brushed up as well as I could. I'd buy new stockings on the way. As for Crop – the boy had done his work well. I gave him sixpence. That left me with about nine shillings, but it didn't matter. The sooner this business was finished now, the better. It was the twenty-fifth of May. The boat sailed for

Amsterdam tonight. Will's money may have gone, but the sale of Crop would buy his freedom and two passages on board. And after that–

–oh, after that: the great adventure of our life in Holland.

It began to drizzle. The rats playing in the drain lifted their heads and sniffed, peering wisely here and there. As I led Crop through the passage and out on to the road, a gust of breeze whisked in off the river and the rain settled into a pleasant singing whisper. I drew my cloak tight about me, pulling down the wide brim of George Teager's hat. Rain in Ratcliffe Highway did not cleanse and bring sweet smells. It sent the rats down into the cellars, but it filled the drains and stirred up the sewers and made of the thoroughfare a filthy running river of muddy brown soup that bubbled and babbled over the broken paving stones, swirling frothily in the gutters and byways, foul-stinking as the whole of hell coming up from beneath. I rode towards Whitechapel, out of it, taking a route recommended by the landlord. I bought stockings from a hosier in a place called Rope Walk, the name reminding me of Ipswich and the Widow Syers, and of all the life I'd lived up until this day: a completeness that seemed to me now so closed, as surely gone as a dream recalled at midday. A little longer and I could be Peggy again, but for now I was Lucas Clements riding his master's roan horse to a sale.

Black Bull Yard was a long alley off Aldgate High Street, narrow for most of its length but widening out here and there where small houses and dark little shops had grown up. The Black

Bull Inn was in the big central yard. I called for the ostler, a scrubby wrinkled little man with a rasping voice that seemed to come up from his belly. 'I'm told this is the place to sell a horse,' I said.

'Could be.' He scratched his nose. 'This horse?'

'This one.'

'He's a fine one, ain't he?'

'My master wants a good price for him. Give him a sup of water and I'll come and see him fed in half an hour.' And I strode in, ordered breakfast and sat down to light a pipe and read a newspaper at a table in the window. The place was practically empty. A girl of about twelve swabbed down the counter. I was mopping up eggs and swilling tea when the ostler came in. 'I took the liberty of calling on our Mr Frogden what keeps the livery stable,' he said. 'He's got a gentleman leaving town this afternoon, wants a strong carriage horse and the one marked for him gone lame. Mr Frogden's taking a look at your horse now, sir, if you wouldn't mind stepping out for a word with him.'

I had enjoyed my breakfast. I had enjoyed my solitary, worldly perusal of the paper, the sunlight penetrating the misted windows to cast patterns over the table, the smell of the suds the girl was throwing out of the door on to the cobbles. So much was I enjoying the freedom of not being Peggy that for a moment I had forgotten entirely who I was. I thought sharp and remembered I was Lucas Clements. Up he jumped. He too was enjoying himself.

Crop was eating in the stable round the back,

saddleless. Frogden, a friendly big-faced man, was studying his right forelock. We shook hands. 'Don't see many like this,' he said, raising his eyebrows and meeting my eyes directly. 'Who are you selling him for?'

'Mr Stebbing of Ipswich,' I said. I'd thought this out. Stebbing was a common enough name in our part of the country. It had a ring of truth, not like Brown or Smith. 'He's coming up to town tonight.' I'd thought this out too. A story. A ring of truth.

'He's a beauty.'

'Best horse I ever rode,' I said sincerely. 'I'll be sorry to part with him.'

'Is there a warranty?'

'Of course,' I said, and my heart began to beat a little harder. It felt as if the world was more real than it had ever been before – as if an artist had drawn the lines too sharply. 'I can write you one now if you like. Or you can wait till Mr Stebbing gets here and deal with him directly.'

It was a masterstroke.

Frogden patted the horse's neck and smiled. He was not a bad-looking man, about thirty. 'When are you expecting Mr Stebbing?' he asked.

'About nine this evening.'

Too late for your customer. I didn't say this; and I saw the calculations passing over his face. He went on examining the horse. 'How old is he?'

'Six year old next grass.'

'Know of any problems with him?'

'I can't fault him, sir.'

'As if you'd tell me any different,' he replied, grinning widely.

'Judge for yourself,' I shrugged, almost, as if it was no odds to me. 'You know a good horse when you see one.'

He walked around the horse once. Twice. 'What's Mr Stebbing want for him?'

'A hundred and twenty guineas.' But I'd let him beat me down to ninety.

He snorted. His eyes kept running over and over Crop's beautiful lines. Any fool could see it was a good deal – but not *too* good, not so as to arouse suspicion – and he knew his horses.

At length he stood back and sighed. 'He's a beauty,' he said again, and started lighting a pipe. Hooked him, I thought.

'You can put him through his paces in the yard if you want,' I said.

Let him once get up in that saddle and the deal was done for sure.

'Bob,' he said to the ostler, 'fetch the saddle.'

It was a good one. I saw him eyeing it. 'Let me do that,' I said as Bob made to tighten the girth. 'This is what you need to do–' and I gave Crop a quick sharp knee in the belly before yanking hard on the girth. He gave a great resigned grunt. 'He holds his breath, sir,' I said to Frogden, patting Crop's neck. 'Holds his breath and puffs himself out just when you fasten the girth. He's always done it.'

Crop turned his head and gave me an affectionate nuzzle. It was obvious he was easy with me, obvious I knew him well. Clearly this was my master's horse.

'Crafty,' Frogden said, addressing him. 'So we can fault you after all, my pal.'

'Every rose is allowed at least one thorn,' I said.

Frogden laughed. I led Crop out into the yard and he mounted heavily. The horse did me proud, picking up his feet like a deer, holding his head up all style and nobility as the livery man trotted him smartly up and down the yard.

'I'd like to see him on my own ride,' Frogden said when he reined in. 'Can I just take him round there quick?'

'I can't let him out of my sight. I'm not allowed,' I said. 'I'll have to go with you.'

He thought a bit. 'Tell you what,' he said, dismounting, 'you ride him round there for me – I'll show you the way, it's not far – so I can see him in action. You can take him up and down my own ride for me.'

'Of course.'

I made to mount. Those damned stirrups were too long now. He'd adjusted them. I yanked them up – God, how I hate stirrups – and then I put my foot in the wrong way like a fool, and my trousers rode up my leg. Rolling my eyes, I hoisted myself up, pulled the stirrups after and crossed them over the saddle. 'I ride without stirrups,' I said. 'I can't stand the things.'

Off we went, I riding, he walking beside. He directed me off the high street and into a long narrow lane full of shops, with a grand church on one side. At the end of this, we turned right into a big stable yard. Four or five horses stood tethered here and there, not one of them anywhere near as good as Crop. The grooms stopped their forking of hay and cleaning of hooves to look at him. 'Will you just take him up and down the ride for me,'

Frogden asked, and I trotted proudly, sitting tall.

'Fifty guineas,' he said when I got back.

I laughed. 'Just look at this horse! He's magnificent. Quiet as a lamb, strong as a lion. My life won't be worth living if I take less than a hundred for him. Honestly, you'd be better waiting for Mr Stebbing, you might find *him* more yielding than me.'

'Hm,' he said, and put his chin in his hand. 'Ride him up and down one more time.'

But I was no fool. 'Come now, a decision,' I said, dismounting. 'I have a lot to do today. A hundred guineas and he's yours. I'll write you a warranty.'

'I'm not fond of cropped ears,' he said ruminatively. 'Sixty.'

'You're wasting my time.' I laughed again. It was all very amicable, and I felt slightly drunk and a little light-headed though I'd had nothing but tea.

I agreed to eighty in the end. He asked if I'd throw in the saddle and bridle but I said oh no, they're my perks, it's a good saddle, that is. And I got four guineas for the both. And there we were, laughing and joking and stroking Crop's beautiful strawberry roan nose, when the constables turned up.

They came into the yard with the ostler, three of them with shiny buttons and white hose. There was a single moment when I both knew and did not know at the same time that it was me they'd come for. When I say I knew, I mean my body knew, my very marrow knew, because a sweat burst out startlingly on the palms of my hands, and my tongue dried up in my mouth. But my mind would not know. I was talking to Frogden. My mind did not know, but my tongue dried up mid-sentence and stuck to the roof of my mouth most ridiculously so that I heard my own voice gibbering thickly in my skull like an idiot as they strode serious-faced and purposeful towards us.

'Morning, Frogden,' one said, 'I think you should look at this.'

He flashed a piece of paper under Mr Frogden's nose while the other two grabbed me. Each had an arm and their hands gripped like the mouths of mastiffs.

'What's happening?' I cried. It came out hoarse. I was most troubled by the dryness of my mouth; it was more distressing than anything else at that moment.

'This is a stolen horse,' the first constable said. His small pale eyes flicked towards me, briefly and regretfully. 'I don't know how you thought you could get away with it,' he said.

How? How could this possibly happen? This was London.

'He's my horse,' I said quickly. 'See how he knows me. He belongs to Mr Stebbing, he's coming up to town tonight.'

They were all looking at me, Frogden with his mouth turned down severely, the ostler bright-eyed and chewing his lip. The word must have got round that the police were in, because the yard had started filling up with gawpers, all of them looking at me. I could have cried. With anger at myself, with pure humiliation. How could I have ruined my life any more completely than this?

The constable took the paper from Frogden and held it before my eyes. It was a handbill. TWENTY GUINEAS REWARD it said in big black letters. My eyes swam over the words: fine strawberry roan grey gelding ... John Cobbold Esq. of St Margaret's Green ... whoever shall give information ... sixteen-hands high...

'You must have known you'd get caught,' the pale-eyed constable said.

No. No, I didn't. I was much too stupid.

'What's your name, lad?' he asked, not unsympathetically.

'Margaret Catchpole,' I said.

That did it.

A woman! No! The word ran, all round every bloody alley and crawl space in that area, and I put my head down and closed my eyes as they marched me between them out of the yard.

Woman stole a horse. Look what she's wearing! There was laughter. Will she hang? Will she hang? Whenever I opened my eyes there were crowds grinning and staring and babbling. People love a spectacle. Stole a horse. Look, woman dressed up as a man! 'Where's your prick, sweetheart?' a man's voice yelled and everyone roared. Not a single clear thought could I muster. I felt sick. They took me to a big building with big doors and polished wood everywhere, left me in a tiny room with nothing in it but a chair. They locked the door. I cried, hard and unbelieving, biting on my fist. 'No, no, no, no...' What would happen to me? Oh God.

Oh God, let it not have happened, God take it

all away.

Will she hang? Will she hang?

Fear settled like a sickness inside me, on my stomach, in my throat, in every limb and every little last hair of me.

I don't know how long I waited. An hour? Two? Then the key turned in the lock and a man all in black, a clerk or something, summoned me out.

'What's happening?' I asked him.

'You're going before the magistrate,' he said softly. 'Mind you say you're sorry.'

'I am sorry,' I said, 'of course I'm sorry. What's going to happen?'

He shrugged and shook his head.

The room was very hot and crowded. There was a constant backdrop of noise. The magistrate was fat and red. I stood there in front of everyone. I held my head up. The magistrate scarcely glanced at me as the constable read out the charge, but when he realised I was a woman he looked up. 'Dressed as a man?' he said and peered at me very intently. I looked back at him. His wig was slightly crooked and he looked very clean. My eyes watered. I looked down.

'Dressed as a man,' he repeated slowly under his breath, writing something down.

Did that make it worse?

He asked me if I'd done it and I said yes. I hadn't a clue what was going on, my mind refused to work. Then the clerk beckoned me again, and I walked towards him and out through a door, and the same constables as before put chains upon my wrists.

The Deadly Nevergreen

57

I was with three others in the cart, two women and a young boy of about seventeen, all dressed up with a nosegay in his buttonhole, whose terror seeped off him like a bad smell. His mouth was continually open. He breathed strangely, as if he could not get enough air. Whenever we jolted over a stone he caught his breath and swallowed, closing his eyes and tightening his pale forehead sternly.

So many great domes and spires, such grandeur of design – this was more of London than I'd ever seen, and I could have admired it if I'd not been feeling so strange, so curiously calm yet so sick in the stomach and light about the head. It wasn't far to Newgate. The streets teemed. We were high up in the cart and all the way I could watch the people and they watched me. I met the eyes of as many as I could. This was very important to me, almost a duty. I would not slump, like that poor girl there, a poxy little scrub of a thing with her eyes seeing only the dirty straw on the floor of the cart. Some smiled. Some of the men made filthy gestures. A lad with affronted eyes stooped and picked up a handful of filth. The wheels of the cart grated over the stones, the wheels of all the other barrows and carts rumbled and screeked, the air was thick with shouting. I suppose the cart passed backwards and forwards, backwards and forwards all day long, shrieking and grinding, a constant dribbling here and there of the felons of London.

A stone hit the boy's shoulder and he flinched and bared his teeth, hissing in his throat. The other woman, a big hard-faced creature in a red dress who'd been in court with me and bled copiously from the hand into a ball of rags all the way, nudged him with her foot. 'Nearly there,' she said. 'What you up for, son?'

'Forgery,' he said breathlessly.

He could hang. Me too. How could I have been such a fool? I'd known this could happen. I knew the law.

I didn't think I'd get caught. Such a sure thing it had seemed. I bet he never thought it either, poor boy. Where was his mother? Wouldn't it break her heart to see him like this?

Fear is a terrible thing, it blocks the throat, paralyses. I smiled at him. He tried but couldn't manage a smile in return.

'What's your name?' I asked him.

'Robert.'

'My brother's name was Robert,' I said.

'Ain't you the one though,' Red Dress said to me. 'Know what she done?' She nudged the silent girl with her other foot. 'Nabbed a prancer. How long you passed as a boy for?'

'Day or two.'

'Rid all the way from Ipswich, the beak said. How far's that?'

'I don't know,' I said. 'About seventy miles.'

'You done well.'

The girl raised her head and looked at me. Her

eyes were small and red from crying and her greasy hair hung in rat-tails across her face. She tried to get it back with her hands, but the irons got in the way. The straw in the cart hopped with fleas. I itched all over but couldn't reach to scratch. How beautiful, I thought, the great dome against the thick white sky. I saw gentlemen going up and down high wide steps, like the steps to heaven almost, fine gentlemen all dressed in black, with white stockings and tall wigs. Some looked our way. I had an urge to wave, but the manacles weighed a ton and it was too much effort to lift my arm.

'Heigh-ho,' said Red Dress, shifting her bloody bundle of rags, 'here we go.'

Newgate was massive. One long huge solid grey wall, flat and merciless like a closed face. Will was on the other side of it. There was a gate, very grand and imposing, at which the cart drew close. I could not take my eyes off that great wall, and had no awareness of anything around me more than the fact of noise and many people, all the mangled babblings of humankind. Will was somewhere in there. You had to laugh. Here was me come all this way to get him out of a pit and all I'd done is fallen in myself. The back of the cart opened; there was a door. A big church bell rang, very close and loud. The guards, hefty beef-faced men, herded us through the door. That pit-faced little scab of a girl, she was the size of a doll when she stood up. Her nails were ragged and bloody. As she was getting out of the cart behind me she put her hands to her belly and doubled over as in a cramp, clenching her eyes and whimpering. She was like one of my children, no different at all, and I thought of all my young ladies and gentlemen, Sophia, William. I thought of them here.

The door closed. The world was gone.

They took the boy away to the left, to the men's side.

'Robert,' I said just before he was led away, 'if you see a man called Will Laud over there, a sailor, please will you tell him Margaret Catchpole's here. Tell him you saw me.'

He made no sign of hearing.

Our side was on the right. There was a room where the surgeon looked us over, a glance it seemed. He pulled the rags from the bloody hand of the woman in the red dress and I saw that she was missing a finger. Blood splashed a table. They took her into another room.

'Do I get women's clothes?' I asked one of the guards.

He didn't reply.

The girl and I went on with him and another man, rooms opening into rooms, a faint sourness in the air, till we came to a heavy oak gate, bound with iron and studded with nails, where a turnkey bullishly stood waiting to admit us. A great jangling of keys and creaking of hinges, an echoing crash as the gate slammed behind us, then a few steps down into a narrow stone passage that led us into a stone maze, the maggoty burrowings and windings of the gaol. We passed through a great many doors, each of which had to be locked and unlocked; through lobbies and corridors, alleys and ginnels, bare open areas with vaulted ceilings and high arched windows opening only on to inner gloom. There was nothing at all in that place to lift the spirit or please the eye, or indeed any of the senses. The further in we proceeded, the deeper grew the smell. Imagine a privy left forgotten and unemptied in high summer. Imagine dozens of them, and the shit-heavy stagnant air like a hand sitting on your face, making you want to cover your mouth and nose. But you couldn't. And as the smell thickened, so did the noise become more and more diabolical, a rabble on a market day, a crowd around the gallows, muffled and moulded by walls, distorted by echoes. We passed places where gratings of criss-crossed iron and huge barred doors gave us glimpses of black-walled courtyards, spiked at the tops, each one very high and narrow and crammed with women, shouting, pissing, drinking, arguing, shrieking with laughter, walking here and there or sitting alone. We walked down a passage with strong black doors on either side, one of which reverberated to great constant blows, as if a mindless monster was hurling itself again and again at the door. Behind another, someone screamed as if demons were nipping at her.

Then down. They put us under the ground in a dark foul place with low shelves all around the walls, and women lying on them. I had a mat and a blanket, a big iron ring in the floor to which the guard attached my shackles, and a chamber pot, crusty inside. A fire winked through the darkness, far away. I made out people sitting about it, the rising smoke of pipes, here and there a candle. There was a constant burble of voices, and someone somewhere moaned. The girl was next to me. A fat woman in rags appeared before us. 'Got any blunt?' she asked.

'What?'

'Money, dear,' she said.

'Not much.'

'Got any booze?'

'No.'

She lost interest and wandered off. You had to pay for everything in here, it turned out. Someone came round later and even took a fee for my mangy blanket. As for that poor child next to me, she had nothing, so I ended up sharing my bread with her when it came, which was no hardship to me. I could never eat in here, not with the stink, I thought, looking round at the others cramming their mouths. What a rabble! Mad, some of them looked. Mad and hard and fierce.

'What's your name?' I asked the girl.

'Rebecca,' she said.

'Have you got a pain?' She kept making a face and holding herself.

'I'm all right,' she said.

I could get no more from her till the woman in the red dress appeared, one hand all bandaged up and raised in a sling. She had no shackles and was free to walk round. Paid one and six to get them off, she said. 'I can afford one and six,' I said, and she went and asked for me, but when the guard came he said Rebecca and me had to keep ours on because we were in court first thing in the morning. It didn't seem a good reason to me, but he wasn't for arguing.

'Bastards,' said Mary of the red dress. 'Stupid bastards.' Some kind of bond was between us three because we'd been in the cart together, and she made a place for herself by us. She and I bought a candle between us, and a small jug of rough gin. We drank ourselves soft at the edges. She was a nice woman, Mary. Big of face and hard as teak. The girl Rebecca turned from us at some point, put her pitted face to the wall and gave herself over to humming in a small sad voice.

'Killed her baby,' Mary whispered loudly. 'She's for the deadly nevergreen.'

I looked at the poor girl's throat. Hymns, she sang. She went on like a gnat, long into the night.

'So am I probably,' I said. I laughed. Mary passed the jug.

'Got a smoke?' I asked her.

She indicated a pocket in her apron. 'Bleeding hurts, this finger,' she said.

'What happened?'

'Bitch in Garden Street. "What you think *you* looking at?" she says. *You* know. Wants a fight. "Give you a kicking, I will," says I. Pulls out a knife.' She made a sound with her mouth exactly like the sound of a chopped bone. 'Gone. Finger gone, blood pouring out, blood everywhere, shite-faced bitch.'

'So what are you here for?'

'Cock knows. Give her a kicking, I suppose. I dunno.'

Mary grew more and more voluble as the day crawled into night. We were under the ground; no light told you the time.

'What about you though?' she said. 'Ain't you the one though, riding all that way?'

'Fat lot of good it did me.'

Someone vomited somewhere. The smell hovered about on top of the other, deeper one. The fleas were bold upon us, fat and glutted, lazy like grazing sheep. It was candles out at ten, but the noise didn't stop. People clustered about, squatting on the floor, smoking, drinking. A fight broke out somewhere but the guards smashed it up. Three or four other women gathered round us.

'We had another lass dressed as a man not seven months ago,' one of them said to me. 'She was let off with a spell in the nutcracker. You might be lucky.'

'Seven months? You've been down here seven months?'

'Not all the time,' she said. 'I'm in and out, you know.'

I didn't sleep. For an hour or so towards morning I lay down. I think I may have drifted, with the talk still going on above my head, but you couldn't call that sleep. I thought of Will somewhere in this place; of Cat and her children, of John Luff out on the sea. I thought about home. Where was home?

I'd slid down, down, down – like in the game we used to play, a game called the tree game when we were young, my mother had it on a board and it was very old. She'd had it from her mother, my old granny in Yarmouth. We never really had any toys, just a couple of balls and a family rag doll called Patchy that we buried with Sue, and the tree game. The board was painted blue, and a tree was carved into it, with spreading branches, some green and sweeping up to heaven like supplicating arms, some black and raining downwards like the big willows at St Margaret's Green. At the top, the sky was bright, with birds like opened books and a yellow sun in one corner with thin quivery rays. At the bottom was black mud and dark-green plants with thick wavy leaves that looked like mouths snapping at you. Just as you thought you'd got to the top you'd make a bad throw and land on top of one of the black branches and come sliding right back down into the mud again. My mum said it showed the fickleness of fortune.

I'll never get up this time, I thought, this is one step too low. This is under the ground, dead and buried and the earth thrown on top.

At seven, just as I was falling properly asleep, a bell clanged and I came to with a start. I tried to sit, but the iron held me down, and I remembered. First came the smell of a thousand piles of rags rising up from the ground, then a great bellowing of orders, a clanging and a clanking, a tramping of feet and a raucous mess of clearing throats and hectoring voices. We had to empty our chamber pots into a shit-smeared privy in the corridor. The guard counted us. Breakfast was watery gruel and brackish water. Then there we were, the three of us and a few more, herded back the way we'd come, up through the maze of Newgate, back to the bright light of a cool fresh day, which made the tears run from our eyes.

58

We were back at the court. They put us in a room, all of us standing in our chains. A door opened. 'Margaret Catchpole,' someone said. The guard pushed me. I went out into the passage and a man took my arm. 'This way,' he said. Another door opened.

I heard Mrs Cobbold's voice. 'I have not the slightest doubt...' she was saying.

I could not bear it, couldn't face her. I turned. 'No,' I said, 'I don't want to see her.'

'Don't be silly,' the man said, tightening his grip on my arm so it bit, propelling me forward into the room. There was a huge table and a lot of shelves and books and tall-backed wooden chairs. She was sitting in one, very stiff, in a pink frilled bonnet. They were both there, him and her. I was filthy. It was horrible.

'I'm sorry,' I said, and burst into tears.

It was Mr Cobbold that came forward and put his hands on my shoulders and looked me seriously in the eye. 'I want you to know that it has not been my own decision to prosecute,' he said very gravely. 'I have been bound over to do so.'

I felt so stupid standing there in George Teager's old clothes that didn't fit. So low. I dropped my eyes. 'I'm sorry,' I said again.

'What on *earth* got into you, Margaret?' That was her, half stern, half sorrowing.

I couldn't look at her.

Mr Cobbold gave me his handkerchief. So white and crisp! It seemed a shame to dirty it. I wiped my eyes fiercely. My nose was running. If I was not so filthy, I thought. If I was not so tired and aching and itching. If I was not weighed down so much by these irons.

Mr Cobbold leaned close. I must have stunk. 'I want you to know,' he said in a low voice, 'that we will do everything within our power to help you.'

'Thank you, sir,' I mumbled.

Of course they would be kind. They were kind people. That's what made it so terrible. He went out and left me with Mrs Cobbold, who got up at once and came and gave me a hug. 'I could shake you,' she said with tears in her eyes. 'I know you for an intelligent woman. How could you have been so foolish?'

I shook my head.

'I was mad,' I said.

'Don't you remember passing the mail coach? They recognised Crop. He's such a very distinctive horse, you know that. It was reported as soon as they got to Colchester. They came and knocked us up at five in the morning. They had the handbills on the nine o'clock coach for London. Didn't you think?'

'I thought I'd be safe in London.'

'Oh, Margaret!'

That was the worst of it. Being green enough to get caught.

'I'm a fool,' I said.

'Yes!' she said sharply. 'You are.'

What more could I say?

'You look very bonny, madam,' I commented. She'd put on a bit of weight since I saw her last. 'Are you expecting again?'

'I am,' she said, 'and I'm very tired. We came up in the coach last night, and that's something I could have done very well without, Margaret.'

'I'm very sorry, madam.'

Her eyes looked hollow. Her mouth was tight and tense. The door opened. 'We'll do what we can but we don't have infinite powers,' she said quickly.

'Margaret Catchpole,' the man said.

I gave her a quick smile. 'When are you due, madam?' I asked her.

'September,' she replied.

'Oh,' I said, 'quite far on then.'

The court was packed with stern men in rows. The Big Wig told me if I said anything it could be read against me when I came to trial. I thought this *was* the trial; but he said no, the offence was committed in Ipswich, so I'd have to be tried up there.

What could I say? I'd done it and they'd caught me. 'Yes, I did it,' I said. 'I took the horse.'

The clerk read out what I'd said and gave me a paper to put my mark to, and I read it through and signed it proudly. See, I can read, I wanted them to know. And I can sign my name in a proper way. Then he said I'd have to go back to Newgate till such time as I could be taken back to Ipswich. I wanted to ask, how long? How long do I have to stay in that place? But he banged his gavel and I had to go.

59

I was in there for two weeks. There was never a place as bad, not in my experience – and I've endured the trip of the *Nile* round the world – never a place as bad in all the world. In Newgate I was never that far from home, but I might as well have been on the moon. I was no longer in the dungeon. My fetters were taken off me for the easement money the Cobbolds paid, and I was given an old grey dress, something once worn by a fat matron, it seemed. There were forty women on my ward, all of us awaiting trial. We had a long table, wooden forms, a shelf of pewter dishes, places for our mats and blankets. A big fireplace dominated at one end. Windows, arched and very high up, let through nothing but a bleak indoor light. Old whitewash flaked from the walls, which were covered in writing and drawings people had done, filth mixed with hymns. From our ward you could go down stone stairs and out into the yard. One side was railed off into a big roofed cage, with iron bars where you could talk to your visitors over a divide. I never had any.

I cried a lot in Newgate. Cried and drank. Thought of Will. We got beef once a week. We got bread every day. The water stank. If you looked close you saw little creatures floating, some swimming. The stink was worst. The noise, night and day. Swearing, gaming, singing, dancing, screaming, wailing. The brawls, the faces pushed against walls, slammed into iron bars. The arses bared and displayed.

I drank. The Cobbolds had left me provided for, enough anyway, more than many. Everyone drank, the gaolers too. I sent a letter to Mrs Cobbold. Please, I said, pay Will Laud out of gaol. That's why I did it. Please please please. Sorry sorry sorry.

What a fool I was to end up here. Please please please, God, turn back time.

Someone died. No one came. Just the guards who took her clothes. I know nothing about her, who she was, what she did, anything. It was two more days before anyone came. To the surgeons, they said. Please God, never, no never, please never, not the surgeons. Bury me in Nacton Churchyard, complete.

60

Thursday 6 July 1797. My dearest Dad and Ned, It is with great joy I pick up my pen to inform you I have this night arrived in Ipswich. Please come and see me. Is Ned angry with me? Please tell him to come. I am happy to be back home. This gaol is so much better than Newgate which is a shocking place. Here there are flower beds in the yard. I have my own cell where I am writing to you now. I am also writing to my Uncle and Aunt Leader and Uncle and Aunt Catchpole and to Mrs Cobbold who has been so very good to me and paid all my costs in Newgate. She has paid Will's costs too so now he is free, that is how kind she is. He has sent me a very nice letter saying all will be well and I have told him he must write and thank her so she will see what an educated man he is. From my cell I can see the willows at St Margaret's Green if I stand on my bed. I can see the fields where I used to take the children for their walks. Dad, can you get me some things I left at the Widow Syers'? A blue cap and a piece of amber and my bit of green muslin with the roses on, I left them all in the top front room. Don't worry about me, Dad. I am to go to the assizes at Bury on 9 August–

Who'd read this to him? Would he take it to Mrs Cobbold?

Again I stood on my bed and held on to the iron grating to look out. It was dark now, there were lights shining in town. It was easy to sound cheerful for Dad. Seeing the back of Newgate did it. Seeing my new prison, a haven by comparison, though if I'd come here first I'd have thought it grim. But I felt I was home now. I was clean, I had proper clothes again. That night I slept in a real bed instead of on a mat on the floor, and I had sheets.

In the morning Dr Stebbing came into my cell and said, 'Well, Margaret, this is a to-do.'

'It is, sir.'

He sat down and touched my hand. 'The question being how we should proceed.'

'That's out of my power to control now, sir,' I replied.

'Not at all.' He coughed politely. 'I've been surgeon to this gaol for a long time now, and I've seen them come and go. I've seen so many things, Margaret, and there's one thing I've learned.' He smiled sadly, looking me fixedly in the eye and patting my hand. 'You must always hope.'

'Everyone hopes,' I said.

He turned away and briskly opened his bag. 'You have some very good friends, don't forget,' he said. 'Now, let's have a look at you.'

Everyone told me to hope. Old Rip, our governor, told me to prepare for the worst and hope for the best. He said the judges were hard on horse thieves. I'd need friends to speak for my character. Mrs Cobbold said the same on that first morning, when she came. I should look on the bright side. She'd send a letter to court saying what a good worker I'd been and strongly recommending mercy, though she wasn't sure she could go herself because she'd be getting near her time by then. But she was sure Dr Stebbing would speak.

'The children won't stop crying,' she said. 'All of them send their love. William said to me this morning, he said, *You can't let them hurt Margaret, you can't. Have you forgotten how good she was, how she sat up all night with me when I was so sick? Every time I woke up she was there. She never failed.*'

She smiled. Her eyes filled with tears.

'Dear Margaret,' she said. 'Dear Margaret.'

'Will they kill me, madam?' For a moment there was a strange equality between us. 'I'm very scared. I don't want to die, madam.'

I buckled over and for a moment thought I was going to be sick.

She gripped my hand. 'Be strong,' she said. 'You *are* strong.'

'But some things are too much.'

My head was dizzy.

'I don't know what's going to happen,' she said. 'I have no idea.'

Our knuckles, entwined, were white and painful.

'It's cold in here,' she said.

'You shouldn't be coming in here in your condition,' I told her.

'Nonsense.' She was brisk again. 'I don't know what's going to happen, Margaret, but for God's sake, don't start giving up. You're not to think of death. There'll be no death, not if I have anything to do with it.' She spoke sharply, as if reprimanding the inevitable.

She'd save me. She'd have to because she knew I was not bad, and I had meant something to her family. She liked us wayward ones. She had a soft spot, you could say. I felt sorry for her in a way. She'd chosen one way for herself, I another. And they could kill me for going my way, but she envied me, I think, in a funny sort of way. She couldn't go wild with the way she'd chosen.

It was a month till my trial. Dad came three times. Ned only came once, and when he did he was awkward and sulky. The good ladies of Ipswich took it upon themselves to continue my education. They deluged me with books. Mrs Sleorgin did, and Dr Stebbing's daughter, which I thought was very nice of her; and of course Mrs Cobbold. Uncle Catchpole sent the papers in for me, so I could read about myself. *Margaret Catchpole, for stealing a coach horse, belonging to John Cobbold Esq. of Ipswich (with whom she formerly lived as a servant) which she rode from thence to London in about ten hours, dressed in man's apparel, and having there offered it for sale was detected.*

Best and worst of all though, a letter from Will.

He could not come. Captain Bargood had advised him to keep his nose clean and stay well away from any criminal connections till another voyage was out and he could make up some of his losses.

Criminal connections: that was me! How twisted things were.

He'd left the note with Dad and Ned, and was gone Dutch-side again. He said he'd do a couple of runs and furnish us a home in Amsterdam, for when I was free. *Don't worry, Pegs*, he said, *all this will soon be over. Bargood knows people. You are the bravest girl in all the world, and the best.* It made me cry.

For an hour I raged, blaming him for everything that had befallen me, and cursing him for a heartless, hateful thing to keep away from me now I was so low. For another hour I ached so from missing him I thought my heart might give up under the pain. But after that I got sense again and started to hope. Why should I not? I had some very good people looking out for me. I was very lucky. Hadn't I always said that? In spite of everything, I could still say I've had very good fortune in my life. And of what did my luck consist of, after all? Friends.

I made friends in Ipswich Gaol. Some of those

girls were so wet behind the ears, they needed looking after. Sometimes it felt as if I were the nursemaid again, me and Alison Lloyd, the woman in the cell next to mine. She was fifty or more, Alison, in for the duration for bashing her husband on the head with a skillet. Only a tap, she said, she hadn't meant to kill him. He hadn't been a bad old soul really, just very irritating, and everyone had vouched for that when it got to court. She'd have hanged, she said, only for the fact that one of the judges had once spent several hours stuck in a snowbound coach with him coming back from King's Lynn. That's why he'd transmuted it, she was positive. Everyone said you'd have to be a saint to live with that man as long as she did, and God knows *she* was no saint. Alison was built like a barn, and walked like a man. She swore and spat and kept a look in her eyes of hard challenge. But was soft and kind to a remarkable degree. Every night in her cell she got tipsy and sang sentimental old songs in a pleasant lilting sort of a way, till Sims the turnkey came and rapped her door and told her to keep it down a little bit now, some of us wouldn't mind a bit of shut-eye. Other times she'd shout out or wail in her sleep, reliving some old terror.

Nights were never quiet in gaol. We mumbled and tossed and turned. Dreams broke through. Weeping happened. Alison Lloyd's breathing was bad sometimes and she'd wheeze all night. Now and then someone would go mad and start screaming and shouting and bashing about in their cell, till Sims and a couple of guards would come and take them away where they could no longer be heard. It happened once with Alison, when she started bellowing about being cut up, bellowing like a cow in labour just the other side of the wall from me. She'd got the horrors, she told me later, but it was all right now. She'd made Mrs Ripshaw promise on her immortal soul never to let the surgeons at her.

'"What are you talking about?" she says.' Alison skilfully mimicked Mrs Ripshaw, our governor's wife, her air of brisk jollity. '"Cut up? What nonsense!"'

It was her, to the life. I laughed.

'But they do,' said Alison, 'and they know they do, and I got no one to make sure about it, so I made her promise.'

'Good for you,' I said. 'Tell you what, if I'm still here when you croak I'll make damn sure she sticks to it.'

Our days consisted of endless washing, ironing, sewing and scrubbing. Wash days were worst. We didn't get out of the big laundry room all day. We didn't get breaks. We ate in there with the hot steam and the damp, and water running down the walls like the sweat pouring down our skin under our clothes. You couldn't finish early, even if all the wash was done. You had to wait until eight then bang on the door for Sims to come and let us out into the felons' yard for our half-hour. Sweet air, though the sky was very high up and far away. There was a long flower bed at one end. Imagine. There'd been nothing like this at Newgate. I'd have died if I'd had to stay there too long, I'm sure of that.

Old Rip loved his flower beds. He'd put in

daisies and polyanthus, and he was having a go at carnations too, but they were looking rather peaky. You got to do some weeding if you were lucky. Nice work, much nicer than scrubbing.

Old Rip and Mrs Rip lived in a house right in the middle of the gaol, and their own little garden ran right alongside our walk on the other side of a paling. I said to Mrs Rip one day when she came to inspect the laundry, 'Don't you feel funny living in such a place, all spikes and bars and echoes and shouts; and then the days they do the hangings just outside – doesn't it make you feel funny?'

She said she was used to it.

'I'm good with gardens,' I said. 'Can I do some gardening for you like Alison Lloyd does?'

We were on the drying-ground. The heavy linen-horses had been dragged round from the long stone passage that ran between the debtors' and felons' yards, and the linen-lines were raised high, dripping with sheets.

'Alison's been here a long time,' she said. 'We'll see.'

At nights I lay awake for hours, tired as my body was, crying sometimes over the separation from Will. Wondering how he could sound so sure I'd be out someday, and soon.

61

The night before the assizes, Mr Ripshaw came into my cell just before lock-up. He was a very portly man, getting on in years, weak-chinned and beady-eyed, with a nose remarkable for the great size of its nostrils. Not a bad man. Each of us up for trial got a jug of watery beer and a few words of wisdom. 'Now, you know what to do,' he said in his podgy, serious way, settling back with ankles crossed and hands linked on his belly. 'You must be very respectful towards all the officers of the court and you must always remember to say "my lord" whenever you address the judge. You must, of course, plead not guilty.'

'That's what Mrs Ripshaw told me,' I said, 'but I don't understand. Everyone knows I'm guilty, I owned up to everything as soon as they caught me.'

He sighed, long-suffering, and his nostrils expanded even more. He put a hand on each knee and leaned forward heavily, about to push himself up to his feet; and he looked at me very gravely with his pale bloodshot eyes. 'I have to explain the law to you,' he said. 'If you plead guilty, the judge will have no choice but to sentence you to death.'

Death.

I repeated it, just to be sure. I smiled. 'I know that, Mr Ripshaw,' I said, 'but I don't understand it. I did it. Everyone knows I did it. Should I not tell the truth? I'm just trying to understand.'

'Of course you tell the truth. But if you plead not guilty, you enable your judge to exercise discretion.'

'The law's beyond me,' I said.

He rose, creaking, to his feet. 'Don't worry too much about it, Margaret. Just take my advice.' He patted me briskly on the shoulder. 'Get a good night's sleep, that's the main thing. It's an early start.'

Of course I couldn't sleep. I drank my hogwash and wrote letters, to my dad, to Uncle Leader, to Dinah Parker and to Mrs Cobbold, because she wasn't coming tomorrow, and there was a chance I may not see her again. *Honoured Madam*, I wrote. I'd asked Mrs Ripshaw, and she'd said that was the right way to address your former mistress. *Honoured Madam, it is with a very full heart I pick up my pen to inform you I am to stand trial in the morning at Bury St Edmunds...*

What could I say? What did I feel? Sentimental. Scared. Cold. A terrible pain in my heart at leaving everyone, a constriction in the throat and a weakening of the bowels if I dared think of the rope. But I must not be a fool. I must appear as I am. How to stand before all those people and be looked at by so many eyes? I must make a good show.

I had my blue gown laid out ready to wear for the trial. Mrs Ripshaw thought it was a good choice: very plain cotton, decent and sober. I wanted to live. What should I do? Fall on my knees and grovel? Never. Would fear make a fool of me? I wanted dignity. Dignity. How could I, having done what I'd done, demand from them dignity? I must be stronger than I had ever been.

It would not be death. Transportation. Was that worse? Hell, worse than Newgate. How could I bear it?

I gave up writing and took to praying.

It was the same routine every night. Sims' footsteps echoing down the flagstoned passage between the yards, where the heavy wooden linen-horses hung on pegs. Then approaching our cells, the jangle of keys, a rap on each door. 'Catchpole!'

'Yes, sir.'

The grinding of the key in the lock.

'Lloyd!'

'Yes, sir.'

Grinding of key.

And the scuffling progress of his footsteps along our restless row, each of us calling out something, yes sir, good night or something worse.

62

We were up, in chains, in the cart by six. Four women and five men trundling slowly onwards to Bury St Edmunds. It was stifling by eight, and still three more hours to go. Great beads of sweat stood up on our faces and dripped from our eyebrows, stinging our eyes. My blue gown was wet under the arms. We shared a few pipes. Passed around a greasy leather bottle of flat warm water. Next to me was a woman called Betty Frame, up for burglary, three months gone and still with the morning sickness. She turned away every once in a while, lifting the lid of a can and retching into it. On the other side was Tom Shop, a lad of such rough, rare beauty it broke my heart to look at him. Across from us was a gaunt and haunted man, mad-eyed, with nails that curved like a wolf's. He sprawled like a pasha and took up far too much room, but no one dared ask him to move.

'Devils!' he hissed from time to time, like Robinson Crusoe, but not quite the same, for he seemed much heavier in his soul. I remembered sailing in Robin's old boat when I was a child. What does he think of me now? He was wrong. Will was not the hell-born babe, I was. Hell-born, hell-bound.

At Stowmarket we stopped for half an hour in the street. All of a sudden I remembered me and Mum and Sue and Ned on Noller's Wagon, going to see my Uncle Leader when I was young: the johnny raw holding out his hand, the back of the driver's head, my mother cracking nuts in her lap. The very creak and rustle and friendly smell of Noller's Wagon. Ned was such a sweet little boy then. Little ratty. Look at him now, such a serious man he'd become. Would he be in court? Look at me – there I'd be with all of them watching, Margaret Catchpole up before the bench.

All those on Noller's Wagon that day were dead now, all but Ned. That was incredible to me.

Now me. My turn. I put my head between my knees and kept it there and realised I'd slept only when the lurch of the cart recalled me.

We were coming into Bury St Edmunds. The crowds held us up. Some palaver was going on ahead of us, a joyous pealing of bells across the sky as if for Christmas, and then a great fanfare of trumpets, and much shouting and whistling.

Tom Shop with his great black eyes looked out, and called: 'What's to do, lads?'

Old Rip, who was riding in front with some of the guards, walked back to us and said it was the sheriff going by; and we got a glimpse of the gilded carriage and white horses, the plumes and braids, the silver and gold, of great fur sleeves on scarlet robes, and a cloudscape of wigs piled high atop the faces of those large, polished men processing robustly through the crowd, which tossed and pitched gaily like a choppy sea. All the inns would be full. There'd be jugglers and bands and a dancing bear, balls in the evening for the quality. Somewhere in all that lot would be my dad and Ned. And who else? Anyone who ever knew me turning up to gawp.

'Who's on the bench? Who've we got?' someone asked.

'Macdonald,' Ripshaw said.

We moved on, the town heaving about us. At the gaol we were given some broth, but I couldn't eat a thing. Neither could Betty, who got her can emptied out and rinsed and was much relieved to be off the cart. Tom Shop ate heartily and said he'd have our bread if we didn't want it. We were put into a very large room with a great host of dross who'd come in from miles around to be tried at the assizes. I was glad we were chained. Some people there I would not at all have cared to see unmanacled. I got a place on a bench, squashed up between Betty and the wild man. The wild man smelled strongly of cloves, which he carried in his pockets and shoved between his teeth and crunched from time to time.

'Look at your nails,' I said. 'You want to cut them, you do.'

He looked startled, held out his hands and stared at his nails as if he'd only just noticed them. It set him off blinking.

'Who'm you?' he whispered.

'Margaret,' I said. 'You want to get them cut. They'll stop you doing things.'

'No, no,' he said, with a worried shake of his head, 'they's useful.'

I'd rather have been stuck with little Tom Shop, who'd fallen into a beautiful boy-sleep of soft flickering lids and open mouth, his swarthy head tipped back against the wall. I looked at his throat and wondered what he'd done.

'The devils!' my companion sighed, and closed his eyes.

We waited. They brought water.

I heard a great clock striking noon.

The guards got us in groups, herding us here and there, separating the men from the women, crowding us on all sides and becoming tense, hushing us and making signals to one another. There was a heavy door that groaned and swung to behind us with a discreet shush, then a long dark place – a tunnel, it seemed – but the walls were of wood, and it smelled of wax. Things twittered in my innards. My mouth and throat clagged. When I tried to lick my lips, my tongue grew fat and powdered and clung like a slug. This would not do. I must not cry. A further door opened and we were ushered through into light. They put us in three cages in the middle of a great room, eight or nine to a cage. So many people! So *many!* Rows of grave-faced, well-fed gentlemen, all looking at us. Everywhere, a vast throng crowding the place like foam, the people all agog and ajostle to see us. It was like an oven. Through iron bars we could see the bench, very high.

I don't know the half of what went on, such a toing and froing, such a great handing up and down of papers for such a long time before the thing got going. They swore in the grand jury. The name of my old master, John Cobbold, was read out with all the other esteemed esquires. There he was, nodding curtly, black-clad and white-haired, very serious.

Then, with huge declamation, those very great men, wide as houses in their robes, their black-topped wigs towering and cascading, took their places on the bench. The Lord Chief Baron Macdonald sat in the middle.

It was two hours before I was called. Time to look around and find faces in the crowd. First I saw my dad and Ned, very close and just beneath me. Then Uncle and Aunt Catchpole, Dr Stebbing, old Mary Cracknell, Dinah Parker and her Dolly. Will was not there. I looked for, but did not see, Uncle Leader. Each one my eye found had a smile or a small wave for me. That moved me wonderfully, but what really did for me was when the tears started trickling from my dad's eyes, because he wasn't a cryer. Was it because he'd already lost so much and weathered it well, that he suffered so badly to see me in chains? I'd been cruel. Stupid. I'd broken hearts. Oh, Dad, now you've gone and done it, I thought as my nose started to run. Now here I am snivelling like an infant in front of everyone. But I had time to collect myself. Time for the fear to subside, time to summon dignity, as one by one we were called up.

Sheep-stealer, death. Stealer of a pair of boots, transportation.

What chance have I?

Each time, great rustlings of papers and passings backwards and forwards.

A girl stole a silver ring and got the pillory. Boy took a leg of lamb, whipped. Beggars, whipped. The wild man had shown his private parts to a lady in Wickham Market. He got three months in Ipswich Gaol. Then Tom Shop. Poor poor Tom Shop. Swearing he'd not known the purse in his pocket was not his own. He'd picked it up by mistake from the grocer's counter. He put his hands together in prayer before the judges and hung his head, weeping, lifting his chains to wipe away snot.

'I didn't mean it,' he sobbed.

I saw a red beard. Uncle Leader waved at me from the back. Will had not come. Poor Tom Shop got death. He was to be hanged just over Sims' doorway, the new drop, they called it. Better than the old, no doubt. Tom Shop's Adam's apple was a soft shading in his pale throat. If they'd hearts they'd never do it. Often they reprieved, last minute to make you sweat.

If the sweat in that room could have been collected it would have turned a mill. At every sentence the crowd reacted, sometimes a sigh, sometimes a jeer, a shout, a booing, a weeping, a waving of handkerchiefs. I looked in vain for the mother of Tom Shop in the crowd, someone to plead for him, but he hadn't a soul.

Then a paper was handed from the jury box up to the clerk, who read it out: *'A true bill against Margaret Catchpole, for horse-stealing.'*

The bolt shot back. I was up the steps and in the dock, standing before the bench. Lord Chief Baron read out the charge, that on such-and-such a night I'd taken a roan horse, the property of John Cobbold Esquire, and had ridden it to London and there offered it for sale. He looked at me very severely over the top of his eye-glasses. 'How say you, prisoner at the bar,' he intoned, 'are you guilty, or not guilty?'

'Guilty, my lord.'

He stared at me silently for some moments, unblinking. At last he leaned forward, knotting his fingers. He had a very fat and swollen face, what I call a gouty face, ruby-cheeked. 'Prisoner at the bar,' he said, 'the crime of which you are accused is a most heinous one, one that, unfortunately, is all too rife in this county.'

I kept my eyes steady, on his.

'Do you understand, prisoner at the bar, that if you plead guilty to this offence, the sentence of the law is death? Prisoner at the bar, do you have anything to say which might give good cause for me to consider why the extreme sentence of the law should not be passed upon you?'

I cleared my throat, looking nowhere but at him, straight into his eyes, for he was only a man and I should be able to talk to him. 'I don't understand,' I said. 'Everyone knows what happened. Should I not tell the truth?' My voice was surprisingly firm. 'I did take Mr Cobbold's horse and I'm very sorry for it. How can I say I didn't? What can I say? They were a very very good master and mistress to me all the time I worked for them, and I don't know how to say how horrible I feel for what I did. If you don't think I haven't sat and gone over this again and again in my mind every second since it happened ... and Mr and Mrs Cobbold have been wonderful to me, my lord. After all I did, they've forgiven me.'

I could say no more. I looked down. There was a spattering of applause from the public. I kept my eyes down and held my breath. I heard the scratching of pens, and a mumbling that passed along the bench like a catspaw of breeze over corn. The judge cleared his throat. He asked if anyone would vouch for my character, and although I'd known beforehand who would speak, what followed shook me to the core. Standing before that hotch-potch crowd and listening as one after another of those good people stood up for me, I wept sincerely.

'George Stebbing Esquire,' the clerk announced, 'surgeon of Ipswich.'

The dear doctor said he'd known me from childhood and I'd always been of good character. He said I was intelligent and hard-working and had done sterling work looking after my mother and sister when they were sick. He look straight at me and smiled.

'If she were to be set at liberty,' he said, still looking into my eyes, 'I would have no hesitation whatsoever in offering her immediate employment in my own house.'

Sweet, sweet man.

Uncle Leader was after Dr Stebbing. He said I'd always been a good girl and had looked after my cousins when their mother died. My aunt, that woman I'd hated, said I'd been worth my weight in gold to her. 'This is completely out of character,' she said. 'We couldn't believe it when we heard about it.'

'I'd take her into my service again,' she said, 'oh yes, I would.'

Poor old Dad was in tears again. So was Mary Cracknell, so was Dinah, snuffling discreetly into her Dolly's brown curls; even some of the crowd cried, because they loved a good show, and Tom Shop had already opened their floodgates.

At last, Mr Cobbold stepped into the witness box.

'You are the prosecutor in this case?'

'That is correct, my lord,' my old master said, clearing his throat and speaking very clearly and precisely, 'and I would like to make it clear that had it been my own decision, I should not have pressed charges. I was bound over to do so, as your lordship knows.'

Macdonald nodded. 'Proceed,' he said, writing something down.

Mr Cobbold gripped the edge of the witness box and stood tall, speaking slowly and strongly like a priest in a pulpit, with long pauses, addressing the room at large:

'Margaret Catchpole worked for my family for three years,' he said, 'both as cook, and nursemaid. During that period, she proved herself time and again to be an invaluable asset to my household – always discharging her duty faithfully – and caring admirably for my children – who are now most distraught at her plight.' He turned towards the bench. 'I must mention, my lord,' he said in a more conversational tone, 'that on one memorable occasion, when my three-year-old son had fallen into a pond and was in danger of drowning – with no hesitation whatsoever, *this* woman–' he waved a hand in my direction '–dived into the water and brought him out.'

There was a hum in court.

'May I say, at some considerable risk to her own safety.'

He paused, licked his lips, surveyed his audience, and continued: 'I have found her to be both resourceful and good-natured. My family and I have only the warmest feelings towards her. I *firmly* believe she acted on an impulse she now sincerely regrets; and I remain convinced that she is neither a hardened nor an abandoned character. For these reasons, my lord,' and he bent his head most respectfully towards the bench, 'may I say that it is my firm conviction that if ever a case called for mercy, this is it.'

If I could, I'd have stepped out of the dock and gone over and given him a kiss.

I looked at Mr Cobbold as he stepped down but he did not meet my eyes.

63

They were a long time deliberating, so they gave me a chair to sit on. I looked around. Will should have been here. My friends smiled at me whenever they caught my eye. I could not smile. I tried. He could have slipped in at the back and stayed out of sight. Maybe he had. A long time, I thought, that's a good sign. A whole half-hour passed, and the crowd grew restive. He *should* have come. He was a coward, that's what. Such a brave man, and a coward. Old Rip came up to me, leaned his elbow on the dock and whispered, 'Bear up, Margaret, not long now.'

At last, the judges settled their wide sleeves. The Lord Chief Baron adjusted his eye-glasses on the ridge of his large red nose. A hush fell. The Lord Chief Baron looked at me very steadily for a long moment.

Then–

He took the black cap from beneath the desk and placed it on his head.

The crowd gasped.

He was glad, he said, that I showed repentance. He said I'd enjoyed many privileges in my life, not least of which was employment by an excellent master and mistress, and the good opinion of my friends. I don't know the half of what he said. Sometimes it sounded kind. But then he made much of the heinousness of my crime. Regrettably, horse-stealing was committed with such boldness and frequency these days, he said, that it was very rare for leniency to be shown. This very night, he would see to it personally that all my representations of good character should be sent to the King, in whose power lay mercy. However, he said, I'd made it abundantly clear that I knew right from wrong, and therefore my transgression was worse than if I were depraved. It would be cruel for him to offer false hope, and the best he could advise was that I prepare my soul for eternity.

'It only remains,' he concluded, 'for me to fulfil my duty by passing sentence of the court upon you – which is that you be taken from the place where you now stand, back to the place whence you came, and thence to the place of execution, and there be hanged by the neck until you be dead; and then may God have mercy upon your soul.'

Someone cried out. I remember nothing more.

Time

64

'Think of those other poor wretches, still waiting. At least you know.'

They said I shall suffer Saturday week.

The woman sitting up with us on watch was huge and fat and peeled fruit in the great valley of her lap, in her apron. We were back in Bury Gaol, me and two other women sentenced to hang. The assizes were still going on and we couldn't go back to Ipswich till all nine who'd set out had been tried. Two days more, maybe three.

The cell was cold stone, a small room with a bench, a rug, a Bible and a prayer book. A candle glimmered in a recess in the side wall. There was a tiny window, very high up, with a double row of bars.

'Yes, well,' said our watcher, who seemed remarkably jolly considering the job she had, 'as I always say, there's many a slip twixt cup and lip.'

'What's that supposed to mean?' a woman with a red eye asked.

'It means he'll pardon some before he goes anyway,' she said, 'because he always does,' and offered round the slivers of apple. We were more interested in the brandy. It put heat in our bellies. I'd asked for pen, ink and paper, and spent my time writing letters to say thanks to all who'd spoken for me.

After the candle was out I wrote in the dark, a

letter to Dad and Ned. I didn't want to go to sleep. I didn't ever want to sleep again. Time was short. I must see Will before I died. Died. The word itself was strange. Sue died. Mum died. James died. Robert died. I died. Two days and nights passed in limbo. I didn't sleep. Will wandered around in my mind. We bad women, I thought: me – and Jane Brewer who I saw from Robert's meaty shoulders, how the death sweat shook her; Ann Beddingfield, burned to fine ash and her lover hung on Rushmere Heath; Mary Bryant, who got away from Botany Bay but lost her babies. Bad women, all of us. Sisters, we were. And brothers. Poor Tom Shop. He could've been Will. Where *was* Will? What was happening to him? Dad must get word to him. I can't die before I've seen him. Saturday week. How strange and ordinary those words. My hands were cold and covered in sweat. The body has wisdom and knows. My life had quivered down to one big prayer from me to everything that was not me: do not cast me off, do not shed me like a skin. I kept thinking about death and what happens when we die. Sometimes I did not feel so bad, but in a second, how it could change. It was the dying, I minded. The pain. When I thought of that I touched my throat and swallowed, and the life within felt inextinguishable; then wild-eyed fear rushed in, shook me as a dog shakes a rat, and left me lying on the floor, sick.

Time marched on, relentless, caring nothing.

It played tricks, stretched long like a leech, grew fat and short, rolled over, fell away like old masonry. It was like weather. You couldn't do anything about it, it would have its way.

Someone watched with us all the time, sometimes the fat woman, sometimes another. Was it only two days and nights? It ran by like sand. It lasted an eternity. There were certain aches. One grinding, impossible, in every part of me, the pull of fear. One cruel and bloody, right in the centre of my heart, and that one was grief, I suppose, stabbing at the thought of Will and my dad and just about anyone I ever knew. Everyone was dear to me now. Even Aunt Leader. Even John Luff. Even Mat Sampson, who'd made such game of me at Priory Farm and got me in trouble. Everyone's dear when you're going to die.

I hadn't thought about Priory Farm in ages. On Saturday afternoon, a week to the day before death, I fell into a strange deep sleep and dreamed I was there, running about under the trees near the little wooden bridge that used to go over the stream that came out of the moat. I was playing with Bosun, the turnspit dog, and it was a beautiful day, glorious sunshine. Spring it must have been, because the daffodils were out. We had a lovely romp, Bosun and me. It was a very happy dream.

Someone shook me awake.

'Rise and shine,' the fat woman said. 'Here's your Mr Ripshaw wanting a word. Quick now.'

Coming up from sleep was hard. It clung to me like honey as she led me out and down a passage into a small neat room with a desk, and a window that startled me with its lack of bars, looking out on to plain blue sky faintly patterned with the branches of distant trees. Two wooden chairs were placed before an empty fireplace. Mr Ripshaw rose from one. 'There, Margaret,' he said, 'it looks as if we're to keep you with us a while yet, and I for one must tell you I'm very glad indeed.'

I felt faint and my head ached.

'You're reprieved, Margaret.'

He sniffed noisily, as if he'd just been taking snuff, took my arm firmly and made me sit in the other chair, then seated himself before me and gave me the news. Mr Cobbold had got up a petition for me. All his friends on the grand jury and the petty jury had signed. The vicar from Nacton had sent a letter.

'What does this mean?' I shouted.

It felt like more fear. I can't explain. Like a thunderclap in my head.

'Your sentence has been commuted to seven years' transportation,' he said.

Australia. I was going to hell for seven years. 'However,' he said, 'you can put Australia out of your mind. The fact is there are nowhere near enough boats. What it actually means is that you'll be serving your sentence in Ipswich Gaol.'

I was dumb. I put my head in my hands.

'With time off for good conduct you could be out in four or five years.'

Tom Shop

65

Those years in Ipswich Gaol a great melancholy came down on me, though I was not by nature a gloomy person. It settled upon me with overbearing arms the Saturday I should have been hanged from the new drop in front of the turnkey's lodge, the day they hanged Tom Shop there instead.

Finally, Will had been to see me. We'd spoken through an iron grating. The sight of his face made me angry. His hair was wild and dirty. He looked naked-eyed, anguished as a whipped child.

'Three weeks and not a word!' I said. 'What do you think it was like for me, thinking I was going to die? And you not here? A time like that! You should have been here.'

'But, Pegs,' he protested, 'it wouldn't have been good for your case! I saw your dad and Ned, we all said – you have all your grand friends working for you, they said, and Bargood was putting in words where he could – and he knows a lot of people – they all said, everyone, I should keep away. I'm not the kind you should have sniffing around at a time like this, that's what they all said.'

'There's not a thing on you now,' I said, 'and you know that.'

He put his lips to the grating. 'But there's talk, Pegs, there's always talk, and I'm in as deep as ever now. There's no end of work, Pegs! It's the only way I can make up for what we lost.'

'What *you* lost, you mean.' I put my teeth around his lip where it pressed at the grating, and I bit hard.

When I let him go, tears of pain stood on the rims of his eyes. 'Oh, Pegs,' he said, 'we're finished with this country, me and you. Two and a half years at most I reckon you'll do – if that, with friends like you've got. I know it's hard, it's foul, but can you get through it?'

'What choice do I have?' I started to cry.

'Pegs, don't,' he said, and the tears on the rims of his eyes spilled over.

He put his fingers through the grating and I took them with mine.

'Oh, what a mess, Will!'

'I know, I know,' he moaned.

'Stop behaving like a child! Grow up!'

'I'm sorry,' he said. 'You think it's all my fault, don't you? You think because I lost the money...'

'Oh, what does it matter? I might have been dead.'

'No, no, no, Bargood said...'

'He doesn't know everything.'

'Oh, Pegs, why did you take the horse? I never meant for you to do that.'

'Two more minutes,' the guard said, putting his head round the door.

66

It was Saturday, the day of my death. I worked my way through the scrawny carnations. A crowd had been roistering outside for an hour, their hubbub rising and falling. I did it for him, I was thinking. That's why I stole that horse. To get him out of trouble. What did he have to go getting himself in trouble for in the first place? Now I was the one paying. I hated this place. I couldn't stand the idea of the time that stretched ahead.

I could not feel grateful enough. Mrs Cobbold, who had been allowed to visit me in my cell on account of her being a lady, went on and on about how lucky I was, and of course she was right, but I hated this place. It wasn't so bad, everyone said, a pleasure garden next to Newgate.

A sudden great cry from the crowd burst up like an explosion from the front of the gaol. I jumped to my feet, dropping a handful of weeds and dirt. It was Tom Shop getting hanged. I saw his face in my mind and put my hands over my eyes. It should have been me. Tom Shop had no clever friends.

The crowd roared again. Was he dancing still?

A woman who was weeding at the other end of the bed got up and came and put her hand on my shoulder. 'Are you all right, Margaret?'

'What a world,' was all I could say.

I was back in my old cell with Alison Lloyd next

door. Every day I did what I should. I was good. I got on with everyone. I wanted to live. Never again did I want to feel fear like that. But it had left its trace, a darkness I had not known before.

A few weeks later Mrs Cobbold had her baby, so she didn't come for a while. Dad brought me in a harvest-cake. He wanted to spend Christmas Day with me in my cell, he said there was nowhere else he'd rather be; but three weeks later got word to me he was feeling poorly. Then suddenly there was Ned to see me, looking very grave, walking in all stiff, holding his hat clumsily by the brim. Ned hated coming to the prison. He felt great shame.

'Dad's worse,' he said. 'He's an old man, he's easily knocked sideways.'

'What is it?'

I went cold.

'A fever of sorts,' he said dully, 'a glut of phlegm on the chest. Dr Stebbing says there's a lot of it going about.'

'But he *will* be all right?'

Ned shrugged.

'You think it's my fault, don't you?' I said.

Ned stared at me. 'I didn't say that.'

'You don't have to.'

He turned away, flushing. 'I'm just telling you,' he said peevishly, 'I'm not saying anything.'

I never saw Dad again. He was never strong enough to come in. He died just before Christmas. They wouldn't let me out for the funeral, but Mrs Ripshaw came up to me in the middle of the morning wash, as I was standing in the passage where the linen-horses hang, my forehead pressed against the cold stone. She told me to go and have a nice rest in my cell if I wanted to. It was decent of her, she didn't have to do that. He was so quiet, Dad. He'd said so little in life, just driven the horses as long as he could, then wielded a spade till he could no longer hold it. He'd never said a word against me. I remembered him lifting me up to stroke the horses when I was little. I remembered him rubbing old Dandy's shoulders down.

Ned was right. I'd upset him and it had made him weak. I cried till I was drained, then I sat up and composed myself and stared at the future.

I could live it out.

Will wrote he was saving hard. He thought of me all the time. This brought me pain. Rube had been asking after me, and so had all at the Neptune. *Last night*, he said, *we drank your health in Portuguese brandy. I am told I can visit you again in March, I will try for your birthday.*

Mrs Cobbold came once or twice, bringing books. She knew everyone, so she could come whenever she wanted. I think she thought it was all rather fun. I wanted her to bring the new baby and she kept saying she would, but she never did.

'I know this must sound ridiculous to you,' she said, withdrawing a lemon-coloured glove and running a finger up and down the spines of a pile of books she had just deposited on my table, 'but really it's quite possible for you to see this in some curious way as a gift from the gods. Had I but world enough and time! Ah, how often have I said that? As the world has contracted into a nutshell, so you have time now to study. A candle, a table and a good book! How marvellous!'

'I don't know about time, madam,' I said. 'What do you think we do all day? We ain't just sitting about on our backsides.'

'Of course you're not. And neither should you be. Hard work and study can be a good combination. You saw Newgate; give thanks you didn't end up in there.' She put both hands on my shoulders, a habit she'd taken to, and smiled into my face. 'One day this will all be over, Margaret, I promise you,' she said. 'Things could have been *far, far* worse. We'll get you a position again. Someone who knows of your past and is prepared to give you another chance. Believe me, such people do exist.'

'Dr Stebbing said he'd have me.'

'There you are then! The thing to do now is settle down and use your time in here well.'

After she'd gone I looked at the books she'd left. One of them was *Roderick Random*, the book Charles and Will had talked about so long ago, the night we left the Cracknells' christening party and walked down to the Orwell shore with Robinson Crusoe. I opened it, turned the pages. It looked very hard but when Will came to see me a week after my birthday, I was able to tell him I'd reached page seventeen. I showed him my copy through the grating and he grinned, showing all his teeth.

'She brought you that, did she?' he said. 'Not so la-di-da as she looks then.'

But he was the bearer of bad news and didn't know how to say it. Ned had gone away.

'Said to tell you he'll write,' Will said, trying to make it sound cheerful. 'A nice long letter when he's got himself settled.'

Someone had ragged him about me in the pub.

'He's been brooding,' Will said. 'You know what he's like.'

He'd gone into Cambridgeshire and got work as a shepherd where no one knew him.

I got a letter in June. Another the Christmas after. Neither said much. My uncles and aunts wrote more than he did.

67

Every day was the same. My cell was always the same. Same smell, same walls, same voices, same steam, same dirt, same echo, same food. Same thoughts going round and round and round inside my head, and life going on without me.

The Female Sailor

68

It was a long time before I first thought of escape. It was after the August assizes two years after my sentence. Mr Ripshaw had recommended me for good conduct to the magistrates and they'd passed the appeal up to the Lord Chief Baron. Old Rip had been quite buckish about it. 'I'm always a one to counsel caution, Margaret, as you know,' he told me the night before he left, 'but to be honest with you, I think you've got a fair chance.' He smiled. 'And if not this time I can almost guaran*tee* the next one.'

The next one was six months away. Two years' good conduct. Had I not proved myself? What more did they want? I could get through another six months. Yes, I could. I could make myself a calendar, it would be something to do. I'd make it nice. I'd write to Mrs Cobbold if tomorrow's appeal failed. I'd ask her to bring me some good paper and a drawing pencil, and I'd draw a picture for each day, something very simple, and the number. She could bring me some colour and I'd make it nice and she could give it to the children for the nursery. That was it – I could make it a nursery thing for the children, it would be a project for the winter evenings. And when it was done, I would be free.

All the while Ripshaw was away at the assizes, for three whole days, I prepared myself for this. I told myself not to mind if we failed this time, it was perhaps only to be expected. I even planned in rough some of the pictures for my calendar. It got so that I almost wished the appeal would fail so I could get on with it.

So why, when Rip came back and said, 'Not this time, Margaret, but bear up, bear up now, we can try again' – why then was I so desolate? Why did my stomach curdle and turn sour, and my cell walls insult me so vilely that night when I tried to read?

They were cold. They watched, they crowded me.

Rip said horse-stealing was still on the up, that was the problem. Macdonald had a particular antipathy towards it. He thought maybe Macdonald had had a horse stolen himself.

69

Six more months.

I could do it.

I asked Mrs Cobbold for paper and made a start on the calendar. It wasn't very good. I'm no artist. Will wrote: *We will celebrate your next birthday in Amsterdam*. That would be next March, I'd be thirty-eight. By the time my mother was thirty-eight she'd had all of us. I began to look up at the tops of the walls. I began to think strange thoughts, such as: what if you wanted to escape? How would you go about doing it? Was it possible? It *was* possible, I knew, because I'd heard of it happening. Someone Rube knew got out of Colchester. Jack Shepherd of old got out of Newgate three times, God knows how. And look at Mary Bryant, *she* got out of Botany Bay.

Just supposing it were necessary, how would you go about getting out of this place?

Planning it was something to do, along with the calendar. Mrs Cobbold loved the calendar. Every time she came she wanted to see the latest. She was pregnant again, and they were preparing to move back to the Cliff, so the house was in uproar. If only I was there to help with the children, she said. She'd never realised I could draw so well. If she'd only known she'd have had me doing pictures for the childrens' walls long before.

'Ah now, madam, you're just being kind,' I told her but she said no, absolutely not, so I showed her my latest effort, which was a number four made to look like a ship in full sail.

'Look at that sea,' I said. 'It looks like porridge.'

'Nonsense, it's pretty. Who is that coughing? Has she seen Dr Stebbing?'

'It's Alison Lloyd, she's had that cough for ages. Dr Stebbing gives her stuff but it doesn't work.'

She listened, cocking her head. 'I'll bring her some ginger punch,' she said decisively. 'So, Margaret! Are we planning for the future?'

'I always do, madam.'

One thing I noticed. For all she kept saying if only I was there, not once did she offer to have me back. That upset me. I suppose we both knew it wouldn't work, not after all that had happened. But still.

Anyway, it was Amsterdam for me and Will, I was sure of it. It was in my bones that it was time for a great change. Too much had gone wrong here. So, as I lay in bed nights listening to Alison hacking steadily away next door, I thought of the English shoreline receding as the ship took us away from Harwich to a new, unknown life. There were so many sailors in Amsterdam, it would be just like home. I didn't tell Mrs Cobbold, I let her go on mulling over this or that good person who might provide me with employment here, in case a stop-gap should be needed. And when I wasn't thinking about Amsterdam, I was considering such things as the spikes on the tops of the walls, and the gaps in between. Could a thin person squeeze through? A skeleton maybe. The spikes along the stone passage were straight up on both sides. You'd never do it, and anyway there was only more yard on the other side. All the outside walls had *chevaux de frise* on top, massive crossed spikes that turned over on a bar. In the felons' yard there was a spike missing next to one of the posts holding the bar.

I bet they'd never leave a thing like that unseen to in one of the men's yards, I thought. I bet they don't think a woman could do it. I could get in that gap, I thought. But I'd never get up there. And if I did, how would I get down the other side? That wall was four times my height. A rope. The linen-lines on their posts. I wondered why no one had thought of it before. Of course they must have, but given up. Too many problems. First of all I'd never be able to throw the line that high. And even if I could, we were locked in our cells at night so I'd have to do it in broad daylight with the guards looking on. *Very* clever.

Even though it was impossible I went on plotting, worrying away at it in my head. By Christmas I was nervous. What if they don't let me out this time? I thought. What if I have to do the whole seven years? I wasn't even halfway through. I started biting my nails as the time approached, and that's a thing I never did before. This time the appeal was going to the Secretary of State himself. It was sure to succeed, wasn't it? But when the time came I was so scared, and what made it worse was the empty cell next door to me the night before, because they'd just taken Alison Lloyd away to the hospital. At lock-up, along came Sims jangling his keys.

'Good night!'

Clang.

'Good night!'

Clang.

And so on and so on, then me, then straight past Alison's cell and on to the next. The disturbance to routine jarred. When his footsteps had passed away I thought of the empty space next door. It was very quiet without Alison. I couldn't sleep. Ripshaw would be back about noon and then I'd know my fate. If my reprieve came through, this time tomorrow I might be in Aldeburgh with Will. Back where we started, but alive. Will was talking to Captain Bargood about two rooms in a house in the middle of Amsterdam. I'd ask for no more. I'd send Mrs Cobbold where she could reach me. It was very cold that night and the wind blustered dreadfully and made itself heard in spite of those walls. I wished Alison were back, coughing or not. Poor old Alison. She'd never go out of here. How strange, I thought, if I'm gone before she gets back. I'll never see her again.

70

The appeal failed.

Horse-stealing was a blight on the country, the Secretary of State said. And the Lord Chief Baron, who could have interceded, agreed.

So that was that.

Alison came back that night. She heard me crying in the night after I'd ripped up the calendar. She called out: 'Next time, Margaret! Don't despair, girl!'

Calling out set her coughing. With a great tearing sound, she cleared her throat and spat. I was glad she was back. 'Alison,' I said, 'Old Rip says I have to wait another year now.'

'Gaarrgh!' she said, and Sims yelled: 'Quiet!'

His reply was a volley of abuse from us all.

All through the ward a hum of communication persisted into the night, tappings and rustlings and whisperings. We slept, Alison and I, with our heads either side of a wall which was solid enough, but had channels and labyrinths within, through which sound travelled; so that if you knew which bits to put your mouths and ears to, you could manage a conversation of sorts.

'I'll never get out,' I said.

'*I* won't,' she replied, '*you* will.'

'I want another judge. It's always Macdonald.'

'Macdonald,' she said after a moment. 'I remember him. He looked like a side of pork.'

'Have you ever noticed,' I said to her, as we were let out after Tuesday wash, 'what a natural ladder one of these would make if you put it up against the wall?'

We were in the stone passage, struggling to haul one of the linen-horses down off its big iron peg. She was a large woman, Alison, very strong, and I was thin but tough, so they'd put us together. The linen-horses were wooden and weighed a ton. If he had time, Sims usually got them down while we were still in the washroom. He'd drag them out into the drying-ground ready for the morning. Today he'd not got round to it.

Alison grinned. 'Oh, you devil,' she said.

'What do you think?'

'I think it would make a fine ladder if you only wanted to go halfway up the wall.'

'I could do it,' I said. 'The horse would get me halfway. Standing on top I could throw a rope.'

She laughed. 'I don't think you could.'

'I could.'

I dragged, she pushed it along the passage and round into the drying-ground.

'See,' I said. 'Look, rope everywhere.'

The lines stretched here and there all over the yard, the props leaned this way and that, and everywhere, women were reaching up with pegs in their mouths.

I could do it.

After the linen was hung it was too cold for the

yard, so we went back to our cells to wait for lock-up. Alison came into mine and we smoked a pipe. 'Go on then, tell me,' she said, 'how would you do it?'

'I'd need your help.'

'Go on.'

It would have to be at night, well after lock-up. I'd need to be out of my cell. If Ripshaw was away so much the better, so much more of a delay. They'd be running round like headless chickens, Mrs Rip and all the guards, wondering what to do. It must be a Monday or a Tuesday, a wash day, so all the linen-horses would be down off their pegs and out in the yards. And somehow I must be out of my cell.

71

'Alison,' I said, 'you remember when you was away that night in the hospital? He didn't lock your door that night. He never does lock the empty cells. I've noticed that.'

A slow smile started. 'Go on,' she said.

I jumped up. 'You stay here.' I ran next door, lay down on her bed and put my mouth to the wall. 'Can you hear me?' I called.

'Of course I can.'

I got up and dashed back feeling quite excited. 'Now stand outside,' I said. 'Stand outside my door as if you're Sims locking me in, and we'll close both the doors and I'll call through the wall, and you tell me what it sounds like.'

We laughed as we did it. She rapped my door and called out, 'Night-night, Margaret,' and I called back, 'Good night.'

'Cling-clang!' she cried. 'That's you banged up for the night!'

All along the row there was talk and babble. No one took any notice of us.

'What did it sound like?'

'Like you shouting through a wall.'

'If you were Sims, would it fool you? Would you think I was in my own cell?'

She said she thought if she were Sims and not expecting anything she probably wouldn't twig. 'I know what you want me to do,' she said. 'You want me to get taken bad one day, very bad so they'll take me to the hospital again, don't you?'

'I do.'

'It's dangerous, you know, Margaret.'

'I know.'

She spat out tobacco.

'When?' she said.

We planned it for the night of the twenty-fifth of March, a Tuesday not long after my birthday, the one that should have been celebrated in Amsterdam. Instead we'd be talking through the grating again, Will and I. Old Rip would be away for a week at the assizes from the twentieth. We decided that Alison would get taken bad just after supper on the twenty-fifth; a stomach ache *and* a chest ache would be called for, she thought, just to be on the safe side. She looked forward to performing. She worried though. 'Where will you go when you get out?' she asked. 'You won't have much time. All hell's going to break loose first thing in the morning.'

'I'll arrange it with Will,' I assured her. When he came for my birthday visit, I had him put his ear as close to the grating as possible and in it I poured all my plans.

He closed his eyes and swallowed. 'No,' he whispered back, 'it's much too dangerous.'

'It is not! I can do this, Will. I've thought about everything. Every little detail is taken care of. All you have to do is find me a safe place to lie low till we can get a boat. I can't stay here any more, Will, it's *killing* me, I *hate* it. It's not right to live locked away like this.'

His face was close to mine so I could see how he was no longer young. How the boy was hiding in there under the seamed and weathered mask of him, and how the creases that cut from the sides of his nose to the corners of his big cruel mouth had grown etched and dark. Did I say cruel? Yes, his mouth was cruel. But *he* was not. 'They'd kill you, Pegs,' he said very softly. 'They'd shoot you like a dog, don't think they wouldn't, if you was caught escaping. I don't want anything to happen to you.'

'Nothing will!' I was fierce. 'I want my life back! I will have it by hell or high water, or I'll die! I don't care.'

He kissed my fingers. 'I don't want you to die,' he said.

'Come here.' And I caught his lip between my finger and thumb through the grating, as if I'd pull him through. 'I'm doing it anyway,' I whispered tenderly, 'even if you won't help me. I'm doing it.

Understand that, my love? There's not a thing in this world you can do to stop me.'

He blinked rapidly a few times, clearing his eyes. We said nothing for a long time, but our eyes held firm.

'Tell me when,' he said.

'Twenty-fifth. Midnight. Wait for me at the church. Bring me a sailor's jacket, and a hat.'

72

They never minded if I had a candle and sat up late. They trusted me. Good as gold I was, night after night with my books and my mending. I'm nifty with a needle. As well as stockings and aprons, I had both sheets off my bed and laid them out on the floor, and cut out a rough pair of trousers like a sailor's, and a loose smock, the kind a shepherd might wear. I have to admit they weren't the finest of duds by the time I'd finished, but they'd serve.

We were late knocking off that Tuesday night, because poor Alison was taken so bad just after we'd had our tea. You should have heard her groaning and swearing, doubled over with her knees on the wet floor. I got to her first. She grasped my hand in her great paw, pulling me close and whispering hoarsely, 'Do well, chick,' before redoubling her cries. There was a convergence. I noticed she was wheezing; that wasn't sham. They never should have had her in this steamy hole. Sims appeared. She'd lain herself out on the stone floor in the dirty water by now.

'It's her stomach,' I said.

'Feel sick, do you?' he asked her.

'Pain,' she croaked, 'terrible pain.'

I swear that woman should have been on the stage.

'Where?'

'Everywhere,' she said. 'Oh mercy!'

'Can you walk?' he asked. 'Can you get up?'

She was too big a woman to carry. Four of us supported her to the door. I have to say she did look peculiar, face all slick and red and greasy, a few tendrils of soaking-wet hair crawling out from under her cap and clinging like leeches to her forehead. But then we all looked like that after two days in the wash-house. We sat her down on the floor in the passage. Sims told me to run for Mrs Rip. My blood was up again, the first time in years, up and running fast, as it did when I stood in the dark stable and whispered in Crop's warm ear that we were off on an adventure; or when I plunged down Bishop's Hill on frisky Jem. Something was afoot that could not be stopped. They took Alison away, doubled over and bravely fighting down the groans. Good. She wasn't overdoing it.

I looked up. The sky was darkening already.

We had to make up the extra work she'd left. By the time we were finally let out in the yard it was full dark. The linen-horses weren't there. He hadn't put them out like he usually did.

'Sims!' I called, hot in the chest and about the head and trying to sound as if it didn't matter, 'didn't you get the horses out?'

'Been rushed off my feet all day, Margaret,' he said. 'All this with Alison, I've not had time. I'll do them first thing in the morning.'

It was a dose of cold water.

The linen-lines were there, on the posts. So were the crotches and clothes-props. Wild thoughts came into my head. I'd throw the rope with herculean strength up the wall, all twenty foot of it and more. Never. Might as well try and fly over the wall. Will would wait all night for me at the church and I wouldn't come. He'd think I was shot. Alison would come back from the hospital tomorrow and find all her fine mummer's skills in vain.

I wandered round the yard, fairly twitching. They'd not keep me here, not now. Never. A ladder. I looked at the palings of Ripshaw's garden – they'd make a ladder, of a kind. Would they hold me? Would they break? I was strong. Surely if – no – Sims was a Goliath compared to me. Tall I may be but I was always a lathy girl. I'd never be able to get one of those horses down alone. And if I did, what a screech it would make dragging it round into the yard. I strolled over to the palings and touched them. I could never get them out, not without anyone hearing. My face began to crumple. I was a child denied a treat I'd looked forward to all week. I would not have it. I ranged about the yard, muttering under my breath, blinking burning tears back from my eyes. It was all up. I was done. Finished.

I sat down on the ground and put my head between my knees.

'Are you all right, Margaret?'

This was Prinny Robin, a funny elf-like little girl who'd robbed her mistress. I scarcely knew her.

She held out her hand.

'You're fading away, poor girl,' I said, accepting it and letting her draw me to my feet. 'Fading away, poor girl.'

Prinny was for the drop, for sure.

My eyes fell on Mr Ripshaw's flower bed, so long asleep through winter and now once more awake. The snowdrops had shown, and the crocuses. Now we were seeing shoots, small and pale and shy, in need of protection from these still cold nights. Old Rip had put the garden frame across the bed, but it had not been covered since he'd gone away last Wednesday. Whose job that should have been I do not know.

I put my arms round Prinny and gave her a squeeze, surprising her. I was all water that night, as if it were my last, as if I were going to die in the morning. Poor child, for the drop, she so small. No use to wonder would it hurt. Yes, it hurt. Yes it hurt, all of us knew it hurt. As if she were a pup bound for the bucket, I wondered in my soul at her. I remember my dad drowning pups. I remembered their blind, unbegun faces. All you knew was they were there and then gone. Getting wherever they were going was a great hurt to them. Of that there was no doubt.

We went our separate ways.

The gardening frame was heavy, I know, because I took a last stroll about the yard. When I passed the flower bed I paused to inspect the state of things and gave the edge of the frame a quick lift, so sudden no one would have noticed unless they were looking out for me. I guessed it to be about twelve foot long and a good three across. It could get me halfway up the wall if I could lift it.

We had our supper and went to our cells. As soon as I got in mine I took the scissors they'd let me have for my mending, and I cut off my hair. See how much they trusted me? I changed into my sailor's trousers and the smock, looked around one last time. I could carry nothing, but I slipped my old bit of green muslin round my neck and knotted it quickly like a sailor's hankie. A souvenir. No more time to think. I stole out, closing the door softly. Next thing I was in Alison's empty cell, tight in at the foot of the bed, behind the door, which stood ajar. I sat and waited, half an hour. An hour. What if I couldn't lift it? What if it fell over when I tried to mount it? The life of our prison ticked on all around, a humming and a scuffling, all serene on this night, no screams, no cries, no fights. I sat in the dark, like part of the wall, and tried to make myself thoughtless. I wanted to be nothing but time itself rolling on relentless, unstoppable. Till at last I heard the weary feet of Sims come shuffling along the flagstones.

'Good night!' Clang!

'Good night!' Clang!

He reached my door.

'Good night!'

I put my lips to the wall. 'Good night!' I called.

The key turned, the bolt shot.

My heart jumped. He walked past and was on his way.

I must wait. Impatience now could scupper me.

When I was sure he wasn't coming back, I lay down on Alison's bed and closed my eyes. Funny to be on a strange bed after all this time. Time did those old tricks again. First it flew on wings. In no time at all I heard St Clement's clock strike eleven. It wasn't a quiet night in the gaol, no night ever was. But there were no footsteps on the stone walkways. I wasn't going to move till nearer twelve. I went over and over the actions to be performed, mechanically, in my mind. Time then stopped and stretched itself out like a lazy cat. I swear it even yawned and popped an eye at me, and thereafter refused to budge. An arid plain was crossed before the quarter sounded. I was cold. Well, I thought, the cold will keep me awake.

A hundred more years and it was half past. Perhaps I should go now? I actually sat up, teeth a-chatter, and was about to go, but I stopped myself.

Patience.

I lay back down. Be a wall, be a stone, be a spider beginning the ascent. Who cares about time?

At quarter to, I sat up, took my shoes in my hand, slipped out of the door and ran down to the stone passage and along to the yard. They never bolted the gates at night. What point? We were all locked in our cells. The gate creaked a little as I pushed it open in tiny stages, stopping at each one to listen. I closed it after me for safety, ran to the flower bed and seized the gardening frame. It came because it had to. I don't know where I found the strength but I did, because I lifted it up out of the ground, with both arms stretched as wide as they would go, lifted it clean off its feet and into the air and carried it, slightly staggering, across the wide yard. I set it endways under the place where the spike was broken.

It reached a bit more than halfway up. I stood panting. Now it was done I realised it was too heavy for me, because my whole body felt sick at the effort it had just made. I had to sit down instantly on the flags and put my head between my knees for the second time that day. But it passed in a few minutes, and I stood up and shook the ladder firmly. It seemed stable enough. If it slipped, I would break my neck. I shook it again, leaned this way and that against it. I was brisk as I took down one of the lines and the longest of the clothes-props. It's been useful knowing sailors as I do. I know all the knots. I made a running noose and slipped it over the notch on top of the prop. Then I climbed up the frame, hauling the prop with me.

My head was about three and a half feet below the spikes. I didn't look down, didn't think. I got my footing safe on the place near the top of the frame, the wall in my face, and I stretched up and up as far as I could reach with the prop, up and up and up till it nudged the iron post next to where the spike was broken. Then I slipped the noose over the iron post and pulled on it hard. Perfect. It was caught fast. I was home.

Now. Now more than ever be a wall, a stone, a

spider, pulling myself up on a slender thread. I left the gardening frame behind. Inch by inch I ascended, hand over hand, grasping with my knees, squirming, calling from every last hiding place of my fibre any inkling of power that ever lurked there. You can do more than you think. That's true. Till you need it you don't know what strength you've got. The top of the wall appeared, the gap where the spike was gone. My shoulders pounded, my knuckles trembled before my eyes. I hoisted my body over and lay across the roller on top of the wall, panting, face down so I looked over the edge. One hand gripped the iron bar. I saw the bank that sloped into the ditch at the foot of the wall outside, very far away, a killing distance to fall. So funny to see the world from up here. I tried for my breath but it was hard, lying there on my stomach with my lungs squashed, no time to wait, no time any more to rest, come sickness, faintness, pain and death there was only one direction now. I hauled up the rest of the rope and let it fall down on the outside of the wall. I could break my skull now. Or my back. I held on to the line for dear life with both hands and rolled myself forwards. The whole body of spikes revolved, the moon and stars revolved, the cold night air bit me in the nether regions, and the stone wall caressed my face. Head over heels I went and found myself a-dangle on the other side of the wall. The town lay before me. I caught my breath. How like a hanging, I thought, then I let myself down, hand over hand. St Clements struck midnight. Only midnight! I was in the ditch. A slope upwards. I was up it in a trice, over the fence and into the road. I didn't run, I walked smartly. No one was about.

And there was Will, waiting in the lane alongside the church. His face was drawn and worried, but when he saw me, he laughed because I looked so silly in my home-made sailor's trousers and smock. He threw his arms around me and kissed me hot on the mouth, and the feel of his body against me was a homecoming, the smell of his face and hair like twigs and honey and salt. He cried and laughed at the same time, my teeth chattered. He'd brought a blue jacket and a wide-brimmed hat for me. In two minutes I was a sailor. We walked. Two sailors on a road is not remarkable. He said we were going to Sudbourne to stay at Lucy's for a few days till Bargood sent a boat, a cutter that would take us to Holland. It was all arranged. We walked and walked through the night, wide awake, hardly speaking but bound together by some strange elation, so that every now and then one of us would say something, anything, not funny at all, and we'd find ourselves laughing. It was near dawn by the time we reached Woodbridge, a shivery morning rising blue in the east. We quickened our pace. The Sutton Ferry went at first light. Cold cut through my thin breeches as we waited in the gloom of morning by the river. By the time the surly boatman came lumbering down the jetty I was frozen stiff. No one else wanted to cross at that hour, and the river was deserted apart from a small fishing boat off in the mist.

Past the ferry it was hard land, a bleak heath of slowly swirling vapours, the kind of place you wished were over. I feared footpads. And I was tired now, suddenly dog-tired, and wanted warmth.

'Not long,' he said, and slung an arm round me.

At last we smelled the sea. We'd walked nine hours. Lucy would have a big pot of stew ready and waiting, he said, then we'd be back in our bed above the Keeleys' shed, the bed we'd slept out the cold weather in three years ago when we were so poor.

The Shingle

73

In my dreams, again and again I am on the salt marsh or on the shingle. A high grey sea tosses and fidgets alongside, and the sound it makes is an eternal lullaby hushing.

Lucy's cottage looked over the marshes. Every day the pattern of land and water changed. Sometimes when you walked out, the ground turned to jelly under your feet and swayed like a living thing. At night the moon was big and startling, low, wreathed in mist.

Strange to think of that place now, so far away. I don't know why it lingers so brightly in memory, I was not there for that long – the first time a matter of months, the second time eight or nine days, I suppose. Each of those times remains dreamy, yet more real than anything else. In sleep, or wide awake, it's the same: the sense of sudden recognition, the shock of it, the whole thing so real again as to make no difference from life – the smell and the sounds and the tingle of it, the very moment. You can believe you've jumped in time. It feels wide and fearsome and lonely, yet magically beautiful, with the lonely things calling, and the great deep blackness of the North Sea rolling away beyond like God brooding on the face of the waters.

We were waiting for the ship.

In the very early morning, while Will was still

sound asleep in our nest above Keeley's shed, I liked to put on my shepherd's smock over a good wool jacket that scratched my ribs, and I'd slip out with Lucy's man Bill and the dogs when they drove the sheep on to the marshes. The wilder the weather, the more I rejoiced. It was part of my trials. I was in a strange way those days. It was something like the feeling after fever, as if I were apart from things a step or two. I couldn't recall how my life had become so dangerous, the many little steps and stumbles that brought me here, but I knew that endurance was the only way. The storms reminded me of that. I was free but still trapped.

Two or three times a day, it was necessary to come down here, looking for a sail. Bill kept a small boat near the stream that came down from the Alde. These mornings it would fill with water. We'd have to tip it over and bail out before we could cross over. The dogs would swim alongside, then streak about madly on the long wild shore.

We'd walk up and down the shingle, seldom talking but companionate, Bill striding brawny-limbed and hard as a rock, the two black dogs hurtling back to him constantly, wild-eyed and laughing. Day after day the wind was never right, so there was never a sail. Bill would scan the horizon, slit-eyed. 'We're at the mercy of the weather,' he'd say, and we'd stand and be thrummed by the wind, scoured by the sound of the cold sea; then we'd row across again and I'd let the wind blow me back and stow me tight away from the world. While Will was just about beginning to sit up and scratch his head and yawn.

In that house, waiting for the boat, we sat by the fire. Made broth. Made up my decent sailor apparel for our crossing. I think of it as a happy time. Lucy I always see with her red apron wrapped about her solid frame, peeling potatoes over a bowl with a knife the size of a cutlass. Bill is always nodding off and dropping his pipe. We lived in near-wordless amity. I suppose talk went on between the four of us, it always does, but I remember none of it. Only once did Will and I talk about John Luff, in bed one night.

'Tell me truly,' I said, 'did you ever tell the man you'd go with him to America?'

'No!' he replied. 'But you couldn't tell John no. You know how he was.'

'Will,' I said, after a while, 'why did you stick with him so long?'

He thought for a moment.

'I don't suppose I'd be alive if it wasn't for him,' he said.

'I don't suppose we'd be here, hunted, hiding, if it wasn't for him!' I shot back.

'Pegs,' he said, mollifying, 'forget him. He's past and gone.'

Will and I were always ready to go at a moment's notice. Bill said my escape was the talk of Ipswich. People went to look at the place where I'd got over the wall; they pointed out where the broken spike had been. He brought in the papers so I could read about myself. They'd arrested poor old Sims. That was ridiculous, I'd never thought of that. They'd have to let him go.

'FIFTY POUNDS REWARD,' the handbill said.

Whereas, on Tuesday night, the 25th of March, or early on Wednesday morning, Margaret Catchpole, a female convict, confined in the Ipswich gaol, made her escape therefrom, either by scaling the wall, or by the connivance of the turnkey, this is to give notice, that the above reward shall be given to any person or persons who will bring the said Margaret Catchpole to Mr Ripshaw, the gaoler; and one-half that sum to any person or persons furnishing such information as shall lead to her apprehension. And notice is hereby given, that any person concealing or harbouring the said Margaret Catchpole shall, after this notice, if detected be, by order of the magistrates, punished as the law directs.

NB – The prisoner is a tall and dark person, with short hair, black eyes, and of intelligent countenance. She had on the gaol dress, and took away with her the two sheets belonging to her bed.

IPSWICH GAOL, March 28th 1800

'It's decent of you both,' I said to Lucy and Bill as we sat drinking rum and smoking by the fire one night, 'risking yourselves for us.'

Bill said they could kiss his arse with their rewards. *He* was sharp enough for *them*. Lucy shrugged. 'It's no skin off our noses,' she said stoutly. 'We don't know no Margaret Catchpole, we don't. Only this yere sailor what come with my brother. I'll swear it to my dying day.'

She poked the fire with vigour. Wind shook the rafters.

'Soon be a change,' Lucy said. 'It's swinging about.' As if the sky was a great cradle.

As for Will. I could see no anger, no humour. He was quiet and serious and slept a lot. He was supremely gentle in his dealings with all of us, soft and courteous, sweet, helpful. But his eyes were dark. His eyes were like the skies. From time to time, as I passed him by, he'd reach out for me with both hands, pull me down on to his knee, nuzzle his head against my neck. Then he would look at me very deeply and give me a kiss, and I'd feel such love for him it was like a burning in my chest.

74

The ship came on a choppy afternoon. We were ready. Down to the shingle with no hesitation when Bill gave us the word; quick kisses for him and Lucy, promises to write, promises of visits then down to the marshes next to the sea. We could see the ship quite far out, too far I would have thought – and I wondered if this was really Bargood's. But Bill said he'd seen the signal.

Will's eyes were better than mine. 'They're putting a boat down,' he said, flicking open the priming pan on his pistol to check the powder.

'How is it?' I asked.

'Perfect,' he replied. 'It'd see off an army.'

He didn't meet my eyes. I'd never been with Will on a run. This must be what he's like, I thought, cold, efficient, removed from everything but getting through the job. So was I. There was no other way to be. The air was cold about our ears, the sea heaved. A lone marsh bird called. I could see the boat coming in for us now, five or six men rowing hard against the swell. It was hard for them. Even I could see that. Will's eyes were slitted, staring.

It took some time to register the barking of the dogs. Will heard them first and understood first too.

He grabbed my arm.

'You must get away,' he said into my face, eyes urgent. 'If they catch you now they'll kill you.'

'What!'

He turned and stared wildly up the beach. A look of sheer despair came over his face. He was so beautiful at that moment, I'll never forget it. Never. As long as I remain, I'll keep that in my mind. Will Laud was a beautiful man. I don't care if anyone else saw it in him or not. I did.

I looked where he was looking. All I saw was empty shingle and flat grey sky.

'What, Will?' I cried, all at once panicking.

'They're coming.'

I turned back to the sea. The boat was nearer, I could see the round heads of Bargood's men bobbing up and down, the heave and thrust of their strong shoulders.

'Here they are,' I said, and hoisted my bundle, preparing for wet feet.

He grabbed my shoulders. I never saw such fear in anyone's eyes. I stared hard as I could up the rising drift of that shingle, far as ever, and there was still no one, still nothing. He hugged me to him as hard and close as he could, and my breath went out of me. I felt him trembling, every little fibre of him.

'Whatever happens,' he said, 'you get on that boat.'

'Of course I will.'

He closed his eyes.

'Will! What's the matter with you?'

He opened his eyes. 'If they get you they'll kill you,' he said.

'No, that's not...'

He shook me. 'Yes, it is. It is. Not for me, for you, don't you see? You have to get on that boat whatever happens, do you understand? They'll kill you, Pegs. They'll really kill you.'

A hollow voice cried: 'Margaret Catchpole!' The wind pulled it out of shape.

I looked. Half a dozen dark figures came running down the slope of the beach.

'Go for the boat, Pegs,' Will shouted.

Then the voice again, familiar yet strange: 'Margaret Catchpole! Give yourself up!'

It was Mr Ripshaw's voice. I saw him, his feet splayed awkwardly on the shingle. A speaking trumpet covered the lower part of his face.

Will stood in front of me, a pistol in his hand.

'What have you to do with us?' he roared over the roaring weather. 'We're not defrauding the revenue. Haven't we the right to get on a boat if we want to? This is not Margaret Catchpole.'

'We have no business with *you*,' Old Rip's hollowed voice called. 'Give her up. *She's* the one we want.'

I saw a red flash. A pistol cracked. The shingle exploded. A revenue man went down on one knee, taking aim to shoot again.

Will fired back. 'Go for the boat,' he said.

I ran into the sea. The shock of icy water winded me. I could see the men in the boat. The sea wasn't having me, it pushed me away.

'Go!' Will shouted and shoved me hard in the back with his elbow.

I ran. Waves slapped, the cold cut like knives. My arms were before me, my feet knocked out from under me, I bobbed shipward like a cork, swallowing a scorching throatful of saltwater. I struck out hard, kicking freely. My head went under. I surfaced to a roaring in my ears. The sound of gunfire cracked like kindling under the sound of weather. The sea gripped me then threw me out on the shingle, face-down, choking and twitching. The stink of burned powder cut through the salt. Someone ran to me. Will's boots.

'Leave her alone!' he screamed.

The whole world flashed white and I passed away.

Salt Horse 2

75

I heard the men talking above me, but could not tell what they were saying.

I was on a rolling water and opened my eyes to see Will's face next to mine, open-lipped, white, the narrow slits of his eyes glittering. We were lying on cloaks, and there were more spread over us. I was wet, frozen. He was soaking wet too, but colder than me. I put my arms round him and tried to rub the warmth back in.

We beached. All the familiar sounds returned.

'Here, she's got herself all bloody,' a voice said. 'We shouldn't've put them together.'

'Margaret, now,' came the voice of Old Rip, 'it's time to sit up.'

Strong hands pulled me from Will and sat me up. I blinked. Ripshaw's face was inches from mine, as ugly as Will's had been beautiful. Old Rip looked very worried. 'Are you all right?' he asked.

I couldn't speak.

'Come on now, Margaret,' he said. 'You must have known you'd never get away with it. We're taking you back.'

I laughed. I suppose they all thought I'd gone mad.

He offered me a handkerchief. 'Wipe your face,' he said.

Blood was bright on the snowy linen. I couldn't take my eyes from it. One of the men put out his hand to me and led me from the boat. Two others came either side of me, each taking an arm. I tried to turn and look as the others took Will out of the boat, but they began to march me away up the beach.

'Mr Ripshaw!' I shouted. 'What will they do with him?'

Ripshaw came alongside. 'We're going to the Ship,' he said briskly, walking with his hands clasped tightly behind his back. 'There's a post-chaise there will take us to Ipswich.'

'I want to see Will.'

'No.'

'Why?'

'No.'

'Are they looking after him well?'

'They are,' Old Rip replied.

'He's a good man,' I said.

He nodded.

There was a gawping crowd in Orford to see our little procession enter the Ship. We stood in the narrow lobby of the inn. Men crowded through the door behind us. I turned my head and saw for a second Will's hands, the thick-veined backs of them all trickled with blood that had run down his sleeves, and the back of his head and neck, his long hair hanging down. He was slung over the shoulders of a revenue man. They took him into a room. 'He's hurt, let me see him,' I said, but they pushed me on, into a small sitting room with no fire in the grate. Ripshaw told me to sit down. He told the men to see the landlady and get some women's clothes for me to wear. When they'd gone he sat down opposite me, put his hands on his plump knees, pursed his lips and told me all that had happened.

They say my screams were heard all over Orford.

76

They brought me women's clothing, clean and dry, made for someone fatter than me. They chained me for the journey. All the way back to Ipswich I kept my eyes closed. The post-chaise swayed and rattled. Thoughts that ran in and out of my head were all of Will. He was a free man till I came over the wall. If it wasn't for me he'd be alive.

'Salt-horse–' I whispered to myself.

The truth could not be.

Salt-horse–

Salt-horse–

Salt

A Savage Land

77

That first night was not as bad as some, because he'd not yet gone. I felt him still near, close by, crouching inside my head, speaking to me in a language with no words. We lay down together for the night, but we didn't sleep. I laid my cheek to his chest and found blood, thick, still running.

When I woke he was gone and I knew again that he was dead. I wondered if I'd die too. It didn't matter now.

God, let it have been quick, a flash and gone. No time for pain.

My hands shook. I couldn't swallow. I had a beaker with water in, but the water dried as soon as it touched my lips.

Morning faded in. I was taken to the Ripshaws' parlour. The constable of Sudbourne came in with three fat magistrates. They sat side by side. The one in the middle had eyes like grey pebbles and long salmon-coloured lids drooping over.

'Is it true you can hang me for this?' I asked before any of them could get a word in.

Old Rip looked distressed.

The chief magistrate's cheeks puffed in and out like the skin of a bellows. 'You're an intelligent woman,' he said crisply, 'you know the law.'

'Not this one, I don't.'

'I shall enlighten you then,' he replied very coldly, leaning forward and folding his hands. 'It's very simple. If any prisoner should endeavour to escape, and in so doing resists the attempt of his gaoler to bring him back, he may be killed on the spot. *You* are extremely fortunate therefore to be alive at all at this moment. In your par*tic*ular case, as one serving a sentence commuted from death, you must now become liable to the original punishment deemed fit for you by the court.'

'You must make your deposition, Margaret,' Ripshaw said softly, bending forward from the waist as if bowing to me. 'It will be written down and you can sign it. You may have your say.'

'What deposition?' I cried. 'Damn the deposition! You know exactly what happened. I've told you. I'd do it again, anyone would. What's wrong with what I did? I could understand it with the horse, but not with this. Who have I hurt? Tell me that.'

Their faces – as if I'd slapped them.

'That will do!' rapped the chief magistrate. 'You can think what you like but the law's the law.' The hooded eyes blinked slowly. 'You broke the confidence Mr Ripshaw placed in you.

'Not only that,' he ploughed on, 'if you had *not* been retaken he would have been liable for a penalty of five hundred pounds.'

I looked at Ripshaw. He looked sorrowfully back at me, poor old thing, for all the world as if *he* was the injured party.

'Not to mention Mr Sims,' said another of the magistrates. 'Do you think he relished his eight days in gaol?'

I stared hard at him. 'He had nothing to do with it. No one's guilty but me. Not Sims, not the

Keeleys, not Will Laud–'

His name tripped me up. I looked at the floor.

'My conscience is clear,' I said.

But it wasn't. It carried Will's death, oddly, like a pain referred.

'Margaret,' Mr Ripshaw said gravely. 'You're not helping yourself.'

'Oh,' I said sullenly. 'I thought I was allowed my say.'

'Make your deposition now, Margaret,' Ripshaw said sadly.

I did, and spoke no more.

They gave me a piece of paper to sign and told me I was for Bury assizes again, August the second.

Four months away.

I'd rather it were sooner. Killing should not take so long. People think it's all in the hanging or the burning or whatever but it starts long before that.

They put me in solitary. Late on the fourth day, after lock-up, they moved me once more into my old cell. I saw no one. The door banged shut. I might never have left. Shivering in the cold, I got ready for bed. For a few moments there was silence, then a chorus began. Alison Lloyd began it. 'You done well, Margaret!' she yelled, banging on the wall.

Other voices took it up.

'You done well, Margaret!'

'Fine girl!'

'You give 'em the runaround, sweetheart!'

I lay in my bed. Tears gushed from my eyes.

A great echoing clang rang through the night. Keys rang against stone.

A roar: 'Pipe down!'

That was Sims. I hadn't seen him yet. Would he hate me? I meant him no harm. I meant none of them harm, nor had poor old Robin meant harm when he'd blabbed he'd seen me all dressed up as a sailor going over the Sutton Ferry, nor Lucy Keeley when the men turned up at her door and she sent them on down to the coast after us. She didn't want to go to prison. Swore she thought I was a man, a friend of her brother's.

'Alison!' I hissed through the hole in the wall.

'Hello, my dear.' Her voice was close.

'Did they bother you?'

'Me?' A little snort. 'No, my darling. How could they? No proof. I was shocked, that's what I said. I am so *shocked*, Mr Ripshaw, I never dreamed she would've done such a thing.'

'Will's dead,' I said.

'I know, darling.'

I couldn't say any more.

After a time, she spoke again. 'The day they hang you, Margaret,' she said, 'I shall give them bloody hell. Trust me, they'll know what they've done.'

78

All was quiet, at least as much as it ever could be in that place, and in the quiet there were thoughts. I wasn't afraid, not then. Berry was the hangman in those days. They say he knew his job.

I knew death. It was where Will had gone, and that was the thought that killed me now. Because suddenly, no matter how hard I tried, I could feel him with me no more. I couldn't recall the moment he left me, but I knew now he'd gone now, for sure. Whenever I opened my eyes he'd not be there. However I listened I'd never hear him again. Grief has a certain purity. It came to me that night as fierce as a sword.

79

Mrs Cobbold came at a bad time. I was in a watery-headed phase and cried at any old thing.

'It's your lady,' Sims said, as if announcing a great treat, coming and getting me from the workroom where I was unable to sew properly because my eyes kept blurring over. I put down my work and followed him out into the long stone passage. Sims and I had become friends. Funny, that, him being so nice when I finally faced him. Eight days in gaol. Imagine him, a turnkey, having the key turned on him. The first morning after going back to my old cell I walked straight up to him and apologised as nicely as I could. 'I had no idea they'd think you had anything to do with it,' I said. 'It just never entered my head.'

And he smiled in a very ordinary way and said, 'Not to worry. These things happen.'

'I don't really want to see her,' I told him now

as we reached my door.

'Well, *she* wants to see *you.*' He shuffled expertly through his bunch of keys. 'Been crying, she has, I'd say. Not a happy lady.

'You go in,' he said, turning the key in my cell door. 'I'll bring her along.'

'I don't know what to say to her.'

'You, Margaret?' he said. 'Lost for words?'

Lost.

When she came in I stood up and curtseyed. Like everything else, the act made me cry. It was funny really, and I don't know why; something to do with the fact that I was going to die and here I was standing on ceremony. I hadn't seen her for a while. Her cheeks were haggard and over-rouged. It's true she'd been crying; her eyes were red.

Sims brought a chair and placed it very neatly for her, backing out respectfully.

She set down a carpet bag she was carrying, came straight to me and threw her arms around me. I hated that. I stood awkwardly, patting her shoulder, wondering who was supposed to be comforting who.

'Oh child, child, child,' she said, 'what have you done to yourself?'

And though I couldn't not cry, I had to laugh. Child? What was she talking about? I stood away. 'Hardly a child,' I said.

'You know what I mean.' She was tight-lipped. 'It's not like last time, Margaret. This is far more serious.'

I smiled nervously. 'Why are you so angry?'

'Oh!' she cried, exasperated, and paced up and down two or three times before sitting down abruptly on the hard little chair Sims had left for her. She wore a pretty blue cape lined with silky grey fur. 'We tried very hard to help you, Margaret,' she said in a rasping way, peeling off her thin white gloves. 'People said we were fools to stick up for you as we did. Do you think it was easy?' She looked at me, hard-eyed. 'What happens now? How can we help you? You make it so *difficult*, Margaret. We all spoke for you before and we were glad to, and *now* look. A year or two more and you'd have been a free woman. What's it going to look like now if we try and intercede again? *Well*, they'll say–' she rolled her eyes '*–you vouched for her once before, didn't you?* And they'd be right too, wouldn't they?'

'I see,' I said. 'I'm sorry, madam. I'm truly sorry I've upset you.'

'Oh, Margaret, don't be stupid! Sit down!'

I sat on the edge of the bed. She leaned forward and took both of my hands in hers and spoke fiercely. 'It's got nothing to do with upsetting me, it's about saving your life! Don't you understand what you've done? It's a death sentence, Margaret! How could you be such a fool? How can I *not* be angry with you? Don't you dare blame fate, Margaret: you put yourself here, you know you did.'

Her face crumpled.

I don't know why the fear chose that particular moment to strike. I will hang, I will hang, I will hang. The words in my mind going round and round as if a cook was beating them in with a spoon. My body knew it. My throat felt the hemp. My belly shrivelled, every nerve screamed.

I put my head down as far as it would go.

Her fingers gripped my hands, hurting me.

It was like a wave of nausea, but I couldn't chuck it up.

In a moment or two the spasm passed. I lifted my head.

'There now,' she said briskly, smiling, 'I've brought you a few things,' and turned to the carpet bag. As well as wise little books of religion and knowledge, out came a great sheaf of pictures the children had done for me, things they'd made me, red silk hearts with M embroidered in blue, sugar cakes with pink icing, pressed flowers, sweet little notes, even one from Rowland. His writing was round and blotched. Dear Margaret, he wrote, I hope you are well. She couldn't have done better if she'd wanted to make me cry again.

'How are they all?' I asked.

'Very well.' She smiled. 'Very well indeed. William's been helping his father. Remarkably, he has a head for figures. Henry's learning to ride. And that's about time too, I'm afraid he's a very lazy boy. And the girls – oh well, the girls are all butterflies–'

She stopped. 'I'm having another,' she said, smiling and raising her eyebrows at the same time. I wasn't sure if she was dreading it, or delighted but not letting on to be feeling happy in deference to my position.

'Who've you got?' I asked. 'Still Louise?'

'Yes.'

'Oh, you'll be all right with Louise.'

'Yes, Louise is very good.'

'You know what the worst of it is?' I said,

swallowing hard. 'Will's dead.'

She looked pained.

'It was my fault,' I said. 'He was a free man. They had nothing on him. He went along with my plan and now he's dead.'

Her shoulders drooped. 'He was a grown man,' she said. 'He made his own decisions freely.'

Proximity to death bestows great freedom. 'You never liked him, did you?' I said.

She wasn't surprised. 'Like him?' she replied. 'I didn't know him. He was a very handsome man.'

'Do you think so?'

'Oh yes! In an odd kind of way. But he was trouble, Margaret. That was always clear.'

80

There were three of us for the next assizes: me, Sarah Barker and Elizabeth Killet. We used to cluster round Alison Lloyd in the sewing room. They were both much younger than me, and very scared. Alison was older than the lot of us. She became our mother. It sounds funny to say it but there were times when we were all quite happy in those few weeks.

At night, before we slept, Alison and I would talk through the wall.

'I still can't see that I've done wrong in escaping,' I told her. 'I just can't see it.'

'Nor have you, darling,' she said, and set off on one of her old coughing fits.

'If it happens,' I said, 'the worst, that is, I'm not going to whinge and whine.'

'You'll do well, darling,' she said. 'Don't you worry.'

I'll be one of those that goes defiant, I thought. I will. I'll say it loud: I am not a bad person, it's this devil law. I won't hang my head. I'll look them in the eye and tell the truth. I want my say. If I'm going to die, I deserve it. I want to give them something to remember. If they were going to kill me, I'd make them look me in the eye.

I said that to Mrs Cobbold one time, I remember. 'I'll never hang my head,' I said.

Her eyes filled with horrible pity. She was very concerned about my state of grace. 'You have to be ready just in case,' she said. 'Be prepared for anything.' She'd got people praying for me, not just the family but Mrs Sleorgin and all her friends. In long dark nights I lay awake thinking of those kind ladies. I wondered if any of them would come and see me hang. I doubted it. They weren't the sort. Who *would* come? God knows. People loved a good hanging. How would *I* be? Would I give a good show? Some joke with the crowd. Some cry and scream and cack themselves. Please God, let me keep my dignity, I prayed.

The night before we were due to leave for the assizes, I got a letter from Mrs Cobbold. First of all, for heaven's sake, don't argue with them, she said. Say yes, I'm guilty and I'm very very sorry. Be respectful. Prepare for the worst. May God be with you.

81

I don't know why I became so calm just when I did.

I stood in the cage with the eyes upon me. The body of people in that sweat-filled room was one thing, a monster with a million eyes that crawled on me like grubs. For one terrible moment I thought I was going to scream. Next I was calm. It was a game. We all had our moves. They'd make theirs, I'd make mine. Someone would win. I stared through the bars. The judge was the good old Lord Chief Baron again. I looked him full in the eyes and smiled. He was only a man. I was not being insolent, not unless it's insolent to look at another person as if you and he are the same in the eyes of God.

He asked for my plea and I said, 'Guilty, my lord.'

The Lord Chief Baron folded his hands before him on the desk and looked at me for a long time. I looked back.

He cleared his throat. Pushed his glasses up his nose.

He said I was wicked. Unfit to live. Those were his very words: unfit to live.

Unfit to live, unfit for any man, a danger to the morals of others. Callous, hardened, unwomanly.

Then he twisted the knife.

'I was fully prepared,' he said prissily, looking

over the top of his eye-glasses, 'to grant your pardon these very assizes if I'd got a good report of you; of course that's out of the question now.'

It was all up. Clearly reason held no sway here.

'I have to say,' he continued with an air of head-shaking regret, 'such bold and intolerable behaviour as you have displayed proves you unworthy to live.'

There was some murmuring in the court.

'Prisoner at the bar,' said the Lord Chief Baron, wearily this time, 'do you have anything to say as to why this court should not pass sentence upon you?'

'I do, my lord.'

'Proceed.'

I smiled. Me to you, my lord: 'You're too hard. I'm sorry, my lord, but I must say as fact that I am not a hardened criminal. I broke the law twice. I said I was very sorry. I never hurt anyone. I've been a prisoner now for three years and all that time I've behaved well. All the magistrates who visited the gaol signed a petition for mercy and you said no. You kept saying no when there was no good reason. If you hadn't said no, none of this would have happened and I wouldn't be here. I'm not hardened. I'm sorry I did it, of course I am. But I'm not a bad person. I don't deserve to die. I may be a fool but I'm not bad. And I'd stand at Judgement Day and say the same thing, my lord.'

I was very pleased with how it came out. I don't think I could have made it much better.

I felt the court with me, a little murmuring surge of approval, and I dare think it came also from the benches where the gentry sat. The Lord Chief Baron banged his gavel. He reached down beneath the bench – the court gasped, he put the black cap on top of his wig and, for the second time, sentenced me to hang by the neck until dead.

I curtseyed and left the dock.

82

I was sick and faint by the time I reached the cell. I lay down, closed my eyes, turned my face to the wall for the three days till the end of the assizes. There was no hope this time. I feared every single moment that lay ahead of me. Sarah and Elizabeth both got transportation. Sarah said she thought *I* was the lucky one; she'd rather die than go out there and be eaten up by savages.

'Or torn to pieces by wild animals,' Lizzie added. 'Or end up on the bottom of that horrible cold ocean and no one to bury you but the fish to eat your bones.'

'I don't want to die,' I whispered to the wall.

But he was playing with me, that cruel judge. He must have always known. For three days I whispered to the wall. Then someone shook my shoulder and told me he'd commuted my sentence before he left town. That it was transportation, to Australia. For life.

83

'And is it true there are wild cannibals living in that country?'

'Oh yes. They all carry tommyhawks and knives and whenever they see a white man they delight in butchering him. But they have to behave themselves when they come into town or they know what they'd get.'

'Are there horses?' I asked.

'Indeed there are. Though I doubt you'd see a Suffolk punch.'

Old Rip's daughter's servant, a red-faced matron called Hepzibah just lately returned from Sydney Cove, had been given leave to instruct us three in the ways of the new colony. We sat in a corner of the yard in the sunshine.

'It's not so bad,' she said. 'The flies are the worst of it.'

'Not so bad for you maybe,' Sarah Barker said. 'You was a free woman when you was there.'

Hepzibah had gone out with her mistress, she said, a free settler; but they'd returned because the climate brought the master up in boils. 'We was in the town,' she said, 'and it's not so bad in the town. Outside the town is just a great wild waste. I wouldn't want to go out of town. That's where all the horrible things happen. There was a man had his arms and legs cut off.'

Sarah squealed.

'And there's the snakes, dreadful things, fangs this long–' she stretched her fingers '–they jump straight up from the ground and fly at your throat. Always the throat. Oh yes, it's certainly a very dangerous country, no use in pretending it ain't. Stay in town if you can. And do what they tell you.'

Might as well send me to another star. I remembered the globe in the schoolroom at the Cliff. Holland was not so far. I pictured a little house. An inn on the waterfront in Amsterdam, an inn where the sailors drank, a cheerful place.

'Cheer up,' said red-faced Hepzibah. 'Some get pardons for good behaviour and settle as free citizens.'

'It's the sea worries me,' Lizzie Killet said. 'I get sick just looking at the Orwell.'

'I burn terrible easy in the sun,' Sarah said.

84

Mrs Cobbold sent a chest of stuff on ahead for me, all the way to Australia, 'full of surprises,' she said, 'so you'll have something nice to look forward to when you arrive. I've put some good books in, and one or two small items you might find useful.' I couldn't believe me and it would ever meet up on the other side of the ocean.

We left in late May. Uncle Catchpole came to see me a week earlier, Uncle and Aunt Leader two days before. Mrs Cobbold was my last visitor. She came breezing in with a cake she'd made for me to take on the journey. It was very pretty, with nuts and a glaze on top. 'Oh dear, I hate goodbyes,' she said fretfully. 'Don't you? Now you'll be sure to write?'

'Of course I will.'

'It will be so interesting for us to get your letters! We'll make use of them in our lessons. Now I in*sist* you write regularly and tell me all about the new colony. It will be fascinating! Send me things.'

'Things?'

'I don't know, a leaf, a flower, any little thing. Something from the new world! How exciting!'

'I feel so scared,' I said.

Her eyes were bright. 'No sadness,' she said, smiling. 'You're going to a new life. May it be wonderful, my dear.'

The terror I felt was beyond words.

85

They struck off our chains when we got out of sight of land. The *Nile* was not a bad ship. No one died. But we were down below for most of the time, a host of filthy women bleeding and sweating together in a hole with dirty bungs that creaked above our heads. When it pitched, people got sick. One hundred and seventy-six days we sailed, and Sarah Barker cried all the way. She cried out from terror of the sea, sickness of the stomach, and apprehension as to the life to come.

I was lucky again. The Mate came for me. 'Here,' he said. 'You done some nursing?'

'A bit.'

He hooked his finger at me. I was very tired and ached all over but I followed him up on deck. There was a fine rain, very refreshing. The sea was dark grey, almost black, and it sat bowed and swollen on the horizon. There on deck was an anxious man with a thin sensitive face, whose lips and eyes relaxed when they fell on me. 'Can you come to my wife?' he asked me. 'She's in quite a state.'

He was Mr Rouse, a free settler. His wife was pregnant and sick, and his little girl had diarrhoea. He took me to a tiny cabin where his pale wife lay scared and twitchety in her bunk, small hands picking at the blanket that covered her belly.

'When are you due?' I asked her, moving my hands over the mound. A sizeable child, by the feel of it.

'About a month,' she whispered. She was young.

Her little girl stood by, fingers in mouth.

'What's *your* name?' I asked her.

She blinked.

'That's Mary,' her mother said.

'I think we need to change your nappy, Mary. Let me just see to your mother first, hm?'

She blinked.

'I'm afraid I'm rather a coward,' Mrs Rouse whispered. 'Will you hold my hand when the time comes?'

'Don't worry.'

I brought baby from her three weeks later. The sea was high, like a wild horse, a bucker.

'This one of all your babes,' I said, 'this one will ride wild horses.'

A Remnant

86

Richmond Hill
New South Wales
21 April 1819

Honoured Madam,

It's been so long since I wrote I don't know where to begin. I don't remember any more whose turn it *was* to *write, nor does it matter. How are you? And all the children, and Mr Cobbold? I am keeping reasonably well, all things considered. Two years ago we had another of our terrible floods–*

It was late. Billy was up on the ridge, me sitting with my tea, looking at the blank paper and doing nothing, musing, remembering. I'm still amazed at being alive. They'd plucked us out of the tree at first light. They said the rivers Nepean and Grose were thirty foot over their banks.

–nearly as bad as those others I told you of. I was delivering Mrs Raby's baby and we all had to go up into a big tree. What a night that was–

A baby crying, the rhythmic wail of a newborn, raw, high and ragged. It had been constant for a while, a little animal calling out with all the other animals: hear me, I'm alive. The sky full of a strange wild music, the bleating and lowing and howling of thousands of beasts. It was a strong healthy gusty sound, and the baby joined in. The chapel bell rang in Richmond across the river. A world of flotsam-rich water swept down to Broken Bay, here and there the tiny hump of a hill poking through.

A soldier called: 'All safe now, ladies!'

'We've a baby here!' Phoebe called back. 'Born last night.'

Downriver we went, and all the hens and geese squawking away on the islands of debris around us. They took us to the church at Richmond. My old shipboard friend Lizzie Killet was there serving tea. When I told her what had happened to me she said, 'Jesus, Margaret, how many lives you got, you old scapegallows?'

–the river flooded again this year but it did not reach us up here. It's starting to get colder now. I got a good soaking the other night walking back from one of my ladies who is coming along very nicely with twins. I'm still nursing you see, and my little farm is surviving, and my shop. I get along very quietly. I have a child that lives with me, and I have my dogs, but I would like a horse, because I have to do a great deal of walking and sometimes I do get tired. I was fifty-seven in March and I am sorry to say I am losing my teeth. But I have nothing to complain about. I am well thought of here. Uncle Catchpole keeps me very well informed about home. My brother Ned is married and doing well, I'm pleased to say. I've had a good few offers myself, but I said I wouldn't marry and I haven't. I'm sorry to say we lost Charles only last year. He was home in Suffolk for one week in March

then off back East and my uncle got news come August he'd fallen down a ladder on ship and broken his back. They buried him at sea. Do you remember when we used to bring you his letters to read for us? And all the strange and wonderful things he told us of those hot places. I never would have thought it would be me writing from the far side of the earth one day. Do you remember when I used to send you those pretty things, feathers and skins and little carvings made by the natives of this place? Do you still have the lyre bird I sent you? Madam, I find myself sentimental tonight.

I was haunted by thoughts of home. This sometimes happens. I went in and got out my box, just an old wooden thing, very battered. All my letters were there, and underneath them my uncles' and aunts' and cousins' hair, and an old cap Mrs Cobbold sent me straight off her head, and the silk hearts with embroidered Ms that the Cobbold children made. Will's hair I kept alone, in a tobacco pouch. I stroked it, silky-fine and golden.

I still think of Will. It's an old wound now

–it was thinking of old times after I'd seen an old friend. I sincerely wish to know how Miss Ann and Miss Harriet and Sophia do and all your own dear family do. I would love to hear some good of Henry. I still cannot believe that Rowland is gone–

These things draw me sometimes, my souvenirs. They drew me that night, after the flood – I remember the heat had broken at last, and the beginnings of dusk were like a very early spring morning in England. The dogs flew to greet us. We hadn't been touched. Henry Morgan had got the pigs in and put them in the stock-yard. They'd made one end of it all mud, and were well content – and he'd milked the cows and turned them out on the front pasture. Our sheep were higher up the hill. I looked out over the still-watery plain, fading away below. Ruined, whatever grew there. A flight of shrill green birds passed overhead. Here we were safe home, and all our things waiting for us, good as gold, dry as a bone, just as we'd left them so long ago. It was not yet three days, but it felt as if we'd sailed the world all round and encountered a hundred great adventures.

My letters. My box.

–I wonder if Dr Stebbing's still alive? He'd be quite an old man now–

'Who are you writing to, Auntie?'

I looked up. Billy had crept in quietly. 'An old friend. Put your nightshirt on, Bill, we'll have supper by the fire.'

The dogs came in, excited, running here and there with their tails bashing wildly about the place. 'Settle down!' I scolded, and put the letter by.

'I have to go and visit Healy tomorrow,' I told Bill, building up the fire.

'Healy in the valley?'

'The shepherd, yes.'

'It's going to pour.'

'All day?'

'Maybe.'

'It's only two miles,' I said. 'You can look after things for me, I won't be long.'

'What's up with him?'

'He's got a sore leg.'

'You shouldn't go,' Billy said. 'You'll get soaked again.'

'Poor man's suffering.'

The fire was blazing up. The dogs settled.

'Anyway,' I said, 'I have a soft spot for shepherds. My brother Ned's a shepherd.'

87

–so I will close, madam, hoping you and all yours are well. But first I must tell you what I have on my table. It's a very small thing, a card table that I place next to me of an evening for my cup and my book and the letter I may be writing. Guess what I have as a cloth for it, madam? It's the old offcut you gave me years ago, when you were making Miss Sophia's dress. Do you remember? The pale-green muslin with the pink roses–

–and here have I been gazing at the fire now a whole half-hour.

On the Pitts' property, near Windsor, Australia, she nursed the shepherd till the influenza took him. She came down with the infection herself and died on 13 May 1819.

Her grave is unknown, but she lies in Richmond Cemetery. The register of burials at nearby St Peter's Church contains the following entry, inscribed by the Reverend Henry Fulton: 'Margaret Catchpole aged 58 years [in fact she was 57], came prisoner in the *Nile*, in the year 1801. Died May 13; was buried May 14, 1819.'

ACKNOWLEDGEMENTS

This novel is based on the life of Margaret Catchpole, a real woman who was born in Suffolk in 1762 and died in New South Wales in Australia in 1819. She made a huge impression on those who knew her and left her mark on both countries. Stories of her courageous rescues and wild rides (she was an excellent horsewoman), of her charm and constancy and freedom of spirit eventually took on a semi-legendary status. Though nowadays few people have heard of her, in Suffolk there remains a pub called the Margaret Catchpole, and there is a house on the banks of the River Orwell pointed out as the Cat House, where it's said she used to place a stuffed cat in the window to warn smugglers about the excisemen. In Australia, the maternity ward of Hawkesbury Hospital, Windsor, New South Wales is named Catchpole Ward in honour of her midwifery services to the early colony, and there is a Catchpole Avenue at nearby Hobartville.

I am hugely indebted to the Reverend Richard Cobbold, whose 1845 book, *Margaret Catchpole, a Suffolk Girl* was an invaluable source. The son of her philanthropic employers, he was a newborn baby at the time of her transportation and during his early years Margaret's letters to his mother from New South Wales were a regular occurrence. However, the Reverend Richard wrote his book some twenty-six years after her death, and was concerned to make of her life a Victorian morality tale about a good and simple girl led astray by a bad man, eventually redeemed by marriage, motherhood and religion. He claimed it was the true story, but played fast and loose with the facts, lopping twelve years off her age and allowing her to live into a ripe old age of domestic bliss, dying surrounded by an adoring and devout family.

The truth was more complex. 'I am not for marrying,' the real Margaret wrote, though by all accounts she had plenty of offers. This was a deliberate choice. In a time and place where women were not only regarded as second-class citizens but whores and chattels, she was one of a tiny percentage of women who carved her own niche and lived independently. 'I live in my little cottage all alone except a little child for to a come and stop with me,' she wrote. Her true voice comes through these letters home. She was one of the very few convicts who could read and write, and her descriptions of the female convict experience and life in the young colony (including the great floods that regularly devastated the Hawkesbury region) are preserved in the archives of the National Library of Australia. They take some deciphering, not just the ornate curlicues of her handwriting and the idiosyncrasies of spelling and lack of grammar, but the rambling, almost stream-of-consciousness nature of her expression.

However, the Reverend Richard's book is full of

telling little details and anecdotes which have the ring of family stories oft repeated. Those that seemed to me to have the ring of truth I have taken for my novel.

I am also very grateful to David Jones at Ipswich Museum, whose vast knowledge was invaluable, and who took the time to regale me with many intriguing and fascinating insights. The staff at Suffolk Record Office and Christchurch Mansion were extremely helpful, as were staff at the National Library of Australia, who supplied me with copies of Margaret's letters home from the fledgeling colony.

Great thanks are due also to Paul C. Ineson and Johnny Latham, my saviours in the laptop realm, to Nina and Dave Bleasdale for their generosity in loaning me a space and time for peace and quiet, to Kim Murden, Mic Cheetham and Lennie Goodings, and last but not least to Martin Butler who gave me the original idea.

The publishers hope that this book has given you enjoyable reading. Large Print Books are especially designed to be as easy to see and hold as possible. If you wish a complete list of our books please ask at your local library or write directly to:

Magna Large Print Books
Magna House, Long Preston,
Skipton, North Yorkshire.
BD23 4ND

This Large Print Book for the partially sighted, who cannot read normal print, is published under the auspices of

THE ULVERSCROFT FOUNDATION

THE ULVERSCROFT FOUNDATION

... we hope that you have enjoyed this Large Print Book. Please think for a moment about those people who have worse eyesight problems than you ... and are unable to even read or enjoy Large Print, without great difficulty.

You can help them by sending a donation, large or small to:

The Ulverscroft Foundation,
1, The Green, Bradgate Road,
Anstey, Leicestershire, LE7 7FU,
England.
or request a copy of our brochure for more details.

The Foundation will use all your help to assist those people who are handicapped by various sight problems and need special attention.

Thank you very much for your help.